2Ø12:

THE ZOMBIE APOCALYPSE

RYAN TOMASELLA

iUniverse, Inc.
New York   Bloomington

2012: The Zombie Apocalypse

This is a work of fiction. All of the characters, names, incidents, organizations, and dialogue in this novel are either the products of the author's imagination or are used fictitiously.

iUniverse books may be ordered through booksellers or by contacting:

iUniverse
1663 Liberty Drive
Bloomington, IN 47403
www.iuniverse.com
1-800-Authors (1-800-288-4677)

Because of the dynamic nature of the Internet, any Web addresses or links contained in this book may have changed since publication and may no longer be valid. The views expressed in this work are solely those of the author and do not necessarily reflect the views of the publisher, and the publisher hereby disclaims any responsibility for them.

ISBN: 978-1-4502-2534-2 (pbk)
ISBN: 978-1-4502-2536-6 (cloth)
ISBN: 978-1-4502-2535-9 (ebook)

Printed in the United States of America

iUniverse rev. date: 4/26/10

CHAPTER 1 - THE BEGINNING

It was Tuesday, February eighth, ironically the day of my birthday. Unlike everyone else, I spent my twenty-first birthday inside, working, instead of going outside, getting drunk and celebrating. Snow was still on the streets outside from the storm last night. However, the little bit of snow didn't stop the morning commuters. Outside my window I still heard people talking, yelling, cars honking - all the normal things you'd hear in a big city. I let out a long drawn-out yawn, rubbing my face to try and shake off the night before.

Today began just like any other day. I rolled out of bed around ten a.m., put on a pair of pants and turned on the TV before walking over to the bathroom. Inside the bathroom I reach for the tooth brush next to the sink before squirting some tooth paste onto it. Once it's covered in toothpaste I stick it in my mouth before swishing it around a few times. In the mean time I decide to walk over to the kitchen and start up my first batch of coffee.

As I am pouring the water into the coffee maker I overhear the news mention something about a nuclear power plant leak in Delaware. I roll my eyes and mumble out loud, "Nothing ever changes in this county." After I finish preparing the coffeemaker and return to my bathroom. I spit out the toothpaste left in my mouth and quickly rinse it out. I place the toothbrush back into the vanity and close it, giving the mirror a good look.

A recently shaved man stands about six foot three. He has long black hair almost perfectly shaping his face. I grin looking at the mirror, "Look at that sexy devil". I chuckle a bit to myself, walking away. I return to my living room, turn on the computer and take a quick peek at the TV. The news is now currently saying fifteen people are reported dead and four more are injured. I let out a sigh and say "Must have been a pretty big disaster."

I leave the living room, giving time for my computer to turn on and to grab a cup of coffee from the kitchen. I return to the living room and turn the TV off before sitting down at the computer. I begin working on my daily website project and don't really take any concern to what I heard on the TV earlier this morning.

My daily website project was one I have been working on for weeks. I had a really annoying customer that wanted his shit done now and by now I mean immediately. If you slept, ate, or even shit when his website wasn't finished he felt that you were conspiring against him. Almost like everyone had an evil plot to stop him from selling his baby bottles to the world.

His name was Mr. Clark. I never met him in real life, only spoke when him through emails or over the phone. He sounded like a real crabby old man, something I don't need in my daily life. I have a website of my own that I occasionally get to work on. I give out free game guides for online games such as *World of Warcraft, Everquest, Aion* and *Warhammer Online.*

My website doesn't offer a large enough pay check to pay for my bills. So I've had to freelance my skills to people like Mr. Clark. It was a good decision overall, even though it added a lot of extra stress into my life.

The day continues on much like any other day. At noon I take my quick break for lunch and head over to the kitchen. I open the refrigerator door and pull out some left over Chinese food from last night before returning to the living room and sitting down onto the couch. I shove a mouthful of food into my mouth before reaching for the TV remote. I turn on the TV to see what the news is with the nuclear power plant leak.

When I turn on the TV our local female news reporter is on. She is wearing her usual garb, all black, pitch black hair and even black nail polish on her finger nails. Today happened to be one of the days where she didn't add her black chap stick into the mix.

She says, "There has been a recent update on the nuclear power plant leak in Delaware. All four people that were injured and were in critical condition have passed away. Also, they found eight more dead bodies, bringing the total count up to twenty-seven. Our hearts go out to the families that were affected by this horrible disaster".

I roll my eyes at the TV before asking myself, "What does that even mean? Our hearts go out to the victims?" I shake my head in disapproval at the TV, disgusted by the media in today's modern day society. I turn the TV off and return to my computer to pull up my website project for the day.

After I pull up my website project I give my computer screen a blank stare as I am unable to focus on anything at the minute. I worry about my family and friends living in south Jersey, close to the power plant leak. I'm also worried if the leak could possibly affect me, even though I'm a long distance away.

The day seems to fly by as I get almost no work done. I was too busy day dreaming and running what if scenarios through my head. It now happens to already be five in the afternoon. I lean back into my chair and stretch my arms back before saying, "Alright, time for dinner!"

I stand up and walk straight over to my kitchen to look through my refrigerator. Once I'm at my refrigerator I open the door and stare inside of it. As usual I make many faces looking at all the goodies I have inside, trying to decide what to eat. With nothing in my refrigerator looking appetizing at the minute I grab a bottle of water and return to my couch. I sit down on the couch and kick up my legs before turning on the TV.

"We've gotten a recent update from the hospital", said the same female news reporter from earlier.

"It seems like a late Christmas miracle has happened! Those who were reported dead at the nuclear power plant incident earlier have come back to life. Doctors think it has something to do with the amount of exposure to the radiation. More information will be given on this when we understand more of what is going on. Until that time the families of those infected are the only ones being permitted to see them."

I smile and lean back, tipping my cup to the TV and saying "Hallelujah", before grabbing the remote and turning the volume down. I place my drink on the table and lean back on the couch. Throwing my legs up on one of the arms and placing my head on the opposite one. I close my eyes and snuggle down, before falling asleep.

I wake up later that day from the sound of the TV. I roll over and rub my eyes before taking a look at the TV. "Hmm, what is going on?" I mumble to myself, wondering why the TV is all static. I let out a sigh and say, "You know… This damn cable company is a pain in my ass... They were just here a week ago..." I grab the remote from the table and turn off the TV before sitting up right.

I let out a long and loud yawn before standing up and walking over into my kitchen. I open the refrigerator door in my kitchen and stare inside of it. I realize something is amiss but can't quite place it yet. Then it hits me, the power is out in my refrigerator! I look up at the top of the refrigerator and hit the switch a few times but nothing happened.

I let out a sigh before saying, "Why's this shit always got to happen to me?" I slam the refrigerator door shut and walk over to the light in the kitchen. I click the light on and nothing happens. I let out breath of air and shake my head side to side. Trying to hold myself together and not smash everything in my house out of frustration.

After I am done venting I return to my living room and lay back down onto the couch. I stare up at the ceiling and place both hands over my face. "Story of my life... Story of my life..." I say before closing my eyes and falling back asleep.

This time I don't wake up until the next morning. "Burr..." I say, a bit chilly from the night before. I roll onto my side and rub my arms, trying to warm myself up. I reach over to the table and grab the remote off of it. I point it at the TV and hit the power button but nothing happens. I sit up on the couch and point it at the TV again, hitting the power button. But still nothing happens.

I grind my teeth together out of frustration before saying, "Dependable, reliable service my ass". I place my hand onto my forehead and cover my eyes. The second I cover my eyes a loud gunshot can be heard from the streets. I jump a bit as the sound echoes through my apartment. I stand up and slowly make my way over to the window.

I look outside and peek around, being careful not to expose myself to whoever shot the gun outside. Unable to see anything I move closer to the window, almost sticking my head up to the glass to see out. Instead of seeing the shooter outside, I see something much more shocking.

There are cars parked in the streets, not just on the side of the streets but also in the middle of the streets. There is shattered glass all over the ground below. Doors to cars and houses are left wide open, clothes and personal items almost litter the streets. Papers can be seen flying around the streets like tumbleweeds in the west.

There are patches of blood on the sidewalks and in the middle of the road with streaks of blood from where bodies were dragged down the road. I shake my head, unable to process everything at one time. The once crowded streets of New York City now don't have even one single soul walking down them.

I step back from the window, still in shock from everything I have just seen. I shake my head in disbelief, not being able to comprehend what I just saw. "There has to be some kind of explanation to this... Are they filming a movie or something?" I ask myself. I start to pace up and down the hallway in my house and then it hits me. The power plant, in Delaware!

"But how could the radiation get all the way up here so fast?" I ask myself.

I walk over to my front door and look out the peep hole into the hallway outside my apartment. The hallway is perfectly clear of life but has a desk knocked over and lying on its side as well as hundreds of pieces of paper scattered throughout it the hall. I step away from the peep hole and pause, before asking myself, "If this is from the nuclear power plant leak... Why is there so much destruction? Radiation wouldn't cause this to happen..."

I continue to pace up and down the hall, confused by everything I see. Occasionally walking back to the peep hole and looking out. Trying to convince myself maybe everything will just go back to normal.

"Think Ryan, think... What could cause this to happen? ..."

Becoming overly frustrated with not being able to figure out what is going on I start to argue with myself. I stop pacing up and down my hallway, still questioning myself.

"There had to be some kind of city wide evacuation... My power was out yesterday, maybe everyone else's was too... So how did they get the word out to evacuate? What about sirens? Maybe they could have used alarms? No... I'm a heavy sleeper, but not *that* heavy. I would have heard that.

I continue to talk to myself while pacing the hallway. Occasionally walking over to the window and looking outside, seeing if everything is back to normal. I stop pacing for a second, thinking that I may be on to something.

"What if no one knew about the evacuation? If the people had no idea, then in a complete panic, bam! Everyone freaks the fuck out and leaves. Although it does not explain how they made no noise when leaving..."

At least five minutes go by with me pacing back and forth in my house. As I am pacing back and forth I continually check the peep hole in the front door and the window at the back of my apartment. Praying that everything is back to normal or this is just some sick joke. Hell, I'm even getting desperate, maybe I'm dreaming!

I walk over to my couch and plop my butt down on it. I let out a long drawn out sigh and stare at the TV. "What can possibly be going on?" I ask myself for almost the hundredth time. I tilt my head back and use my right hand to smack my forehead a few times, trying to knock some sense into myself.

Almost five minutes go by without me figuring out what the hell is going on. I stand up again and start to pace around, now with a fresh headache from all the thinking. I walk by the front of my TV, accidentally kicking my X-box which is somehow off its normal shelf. I roll my eyes before bending over to see what damage I caused to it.

I examine each side of the X-box carefully, glad that I didn't damage it at all from the kick. I place it back on the shelf where it belongs, right next to all of my games. One game in particular happens to catch my attention, *Dead Rising*. My heart almost sinks down fully past my stomach as my eyes light up with excitement.

"I figured it out!"

"They're zombies! They're all zombies!"

CHAPTER 2 ⁓ DEPARTURE

It's all so clear to me now.

"Everything I'm seeing resembles a post-apocalyptic world. Ah, I feel so stupid now!" I mumble to myself while running different scenarios and ideas through my head. "What kind of zombies though... what kind..."

"Well you have more than one kind here; you have your "infected" zombies that aren't dead, but really infected with a virus. Then you have your dead zombies that come back to life. Then you have your zombies that only come out at night..."

I pause for a second and spin around to my bookshelf. I quickly look over my bookshelf until I see *28 Days Later* and *28 Weeks Later*. Once I find them I slide them out and quickly flip them over to read the back of the cases.

"Hmmm, mmmhmmm" I mumble to myself while reading the backs. Agreeing almost with everything I am reading. Still a little bit frustrated, I stop reading and throw both movies onto the couch. "The power plant, the radiation..." I say to myself while pacing around the house.

"The news said people died and miraculously came back to life... It couldn't have been an infection, the people infected die, then return to life."

I keep rooting through my bookshelf looking for movies until finally getting frustrated and going back over to the front door. I peak through the peep hole to see if anything new is happening outside. I take a look around, scanning over the hall.

"Ok, It all seems to be good" I say out loud. "Hmm, first things first I need protection"

I run into my living room and grab my Sofa Chair. I drag it over to the front door and wedge it in my hallway. "That should stop anything from getting in and give me time to prepare".

I start to bite my fingernails and pace the hallway "Why haven't I seen one of these zombies yet?" I say out loud, questioning my original assessment.

"Maybe they only come out at night!" I yell, "Just Like in *I Am Legend*, those zombies could only live in the dark, then they came out to feed at night." I smile, my confidence shooting up for what seems to be a ground breaking new discovery.

"But wait," I say. "The zombies in *I Am Legend* were just infected and could be cured, not similar to these types of zombies." I sit down on my couch and scratch my head.

"I'm being so childish here; I'm comparing what is happening right now to movies. I need to figure out what needs to be done." I say before pushing myself off the couch and walking into my office.

I grab a notepad from the desk as well as a pen before returning to the couch and sitting down. I push everything off the table and onto the floor before placing the notepad on the table. "Alright first things first I need to bunker down and hold my position for the night. First thing tomorrow morning I need to get out of the city, it isn't safe here, the population is too high. I can easily get overwhelmed and eaten". I chuckle to myself at the thought of this all being real.

"Alright so, I need to make a list of exactly what to grab while I am still in town... Hmm, where should I start?"

"I'll need some food! Everyone needs food! Canned food... It will last the longest"

"Oh and I'll need some water too! Everyone needs water, same logic as food. Hmm, bottled water can get it from the super market"

"Hmm, I could also use a watch..." I say out loud before looking down and tapping my current watch, "Been broken since December" I say jokingly.

"Of course I will also need some sort of transportation..." Something that I don't have... Hmm, I'll need to find an SUV of some kind, something all terrain and that can carry a lot."

"I should also collect some medical supplies. Such as antibiotics, gauze, butterfly stitches, really any first aid kit that I find lying around"

"Once I find a vehicle I should probably try and find gas cans to stock up on gas. After all I've got to keep the car running somehow."

"Also if I could find some paper that would be good too. It's a great fire starter and I'd like to keep a note of everything that happens here. Hmm, speaking of fire starter..."

"Wood, matches, lighters. All your basic pyromaniac ingredients"

"And finally I will need weapons for protection. I should probably grab a few pistols, a shotgun or two and a rifle. Oh yeah, don't forget about two machetes!"

"On a similar note, I will need all the ammo I can carry as well as a backpack and a belt to properly hold all of my weapons."

I read over all the items on the notepad and then put it down back onto the table. I lean back before giving my TV a long, blank, stare. "Hmm, I know I am forgetting something..." I say out loud still thinking to myself. A few more minutes go by with nothing coming to my mind. "Forget it; I'll grab anything else I need when I remember."

"Alright, first thing I need to do is set up some sort of protection. I should board up the house in case the zombies do come out at night. While I highly doubt this is the case, better safe than sorry".

I walk over to my bedroom and quietly flip the bed onto its side, sliding it up against the only window in that room. I return to my living room and move the couch away from the front of the window. I then slide my bookshelf over across the window to cover it. Lastly, I walk over into my kitchen and unhook the microwave, placing it in front of the small window that even a cat would have a hard time fitting through.

"Alright, if anything does want to get in, they can still get in. But luckily they can't see in to know someone is in here." I smile while continuing to talk to myself, realizing that it is just the illusion of security that will help me through the night.

Unsure of the exact time, I can tell it is late afternoon by peeking outside my kitchen window and taking a look at the sun. I stand and admire the beauty of it for a second, the air seeming to be a bit clearer today than it has been. This is probably a direct result of no cars and buildings feeding their pollution into the air. After gazing outside I pull the curtain shut and back away from the window.

I open my cabinets and take out a few knives for protection throughout the night, just in case. I place the knives in my living room before walking over to my bedroom and grabbing some blankets from my bed for the night. I collect the blankets from the floor and return to the living room before I am startled by a weird sound in the hallway.

My heart drops down into my chest, my fear almost palpable. I take a huge gulp and slowly creep towards my door, bending down and picking up a knife on the way. I place one foot on the sofa chair by my front door and lean in too look out the peep hole. Nothing is visible in front of me. Sweat is now dripping down my face; and I'm squeezing the knife so tight it is hurting my hand.

My breathing has quickened and become much heavier as I continue to squeeze the knife even harder. I think to myself "Something is going to pop up right in front of my door and scare the shit out of me isn't it". I swallow harder, my conscious obviously not helping at a time like this. A minute passes but it feels like an hour, my eye still glued to this hole. I just can't look away.

I can't stop asking myself, "What's out there? Is it a zombie? Is it a cat? Is it a dog? Is it a survivor?" I can't help but think; I only heard the noise once and then didn't see anything. I'm beginning to question my own sanity. I finally convince myself to back away from the door and start to calm down. I take my foot off the sofa chair and slowly back up, down my hallway. Staring at the door just waiting to hear the noise again or see my front door bust open.

Once I am finally calmed down I lie down on the floor in my living room. While trying to fall asleep I stare at the front door, refusing to let it out of my sight. I try to close my eyes but continue to open them every few seconds to glance at the front door, just waiting for something bad to happen. After about forty minutes, I start to become really drowsy and finally fall asleep on the floor.

Seemingly minutes later I am awoken by a loud bang in the alleyway outside my house. It almost sounded like a trash can being slammed into another one. I quickly grab the knife and stand up before rushing over to my living room window to take a good look outside. "Shit it is too dark, I can't see a fucking thing" I say out loud, frustrated and curious as to what is going on.

I run to the other side of the window, moving the bookcase over to see if I can see anything different on that side. "Damn, still nothing" I say, becoming more and more agitated. I try to slow down my breathing to see if I can hear something else. All sense of security now lost. Time drags on while I stare out the window, occasionally running over to the peep hole in my door to see out.

"I can't see anything" I said to myself, before letting out a sigh.

Just as I stop wondering what the noise is I hear a loud scream in the distance. I start to move the bookcase away from the window so I can step out onto my catwalk to get a better look around. I hear another scream,

"Ahhhhh, get away from me. Someone please help!!" I hear a female voice yelling.

I start to yell but hesitate. "Could this be a trap?" I thought to myself. "No. Someone needs my help" I said out loud before yelling "Can you hear me? If you're out there can you hear me?" I go completely quiet, listening into the night for a response.

"Yes! Yes I can hear you! Please help me!" I hear in the distance from the mysterious female voice.

My heart almost jumps a beat; I start to panic, excited to know that I am not the only one left. I try to yell back but I am out of breath from the excitement. I take in a big breath and then yell "Are you hurt? Are you injured? Can you come to my voice? I can help you, please answer!"

"Yes, I can come to you, I'm not hurt. Where are you?"

I yell back, "Uhm, It's... I am going to do a countdown, come to my voice. Just run as fast as you can I am on a catwalk in my alley way outside of my house. I will help you when you get here. Ok, come to my voice... ten, nine, eight, seven, six, five, four, three, two, one..." I slowly count down from ten, listening in between each number to see if I can hear footsteps.

I reach one and don't hear or see anyone, so I start over "ten, nine, eight, seven, six, five, four, three, two, one..." When I reach one again I stop and listen, still nothing. I start the countdown over, hoping that she is ok. This time when I reach five I hear something jumping over a car nearby. Then a young lady, roughly in her early twenties run around the corner into my alleyway.

I run down the stairs on my catwalk dropping the ladder down for her. She grabs a hold of it and starts to climb up. I take a look behind her to see if anything was following her, but there wasn't. When she gets close to the top I quickly pull her up and pull the ladder up behind her. "Come on, follow me up to my house" I say, stumbling over my words.

I grab my knife and run up the stairs of the catwalk. I stop at my window and enter, looking around really quick to see if anything happened to get inside while I was gone. "Clear" I say, turning around to take a good look at the girl I just saved. She was standing there with a smile on her face, roughly five foot seven, long brown hair down to her shoulders and beautiful blue eyes. She had on a green top and a tight pair of baby blue jeans.

You could tell she had grown a bit since she bought the jeans. Her belly created a little bit of a muffin top over her jeans but she was far from over weight. Her cheeks were still rosy red from the brisk cool weather outside.

I toss her a smile and put my hand out "Hi, My name is Ryan".

She takes my hand and says "Hello Ryan, mine is April". After our introductions I run into my bedroom and grab a blanket from the ground, returning to April.

"Here you go, you look cold", I say.

"Thanks", April responds smiling back at me.

"So I assume the mutual question here is do you have any idea what is going on?"

She smirks, "Nope, do you?"

"Nope, I haven't got a damn clue".

I motion for her to follow me over to my kitchen where I opened the refrigerator door. All the food inside my refrigerator is now spoiled. Pushing the food out of the way, I grab two water bottles from inside, still somewhat cold. I hand her one and open the one that is for me. She smiles and says, "Thanks, I haven't had clean water in days". I nod at her "So have you seen anyone else?" I add.

"What do you mean?"

"Well correct me if I'm wrong, but a few minutes ago you were calling for help. So you must know a wee bit more than me as to what is going on."

"Oh yeah, One of those things was after me."

"What do you mean things?"

"You, you've never seen one of them?"

"No, no I haven't what are they? Are they human?" I ask before taking a sip of my drink.

She nods and says, "Yeah, vampires"

I swallow the water in my mouth; it feels almost like a rock traveling down my throat. My eyes light up in fear as she asks "What's wrong?", "V-vampires?" I ask. She nods and says "Yes, I think so, bloodsucking creatures". I stand up and grab her arm, rushing her into my bedroom and opening the closet. "We have to get inside", I say while pulling clothes and shoes out, throwing them onto the floor of my bedroom behind me.

Once the floor is devoid of shoes and clothes I pull April into the closet with me. Slamming the door shut behind me and bracing my back against it. The closet isn't big enough for the both of us, so she is forced to sit on my lap inside. She can obviously tell that I am scared; my breathing was so heavy that my fear was noticeable. The closet was too dark to for either of us to see each other, but I felt her looking at me before she said "Don't worry, they move really slow and make a lot of noise as they approach".

I pause for a second and say "Wait, so you're telling me that they move really slow and moan as they walk?"

"Yes! Moaning! That was the word I was looking for."

I sigh and say, "Do they by any chance look like they have decaying flesh?"

"Hmm, maybe I'm not sure", she says after pausing for a moment.

"Do you know what a zombie is?"

"Like *Resident Evil*?"

"Yes Exactly!"

"Good, so they're zombies, not vampires?"

"What's the difference, they both want to kill you"

"Yes, but both use different methods to get to you. For example zombies can't run up walls or jump really high, they are very slow and don't have super human strength, were as vampires do."

April was silent for a second as she was thinking. "Oh. I see. So, It is better that they are zombies and not vampires?"

"Yes, much better. Now we can get out of this closet too." I try to stand up but April doesn't budge. "Wait! I like it in here. I feel safe and comfortable with you." A bit confused, I respond, "I see, well, alright. We should get some sleep so we can be ready to move at morning".

"Ok, oh and thank you... for saving me".

I smirk and tilt my head to the side, leaning it against the door that my back is against. Her legs are lying over top of mine; both of us are crammed into the closet, but oddly comfortable. I lay there, still thinking of the conversation between me and April from earlier. The fact that I was right everyone that used to be alive is now a zombie. Everyone I used to know, my friends, my family...

I wonder if they are still out there, if they're safe. How much of the world was affected by this? Is it curable? Many questions fill my head, all of which I know I won't get the answer to any time soon. Knowing I won't get the answers any time soon doesn't stop me from wondering. The only thought on my mind now is getting me and April out of this city.

Tomorrow is the first possible step in the right direction that I can take and I plan to take it.

A smile forms on my face, knowing deep down inside that I'll be ok. I close my eyes and clear my mind, almost at peace with what has happened the past few days. I may have lost all my old friends, but I found a new one and tomorrow we are going to make it out of this city alive.

———————————————

Day breaks as I open my eyes. I let out a long yawn, stretching out my arms. Once I'm fully awake I lean over and shake April to wake her up. I startle her at first but then she seems to remember what is going on and where she is. Once we're both awake I pull myself to my feet and help her up after me. When we're both up, I open the closet door and walk out into my apartment. Sunlight is bursting into my apartment at every opening it can find, lighting my way around the place.

I continue to yawn as I walk over to the kitchen and grab two bottles of water out of the refrigerator. The two bottles of water that I grabbed are the last two that I have. I toss one to her and open mine, sucking down half of it almost immediately. As we drink our water we both stand there, staring at each other. Neither of us exchanges words as we are still tired and cramped from the night before.

I snivel and rub my nose before saying, "Here is my list of supplies, tell me if you think we need anything else before we get out of the city". I reach into my pocket and pull out a crumbled piece of paper and hand it to her.

She takes the paper and rubs her eyes before quickly reading it over. April nods every time she goes by an item that she agrees that we need. When she is finished reading she adds, "You forgot vodka".

I stand there, arching an eyebrow at her and say in a sarcastic voice, "By any chance are you Russian?"

She smiles, letting out a slight chuckle, "On my father's side, but alcohol has more medical elements then you think".

I quickly add in a sarcastic manner, "Like what, getting shit faced so you can't feel any pain?"

She nods, agreeing with me, "Yes. It has been used as a pain killer before. It has also been used to lower someone's core body temperature, Inflammation and Disinfectant"

I scratch my chin, happy that I have someone who is knowledgeable on my side. "So, since you know all these things about medicine. I assume you went to med-school. May I ask where?"

"Massachusetts Institute of Technology.", she says, blushing just a bit.

I nod grabbing my water bottle and bringing it up to my mouth. I take in a mouth full from the bottle not fully realizing what she just said. With the water still lingering in my mouth, it hits me. I think to myself... M.I.T? Like *the M.I.T*? I pause for a second, wondering to myself if it can even be true. I mean, if it is true... How did she confuse zombies and vampires?

I swallow my water, shaking my head in disbelief before quickly saying everything on my mind. "M.I.T, *the M.I.T*? So you went to M.I.T, the med-school at M.I.T?" Getting a bit more frustrated, "How... Let me ask you this. If you're smart enough to go to M.I.T, this would imply that your I.Q would be somewhere in the one-twenties. Now, don't get me wrong I believe you. But I don't understand how you got zombies and vampires confused."

"Well..." April starts to talk but I quickly interrupt her and continue. "I mean come on, one has a completely normal face, aside from abnormally large fangs and the other is a completely decaying body. One moves really fast, jumps really high and can run up walls. Oh yeah, don't forget change into bats. While on the other hand the other one moves *really* slow and only wants to eat your flesh."

She sighs and puts her head down, making it more than obvious that I hurt her feelings. I put my hand on her shoulder and she looks back up at me with a tear rolling down her left cheek. I smile and say to her, "I'm sorry". She nods and walks into the kitchen, moving the microwave out of the way to look out the window. I stand there and watch her, feeling bad for the pain I have caused her. I put my head down and turn to walk towards the bedroom to grab my backpack.

The second I turn to go towards my bedroom she says in a crackled voice, "My parents... They sheltered me from the world. They always told me, Oh April you're our number one, you'll be the first person in this family to go to college. They forced me to study, never letting me outside to experience things myself. They suppressed my creativity..." I open my mouth and start to talk but am quickly interrupted by April.

"Please... Let me finish"

"I've seen a handful of movies in my life; I've never had any real friends. My parents wouldn't let anyone over. They said it would be a distraction from my school work..." She pauses and then continues, "I've always said how much I wished they were out of my life... and now they are..."

I can hear her voice starting to break up more. Her nose is starting to get stuffy and I can almost hear the tears now starting to pour down her face. I walk over to her to give her some comfort. When I reach her and put my hand on her shoulder she almost immediately spins around and throws her arms around me. Her eyes are red as the tears are rolling down her face.

"Now that they are gone...and... I'm... I'm happy".

She looks up at me, "Is it wrong? If your parents mistreat you their whole lives... Is it wrong to hate them?"

She is staring up at me, the tears still rolling down her face. This makes it very obvious that this is a tender topic for her. I smile down at her, placing my hand on the back of her head before saying,

"No."

It was almost like pressing the trigger on a gun. The second she heard me say no she burst into tears slamming her face into my chest almost immediately soaking my shirt. Almost a minute passes before she pulls her head out from the hole she created. She looks up at me and snivels before adding "We really should get moving."

"Yeah..." I say while patting the back of her head, "Yeah..."

She breaks her grasp from me and allows me to turn around and walk into the bedroom to grab my backpack. Once I have my backpack I return to the living room and grab my knife. I look over at April still standing in the same spot as before. "Do you want to stay here another night?"

She shakes her head side to side, letting me know she wants to get out of here. I nod and hand her one of the knives from the ground. She looks up at me, almost confused. I smile at her and say, "Aim for the head, it's their only vulnerable spot." She nods as I walk over to the front door to my apartment. I put my foot up onto the sofa chair and take a look out the peep hole. I don't see anything in particular, aside from a door open in the hallway.

I hesitate a second before questioning myself. Wondering if the same door was open yesterday and I just didn't notice it. I continue staring out the peep hole until it becomes obvious that something is wrong. "What's wrong?" April asks. "My Neighbor, Mrs. Clide's Door is open, I'm not sure if it was open yesterday or not." April swallows hard before asking, "Do you see your neighbor?"

I shake my head, "No, but I'm not worried about her. She was in her death bed, on life support…" "What I am worried about though are her cats. I mean if animals can get infected too… Well then needless to say we would have twenty some zombie cats running around."

April bites her lower lip, scared and thinking about what to do. "What about the catwalk that I came up on last night?", "Yeah, that probably is our only option." I step down from the sofa chair and walk over to my living room, sliding the bookshelf out of the way and open the window leading out back. As I step out onto the catwalk, the cold chill of the February air blasts me in the face.

I take a look around outside before helping April out from the house. I look her in the eye and say "Alright, it looks clear. Now, when we get down we got to move quickly and quietly. If you see something, you have to let me know. There is a gun shop two blocks from here. That is our first destination."

April nods to me, letting me know that she understands the plan. I lower myself down the ladder slowly and quietly into the alleyway. I climb down it first and motion to her at the bottom that she is all clear. She reaches the ground and quickly follows behind me and up the alley. When we reach the sidewalk I look out, checking both ways to see if it is clear.

"Clear", I say before making a right and quickly walking down the sidewalk.

Looking at the destruction from ground level allowed me to see how bad it really was. Cars were over turned and driven into buildings as well as into other cars. Glass littered the streets, covering the streets almost as much as the snow from the night before. The damage amongst the city is almost unfathomable.

You could see blood smears from where bodies have been dragged and even bigger puddles of blood from where they laid. However, no bodies could be seen anywhere on the road or sidewalks. Meaning they must have been either fully eaten, or they got up and walked away. I'm going with the latter.

April follows me closely, looking around the streets of New York frantically. Each time we pass a building I glance at the doors and windows to see if there is anyone or anything moving inside. When I reach the intersection farther up the road I check all four streets for any zombies before continuing. I make a right and continue down the street with April still close behind. As we're making our way through New York curiosity arises in April and she asks,

"Why haven't we seen a zombie yet?"

"The city was evacuated. Everyone that didn't leave probably boarded themselves up in their houses. This is where they will stay zombie... or Human."

We continue up the street, the conversation between us coming to a halt until we get closer to the gun shop.

"Alright, right up here on the Corner is the gun shop."

The gun shop is a very small building, no bigger than your average sized apartment. Not many people knew about it in New York Since it was tightly tucked away. The front door was almost in an alleyway. All the windows to the front of the shop were broken, meaning someone was here before and already has looted some of the store.

"Alright, the safest thing you can do is stand out in the middle of the street on top of a car, while I go in and clear it."

"No, I'm staying right behind you." April says while frantically shaking her head side to side.

I grip my knife tightly before opening the door, holding it for April until we're both fully inside. "Shh", I add, before listening to see if I hear anything. I walk down the aisle to check out the store. After I check that aisle I turn the corner and check the remaining two isles. Once I've fully check the whole store I nod my head to April, signaling it is clear. Once I know it is clear I walk over to the cash register and peek behind it, finishing my search.

"Alright, it seems clear." I put my knife on the counter and smash the glass to grab the guns on display. "Alright, I want you to grab two pistols for yourself and a shotgun." She nods, taking a second to process what I just told her to do. "Oh and be quick."

I grab a pistol from the display case and then hop over the counter to grab a similar pistol from the other side of the counter. While I am on the other side of the counter I also grab a shotgun and a rifle. April comes back to the counter and places down a magnum and a shotgun on the part of the glass that isn't broken. I shake my head in disapproval before saying, "You don't want a magnum, it will take you too long to reload it." I hand her my Glock and add, "Here take this, I'll grab another from the wall".

She takes the gun and holds it in her hand, pointing it at the wall. I smile at her, "Find all the ammo you can for this gun and put it in my backpack". I hand her my backpack and she nods going back through the store to find some ammo. I grab another Glock from behind the counter and a belt. I strap the belt to my waist, at the same time April arrives with ammo. I grab the backpack from her and ask, "Is this everything you could grab?" She nods, "Yes, It's all they had."

I smile reaching into the backpack and pulling out a few magazines. I slip one into both of my gun and another into hers. I hand her the backpack again and ask, "Now see if you can find ammo for an M4 rifle and a Remington 870 shotgun."

"How do you know this much about guns?" April asks.

"I played a lot of FPS'" I reply.

She smiles at me and starts to walk away. She scratches her head before spinning around curiously and asking,

"Yeah, I don't know what that is."

"First Person Shooter, It is a time of Video Game."

"Ahhh" she adds, turning around and looking for the ammo I asked her to. A smile comes across my face as I watch her walk away, back into the store. I take the Glock that I got from behind the counter and place it in my belt. The Glock I got from the counter I hold on to, planning to use that as my primary defense.

April returns with the bag, now filled with more ammo. I load the M4 rifle and my shotgun that I got from behind the counter as well as two that I grabbed for her. I throw the shotgun and M4 over my back before handing April an M4 and a shotgun. I hold the pistol I got from the counter in my hand. "It's time to leave, let's go". She nods and follows me out the door.

We step out onto the sidewalk, the cold chill once again finding us. I shiver, looking both ways before letting April know that the roads are clear. We both step back out onto the street, looking both ways to see if we can see anything. While looking up and down the street I say to April, "Alright, next we need a car."

"What type?"

"An SUV preferably"

She nods, looking up and down the street for an SUV. April spots one and jumps in excitement, pointing down the road nearby. "Over there, It looks like a Ford Escape." I take a look over to where she was pointing and notice the SUV sitting in the middle of the road. Compared to the shit heaps for cars around it, the SUV looks like it is in almost mint condition. "Let's go" I say before hoping off the top of the car I am standing on now. We quickly move down the street towards the parked car.

It doesn't take long for us to make our way over to the car. When are arrive April jumps in excitement, pointing out the fact that it is a hybrid. I scan over the area around us, at all surrounding buildings, making sure it is safe. "Clear" I say, before opening the car door and motioning for April to get inside. She nods and hops inside of the car.

"Please tell me the keys are in it, are the keys in it?"

"Yup they are!"

April turns the keys in the car and we both celebrate as it starts up without a problem. My eyes light up with excitement before saying out loud "Ha ha, what are the chances!" I run over to the other side of the car and get in. I look over at April and say, "You guessed it, you're the driver!" She nods, throwing her shotgun into the backseat and turning the car out of the spot it is in. We dodge any abandoned cars as we slowly drive down the road.

Following April's example I throw my shotgun as well as my rifle into the backseat of the SUV. As we're driving I look over to her and say "Alright, now we need to stock up on some food and water." April nods and says, "I know a super market about five blocks away". I shake my head "No, no, no, no, no, no. No super markets, they are too big, too dangerous."

"Good point" April says, now agreeing with me. "Find a gas station. We can put some gas into the car and also grab some for later. Also inside I'll grab all the water and food I can get." April nods, continuing to drive down the road, keeping a look out for zombies as well as any gas stations. Spotting one she throws her arm across my face, pointing out the window. "Hey look there!" I turn to the side, looking directly at where she is pointing and see a gas station.

April slams on the breaks, jolting both of us forward causing me to look over at her, puzzled. She giggles and says, "Sorry, not used to this car". I laugh, a bit reluctant to the fact that she is a competent driver as we pull into the gas station. She parks next to the pump and swipes her card to activate it. I run over to the store, opening the door and taking a quick look around before walking inside. Once inside I work my way over to the water in the back of the store and start to grab some. Stuffing it into my pockets and grabbing as much as I can carry.

I pause for a second after hearing a noise that came from the back of the store. It sounded almost like a can being kicked around along a concrete floor. I drop the water that I am holding before tightly gripping my gun. "Hello?" I say out loud before pausing and expecting an answer. After a few seconds go by without getting an answer I take a few steps forward and yell out again, "Hello?" Without hearing an answer I walk over to the storage room door and open it up. As I walk inside the fear in me is quickly rising. A few seconds after entering the room I hear the noise again. Now my heart is racing and I am scared while just wanting to know what the noise is. When I round the corner in the storage room, I see it.

There is a man standing in the back of the room with his shirt all torn up and blood. The man's face is covered with dried blood as well as torn. He could have possibly been mauled by a dog or something of that nature. His eyes are bloodshot and lips are curled as he is staring straight at me. I swallow hard, almost as if a rock was traveling down my throat. I've finally made confrontation with the enemy, a zombie.

The zombie stumbles towards me as I point my gun directly at his head and pull the trigger... I hear a click but nothing happens. My heart drops into my chest as my fear is so strong I can almost taste it. The zombie places an arm on my shoulder and lunges towards my neck which causes me to stumble backwards. As I am moving backwards I accidentally step on a lead pipe. The lead pipe rolls out from under me before shooting across the room and causing me to fall to the ground.

As I fall to my back the zombie collapses on top of me, now having the advantage. The zombie lunges and bites at my face with blood dripping from its mouth. The blood drips onto my face as I struggle and try not to let it get into my eyes or mouth, avoiding the risk of infection. "You are the ugliest mother fucker... I've ever had on top of me", I mumble before raising my knee and hitting the zombie in his balls.

I stare into his eyes as I thrust my knee into his balls. But the zombie continues, seemingly unaffected. "I'll tell you what, that would of worked on me." I say as I realize I can't stay like this forever.

I grab hold of the zombie's shirt and roll him over, making it so I'm the one on top now. I pin his head to the ground by grabbing his neck as I reach for my sidearm. Once I have my sidearm out I plant the gun to his forehead and stare at him. The zombie is still snarling and biting at me, struggling to get to me. You can tell that is the only thing on his mind, he just wants to rip me apart. He seems to not even notice or care about the fact that he is about to die.

I close my eyes to avoid blood getting in them before firing off a shot into the zombie's head. As the bullet tears through his head blood sprays all over the floor and surrounding area. A few seconds after hearing the gunshot I open my eyes to see the mess I created. Releasing the grasp from his neck I stand up and stare down at him "Dead now? Huh bitch?" I say out loud before picking up the gun that misfired and taking a look at it.

I check the safety on it and aim it at the wall, pulling the trigger a few times. Nothing happens. I sigh before realizing what was wrong with it.

"Fucking firing pin was taken out." I take the magazine out of the gun and throw it on the ground next to the corpse.

Outside I hear April yelling "Ryan, what was that, what happened in there? Are you ok?" I yell back, "Yeah I'm fine, but this son of a bitch isn't". April comes running inside and rounds the corner, looking at me standing over the zombie's lifeless corpse. She adds, "Oh my god is it dead? Are you ok?"

I nod, "Yeah I am fine, let's just grab the water, some food and get the fuck out of here."

We return out into the store, closing the storage room door behind us. We round up all the water and food we can hold and return to the SUV, putting it all inside. We return to the store for a second trip, grabbing everything that is left. When we return to the car April takes it off the pump and closes up the gas tank.

After we've finished loading the supplies I close the back door to the SUV and hop in the passenger's seat. April hops into the driver's seat and turns the car back on before pulling out of the gas station. As we're driving away from the gas station I look into my side view mirror, wondering if I'll ever be able to forget what I just did.

"So where do you plan to go now?" April asks, snapping me out of my trance. "Uhm, well I need a watch and we still need medical supplies"

April nods and asks "Where do you think we should go for that stuff?" I sigh and put my head down, "Heh, another gas station."

"But let's get out of the city first; we'll hit one up at the suburbs. It is too dangerous in the city."

"Do you know where you are going?"

"Yes, we're traveling west towards Jersey. The Holland Tunnel isn't far."

"Wait, The Holland Tunnel? Can we even get through that?"

"Of course we can, why couldn't we?"

"Not sure, just evaluating all of our possibilities."

She chuckles, "Don't worry and just take a nap or something. You've been through a lot today." I take a look at the interior clock, it reads two p.m. I sigh; the day is flying by already. Hopefully we will be out of the city by nightfall I think to myself before taking a look in the passenger side mirror. I take one final look behind the car at New York City and all of the damage that has been done to it the past few days.

I place my head against the interior of the car and stare out the window. While listening to the sounds of the engine before I slowly fall asleep.

CHAPTER 3 ~ TROUBLES

"Ryan, RYAN!! Wake up!" April yells, causing me to jolt awake.

My eyes open wide; as I look around, already fully awake. The first thing I realize is it is completely dark outside. April shakes me again, making sure I am awake "Ryan there is another car, it's coming our way." She is talking fast, scared, unsure of what to do. I look out the windshield and in front of the car. I see another pair of headlights and they're coming right at us. "Keep driving, don't stop." I warn April.

"But..."

Interrupting her, I say, "No buts, you need to keep driving. They could be scavengers."

April nods, continuing to watch the head lights with me as they get closer and closer. The car passes us and both of us let out a sigh of relief. Shortly after they pass us we hear a loud screech, piercing the silence of the night. Both of us spin around and look behind us. We notice that the car did a tail spin and is now heading directly for us.

"They're coming at us fast!"

"Should I stop?" April says hesitantly.

"No. Don't stop." I say, masking my fear with anger

"April, do you know how to drive this car?"

"What do you mean, drive?"

"I mean evasive driving, can you lose them?"

"Uhm, I guess, I've never done it before."

"Forget it then."

In no time the car catches up to us, it hangs behind us and starts to match our speed. Both of us are confused and scared of what is to come next. Almost like they were answering our question we hear two gun shots. April yells, "Oh my god they're shooting at us!"

"No they aren't." I add, "They are signaling for us to pull over."

"Do you want me to pull over?"April says, her hands are shaking, not knowing what to do.

"Start to slow down, not too fast. Enough to let them know we comply. Now listen to me. I want you to place your gun against the side of your door. When we stop the people will come out of their car and over to ours. They will point guns at us."

"What I need you to do is point your gun at your door. Don't move until they get impatient. They will come to the doors and try to open them. At that time fire two shots into the guy on your side and I will fire two shots into the guy on my side. Understand?"

She shakes her head side to side still shaking uncontrollably, "I can't."

"You have to."

"I'm scared, I can't."

"Fuck."

"Alright then new plan, give me your gun and roll down the windows." April hands me her gun and hits the buttons to her left to lower the windows. "When they come up to the doors pointing guns at us I want you to flash your brake lights on the car. Just quickly press it down, flashing then as much as you can. Make sure the car is in park. Wait for me to tell you to start flashing them."

Our car now fully comes to a complete stop. April asks, "Why?" I shake my head side to side as I hear two car doors open and slam shut behind us. Two men arrive at both sides of our car. Both wearing ski masks and pointing guns at the car. They yell, "Get out of the car and no one gets hurt!" I look over and notice that April is shaking and crying, scared out of her mind.

"What's up with the ski masks? Don't want the cops to know who you are?" I ask with a smirk.

"Oh, one of you is a smart ass. Cute, now get out of the fucking car.", One of the masked men replies.

Both of us sit in the car motionless, waiting for them to become impatient.

"I said; get out of the fucking car!" One of the masked men yells again.

I say out of the side of my mouth, "Now".

April turns and just barely says, "What?" It's obvious that her fear and tears making it hard for her to speak.

"Everybody freeze! Nobody move! Get out of the car! This is your last chance!" The masked men yell again.

"Now April, Brake Lights.", I murmur.

My heart starts racing and time seems to slow down. April starts to rapidly press the Brake Lights of the car, just like I told her to. Out of the corners of their eyes, the two masked men catch a glimpse of the flickering light. Confused and curious, they both turn toward the back of the car. The second I notice the men turning, I point both guns at them and fire simultaneously, breaking the silence between us. Less than a second after both gun shots ring out in the car both men drop to the ground.

I open the car door and jump out and drop April's gun on the ground. I quickly move back to the scavenger's car behind us. April is still sitting in the driver's seat, shaking and still flashing the Brake Lights of the car, her fear has made her oblivious to everything around her. The second I see the car behind us I raise my gun and plant two gun shots into the passenger's seat. Quickly following the two in the passenger's seat I plant another two in the backseat behind the driver's side.

April gets out of the car and runs around to my side of the vehicle. She comes up right behind me and puts her hands on my shoulders "There... there were more of them?" she asks. I shake my head, "No idea, but I'm not taking any chances."

I continue to approach the car and smash the driver's side window when I reach it. Once the window is smashed I stick my gun inside firing two more shots into the back seat. April jumps and says again, "Oh my god! Was there someone else?" I look back and say "Don't know, but if there was, he is dead now." I smile and stick my head inside, taking a look around. Nothing is inside aside from my gun shot holes and a few crates of supplies.

"Hey April, Let's get these supplies back to the car." I say out loud, beckoning her over.

She stares at me, not moving an inch. "I understand you're scared, but what was done, needed to be done."

"How do you know they were going to hurt us?" She says.

"I didn't, but I wasn't going to let them take the chance." I say trying to reassure her. "Plus the gun was a pretty big give away."

April nods at me, understanding that I did what I had to do. I reach into the back of the car grabbing two of the four boxes and bringing them to our car. April leans in behind me and grabs the other two. After placing the loot in our car I grab the guns that the two scavengers were wearing and pull off their masks. Curious to see the faces of the very first people I've killed.

April gets in the car while I am grabbing their guns and taking off their masks. Once they're disarmed I drag their bodies off the side of the road and place a bullet in each of their heads for good measure. Making sure that no matter what, they'll never walk again. After I'm done I motion to April for her to come out of the car. She steps out and is questioning my reasoning

"Come here, I want to teach you something." I say to her, motioning for her to come in front of the car and stand next to me.

April comes over and stands in front of me, the headlights lighting the area we are standing in. She is still shivering from the midnight air and the events that have unfolded tonight. I stop for a second and admire her beauty. April's skin seemed a bit more pale than usual and her cheeks rosy red from the cold weather.

She stands in front of me and I hand her my gun "Here take this." She nods and takes the gun, holding it gently in her hand, shaking a bit, scared of the power she now holds. I say, "Don't worry, it is ok." I walk around her and lightly grab her hand with mine, lifting it up into the air.

"Now see that tree over there?" I ask while pointing straight in front of her. She nods.

"Alright, what I want you to do is point the gun at the tree and pull the trigger." I say to her, lifting her hand up to the tree and then letting go.

I take a step back and say, "Go ahead, shoot." April turns and looks at me, letting out a slight smile and then looks back at the tree. She fires a shot and jumps, after hearing the sound of the gun. Her shot just barely nicking the tree I told her to shoot at. I walk over to her and lightly grab the hand the gun is in.

"Alright so what you want to do is hold this hand steady..." I grab her other hand and place it under the one holding the gun. "Alright, now this is what you want to hold it like, to give yourself more support."

April nods as I let go of both of her hands and back up. "Alright, now let's hit that tree!" April raises her hands just like I told her to and fires at the tree. This time she hits the dead center of the tree. "Good!" I yell excitedly. "Now try it again." April raises her hands again, pointing at the same tree. She fires the gun and hits the tree again.

"Good job!" I yell while also giving her a little round of applause.

"Now for another quick test before we get going. Take the gun and point it at that tree. Shoot at that tree, hit it then hit the two trees on either side of it."

April nods and says "Alright". She aims the gun at the tree she previously hit. Firing at the tree and then firing two more consecutive times at the trees to each side, hitting all her targets. April turns to me, lowering the gun and jumping excitedly that she hit all of her targets. She runs over and gives me a big hug while smiling.

April looks at me and says, "Alright, let's get out of here I'm cold."

I smile, chuckling a bit, "I'll drive this time. You need to get some sleep."

April smiles and nods before walking over and getting into the passenger's side of the car. I walk over to the driver's side, opening the door and getting in. I shift the car into drive and glance over at April. She has her head leaning against the window, making it look like she is already passed out. I smile and look back towards the road, rolling up the windows and pressing forward.

With April asleep I now have time to think and process what is going on. I lean back in the seat, focusing on the road but letting my mind wonder... I can't help but think I have killed three people today; of course one of them was already dead... But this still goes down as quite an interesting day in my book.

I let out a long drawn out sigh. Well on the plus side I met a really beautiful girl. I also killed one of the many zombies that infest this world now. Smiling a bit I look over at April, admiring her beauty as she sleeps. Looking back at the road I wonder... We just came from New York City... New York City... One of the largest cities in the world... Why didn't we see more zombies...?

My mind can't help but wonder where all the zombies are. Are they all dead? Do they travel in packs? Why have I only seen one of them? My head starts to hurt just from thinking about everything. More importantly we have yet to pick a destination yet.

"I wonder where April was driving..." I murmur as I am thinking to myself.

"Well, she was heading west so... I mine as well keep heading west too."

Hours pass as I mindlessly stare at the road and let my mind wonder... Day break creeps up on me as I see the sun rising in the rear view mirror. Knowing which direction the sun is rising from lets me know that I am heading in the right direction. As morning breaks, the car starts to grow cold and the frost from the night before is now melting off of the trees and grass outside. I let out a yawn before rubbing my eyes, trying to shake off the cool morning chill.

While driving the only time I take my eyes off the road is to look down at the gas meter. When looking down at the meter this time I realize that we only have a quarter tank of gas left. "This could be bad." I say while letting out a sigh, realizing I got to start looking for a gas station. I continue driving down the road, keeping my eye out for any gas stations. One gas station catches my eye, down the road on the left hand side.

I get out of the car and lock April's side so nothing can get in from the outside. I quietly close the door before I start pumping the gas. Once the gas is pumping, I approach the door and try to open it but it is locked. "Damn!" I yell out loud. I step back and use the bottom of my gun to shatter the glass on the door, reaching inside to unlock and open it.

Light is still trying to burst through the trees outside. Making it hard for me see inside the store and to clear the gas station safely. I clear the front room before holstering my gun. I grab a map book from the counter and a few water bottles as well as some food before exiting the gas station. I return to the car and open the back door, tossing what I found in the back seat before closing the door again.

April moves around in her seat a bit. I must have disturbed her, I thought to myself. I return to the gas pump and place the nozzle back into it. I close up the gas tank and pull twenty dollars out of my pocket, throwing it at the pump I say, "Keep the change." I walk around to the passenger's side of the car and take a look at the road to the north. I immediately notice something walking around the road up there.

It's far away, maybe one hundred yards. I hop back into my car and reach into the backseat grabbing my M4 rifle. I run back around the car and stare down the scope of my gun. I see a man hobbling around on the road. "Another zombie." I mumble to myself before lining him up in my sites. I tap on the passenger's side window to wake April up. When she wakes up she looks at me sleepily. Completely dumbfounded by what is going on.

"Hey!" I yell to her "Just waking you up to let you know I am about to fire at that zombie over there. That way the shot doesn't scare the shit out of you". April smiles at me and gives me a thumbs up, letting me know she heard me.

Once I see her give me the thumbs up I focus down the scope again. I place the crosshairs right over top the zombie's head and fire. Less than a second later I see a mist of blood come out from the side of the zombie. Right after the mist of blood it drops and falls to the ground. "BOOM HEADSHOT!" I yell out loud, laughing.

April leans over and knocks on my window "Uhm, Ryan? There are three more behind us." I quickly spin around, not knowing how close they are. Once I turn around I notice three more zombies hobbling down the road towards me. Without any hesitation I fire at the first zombie, hitting him in the head and taking him down. I line up my cross hairs with the second one, firing at him as well and taking him down.

I line up with the third one and fire at him, but I miss and hit the car right next to him. "Damn!" I yell out loud, a bit frustrated. "First time I've missed." I refocus my sites and fire, hitting the zombie in the head, dropping him to the ground. "Ryan! There is another one in the tree line just over there!" April points in front of the car and a bit to the left.

I lean over top the car and aim at the zombie, firing him and hitting him in the head. I look down the street that I came from, noticing five more zombies walking my way. "Well, it looks like the fun is over." I say to April before hoping back into the car. I turn the car on and look over at April, "We've alerted too many and got to get out of here."

April nods, letting me know that she agrees with me. I hand her the map book I got from inside the store and ask her how to get to South Jersey. She flips through it before pointing in the direction that I need to go. I pull out of the gas station and start to head down the road in that direction. A few minutes after leaving the gas station she asks, "What is in south Jersey?", "Family.", I reply.

"You don't think they're..." She says trying not to hurt my feelings.

"I know they're dead. If they aren't they sure as hell are not still home." I chime in reluctantly.

"I'm... I'm sorry."

"No reason to worry. It's better this way. I won't get hit with a surge of emotions when I get home and realize no one is there." I say, trying to reassure April.

"May I ask then, why are we going to south Jersey?"

"Supplies, I know what I have at my house. A lot of stuff there will greatly benefit us. Plus, I have a few friends there that collected shit in the event of a global disaster, much like this. Knowing those kids, they're still alive." I smile glancing over at April.

"So, how far away is your house?"

"We'll be there by noon", I reply. "I figure we will gather the supplies, load the truck and bunker down for the night there. At least we can then get a good night's sleep in a bed."

April smiles and says, "Thank you."

I look over at her and ask, "For what? Giving you a place to sleep?" I laugh, "No reason to thank me for that."

April smiles and looks over at me, "No, for that night... You remember, the night that you saved me. I was so scared. I had those things behind me, following me. I didn't want to tell you at first because I thought you wouldn't let me up the ladder. I'm sorry."

"No reason to be sorry, I would of let you up anyway. Just do me a favor from now on, alright? When one of those things is following you, let me know!" April laughs while nodding her head.

We both go silent, as I am now focusing on the road ahead of me. Now thinking more about what I will find when I arrive at the house in South Jersey. I turn to April, bored and looking for conversation.

"So, where are you originally from?"

"My family is from Russia, but I was born in New York City."

"Ahh, so you're used to the cold?"

She nods, "Yes, yes I am. Why do you ask?"

"Was just curious, I'm bored while driving, looking for conversation."

April laughs and says, "Oh you want conversation do you?"

I smile, a bit confused, "What are you implying?"

"So I remember you mentioning FPS before, as to why you know so much about guns. Where did your knowledge of zombies come from?"

"Well, let's say I'm kind of a fanatic. I've been waiting for something like this to happen for quite awhile."

"Oh really, have you now?" April asks.

"Yes, yes I have."

"What are your plans for survival then?" April asks sarcastically.

"Well you're watching it work right now!", "Grab weapons, food and water and let's keep moving. Eventually we will find a survivor colony or more people and be able to start a colony."

"Well I guess the right person answered when I called for help, huh?"

I smile and turn to look over at her, "Well I guess you did."

The conversation ends abruptly as I continue my long drive south back home. After another hour passes I look down at the gas tank, realizing that I am just below quarter. "We're going to need gas soon. Keep an eye out for any signs or gas stations." I say to April as she nods and acknowledges what I said.

A few minutes later April breaks the silence and points out the right hand side of the car. "Oh! I see a sign; it says two miles exit twelve." I look over at the sign and notice it shows a little gas symbol on it as well. I put on my blinker and switch lanes, getting ready to board the exit ramp. Once I switch into the other lane I chuckle to myself, April laughing and realizing what I did as well. "Some habits are hard to break, huh?"

Two miles up the road we get off at exit twelve. We circle around the exit ramp until we're dumped out onto a small highway. An eerie chill runs down my spine as I slow down the car almost to a crawl. "Something just doesn't feel right here..." April nods in agreement, "What... happened here..."

We pull into a small town area. Windows in the cars around us are broken as well as the stores on each side of the road. Blood is splattered all over the sidewalks, streets and the side of buildings. Body parts can be seen scattered across the landscape. There are bullet-holes in cars as well as paper and hats blowing across the ground. April and I are looking around, almost speechless of what we see. "This place... Is devoid of life", I say to April. April adds, "I haven't seen anything yet..."

I see the gas station that the exit sign pointed out and start to drive over in that direction. Before pulling into the gas station I look over at April and say, "Alright, we're going to get in and out of here as fast as fucking possible. You get out of the car and pump the gas. I'll grab the rifle and cover you." April lets out a shaky breath of air before saying "I have a bad feeling about this place." I agree with her, "Yeah... That makes two of us."

I pull up to the gas pump and stop the car. I shift it into park before reaching for the rifle in the back seat. Once I have the rifle in my hand I hop out of the car. April opens the door and gets out before she starts to pump the gas. She opens the tank of the car and places the nozzle inside. After hitting a few buttons she spins around to me. "Ryan! It isn't working". I continue to stare down the scope of my M4, making sure nothing else is around. "Try the other pumps."

April nods at me before running to each of the other pumps checking to see if they work. She tries the other two pumps in front of the car with no luck. Afterwards she heads over to the last pump at the gas station and says a little prayer before pressing a button. She jumps with excitement "It works! It works!" I chime in, "Good, now move the car over there and fill it up."

April runs back to the car, shifting it into drive and circling around the gas station. She pulls back in and parks the car next to the pump before getting out and quickly placing the nozzle in the tank. My heart is pounding, wanting to jump out of my chest. I frantically continue to check each of the roads around the gas station, every few seconds spinning to look at each road.

I'm caught off guard by April yelling. "Ryan! They're inside the gas station!" I run to the other side of the car that April is on, closer to the front of the gas station. On the other side of the car I notice a zombie slowly limping and making his way through the front door of the gas station. I aim the gun at the zombie's head and pull the trigger, blowing his brains out all over the front of the gas station's store.

"We need to get the fuck out of here." I say to April before spinning around and looking down the road we came in on. "Clear!" I say before turning to the other road to the west. When I turn and look down the road to the west I notice two zombies walking down the road right towards us. "They must have heard the shot!" I remark before aiming at them and firing twice, taking them both out.

April yells out to me, "The other direction, Ryan, the other direction!" I spin around, looking down the street she is pointing towards. When I turn to look down the street I see two more zombies limping and stumbling down the road. I fire off two more shots, dropping both of them to the ground. "How much longer until you're done April?", "I only need a few more seconds!"

I turn around and look down the road we came in on which is still clear. Knowing the road is clear and that we can easily escape from this mess comforts me some. I spin around and look down the road I previously shot two zombies on. Only to see six more crawling towards us. Without firing at any of them I check the final road leading towards the gas station. When I turn to look down this road I see another seven coming right towards us. "April..." I say really slow, "We need to get the fuck out of here."

"Ok! Ok! We're done let's go!" She hollers out before running back around to the driver's side of the car. We both get into the car before April slams the car into drive and peels wheels back onto the highway. We drive down the road until we find the on ramp leading up to the highway. We board that and within seconds are back onto the highway leading south.

"Now that... was interesting." I remark. April continues by adding, "Ryan... I never want to do that again." I smile a bit and laugh, "Agreed." We both sit back and go silent, trying to relax after what we just did and seen at the gas station. I lean into the backseat of the car and trade my M4 for the map book. Still fidgeting a bit I flip to the page covering South Jersey to see where we need to go.

"About two more hours in this direction", I say out loud. "Once we get closer, I'll start driving since I know the roads"

April nods to me, still a bit shaken up from the confrontation earlier. I place my hand on my forehead and look out the window, watching the stripes on the road go by as I think. After a few minutes I lean up and look over at April. "Alright so let's get these facts on the board." I say out loud in a very angry voice. April looks over at me, confused and scared.

"Every time we fire the gun, the zombies start to come." I can hear April let out a drawn out breath, happy to know I'm not mad at her.

"So, this could mean one of two things. One, they smell us or two they hear the noise and are attracted to it." I continue to think a bit more before coming up with another possibility. "Or... They could sense heat, and come towards that."

April arch's an eye brow before looking over at me, "Don't you think you're over exaggerating with your methodology? We have to use facts here. Every time we fire the gunshot the zombies come. So they have to be attracted to the noise."

"You're right, but also wrong." I continue, "We have to fully assess all possibilities. What if a week later we're being extra quiet but get surrounded while we sleep because they actually sense heat? We have to be ready for anything!"

"Alright, I guess that makes sense."

As we continue driving the early afternoon is now setting in. I still can't help but wonder if anyone I know is still alive. Along the same lines, why am I still alive? I place my hand on my chin and rub it with my pointer finger as I think. "Maybe some people are immune to the virus? Better yet, is it even a virus?"

I look over to April, "Hey, April. Do you think what is happening now; do you think it could be a virus? Or what else could it possibly be?", after I ask the question April tilts her head to the side as she thinks. "It has to be a virus, if you're right and it originated from the nuclear power plant, those infected there spread it." I nod to April before responding with, "But why are we not infected? I mean there is no way all of these people have been bitten so far."

April arches an eyebrow and asks, "Bitten? What makes you so sure it is spread by bites?" I continue, "Well, in every movie I've ever seen about zombies it is their only means of offense and defense. They hunger for flesh, biting and tearing at every living thing they can find. It is the saliva in their mouth, if it comes into contact with you, you can get infected. You can also get infected if you get some of their blood into your mouth or an open wound."

I turn and look at April in the driver's seat. "Look at it like this, picture AIDS right? It works in a similar way. If you get their body fluids into you, you're fucked!" I remark before leaning back into my seat. April looks over and nods, "We can't base our survival through this off of movies. We have to learn ourselves."

"We will. However nothing has ever happened like this before and the only documented or even theorized ideas come from movies. If you ask me so far they have proven to be right."

I smile at April before adding, "Don't worry. I have enough knowledge of the zombie epidemic in my head for the both of us." April chuckles before refocusing on the road. I tilt my head down for a second before looking out the passenger's window. Still having some questions unanswered, such as... Can Animals be infected by this? Can Mosquitoes carry this virus?

I linger on the Mosquito part for a bit, causing fear to build in me. If Mosquitoes can carry it, we need to get south in a desert like area sometime before spring. I continue to stare out the window, day dreaming before I eventually fall asleep. What seems like minutes later, April shakes me while yelling "Ryan, hey Ryan! We're at a quarter tank of gas; we'll need to stop soon."

"Where are we?" I ask trying to shake off the fatigue from the night before. "Uhm, Jersey?" April answers sarcastically. "No, no, I know that part... Which part of Jersey though?" April smiles and giggles a bit, "I know, I was just kidding. I seen signs saying Atlantic City was coming up."

I quickly rub my face, making sure to fully wake myself up. "Atlantic City?" I say in a fearful voice. April looks over and asks, "Yeah, uhm, is that bad?", "Bad? It's horrible. Atlantic City has an unbelievable amount of people in it." April swallows hard, "Shit. Where do I go from here?"

"Pull over and let me drive." I say, hopefully reassuring April.

April nods before pulling the car over to the side of the road. Once we come to a complete stop I get out and switch sides with her. Once I'm in the driver's seat I switch the car into drive and continue five or so miles down the road. After driving a few miles I get my bearings of where we are and turn off the first exit I see. Once off the turnpike I start to drive in the right direction towards my house, now remembering where I am.

"Don't worry", I tell April. "You had no idea of knowing."

"Well, the city part of Atlantic City should have caught my eye and warned me."

"We all make mistakes you can't beat yourself up over it."

We continue driving for another ten to fifteen minutes before pulling into a gas station nearby my house. "How are we on water and food?" I turn to ask April. "Could use a bit more", April answers.

"Alright, there is something you should know about this gas station... The owner and a worker always slept here. Stay out here by the pump and fill our tank and I'll go inside. I'll clear the building and grab some supplies." April swallows hard and nods.

I reach into the backseat and grab my shotgun before opening the door and exiting the car. I walk towards the gas station's store and stop when I reach the front doors. Before opening the front doors I look around inside. Once I see that it is clear I open the doors and burst inside, pointing my gun at every possible area they could be. "Here, kitty, kitty, kitty, kitty..." I say out loud, hoping that if anyone is in here they are attracted to the noise and show themselves.

I clear the first bit of the building before making my way to the bathroom door. I place my hand on the handle and my heart rate increases. Still not used to all the danger I am putting myself in. I pull the handle down and take in a deep breath before throwing open the door and pointing my gun inside. "Clear", I mumble while letting out a sigh.

I turn around and walk toward the storage room. Re-checking all the aisles of the store, making sure I didn't miss any zombies. I make my way over behind the cash register and to the storage room door. I slowly open the door, just enough to point my gun inside. Once my gun is inside the storage room I take a look around but don't see anything. My stomach started to churn. Wondering where the two could be.

"They never left this gas station..."

I walk out of the storage room and back into the store to grab a shopping cart. I fill it with all the water and food it can hold before returning to the car with it. When I open the front door I see April still pumping the gas and shooting me a smile. "Clear inside, but let's still get out of here quick." I say to April as she nods and finishes up with pumping the gas.

On my way back to the car I stop in my tracks, remembering something. "Hey April give me a second." I place the shopping cart down on the ground and run back inside the store. Once inside the store I return to the storage room and grab five gas containers from inside as well as a few flash lights and lighters. Anything I could shove into my pockets and hands.

I run back outside to April and hand her the gas tanks "Fill these up". She smiles at me, "Guess we won't have to stop for gas next time, huh?" I shake my head in disagreement, "We'll hold onto these for emergency reasons."

I empty the shopping cart into the car and head back inside the store for some more supplies. When I open the door to go inside I hear a strange noise, grinding up against the outside wall of the gas station. I drop the shopping cart on the ground and reach for my gun. "April!" I shout. "Grab your gun; you got one coming around the right side of the building".

She lets go of the nozzle in the gas can, causing it to fall over and spill gas everywhere. April opens the back door of the car and grabs my M4 rifle. She then aims it at the right side of the building until she sees the zombie come around the corner. I shout, "Remember what I taught you April, Point, Aim and Fire." She nods before pointing the gun at the zombie. She hesitates a bit before taking aim and firing. April stumbles backwards from the kick in the gun.

First shot was a miss. "Don't worry April, keep trying", I holler to her again. April points and aims the gun again, the knockback taking her by surprise. Once she has the zombie lined up in her crosshairs she fires again, this time taking the zombie down. Once the zombie falls to the ground April jumps with excitement, her first official kill. "Finish up with putting gas in all the cans so we can get out of here."

April places the gun back into the car and continues to fill each of the gas cans. I grab the remaining water and bagged or canned food from inside the store. Even after filling it up with all those supplies there is still plenty of room in the car. I walk over to the liquor section and grab some vodka as well as the first aid kit behind the counter.

With the shopping cart now full I run out of the gas station's store and quickly unload it into the car. After I finish loading all of our supplies into the back of the car I grab my M4 rifle. I look down the road through the scope to keep an eye out. Firing at the zombies now walking down the road, obviously attracted to the noise. "April, ETA", I yell. She responds with, "Thirty seconds". I remark, "To mars?" She continues what she is doing and says, "What?!" I chuckle, saying in between shots, "Nothing... Good band though."

April doesn't understand my humor at all and quickly finishes up pumping the gas. While April is finishing with the gas I continue to shoot at all zombies on the roads around us.

"Alright I'm done."

"Hey I think I know that Guy.", I say quickly followed by the sound of my gun going off.

April says in a hasted manner, "Ryan! Come on let's go!"

"Alright, Alright, Ruining my fun", I add running to the driver's seat of the car and hoping in.

I shift the car into drive and quickly pull away from the gas station, running over a zombie on my way out. "Whoa! Did you see that?" I add while the car slams into the zombie and he flails about over top of the car before smacking back onto the ground. April responds, "Of course I fucking saw it! There is blood all over my side of the fucking windshield."

"Don't worry!" I say before hitting the windshield wipers and clearing most of the blood off the window. With all the blood cleared off the windshield there is now a large noticeable crack in it. I look over at April and notice that she is obviously disgusted with the way I handled things. "What the fuck has gotten into you today? You're acting like a fucking idiot." April says while trying not to yell at me.

"I'm just trying to make the best out of what we have."

"These zombies are all over the place and they will keep coming, the more people they bite and infect. They need to be killed anyway, so why not have it done by me? I'm trying to prevent anyone else from being killed. That zombie I hit with the car could have bitten and eaten a little girl thirty minutes from now. But now maybe she gets another week of life."

April leans back in her seat, a tear rolling down the side of her face. "Look, I'm sorry." I say sympathetically. April shakes her head, "No, no reason to be sorry. You're right. They do need to be killed. I'm just... I'm just not used to this... I'm sorry I need time."

I nod in agreement before saying, "But April, we can't give you time. When a zombie is walking towards you he isn't going to stop because you're not ready to believe he really exists. You need to point your gun at his head and pull the fucking trigger."

April nods, agreeing with me. "You're right." We continue driving, now with a silence that has come of us. April is a bit shaken up but she seems to be improving and getting more used to everything. About five minutes away from my house I see a zombie on the side of the road feasting on a dead deer. I start to slow down and come to a stop. I turn the car to the side, leaving April's side of the car fully vulnerable.

April looks over at me shocked and curious as to what I am doing. "Take this gun, point it at the zombie and pull the trigger." I tell her, handing her the pistol that was strapped to my waist. "Remember April, only head shots will kill it." She looks at me, taking the gun and nodding. She points it at the zombie and pulls the trigger.

The gun doesn't fire. April turns to me and says "It's jammed." I smile and say "Safety is on the left side." April nods, turning off the safety and aiming the gun at the zombie. She fires at the zombie and hits it in the shoulder. "You've got its attention now." I remark. "Don't forget you have to hit it in the head."

April points the gun at the zombie and fires again, hitting it in the chest. "April, remember what I taught you." April nods, pointing the gun at the zombie yet again. She pulls the trigger and the bullet flies straight and true. It hits the zombie in the head dropping him to the ground. I roll her window back up and start to pull away from the area. As I'm driving past the zombie I run over its head. My front tire lifts up at first before it crashes to the ground and I hear a loud pop noise outside. Both April and I look a bit disgusted at each other, knowing that we now have brains along the underside of the car.

After driving a bit longer I turn to April and ask, "How did that feel?" April looks over at me and says, "Different, I'm not sure how."

Upon arriving at my house back in south Jersey I pull into an open parking space before getting out of the car. After getting out of the car I run up to the front door with my rifle in hand. April runs up next to me, holding her gun and pointing at the ground, following my example. "You ready?" I ask. "As ready as I'll ever be" She responds. I open the front door and rush inside with April close behind me.

The inside of the house was the exact opposite of the outside. It showed no signs at all of any sort of damage or desertion. All of the lights were off, the shoes were still by the front door and perfectly parallel with one another. There was no sign that anyone was here recently or had left in a hurry. Everything was so neat and still inside that it was even kind of weird.

After I'm inside I reach to the couch right next to the door and grab a pillow from it. I place the pillow over the front of my gun to use as a silencer just in case we do see anything. I clear the first floor of the house and turn to April saying "Clear". She nods before following me upstairs.

I do a quick sweep of the upstairs part of the house before turning to April and saying "Clear" again. We both return to the first floor of the house before venturing further down into the basement. Once I'm down in the basement I look around quickly and check the three rooms nearby. After I know it is clear I throw the pillow to the side and relax a little.

April places her gun on a nearby table. "You can make as much noise as you want down here", I mention to April. "It is sound proofed because of my drum set." I add. April smiles at me and asks, "Wouldn't happen to have running water would you?" I laugh, "Hah, I might be able to rig something up for us."

April smiles and adds, "Don't worry, it will make too much noise.", "Good Point." I continue by saying, "Let's grab a few things out of the car, and bring them inside. We can count our supplies and go from there."

She nods as she follows me outside and helps unload the car. We make at least three trips each as we carry the supplies back into the house. We set all of the supplies that we bring in, down on the living room floor. Once everything is inside I sit down on the living room floor next to everything to go through it. I open all four of the flashlights that I grabbed from the store before realizing that I forgot batteries. I let out a sign before saying to April, "Wait here." I stand up before walking over to the kitchen and checking the drawer for any batteries

While searching through all the drawers I find an un-opened pack of twenty four batteries. "Yes!" I say out loud before returning to the living room with the flashlights. I toss the batteries on the ground and return to the kitchen, remembering that I forgot to grab duct tape. When I return to the living room I sit down and start to load the batteries into the flashlights. Once all the flashlights have batteries I duct tape them to the side of each of my guns.

Smiling I turn the flashlights on and point them at the wall, checking to see how much of an area they light up. "Perfect", I remark out loud before shooting a smile to April, "So how are we on food and water?" She lets out a sigh, "Well we will make it through the night and all day tomorrow. After that I'm not too sure".

"Well let's drink the soda inside the fridge tonight and any water in there too. This will net us some extra time with what we have. Also there is some canned food to the right of the refrigerator in the pantry."

April smiles, "Good, so now we have two to three days of supplies." I nod my head in agreement, "We need to board this place up for the night, just in case."

I pull myself to my feet and slide the bookshelf in the living room over to the front door, placing it up against it and bracing it. Afterwards I walk into the kitchen and move the curtains over the backdoor, so nothing can see inside. I then grab the table, flipping it and placing it over the door. I turn to April and say "Well, It won't stop much from getting in the back door, but it at least makes me feel a bit better.

April smiles at me before nodding. She agrees with me that, just like before, the illusion of security will help her through the night. I glance at the clock on the wall and notice that it is almost four in the afternoon. "Time flies when you're having fun, huh?" I jokingly ask April. She laughs a bit, smiling at me.

"I think it is time we discuss our plan."

"What do you mean?"

"Well, first things first we know they are zombies. Not vampires." I add sarcastically to make April laugh.

"So, what we need to do is find out a way to the least populated area, or a possible Survivor Colony."

"How do you know there is a Survivor Colony though?"

"Usually in an event like this a Survivor Colony forms outside of every major city. Or sometimes they retake a major city to repopulate it and start over."

"Our best bet would probably be something far south. We need to get out of the cold for one, especially with no heat. Also we need to get away from mosquitoes. If they bite you and they carry the virus, well let's face it you're fucked."

April nods agreeing with me. She lifts her hand up and moves her hair out of the way before adding. "Well what about something like California? Or one of the warmer, desert like states to the southwest."

"Yes, one of those states would work. I'm placing a bet on Las Vegas."

"Why do you think Las Vegas? The population there is extremely high."

"Yes, it is very high there but you also must take into consideration that it is surrounded by desert and mountains. You'll be able to see zombies coming at you from very far away. You will have hours maybe even a day to prepare."

"Also you have to take into consideration we're talking about Las Vegas here. They city was probably mostly evacuated; meaning the amount of zombies there would be dramatically lowered. The terrain fits perfectly, since all animals there that could be infected, are poisonous and would have killed you already."

"Plus, if all else fails. I have a friend there and I made a promise to my friend. I said if anything ever happened with a zombie invasion. I'd come for you... And I plan to go to him."

"Sounds like you got it all planned out already."

"Yeah, pretty much."

"Just getting there is the only problem I foresee."

A long pause over comes us as we both think of how we can possibly go about getting to Las Vegas. I also wonder to myself if Las Vegas is the best option for us. I mean we could be walking right into a death trap. I look over to April and ask, "Do you think Las Vegas is the best choice?"

"Well your logic does seem pretty sound.", "It's worth a shot." she adds.

"Let's gather some supplies from my house, blankets, extra clothes and anything else we might need."

"We'll place it in the living room then head down into the basement and sleep for the night."

Both of us walk up stairs and grab clothes as well as other assorted goodies that we can use. The two of us make three or four trips down into the living room, carrying everything we may need. When we're done upstairs we clear out anything useful from the kitchen as well and bring that back to the living room. Lastly, we gather anything useful from the basement.

"Hey April." I say out loud to get her attention.

"I'm not trying anything here, but it would be safest to sleep in the same bed, are you ok with that?"

"Yes, I was going to ask the same thing." She says while blushing a bit.

We carry everything useful that we can find up from the Basement. After we're done I return down stairs and sit down on the couch next to April. April is sitting there quietly, staring at the blank TV, her mind obviously wandering off about something.

"You know if you stare at it long enough, it may turn on." I say jokingly to her.

"Oh, no, I'm just thinking."

"It's been a long day." I say placing my gun between my legs and leaning back to stare at the ceiling.

April snivels and looks over, "You're taking this all really well..."

"Yeah... I've been looking forward to something like this. It sounds weird, I know. But life hasn't exactly been perfect for me."

"I know how you feel. We'll if you've really thought this all out. I guess I am really lucky to of found you."

"Yeah... Yeah I guess so. We should probably get some sleep, tomorrow we got a long day ahead of us."

April nods as I stand up and show her to the Bedroom nearby. She follows me inside and I turn on a light right next to the bed. April is a bit shocked, so she asks, "How did you get power down here?"

"Battery Powered Light.", I reply "Ahh, I see."

"We should probably slide my dresser over the door just in case."

April and I slide the dresser over top the door leading into the room, blocking it completely. "Alright, good nothing will get in now and if it does... We'll hear it." After barricading the door I walk over to the bed and lay down on it, staring at the ceiling. April comes over and lies down next to me, snuggling under the covers.

"I wonder how many people are still alive..." I say while looking over to April.

"Don't know."

"Well you're a good conversation starter." I say sarcastically remarking to April.

"Well out of the two days we were in New York City we're the only two people we know that even made it out. We killed two people on the roads right outside of the city..."

"Wow someone is negative Nancy." I say sarcastically.

"That's usually why I don't talk"

"But no, really, there are more survivors out there, April, don't get your hopes down. We'll find more and we will be ok."

April smiles before rolling over on her side and closing her eyes. I stay on my back, sprawled out across the bed with my M4 laying on top of me. I close my eyes and place my right hand gently over top the rifle and smirk before falling asleep.

CHAPTER 4 - THE STANDOFF

Morning arrives as April reaches over and shakes me, waking me up. "What, huh, is everything ok?" I mumble out loud, still drowsy from the night before. April reassures me, "Yeah, everything is fine."

I sit up and wipe my face before rubbing my eyes. I turn to April and ask, "Any idea what time it is?" She shakes her head side to side before rolling out of bed. I follow her example and crawl out of bed. Before standing up I stretch my arms a bit and crack my back. Once I stand up I toss my rifle over my shoulder and help April move the dresser out of the way that is blocking the door.

Once the dresser is out of the way I open the door and walk out into the basement and take a quick look around before heading upstairs. Once I'm upstairs I shout down to April, letting her know everything is ok and there is nothing to worry about. Right after she hears me she comes up the stairs and into the living room. I walk over to the kitchen and move the curtain out of the way, looking out into my back yard. "The sun is just coming up", I say out loud to April.

"We should load up the supplies and get going", April adds.

"Yeah", I say in agreement. April helps me move the bookshelf out of the way that is currently blocking the front door. Once the bookshelf is out of the way we open the front door and begin to carry supplies out to the car. It takes us five trips each to get everything out from the house and into the car.

After placing the final load into the car I turn to April, "I think that's about it." April nods before responding, "Yup, looks like we got everything... Let's head out." I nod before hoping into the driver's seat of the car and turning the key in the ignition. "Sure we're not forgetting anything?" I turn and ask April as I shift the car into reverse. April looks over, "Nothing I can think of"

I smile before pulling out of my Parking Spot and shifting the car into drive. I take a look at the long road ahead of me and let out a sigh. "It's going to be one long day." I say out loud before pressing down the Gas Pedal and pushing forward.

As I drive down the road I occasionally glance into the backyards of houses that I pass. Most of the backyards are clear but every few houses I see a zombie going for a morning stroll. Every time I see one just wondering around in the fenced in backyard I'm tempted to stop, pull over and kill it. But that would be a waste of time and certainly delay us. I continue driving south; my current destination in mind is my friend Mike's house.

The day drags on and time seems to be flowing slower then it normally does. We reach my friend Mike's house around nine am. I am forced to park in the street, his driveway still filled with cars, possibly meaning no one has left the house since the zombie outbreak. I turn to April, "All the cars are still in the driveway. Someone or something is going to be here, grab your gun and be ready."

April glares at me, an obvious fear rolling over her face. She grabs her gun and steps out of the car. We both slowly walk up to the house with our guns pointed at the ground. Both of us are ready to fire at any suspicious movement or any sounds that we hear. When we reach the front door I turn the handle, "Locked", I say out loud to April.

I lean down and lift the floor mat in front of the door to grab the spare key. I place the key in the lock and turn it, unlocking the door. Once the door is unlocked I twist the handle and take in a deep breath before opening it and bursting inside. I stand in the living room, silent for a few seconds. Before being interrupted by April asking "What's that sound?", "I don't know..." I reply. It sounds like tearing and gushing blood can be heard from the kitchen.

My heart rate quickens as I am fueled by emotions I quickly make my way to the kitchen, pointing my gun anywhere I look. Inside the kitchen I find a zombie sitting over top Mike's body. Pulling, tearing and ripping at his flesh. Bodily organs can be found littering the floor all around him, his chest torn wide open. Around the floor of Mike's body is a fresh puddle of blood.

The zombie notices me and looks up at me, hissing and barring his teeth. "You fucking son of a bitch!" I yell right as the zombie lunges at me. I fire off my multiple shots at the zombie, hitting him all over the

Torso as well as a few times in the head. The zombie collapses right next to Mike's body on the ground. I walk over top of the zombie and fire off the remaining three shots in my gun into his torso.

I continue to pull the trigger even well after my gun is out of ammo. I try to resist crying but I am unable to. A tear rolls down my cheek as I look down at Mike's body. I point my M4 at his head and close my eyes before saying. "Sorry old friend." I squeeze my eyes closed tighter, not wanting to witness what I'm about to do.

I pull the trigger on my gun as the sound rings through the house, piercing my ears. The gun shot leaves a permanent scar that I will never forget. Shortly after the gunshot rings out throughout the house April runs into the room. She takes a long look at me and then back at the two bodies lying on the floor. She throws her hand over her mouth and quickly runs out of the kitchen and back into the living room, obviously sick from what she just saw.

I place my rifle on the kitchen table and open the back door to drag Mike's body outside as well as the zombie's body. I walk over to Mike's shed and smash the lock off with a rock nearby before grabbing a shovel from inside. I return to the area next to his body and start to dig a hole. As I am digging the hole for Mike's body tears start to pour down my face. The tears start slow at first but as time goes on the amount of them increases to the point of where I can barely see.

When I finish digging the hole I grab Mike's body and slowly lower it in. The tears start to quicken, rolling down my face as I struggle for words. I stand up and grab the shovel again, shoving it into the dirt pile right next to the hole. I raise the shovel which is now covered with dirt. Hanging it over the top of Eric's body I say, "Sorry I couldn't have gotten to you sooner... I'm sorry..." I toss the dirt down into the hole over top of Eric's body.

Tears are now flowing out of my eyes like a waterfall. The tears don'ts top until I am fully done burying him in the ground. Once his body is fully covered I jam the shovel into the ground over top of his newly formed grave and walk back inside to find April sitting on the couch. April is covering her face with both of her hands and is crying like she just lost a loved one. It makes it more than obvious to me that killing the zombie in the house and everything before it is taking its toll on her.

I sit down next to her and place my arm across her shoulder, pulling her in closer to me. April throws her arm around my back as I say, "It's alright we're going to get out of this mess. Don't worry." My words seem to be a trigger for more tears as April is now crying more and pulling me tighter to her. Minutes go by without any words being said between the two of us. Finally April looks up, at me with tears still rolling down her face and says "I'm sorry... Sorry about your friend."

I put my head down, refusing to make eye contact. "It is ok."; "At least I still have you." I add before making eye contact with her. April smiles before standing up and looking down at me, "Let's get out of here." she says, sniveling a bit. "Alright", I say before walking back into the kitchen. I grab my M4 off the kitchen table and throw it around my back before opening the pantry. Inside the pantry I grab two crates of water and some canned food, anything I can hold with my two hands.

While I am clearing out the pantry April grabs a few things from the medicine cabinet that catch her attention. We both meet up in the living room when we're done and walk out of the house, leaving the front door wide open. We return to the car and offload our supplies before getting in. No words are exchanged between us for the next forty five minutes as we continue our trek southwest.

We start to approach a bridge as April breaks the silence between us, "What bridge is this?" April asks, curiously. "Benjamin Franklin", I reply. Silence comes between us again as we approach and begin to finally cross the bridge. I am forced to go slow over the bridge; police cars and cruisers flipped over, rolled and pushed all around the bridge.

Glass is shattered all over the road with dried blood covering the side of some cars as well as shattered windows. Much like every other area that we come across with this amount of destruction, no bodies can be seen on the ground. There was an apparent struggle probably from the police trying to create a blockade on top of the bridge. While looking around the outside of the car at the destruction on the bridge I say to April, "They must have tried to make a road block" April looks around outside adding, "Apparently it didn't work."

When we reach the middle of the bridge I stop the car and get out. I walk over to the side of the bridge and look over. "The destruction... It's unlike anything I've ever seen... unlike anything I've ever imagined..." I say while staring out over the Delaware River. April runs up next to me, when she gets next to me I notice her jaw dropping. Speechless of what she sees', much like I am.

There are buildings are on fire on either side of the river causing smoke to billow up into the air. Cars are flipped over and abandoned on the roads all over the city. Boats are taken from one pier only to crash into a building or another pier on the opposite side of the river. There are dozens of bodies along with other debris floating down the river. I turn to April and notice a tear rolling down her cheek. Her eyes are taking in too much sorrow all at one time.

I take a step back from the railing and lean up against my car, unable to control my emotions anymore. I place my head into my hand and stare at the ground. "They're dead... Everyone is... dead..." I say out loud which catches April's attention. April comes over to me and says, "Not everyone." she adds, putting an arm on my shoulder. "There are others like us, other survivors. We will find them. We just need to keep moving."

I don't respond to April, my eyes still fixated on the ground. "I'll drive" April says, "You're too overwhelmed. You should take a break", she adds. I nod and get in the passenger's side of the car. I stare out the window, still looking at what is left of Philadelphia. April gets into the driver's seat and shifts the car into drive. She puts on her seat belt and looks over at me before asking, "You going to be ok?"

I nod to her, "Yeah..." She smiles and starts to drive along the bridge into Philadelphia.

"Follow interstate seventy-six..."

"What?" April responds.

I clear my throat before saying again, "Interstate seventy-six... It is an interstate", I add.

April nods, "Where is it going to take us?"

"Central Pennsylvania", I respond.

I look up, seemingly a bit more cheerful, "When you're on interstate seventy-six west keep an eye out for signs for interstate ninety. You should start seeing signs for it about halfway through Pennsylvania. This will take you in the direction we want to go. Just make sure you keep west bound." I say to April.

April nods, looking over to me she says "Alright, now get some sleep." I smile placing my head against the seatbelt and wiggling until I find the perfect and most comfortable position possible. When I find the position I close my eyes and slowly drift into sleep.

Moments after falling asleep I see Mike in front of me, still young, from a time back when we were both kids. I could feel the friendship between us was strong. Unlike recently were me and Mike both started to grow apart.

He went on with his life, following in his father's footsteps to become an auto mechanic. Eventually set to take over his father's business.

But I went in a completely different direction. Neither of us set out to do what we dreamed of when we were kids. We used to always talk about things like joining the Military together. Or even going out and living in the wilderness. As long as we both were together in the future. We know we'd be happy.

Everything changed though, when I was still young I moved away and lost contact with Mike. We spoke a few times after the move but rarely ever seen each other. Time forced us to grow apart. We both were taking our lives into different directions. I lost contact with Mike for three years at one point. Just recently, we started talking again.

We didn't become really close. Mike had a wife and kids, no time for me. All of these feelings came back to me the moment I saw Mike in my dream. I remember this day, I thought. Mike and I were playing in his backyard with a set of plastic army men his parents recently bought him.

I was controlling the tan army men while Mike was controlling the green ones. We each had twenty army men, four tanks and four other assorted vehicles. Mike and I would always play Army Men, making sure we took turns winning. Mike and I wanted to both join the military, more than anything in the world.

Joining the military was all we would talk about. We used to run around his house shooting at each other with nerf guns. Constantly getting them stuck to the wall or ceiling, out of reach. As we got older we moved up to paint ball guns but never moved past that. Mike and I had a lot of fun that day, playing army men with each other.

A tear rolled down my face. It was almost a blessing being able to experience such a memory again. After all, Mike was one of the reasons I am still alive today, after the zombie epidemic. We used to plan it out; we even had a zombie escape plan. We were just children; we never knew it would actually come in handy.

Mike was one of the few people I always told... "In the event of a zombie apocalypse... I'll come for you". That story always had a happy ending though. Just this time, I was too late.

I sat back for awhile, keeping my mind clear just watching Mike and I play. We rarely exchanged words besides "Bang you're dead", "Argh!!" and "Oh, I'm shot!". Almost everything that came out of our mouths was sound effects. I continued to watch, just smiling and laughing. The memory of us, happy, together, was warming my heart.

"Ryan! Hey Ryan!" I hear. I turn to the side, and see Mike's mom at the backdoor she repeats "Ryan! Hey Ryan!" before I am shaken awake, April looking over at me with a hand on my shoulder, shaking me.

A bit disoriented I turn to April, rubbing the sleep off my eyes, "Where are we?" I ask. She turns and looks out the driver's side window before responding, "Somewhere around the center of Pennsylvania".

I rub my face a bit and take a look around, still getting adjusted to where we are. Just as I look outside the passenger's side window April says "We're at a gas station. I wanted to wake you incase anything went wrong". I beam a smile at April while reaching into the back of the car to grab my shotgun.

With my shotgun in hand I open the door and do a quick once over of the area around us. "Clear!" I yell to April letting her know it is ok to come out of the car. Right after she hears me say clear she opens the door and hops out of the car. She than walks over to the gas pump and places the nozzle inside the car before informing me that she is ready to go inside.

"Forgetting something?" I ask. She arches an eyebrow asking, "What do you mean?" "What I mean is a gun." I add. April smiles, reaching around her backside and pulling her pistol out from her waist band. I smile before saying "That's my girl!" We cut the chit chat and quickly make our way over to the gas station's store. Since both of us want nothing more than to get out of here and back on the road, stopping isn't very safe and both of us know it.

We reach the stores' front door and take a quick look around inside. "Looks pretty clear", I say out loud while grabbing the handle to the front door. With a light tug the door comes open. "Well aren't we the lucky ones today?" I say "It's unlocked!" I open the door and hold it open for April, "Ladies first!" I add while laughing.

April laughs, looking over to me "Well aren't you just the gentlemen today?"; "Making the lady go first into the dark scary building". "Hah" I add.

April enters the gas station with me quickly following behind her. Her first destination inside is the cash register. She leans over the counter and hits the button to activate the gas pump. In the mean time I am making my way around the store quickly clearing each aisle, making sure everything is safe. After I've cleared the whole store I look over to April and say, "Clear."

I look over and notice that April is still near the counter, collecting all the bagged foods that are in the store. After going through everything she lets out a long drawn out sigh, dropping her shoulders down. "It's all candy and chips", She says out loud. "No Beef Jerky?" I add a bit disappointed. "Only two packs", April replies. A bit disappointed, I let out a sigh, neither of us having a real meal in over two days.

"I'll grab the water, you grab the food", I say while looking over to April.

She nods sliding the gun back into her waist band and grabbing as much of the food as she can hold with her two hands. I throw my shotgun over my back and bend over, picking up three crates of water. I navigate my way to the front door, not being able to see very well in front of me.

April opens the front door wide enough for me to get out and says, "Ladies first", chuckling a bit to herself. "Well aren't you just the cute one today?" I reply while both of us are laughing and giggling. We both walk back to the car and unload what we were holding before starting the pump.

Right after April starts the pump she looks over to me and says, "I got to pee". I arch an eyebrow while looking at her before saying, "Well, then go pee!", "I'm not going pee here!" she exclaims.

I let out a sigh before saying, "Well you're not going to make this like a horror movie where you go a quarter mile away into the woods then wind up getting eaten by some sort of monster."

April stares at me, dumbfounded for a second before saying, "Yeah... I was going to go inside. You know, in the store?" Feeling stupid I respond, "Oh yeah... The store has a bathroom." April smiles and says "I'll be right back!"

I quickly interrupt her and say, "Wait a minute! You're not going alone." She pauses and responds with, "I'm a big girl, I think I can handle myself." April expresses herself while running back towards the store. "Besides, we cleared the store anyway!" April yells before she opens the door and runs inside. "I didn't clear the bathroom!" I holler, April just barely being able to hear me as she enters the store.

April sticks her head back out the front door and yells back, "I'll bang on the door, if I don't hear anything I'll open it, take a look around. Either way, a gunshot to the head kills them, it's not rocket science."

I scratch my head, a bit surprised that April can already handle herself. I take the nozzle out of the car and place it back into the gas pump. Afterwards I lean onto the car and stare at the building, waiting for April to get done.

I day dream a bit, thinking how funny it would be to point my gun up into the air and fire off a few shots screaming "April! Come on we need to go!", "Ahhh". I laugh to myself; I'm such a cruel Bastard.

April comes running out the front door of the store stopping in front of me and scratching her head, "I couldn't flush the toilet." I pause for a second, arching an eyebrow and a bit confused. "And...?" I ask.

April smiles, "Hmm, good point".

"Let's get in the car and get out of here."

"Alright, we got everything?"

"Yeah", I add before getting into the driver's seat of the car.

April hops into the passenger's seat as I shift the car into drive. I back onto the highway and continue west. Time always flew by while we were driving since all the highways were always clear. You could zone out with nothing getting in your way besides you and the road. The only time we ever saw another vehicle on the road was if it was abandoned.

Occasionally you would see them flipped over on the side of the road, but never any bodies. I always figured that the people turned into zombies and got up and walked away or actually managed to survive the crash. Every ten or so miles you would see a zombie taking a stroll down the road or feasting on some old road kill.

I never worried about the zombies that we passed. After all we were in a car, traveling seventy-five miles per hour and they were outside of it, stumbling and trying to walk. Occasionally when getting bored or frustrated I would stop and kill any zombies that I see walking along the side of the road. But I don't usually waste any bullets unless I absolutely needed too.

I always told myself, one less zombie, one less thing to worry about in the future. Also while driving my mind always wondered off. I ran every, what if, scenario through my head all the time. Sometimes I would even upset myself thinking of everything. Though looking over at April always fixed it, putting a smile right back on my face.

I kept thinking how lucky I was to meet someone like April in a situation like this. Besides being attracted to her, she also knew a lot about medicine. She was a very intelligent person, which is invaluable in a time like this.

Nothing could take my mind off the fact that everyone I knew was a zombie. Family, friends, everyone I went to high school with. I snicker a bit and think to myself; well that last part isn't that bad.

Time seems to fly while I am driving in no time at all I reach the tunnels right outside of Pittsburgh. While I am driving through the tunnel I place my hand over top the horn and excitedly turn to April. I notice she has her head pressed against the window in a sound sleep. I smile and become a bit disappointed, lifting my hand off the horn.

I return to my trance, staring out the front of the car. Occasionally glancing down and checking to see how much gas is left in the car. Everything seems to be so serene while I am driving, almost like I am at peace with the world. I lose track of time until I see the large green sign that says, "Welcome to Ohio!"

I lean over and place my hand on April's shoulder shaking her to wake her up. She slowly comes to her senses, looking over at me, mumbling incoherent words.

"We're in Ohio!" I exclaim.

She stretches her arms out and lets out a big yawn. "Already? What time is it?" I glance over at the interior clock in the car, "Four forty-five." April mumbles, snuggling against the seat belt more and yawning again before asking how much gas is left in the car. I lift my hand up to get a good look at the gas meter and let her know we have a quarter tank of gas left.

"I'm going to keep driving till we're a bit below quarter and then use the emergency reserves in the back. Then I'll stop at a gas station outside of Cleveland and fill everything up. I don't want to stop in Cleveland and take that kind of risk."

April nods, fully agreeing with me, she then snuggles back into a comfortable position and says, "Wake me when we're at the gas station". "Alright", I say with a smile.

I focus on the road again, letting my mind wander off where ever it wants to go. I keep a close eye on the gas meter waiting until the fuel light comes on before I stop and use the emergency reserves we had in the back. I continue along the road until we reach a quarter tank, about twenty five miles out of Cleveland.

Once the car reaches a quarter tank of gas I start to look around for a nearby gas station before reaching Cleveland. I notice a large green sign on the side of the road that says, "Final stop before Cleveland". I switch lanes and hop onto the deceleration ramp, pulling into the gas station recreational area. I park next to the pump and lean over to shake April awake. "We're at the gas station", I say to her.

April lets out a yawn while grabbing her pistol from the back seat and getting out of the car. I grab my M4 from the back seat before meeting April on the other side of the car. Still groggy from her nap April starts to make her way to the front door of the store. April only takes a few steps before we both stop and take a look inside the store. All the shelves in the store are knocked over and food as well as water is spilled all over the floor.

The cash register is smashed and off the counter it normally sits on. The money from inside of it is scattered all over the floor, soaking in the water. Tiles from the drop ceiling are smashed and hanging all around the store. After seeing the inside of the store I swallow hard and turn to look at April,

"This place looks like hell…"

"Yeah…" April responds staring inside. "But we have no other choice", April adds.

"Let's just get in and out.

I open the front door and hold it with my foot while pointing my gun around inside. While I am holding the door open I let April pass by me and enter the store. Once April is inside I let my foot off the door and walk in right behind her. After we're both inside the door slams shut behind us, causing both of us to jump out of our skins. We both turn to each other, the fear noticeable in both of our eyes. We were about to exchange words before hearing a loud bang coming from then storage room of the store.

Neither of us jump this time when we hear the bang, almost as if we were ready for something to go wrong. We both look at each other and nod. Almost like informing each other that we knew we weren't the only things here. I move up the center of the store towards the storage room while April activated the pump we are parked at.

April heads over to the front door and opens it before nodding to me. Letting me know she is going to get the gas pumping while I clear the store. When I reach the storage room door I notice the door is off its hinges lying across the floor. I grip the handle of my rifle tightly as my heart is beating faster than it ever has before. I use my thumb to turn the flash light on that is on the side of the rifle.

Quivering from fear I take in a long deep breath before entering the storage room. Once inside I point my gun around sporadically, shining light all over the room. Without seeing anything I point my rifle down the hall in the storage room. I swallow hard knowing there is still another hallway and room I have to clear.

I slowly move forward, starting to approach the next hallway. As I approach the corner I grip my gun even tighter and try to control my sporadic breathing. I take another step forward before hearing a familiar noise. The sound of tearing flesh, the same sound I heard in Mike's house. My fear almost completely washes away as I am filled with anger.

Now controlled by an insatiable lust to kill I quickly round the corner pointing my gun directly at where I hear the noise. Unable to even get a good look at my target I am immediately distracted when I hear April scream from outside. I look away from my target and stare at the wall, trying to listen for more.

"Ryan, Help! They're everywhere!"

April yells out to me, her words followed by four gun shots. Still distracted I start to turn and make a break for the door, my mind only focusing on helping April. Once I turn around I hear a loud snarl coming from behind me followed by the sound of feet pitter patting across the floor. I quickly spin around aiming my gun at eye level. I am caught off guard as a zombie is running at me. His teeth showing with his lips pulled back, blood dripping from his face.

His arms are hanging at the sides of his body flailing in the air as he is running towards me. As he gets closer he throws his arms out towards my neck, reaching to grab me. I snap out of my trance and fire off three shots. One bullet hits him in the chest, the other in the shoulder and the third right between the eyes. The third shot, the kill shot, causes him to fall to the ground with a loud thump.

Still panicking I clench my gun even tighter, freezing for a second, confused as to exactly what is going on. Outside I hear more shots firing from April's gun quickly followed by another one of her screams for help.

I snap back to my senses as three more zombies come running around the corner in the storage room. I fire off five shots, missing twice and killing all the zombies with the other three shots. I point my gun at the ground and run out of the storage room to the front of the store. I see April outside with her back to the wall firing at the zombies slowly moving towards the vehicle.

I race outside aiming my gun at any of the zombies around the car and firing. I fire off seven shots before hearing a click. Once I hear the click I let go of my rifle and let it hang by my side, now out of ammo. I reach down to my waist and grab my Glock pointing it at the remaining zombies around the car. I fire at them, being extra careful to try and only use one bullet per zombie.

When I reach the car and take a look through the windows to see that we're completely surrounded by zombies on that side. After I see all the zombies I spin around to look all around us, noticing the zombies are coming from all sides. They are coming from off the highway, out of the woods nearby and even from behind us around the building.

"They're everywhere!" April yells.

I quickly smash the back window of our car and grab the backpack with all of the ammo out of the back seat. I back up to the building behind us and look around for a way out.

"Let's go around the side! There has to be a ladder somewhere!" I shout out to April before running around the side of the building.

I look around frantically for a way up onto the building. April right behind me, her body pressed up against me trying to stay as close as possible for protection.

"Not on this side, the other side!" I yell.

I grab April's hand and pull her around back of the building firing at any zombies that get in my way. We run around the back of the building, pausing for a second while behind it, checking for a ladder. Without seeing a ladder my heart drops into my chest, hoping that I didn't make a mistake looking for a way up onto the roof.

I continue counter clockwise around the building, firing off shots and killing any zombies that get in my way. When we circle around the other side I immediately spot the ladder I was looking for. The ladder has three zombies standing around it and over twenty rounding the corner alerted by the noise we have caused. I let go of April's hand and aim the gun at the zombies, firing off three shots, dropping all of them.

"April get up on the roof." I say out loud.

As April is climbing up onto the roof I kill any zombies that get close, giving her cover as she climbs the ladder. Once April reaches the top she leans over and catches the backpack full of ammo that I throw up to her. I place my foot on the first step of the ladder and throw my hand up as far as it can go grabbing on to another step.

I point my gun at the pack of zombies behind me, firing two more shots at them. Neither one of the shots kills anything. My gun clicks, letting me know I am out of ammo but I keep pulling the trigger, oblivious to the sound. Once I snap back into reality I throw the gun on top of the building and finish climbing up the ladder.

Right before I get out of reach a zombie lunges and bites the heel of my shoe. I move my foot forward before thrusting it backwards, hitting the zombie in the face and knocking out his teeth. I continue up the ladder until I reach the top of the building, April helping by pulling me onto the roof when I reach the end of the ladder.

After catching my breath I look to April and say, "We're really fucked now, huh?"

"Yeah..." April adds, "They just came out of no were... Some of them were even running at me!"

"Yeah I had a few Runners too."

"Wait, you knew they run? I thought you told me zombies don't run?"

"Of course I didn't know that they ran! How could I know if they run or not if I've barely ever seen them?"

"Well you watched movies and played games that I didn't. I figured you'd know this."

"Well, in some movies they ran, but I figured since they are indeed decaying bodies they wouldn't run."

"Well this is important information you should get down on the table before bringing someone into a situation like this."

"Look, we can't keep arguing. We need to figure out a way to get back to the car from here and get out alive."

"Well good job bringing us up here, we could of made it out alive before if we had just got into the car."

"Alright! That's enough!"

I say before throwing my rifle down on the top of the roof. I walk to the front of the building and a tear rolls down the side of my face as I stare off towards the highway. Zombies are everywhere, hundreds of them. I can't even see the grass around them, their bodies pressed against each other almost as if they are forming an angry mob. On the other end of the highway is a large grassy field. Throughout the field there are hundreds of zombies that are all spread out across it. From where April and I are standing they look like small specks limping and stumbling over to us.

The zombies closer to us are smashed up against the windows and walls of the building. Moaning and banging on it, almost like they can sense that we are up top. Around the back of the gas station and on both sides is a dense forest. It is almost impossible to see any more than twenty feet into the woods with all the brush and trees blocking our view. A dark feeling comes over me, a feeling that tells me you're going to die here.

"How much ammo do we have in that backpack?" I shout over to April.

"Eight mags for the M4, Six for the pistols and two boxes of shells for the shotgun"

"Shotgun is in the car, so they're useless to us right now"

"So, what are we going to do?"

"I'm not sure yet. I need a minute to think."

I sit down on one of the vents on top the roof and lean back, looking up at the sky. I try to think of a resolution to the predicament I have put us in. But the only thing going through my head is "We're screwed, we're screwed, we're screwed."

April is walking around the roof taking a look at all the zombies surrounding the building. When she gets close enough to the side of the roof they all try to grab and bite at her. They are all flailing their arms in the air, trying to reach her even though it is obvious that she is far out of reach.

I look up, thinking maybe there is some way we can shoot our way out of this one. But when I look around all I can see is zombies pouring out of the woods and streets and coming straight go the gas station. All the zombies from Cleveland must be migrating east, I thought to myself. I wipe my forehead clean of all the sweat that has formed on it before turning around to face April.

"I'm sorry."

"I fucked up big this time. I got us into a situation that I can't get us out of. I'm sorry."

"It's ok", April adds "I'm sorry for getting mad earlier. But don't give up. We can find a way out."

April's words put a smile back on my face. I walk over to the backpack on the roof and slide a clip into my pistol and M4 before walking over to the side of the building. I aim the gun at each of the zombies, making sure I hit them in the head so I don't use much ammo. Every time I kill one zombie his body drops to the ground and another zombie moves up to take his place. Stepping on each other to get themselves a few inches closer to the roof.

I continue to fire my M4 at the zombies over the side of the building until I run out of ammo. Making sure each bullet hits at least one of them in the head. Sometimes one shot will travel through one zombie and into the other right behind it. Once my gun runs out of ammo I continue pointing it at the crowd below and pulling the trigger. The clicking sound of it out of ammo can be heard loud and clear but I tune it out like I don't notice it.

After finally realizing my gun is out of ammo I spin around and throw it onto the roof, obviously frustrated. I walk over to the vent atop the roof that I was sitting on earlier and sit back down. I bend down and place my hands over my face, gently rubbing my face with them, trying to calm down. April comes up behind me and places her hands on my shoulders.

"It's ok Ryan, it is ok."

"What do you mean it is ok?" I say pausing for a second, "We're trapped up here."

"If they don't eat us we will die of starvation or dehydration."

"It could have been a lot worse." April adds, "We could have tried to get in the car and got torn apart."

I lean back and look up at April who is sitting right next to me on the vent. April is smiling at me; I make eye contact with her and can almost see the sorrow in her eyes. She thinks we're going to die as well but refuses share her real feelings. I close my eyes and turn my head to the side, almost wounded just by looking at her.

I keep shaking my head, telling myself we'll get out of this mess. I feel horrible lying to myself but false hope is better than no hope. After awhile of just sitting there I stand up and take a look over at the forest to our west. The sun is almost fully set over it, the last rays of light for the day piercing through the branches of the trees. It's such a beautiful sight, too bad it is ruined by the zombies snarling, clawing and moaning all around the building.

April sits down on the roof and leans her head up against the vent, trying to get comfortable. I walk around the building and look at all the zombies that surround us. I'm amazed that even as time goes on and the sun is now starting to set, zombies continue to walk out of the woods and off the highway to the building we're imprisoned on. A few minutes later I turn to April who is now lying on the roof, quivering from the cold.

She emptied out the backpack full of ammo and is now using the emptied backpack as a pillow to rest her head on. You can tell it is not very comfortable by how much she keeps adjusting her head on it. I let out a smile from just looking over at her. Just seeing her lay there, so still and serene gives me a warm fuzzy feeling inside. All of a sudden I feel like everything is going to be ok.

I walk over to April and lay down next to her, tossing my arm over her and letting it lay across her belly. April let out a slight whimper, a bit shocked from my cold hand touching her. Once she realized it was me on the other side, she snuggled up against me to get warm. Every time I get close to April I can't help but smile.

It's almost like that right now, on top this roof, nothing else mattered in the world anymore. I pressed my cheek against the back of her head and pulled her close to me for warmth. It seemed like only seconds later I fell asleep.

The next thing I hear are gun shots ringing out from atop the roof. I wake up and quickly scurry over to my rifle to grab it. Once the rifle is in my hand I roll over and point it towards the back of the building aiming it directly at where I hear the shots come from. Right after I point the gun towards the back of the building I notice April standing there. She is holding her gun with smoke still coming out of the barrel, pointing it over the side of the building. April quickly turns around and sees me pointing my gun at her.

"Whoa!" April exclaims.

"I'm just shooting zombies, no need to worry!"

After seeing April holding her gun I let out a sigh before rolling over and sliding my rifle across the roof, away from me. I let out a yawn and stretch my arms, still trying to adjust to the morning. Once I can actually consider myself awake I stand up and walk over to April, staring off the side of the roof with her.

"Well I see everyone is still here."

April laughs, "Yeah, we've even got some more visitors too."

April spins around and walks to the front of the building. She stands at the end of the roof and stares off at the highway. Zombies are still flooding in off the highway, usually in packs of three but sometimes they come in single file. What used to be five hundred to a thousand zombies before we fell asleep has easily increased to two thousand.

"Well we're just fucked." I remark.

April slaps me on the back of the head. As I turn to her, questioning her motives and she says out loud "Don't say that!", before giggling and walking over to the backpack across the roof.

"Have they gotten inside the building yet?" I ask.

"Nope, I haven't heard anything inside all morning."

"Hmmm, well that gives me an idea! I'm going to go through that vent and down into the store. I'll be able to hand up blankets, supplies and maybe something to light a signal fire.

As I finish talking April's face lights up with excitement she nods her head, totally agreeing with my idea. Without waiting any longer we both run over to the vent on the roof and examine it, looking for a way to open it. The vent is very old and seems to move quite a bit just pushing and leaning on it.

I step back and give the vent a few kicks, knocking it off its hinges and fully exposing the ductwork inside. I look inside before sticking my foot in and smashing the ductwork out causing it to fall in the store. April and I both jump when the ductwork hits the ground in the store below, neither of us expecting the crash to be nearly as loud. Once the ductwork is out and the inside of the store is fully exposed I lean over the gap and take a look around inside.

"It's about ten feet down... Once I am down, I don't see how I will get back up."

"I can help you back up!"

"You can't lift me... I'm too heavy. Plus you can't even reach down that far. Once they see me down there, I won't have enough time to grab supplies and devise a way back up."

I lean back and start to pace around on the roof thinking for another way to get the supplies out of the store. April stands near the vent and trades looks between me and the vent

"I'll go."

"No, no way, it's too dangerous."

April volunteer's herself for the job. She walks over to the vent and sticks one leg in. She turns to me, smiling and nodding her head.

"I'll fit right in; you're big and strong enough to pull me back out too."

"We can't take that type of risk!"

April ignores my warning and pulls her other leg over the side and slips down into the store. I run over to the vent and throw an arm down, ready to grab her before looking down.

"I'm ok!"

"Be quiet, stay low to the ground. They don't know you're inside yet."

April looks up at me and nods before scurrying off into the store. I bite my bottom lip as I worry for her safety. I keep looking down into the vent until I am unable to see her anymore. Once she is out of my sight I take a stroll around the outskirts of the roof. The zombies are still biting and reaching out for me on the roof, completely oblivious that April is inside. I continue to circle the building, making sure all the zombies around the building see me up top and keep their eyes focused on me.

While I am walking the buildings perimeter I see a few things fly up out of the hole April dropped down inside from and land onto the roof. Excited I quickly run over to the hole and throw my upper body over it. April throws up a first aid kit which whacks me right in the nose. A loud crunch can be heard atop the roof as I throw my hand over my nose. Blood starts to flow around my hand as I jump backwards and yell.

"Aw, the irony!"

"Sorry!" April yells from down inside of the store

I come back over the top of the hole to grab a few blankets that April hands up to me. April also passes up a crate of water, about a dozen bags of chips and beef jerky. The whole time I grab stuff from April blood is gushing out of my nose and covering the ground below.

"Watch out!" April exclaims.

I quickly move away from the hole, almost diving to the side, avoiding whatever comes up next. I look behind me while covering my head only to see a few lighters fly past me and land next to me on the roof. Following the lighters is a pocket knife and a pack of plastic silverware. I grab everything and round it up into one pile.

"What the fuck do we need all this shit for?" I ask myself. "Better yet where the fuck did she find it."

"One more load!" April yells up to me.

I lean back away from the vent, tilting my head back. Blood is still running down the front of my body, my nose flowing like a river from being hit. April throws a few more things up while I am trying to suppress the blood coming out of my nose.

"Alright! Pull me up!" April yells up to me.

I walk back over to the vent and throw both my arms down inside, reaching as far as I can go down to her. April reaches up as far as she can but is a few inches away from my hands. She struggles to reach my hands while trying to dodge the blood that is flowing out of my nose like a waterfall below.

"I can't reach", I yell down to April while struggling.

"Hold on a second, I need to get something to stan..."

April is interrupted by a loud bang on the window out front of the gas station's store. She spins away from my hands to look at the window. After she sees the window she slowly turns up to look at me again, her eyes now filled with fear.

"They know I'm inside..."

The banging gets louder and louder as more zombies start to pound on the window. My breath starts to quicken and I begin to freak out, not knowing what to do. I sit there, motionless while looking down at April as the blood from my nose continues to drip onto my arm. After a few seconds of the blood dripping onto my arm it hits me.

"It's the blood!" I yell down to April.

"It's the blood from my nose! You need to find something to stand on and get up here. I'll worry about the zombies."

April is filled with an instant burst of happiness, knowing that she may actually make it out of this alive. In no time she runs out of my site again and into the store. Once April is out of my sites I run over to the front of the store and begin bleeding down onto the zombies. When I rub my nose and sneeze all over the crowd of zombies below they go crazy and focus their attention on me. As I continue to bleed on them the zombies immediately start focusing on me more. They follow me away from the front window and around to the side of the building.

"Hurry up April!" I yell to her, hoping she figures out something soon.

The blood is starting to slow down flow out of my nose is starting to slow down and the zombies are starting to lose interest. The more blood I lose the harder it is to remain conscious as well. I start to become very light headed and fumble around with my footsteps. Just as my nose stops bleeding I hear a yell from inside the store. The second I hear the yell I snap back to attention and run over to the vent.

"Ryan! They're at the window again! Hurry, it's cracking!"

I look around and see that April is lining up shelves and other assorted things to stand on. After looking down in the vent I run back to the front of the store and fling any blood on my hands off to the crowd of zombies below. There isn't enough blood for any of them to seem to care about me. They are all hell bent on the fresh meat inside.

I look around frantically while trying to think of something to do. Without any other idea coming to mind I stick my arm out in front of my face, pull my shirt back and sink my teeth into it. Blood starts to squirt out all over my teeth and in my mouth. I spit out all the blood into the crowd of zombies and hang my arm over top of them.

The blood rushes down my arm and all over the zombies below. They immediately respond by grabbing and reaching for my arm. I tease them by lowering my arm closer and closer to them but making sure it stays just out of reach. As my arm hangs over them for longer they start to get fiercer. They start grabbing and lunging at my arm as they get more desperate. They start to climb on top of each other and get closer to me, forcing me to back up in order to not get pulled down.

I hear April banging around in the vent behind me, struggling to get up to the roof. Without hesitation I leave the zombies and run over to the vent. I throw my arm down and grab a hold of April to pull her up. As I am pulling her up I hear the window shatter at the front of the store. Once her upper body is above the top of the vent I throw my arms around her, almost bear hugging her. I yank her up and out of the vent with her collapsing on top of me.

"Umph", I say out loud.

April props herself up on top of me before looking down at me and saying, "I never want to do anything like that ever again." I smile and look back at April, "Yeah, I never want you to do that again."

We both catch our breath before standing up and walking over to the neatly organized pile of loot on the roof. April starts to ruffle through everything making sure everything she collected is there. April brushes her hair to the side and looks at me before saying, "You can't believe how much shit is down there. I mean, I could have been down there for hours."

"May I ask, what the fuck is the plastic silverware for?

"Don't know." April adds "I just grabbed it."

I sit down next to her and help her sort through our newly acquired pile of loot. We examine each item closely and discuss its' uses before pushing it to the side.

"Alright, so it seems like we have about two to three more days of water and food here." I say to April

"I really don't want to be stuck on this roof that long..."

"I know me either. I think I came up with a good idea though."

"What we can do is use the remaining shotgun shells to cause the gas tanks at the gas station to explode. That will kill all of the zombies out front, if not most of them, giving us time to run."

"Well, that sounds like a good plan aside from the running part."

"Well, it is better than nothing."

"So fully explain this plan to me."

"Alright, so what we are going to do is place the remaining shotgun shells into this backpack. Light it on fire and toss it over to the gas storage area near the propane tanks. Once the fire reaches all the shells they will all fire off and explode." I pause for a second before continuing.

"Now the most important part is running. It is going to be a pretty big explosion. Chances are it will blow all zombies up outside the front of the store and knock any other nearby ones down and back. It will still be risky running, but I'd rather try to make it out of here then die up here."

April nods as she silently agrees with me. She sits back and goes through everything she gathered one more time. April separates the items into two piles, one pile for items that are compatible with my plan and the other pile is a junk pile. For the compatible pile she sets aside the plastic silverware, the lighter and one of three blankets. Everything else goes into the junk pile for now.

"Alright, so how are we going to light it on fire and keep it lit?" April asks.

"That... is the part I am not sure about."

"So you came up with this elaborate idea but you're not sure how to execute the main part?"

I lean back against the vent and put my arms behind my head, "Well you went to M.I.T, let's hear your theory."

"Give me a minute. I need time to think."

I smile before standing up and walking over to the first aid kit lying on the roof. I pick the kit up before walking over to the other side of the building. I pull back my sleeve to secretly look at my arm, being sure to hide it from April. I open the first aid kit and pull out some gauze as well as antibiotic cream. I squeeze a little bit of the tube of cream out onto the bite. Forced to clamp my teeth together from the pain. The wound is still tender, but I need to treat it quickly.

After I finish placing the cream overtop my wound I wrap it with gauze and make sure it is secure. When I finish I pull my shirt overtop the gauze, still masking the fact that I bit myself. When I am finished doctoring my wound I walk over to the side of the building and look off. The zombies are still flooding in from all directions, circling the building. It doesn't seem like they are ever going to stop coming.

I enter a deep train of thought, what could possibly be attracting them? Well there are a few different possibilities... Blood or sound is my best guesses or it is possible that they travel in packs, like some sort of rabid dog. Of course, there is always a chance it could be all three of these. Either way, I think it is safe to say they are going to keep coming and surrounding this building.

After I stare off the side of the building for a few minutes I walk back over to April and sit down right next to her. I shoot a smile over to her and start to talk before she interrupts me.

"Alright, so I got a little bit of an idea going. Lighting the backpack on fire is the easy part; it's just keeping it on fire. We have four lighters that I threw up here, right?"

"Actually we have seven. Well, you threw up four but I have three in my pocket at pretty much all times."

"Oh, I didn't know you smoked."

"Whoa! I don't smoke, I just like fire."

April laughs while taking the other three lighters out of my hand and placing them with the others. April moves all the items around on the roof before continuing to explain her theory.

"Alright so, Plastic will hold its heat and flame for quite awhile. So, the plastic silverware will come in handy. We'll place them over top the shotgun shells so when they start to melt they will seep down onto the shotgun shells, in theory setting them off. As for keeping the backpack lit, well we have seven lighters; we should have enough lighter fluid."

"Well won't the lighter fluid evaporate?" I ask.

"That's what I am worried about. The lighter fluid will evaporate quickly which will make this whole thing a real pain in the ass."

"Well we should light the blanket on fire and have the lighter become exposed to the flame. Once this happens it will explode and light the whole backpack. It will be like a mini Molotov... Worse comes to worse I can always shoot the fucking backpack."

April laughs, "Shooting it will be too dangerous, plus you won't be able to get a clear shot with all the zombies in the way."

"That gives me an even better idea! The zombies are all wearing clothes, right? They may be tattered, dirty and wet. But what if we make a Molotov cocktail type of thing and explode it over them? It should set them all on fire."

"We don't have the ingredients for the cocktail", April adds, "We need gasoline, fire and a container for it."

"Take a look around! We have gasoline everywhere we just need an open flame. Granted it will be dangerous, I'll give you that. But we're running out of options here."

April shoves the plastic silverware, four lighters and the shotgun shells inside the backpack. She makes sure the placement is correct inside the backpack before tossing it over to me. With the backpack in hand I wrap it in a blanket, leaving a small portion of the blanket sticking out like a pyramid.

"Alright let's cross our fingers and hope this works!" I say to April

I walk over to the front of the building and look off, shaking my head in disgust at all the zombie spectators below. I turn to April who has followed me to the front of the building. I notice she has a look of fear in her eyes.

"We only got one shot at this, so we better make it count."

April backs up and nods to me as I set the backpack down and place a lighter in the pyramid of the blanket. I stomp on it with my foot causing it to shatter and lighter fluid to soak that area of the blanket. Right after I shatter the lighter in the blanket I lean down and light the blanket. This causes it to almost completely ignite into flames.

I pick the backpack up using the straps on the back of it and swing it back and forth. I line up my throw with the large gas storage tank and toss it over. It lands on a few of the zombies right near the storage tank before falling to the ground.

"Yes!" I yell excitedly.

"Alright let's get back and take cover!" I say to April while grabbing her hand and leading her towards the back of the building.

We run behind the Air Conditioner on the roof and crouch down to take cover. Both of us stare off into the woods, expecting to hear something any second besides the moaning and clawing of zombies. Minutes go by without hearing anything. April and I look at each other, starting to doubt that this plan was a good idea.

"What do you think?" I ask April

"Don't know, but it is too dangerous to check."

"Yeah... How long do you think it will take?"

"Well, if it didn't land in a patch of snow or extinguish itself... Then it shouldn't be any more than ten minutes."

"So, until then we just wait?"

"Yup.", April adds.

Time continues to pass as doubt starts to cloud our minds. Out of boredom I start to bite at my fingernails. When I look over at April I notice that she has her head leaned back against the air conditioner with her eyes closed, almost looking like she was taking a nap. A devious smile fills my face. I lean a bit closer to April and yell at the top of my lungs,

"BOOM"

April jolts forward obviously startled by my voice. She looks around real quick, trying to figure out what is going on before turning to me. "You're such an asshole", She says sarcastically. April starts to laugh while punching my arm jokingly as I use it to shield my face.

"Oh, what are you scared of getting hit by a girl?" April says out loud while laughing.

"Haha, you should have seen the look on your face when I yelled. It was classic."

"I'll get you back!"

"Oh yeah? How do you plan on that?"

"Oh, I'll think of something..."

We both continue to laugh and playfully push each other around. Until moments later were we are both caught off guard by a gunshot. Both of us immediately stop what we were doing and look at each other.

"Is that?"

"Yeah I heard it too", April adds.

The two of us stare at each other before slowly peaking up over the Air Conditioner. We look around in the direction of the gas storage area but it all looks exactly the same. I start to stand up and move out from the Air Conditioner, curiously wanting to investigate.

Right as I step out from behind the Air Conditioner I hear another gun shot. I quickly dive back behind the Air Conditioner, scared of getting hit by a rogue bullet. As I am lying face down on the ground I look up at April who is now giggling at me

"Yeah real funn..." I start to say but am interrupted by the sound of two more gunshots.

I quickly cover my head with both of my arms and pull my legs in behind the Air Conditioner with the rest of my body. We hear another shot go off, the time between them bow rapidly increasing. Two more shots fire off, causing me and April to cower even more.

Seconds later we hear a chain of shots, one after another sometimes two at the same time. About twenty seconds go by before everything goes silent. April and I both look at each other, worrying that our plan didn't work. I shake my head in disappointment before looking up at April.

"Well, I guess another one of my plans miserably failed..."

"Well at least we tried..." April starts to talk but is quickly interrupted.

We hear another gunshot go off, this time the gun shot was followed by an even louder explosion. This sound was no gunshot, that's for sure. The gas tank exploded, causing the whole area around us to shake.

The whole area around us lit up with a red hue, the black smoke coming from the explosion already billowing up and almost filling the sky. Body parts from the zombies closest to the blast can be seen flying in every direction. Some of the body parts land right next to us, April and I both kick them away, gagging as we touch them.

After the explosion April and I both stand up and grab any ammo that is left on the roof. Once we have the ammo we start to run for the front of the gas station's store. Our plan is quickly halted, though, as the building itself starts to shake and crumble.

"It's going to collapse! This way! Quick!" I yell to April while grabbing her hand and pulling her back towards the air conditioner

The building starts to shake even more as it beings to collapse. The front of the building collapses creating a slope down to the pavement below. As the slope is created it pulls me April and I apart, pulling her down to the pavement below.

"April!" I scream as I watch her fall to the ground below.

I take a quick look around, tempted to slide down after her and make a run for the highway. But not enough zombies were killed by the blast. They still fully encircle the gas station making it so running would be suicide.

I look back down at April; she is lying on the ground, seemingly unconscious. I continue to scream her name, getting louder and louder with each yell, praying she wakes up. After about a minute she finally puts her arms out in front of her and pulls herself onto her knees. She places a hand on her head and shakes it as she regains consciousness. Once April is awake again she turns and looks up at me

"Come on, come on, come on!" I yell at her, motioning for her to come to me.

The zombies are now starting to notice April is on the ground and vulnerable. They start to stumble and crawl there way over to her. Some of them even walk through the fire that the explosion caused, seemingly unaffected by it. April shakes her head one last time before she fully regains consciousness. She pulls herself onto her feet and runs up the slant leading up to the roof. She makes it a few feet up before throwing me her hand. I reach down and grab it. Once I have a hold of it I pull her up to the roof right next to me.

Almost immediately after I get April up the zombies below lean on the slant but are unable to get up on their own. I stare in fear and anger down at the zombies, watching them as they start to pile up on each other. They are clawing and grabbing at April and I both on top the roof.

As they begin to pile up on each other the zombies on the top of the pile get closer and closer to making it on the roof. Any zombie that gets close to the top is greeted by a pulled out of my M4 or the back of my shoe, pushing him back down.

When I fire at them, my bullets penetrate their skulls. Killing them instantly and causing their lifeless bodies to roll down the slant knocking every other zombie down as they roll. After resting for a few minutes April quickly comes to her senses and helps me by firing at the zombies below.

Less than a minute goes by before April's Glock runs out of ammo. She turns around and reaches behind me for the only other two Glock clips on the roof. She reloads her gun and sticks the other clip in her pocket, throwing the empty clip at the zombies below.

Shortly after my M4 runs out of ammo I turn around and grab the four remaining magazines off the roof behind me. I place three of them into my pockets and the fourth one into my gun. In an attempt to conserve ammo I start to kick any zombies getting close to the top of the slope. As time goes on the bodies start to pile up below us, giving the zombies something to stand on. This is slowly making it easier for them to reach the top. I turn to look at April who is focused on killing any zombies that get close to the roof.

"We're not going to make it much longer." I yell to April over the sound of our guns.

"We got to keep trying."

I nod to April while continuing to fire at the zombies below. "I'm out of ammo..." April yells out to me before giving her gun a blank stare. A bit preoccupied I reach into my back pocket for a magazine for my M4. I pull out the old one and slip in the new one.

"My sidearm, take it!" I say while looking at the Glock that is strapped to my waist.

April lunges at my side arm, almost ripping it off my waist. In no time she points it at the zombies below and starts to fire again. Now that so many zombies are dead at the bottom of the slant their corpses form almost a stairwell. Allowing the zombies easy passage right up to us.

Our moral is rapidly decreasing until we hear an unfamiliar sound over the woods to the west. April and I both turn to look to the west. We see a large helicopter flying over the woods and then quickly pass over the building.

April and I both look at each other, our moral instantly restored by the sight of the helicopter. Both of us start to jump around and flail our arms in the air in a desperate attempt to get the helicopter's attention. The helicopter flies out into a wide open field right on the other side of the highway. Just when we thought it wasn't going to turn around it does a large one eighty and flies directly at us.

The helicopter flies directly over top the gas station before stopping and hovering above. April and I both continue to jump around, screaming at the top of our lungs for help. We are able to see a minor amount of movement coming from the helicopter above us. As it continues to hover above us we hear a large caliber machine gun start firing. Both of us jump to the side and cower in fear, unsure of who is being shot at yet.

We look over at the pack of zombies that previously threatened us. Their bodies are being torn asunder by the large 50 caliber rounds that are firing out of the helicopter. While we're watching the zombies being torn apart a ladder falls down from the helicopter onto the roof behind us. The people on the helicopter give us suppressing fire, killing any zombies that get close to the roof. I shout for April to get on the helicopter before me but the sound of it above us muffles my voice. Unable to talk to April I grab her hand and pull her over to the ladder, motioning for her to go up first. She nods and grabs a hold of the ladder, starting to climb up while I use my M4 to kill any zombies the helicopter missed.

Once I see that April is safely on the ladder and half way up I grab a hold of it and start to climb up. As I am climbing the ladder I watch April above me as she reaches the top and is pulled in by a few different sets of hands. I climb the ladder quickly, almost throwing myself from step to step. When I reach the top three different people reach out and place their hands on my shoulders, helping me inside.

I look over and notice April sitting on what looks to be a bench inside with a blanket covering her body. April beams me a smile, happy to see me and also thanking me for getting us out alive. One man extends his arm out to me, wanting to shake my hand. I smile and him and throw my hand into his.

The man has short black hair and a full beard, like he hasn't shaved for weeks. By the strength of his handshake it feels like he works out every day.

I notice he has a rifle thrown around his back with the strap coming over his chest. He is wearing some sort of tactical suit that matches everyone else in the helicopter besides April and I.

After I shake his hand he uses his other hand to pull himself to me. He places his head right next to mine he yells into my ear,

"Nice to meet you, I'm Fredrick."

CHAPTER 5 - SURVIVOR COLONY

While riding in the helicopter nothing else can be heard in the cockpit over the roaring blades cutting through the chilly winter air outside. I turn to my side and look at April who is sitting next to me. She has a blanket covering almost her whole body and still has a vibrant smile. April throws her arm across my shoulders and pulls me into her. She pulls me into her before whispering in my ear, "Thank you."

"What do you mean?" I reply.

"You got us off that building alive." April says.

I smile at April and lean in to say something but just as I start moving Fredrick taps me on the shoulder. I lean across the cockpit, placing my head next to Fredrick to hear what he has to say.

"About five more minutes and we will be there."

"Where is there?"

"We have a survivor colony, inside Cleveland. We're located at a hospital just inside city limits."

"How many of you are there?"

"What?" Fred asks, the helicopter muffling my last question.

"How many of you are there?"

"How many of what?"

"Survivors."

"Two hundred and thirty seven."

"Two hundred and thirty seven? Are you just bull shiting me?"

"No. We do a head count every few days. It helps us ration supplies."

"I see. How did you find us?"

"Take a look out the window!"

I lean back and look at Fredrick confused with what he means. He grabs my shoulder and turns me towards his hand as he points out the side of the helicopter. I notice large clouds of black smoke billowing up into the air from the gas station April and I were just stranded at. The smoke must be visible for miles, I thought to myself.

I continue looking out the side of the helicopter at the city of Cleveland below. The sight is almost the same as New York City. Cars are overturned and abandoned their doors wide open with a giant puddle of blood right outside the door. Buildings windows are shattered and some even have severe structural damage from vehicles crashing into them. There are blood smears covering the sidewalks below, accompanied by an occasional body part.

As I continue to look out the side I shake my head, trying to disbelieve the destruction that I am witnessing. I lean back into the helicopter and sit down next to April, my face a little bit more pale then it was before. After I sit back down I look over at Fredrick and toss him a smirk, thanking him for giving me the privilege to look out. Even though I wish he didn't.

Not long passes before we reach the Survivor Colony inside Cleveland. Once here we hover over top the hospital for a minute or two, making sure the Landing Pad is clear before setting down. Right after we set down Fredrick and his team hop out of the helicopter, motioning for April and I to follow. Fredrick and two others assist me in stepping out of the helicopter, making sure I don't slip and fall while getting out. Once I'm out I turn around and help April out, much like Fredrick did for me.

While I am helping April out of the Helicopter Fredrick and one of his friends rushes inside. Fredrick's other friend is standing at the door leading off the roof, holding it open for us. His friend is a shorter man, about five foot nine with short brown hair and a goatee. He has a boyish face and light blue eyes, not really matching the rest of him. Much like Fredrick, his friend looks like he spends way too much time on the weight bench. As April and I pass him we both nod to him, thanking him for holding the door.

Once we're inside the door we start to walk down the long flight of stairs leading off the roof and down into the hospital. None of us talk while walking down the stairwell, our ears still ringing from the short helicopter ride over. We only had to walk down a few floors in the stairwell until we came out into the hospital. The first room we entered from the stairwell was a long hallway with dozens of rooms off each side of it.

The hallway is filled with people sitting out on blankets and wondering the halls, too depressed or anxious to sit. Everyone in the halls seems to be restless and either crying or holding their loved ones closely. It's easy to see who has lost a loved one just by looking at them. April and I quickly make our way through the hospital, following Fredrick closely. All the other survivors give us mean looks as we pass. Making it seem like they're not too welcoming to new people. Both April and I try to avoid eye contact with any other survivors to prevent any trouble.

Fredrick leads April and I down another staircase and through another hallway to a large Assembly room. In the Assembly room there is a large table right in the center of the room with over a dozen faces I've never seen before sitting down at it. These survivors seem different though, they are more upscale and upbeat. Instead of focusing on the now, they are focusing on the future. They seem more worried about how to make things better and not worried about what happened a week ago.

Sitting at the front of the table is an older man. As we walk in the older man motions April and I to sit down next to Fredrick at the table. The man at the head of the table is looks to be in his early sixties. He has a receding hair line but the hair he does have is gray. He has on a small pair of glasses, which look to be more for reading than for actual sight. Next to his seat leaning on the side of the table is a brown cane, how someone who has a hard time walking is calling the shots is beyond me.

Once everyone is seated the older man at the head of the table stands up and starts a speech, "I've called this meeting together today to welcome our two new members. Fredrick and his team found them within a reasonable distance to our colony. After they notified us of their presence we made the executive decision to go save them. Fredrick will you please stand up and introduce our two newest members."

Fredrick stands up before motioning to April and I to follow his example. April and I nod, standing up and turning to the older man sitting at the head of the table. I brush my shirt off while Fredrick clears his throat to start talking.

"Mark found these two stranded on top the gas station right off interstate ninety. When we got there they had caused the gas station to explode and were surrounded by nearly two thousand zombies. We killed as many zombies as we could before air lifting them to safety."

Fredrick holds his hand out with his palm up and his hand flat in the air, just like he was displaying us. He introduces me first and then introduces April, "His name is Ryan and her name is April if I am not mistaken." After Fredrick finishes talking he plants his arm on my shoulder and shakes me, informing me to speak.

"Yes, uhm, I am Ryan and this is my friend April. We are both survivors of the disaster."

After speaking, the man at the head of the table turns to another, younger, man sitting to his right. He leans close to him and whispers into his ear, discussing something. April and I both look at each other, wondering if we are in trouble. A few seconds go by before he leans back into his chair and asks me.

"Where are you from?"

"April and I both lived in New York City and made it all the way to that gas station before becoming stranded on the roof."

"May I ask why you are heading in this direction?"

"I don't know, maybe because the ocean is in the opposite direction?" I reply

"I'm sorry?" The man adds, obviously confused by my response.

"West is the only logical path to go. The ocean is to our east and without a boat it would be impossible to cross. We don't own a boat and could only find a car, thus we decided to travel west."

You can tell the man is a bit frustrated by my response. But he bites his lip and decides not to argue with me.

"Did you have any idea about this survivor colony or any others?"

"Yeah, we picked up a flyer at a gas station. It said this was a nice place to vacation at this time of the year."

The older man growls at my sarcasm and changes the subject, "How much do you know about the zombies?"

I chuckle a bit before starting to talk, "Well, I don't like to brag, but I'd like to say that I know almost everything there is to know about them. I know they can't be tamed once turned. They cannot be stopped unless they receive a bullet to the head. I know once bitten you will be transformed into one. And, I know they also possess the power to run."

"A zombie that is able to run?" The older man asks, alarmed. "What do you know about this Fredrick?"

"This is the first time I have heard about it." Fredrick replies.

The older man turns to the man to his right again, speaking quietly so no one else can hear him. I let out a sigh, now becoming frustrated with the secrecy.

After he finishes whispering into the other man's ear he turns back to me and continues, "I'm having trouble believing you found a running zombie."

"That sucks."

"Excuse me?"

I continue by changing the subject, "It was actually at the gas station Fredrick found us at. In the storage room, I shot four of them, if I recall correctly. I will admit, I was taken off guard and did not know they were capable of running either. However, the ones I shot were running and it is something you should prepare for the in the future. After all, this zombie stuff is new to us all. We can't always know what to expect aside from expecting the unexpected."

"Very well put. What about you young lady? What is your story?" The man asks, looking to April.

"Well, I lived in New York City with my parents at the time of this disaster. When it all happened I boarded myself up in the house. I didn't know what else to do, so I hid. When they finally made it inside my house, I ran and screamed for help. That is when I met Ryan."

"So Ryan saved you?" The old man asks, questioning April.

"Yes.", April replies

"Well that is interesting. Well, we welcome you both to the Cleveland Survivor Colony. We have a few rules here; we give out rations every day at five p.m. It's not a lot but we try to divide what we have equally and fairly to everyone. Our other rule is no starting trouble. If you start trouble you will be placed into a holding cell."

"If you have any tactical experience, please speak with Fredrick. He is our Chief Officer, if you will. He leads all the raids and missions to resupply and rescue anyone on the outside. It seems like you two have knowledge of our enemies and we could use you in assisting Fredrick. Fredrick, if you wouldn't mind please show them around."

The old man stands up and reaches for his cane. He raises his other arm and brings it down, bowing to everyone in the room. Once he finishes his bow he continues, "As of now, this meeting is adjourned, until next time."

Everyone in the room stands up and collects any papers or other miscellaneous items they may have brought in. They all exit the room from a different direction that Fredrick brought us in from. Making me assume that leads to their upscale quarters.

Fredrick turns to April and I before saying, "Alright, let's get out of here. I'll show you around our facility."

Fredrick hastily exits the room from the same doorway we entered. April and I almost have to start running in order to keep up with Fredrick. As we are walking through the halls I spark a conversation up with April.

"Well that was weird"

"Yeah, I guess he is there leader?"

"Apparently so, I don't see how he got the leadership title though, being so old and all."

"Yeah, I found that a little awkward as well."

"Yeah... What do you think of this place? I think it is a little weird to be honest."

"Agreed, we should keep that to ourselves though, they deserve our trust since they rescued us."

"Rescued us? Nah, I was just about to invent a Jet Pack to fly us out of there."

April giggles uncontrollably as until we arrive at the place Fredrick was bringing us. When we arrive Fredrick throws open the double doors in front of us which leads into a large room that looks like it used to be a lobby. Now instead of it being wide open and filled with seats it is packed with bookshelves, tables and benches. Each of which have guns, ammo and knives covering them.

"This is our Armory." Fredrick says out loud.

"And this is the person who overlooks the armory, Braydon. Braydon show them around and bring them to Troy when you're done."

Braydon nods, letting Fredrick know he understands. Fredrick walks out of the room and harmlessly jogs down the hallway in the direction from which we came. Braydon turns to us, extending his hand to introduce himself.

Braydon stood tall, about the same height as me. He had shaggy dirty blond hair; straight at the top but getting curlier the closer it got to his cheeks. As with Fredrick and his other friend, it seems like Braydon spends some time on the weight bench. Not nearly as much time as Fredrick though.

After the introductions Braydon throws his arm into the room. Showing us all the Ammunition and guns he has. The room is jam packed with almost every type of gun ever made and plenty of ammunition for that gun. Putting aside the fact that the room has so much in it, everything seems to be neatly organized. And it doesn't look like anything is out of place.

"So, you like what you see?" Braydon asks.

"Yeah, I most certainly do.", I reply

"Fredrick told me you were going to be joining our Tactical Squad. So I dug out two body suits for you. Here you both go."

"Thanks!" April and I both say at the same time.

"Put them on when you guys get out of the shower later and never take them off. They protect you everywhere but your head and neck. They won't stop a bullet but zombies can't penetrate them with their teeth."

"I would offer you two side arms, but I see you still have yours from the rooftop. However, I figure you probably need ammo after that little adventure. So here you guys go."

Braydon hands April and I five clips each for our sidearm's and hands me an extra three clips for my M4. I look around my waist trying to find enough pockets to put all the ammo. "Now you can't go firing them inside. You'll piss off the local residents and get into big trouble." Braydon says with a huge smile across his face. "Well, of course." I reply with a slight laugh.

While we're joking around another man from the helicopter enters the room. It was the same man who held the door for us earlier while we were on the roof. He walks in the room and stands off to the side. When Braydon sees him he lights up as a smile comes across his face. "Ah Troy you're here, come in, come in."

I extend my hand out to Troy, greeting him with a hand shake. April follows my example in greeting him. After we've both introduced ourselves to Troy he smiles and steps back before saying, "Fredrick told me to come down here and show you two to our HQ. When you're ready let me know."

I take a look around the room checking to see if there is anything else I still need. With nothing catching my eye I turn to Braydon and ask, "Do you have any tactical knives?" Braydon places his hand on his chin, thinking for a second before answering. "Yeah."

Braydon turns around and slowly makes his way through the room, being careful to not knock anything over. Half way across the room he opens up a drawer in a desk and yells, asking me,

"How many do you want?" Braydon asks.

"I want two. April, do you want any?" I ask.

April looks at me curiously, "Uhm, yeah, sure I'll take two as well."

"Do you have any ankle and waist straps?" I ask

"Yeah sure, ill grab you both some."

Braydon grabs everything I asked for and slowly navigates his way back to us near the front of the room. He hands me and April our Tactical Knives as well as the straps that I asked for.

"Can you take us to our sleeping quarters first, so we can drop this stuff off? Then take us to HQ?" I ask Troy. "Yeah, sure, follow me.", He replies

Before all three of us leave the room I tip my head to Braydon, thanking him for everything. When we get out into the hallway Troy leads us back to the stairwell. On the walk over to the staircase he turns to us and says, "Sorry but we got to take the stairs. The elevator is out and Mark hasn't figure out how to fix it yet."

"Mark?" I ask, curiously.

"Yeah. He is our head engineer so to speak. He is the person who runs and operates the HQ. That is who I am taking you to meet."

"Ahh, I see. Is he one of those computer geeks?"

Troy laughs wholeheartedly, before saying, "I think that is an understatement. His IQ is just south of one hundred and ninety. Very book smart but lacks all levels of common sense."

April and I both smile before breaking into laughter, happy that everyone here isn't as up tight as that meeting. Right after we finished talking we arrived at our sleeping quarters. April and I walk into the room and take a look around. It's a small room, nothing more than a queen size bed and a dresser are in the room. April turns to Troy who is standing in the doorway and asks, "Only one bed?"

"Yeah, it's all we can spare. If it is a problem I can probably pull some stri..." Troy says before being interrupted by April.

"No, no, no. No problem, I was just asking."

Troy nods and smiles to her before turning around and looking out the hall, giving us some privacy. April and I both put everything Braydon gave us and everything we came with on the bed. After we've both placed everything on the bed I lean over it and ask April, "It's not a problem, the one bed?"

"No, it really isn't. I don't know why I brought it up."

"Are you sure? Because I can get you another one if you want, or sleep on the floor or something."

April leans back and places her hand on her forehead, a bit frustrated with me. When she removes it she looks at me and says, "Please don't make a big deal out of this. I nod, "Alright, let's go meet Mark", I say in a sarcastically excited voice, trying to cheer her up.

I manage to make April smile before turning and walking out of the room, over to Troy. Once we're out of the room we nod to Troy, letting him know we are ready to go. He leads us back over to the stairwell and stops at the door right before we enter.

"Alright, this is a really long walk; we're going to the basement level. We'll take a break halfway if you need It.", Troy says before entering the stairwell and holding the door for us.

When we enter the stair well I take a look off the side, to see how many floors there are. When I look off to the side my eyes almost immediately double in size as my jaw drops down. I turn to Troy and say in a worrisome voice, "Dude! That is like, twenty floors!"

"Twenty six if you count the sub levels."

"Wow. Who should be working on the elevator right now? Because when I see them I am going to rip their fucking throat out."

"Mark, the person we're going to meet."

"Well Mark needs to get his priorities straight"

"Fredrick told you Mark was the one that found you, right?"

"Yeah, he told me."

"If it wasn't for Mark, you'd probably be dead right now."

"Pssh, I was twenty seconds away from inventing a Jet Pack and flying out of there."

Troy stops in the middle of his staircase and starts uncontrollably laughing. April and I both turn to each other, both thinking the same thing, It wasn't *that* funny. Troy starts to talk, his words broken up by laughter.

"I don't... I don't... know why, but that was really funny. I haven't had a good laugh like that... in a really long time..."

"Ahem, I'm sorry", Troy adds. "Let's continue down."

We continue down the staircase, having about twenty three more floors to go. Since I easily get bored on the way down, it doesn't take long for me to spark up another conversation with Troy.

"So what is up with that council?"

"What do you mean?"

"The people in the Assembly room from earlier. Who appointed them leadership?"

"No one, they are the CEO's of the hospital and other office buildings nearby."

"So, in other words they are just mooching off what we do."

"Yeah, pretty much."

"Hmm, well that is interesting. So how long have you known Fredrick, Mark and Braydon?"

"What has it been, about a week since this all started?"

"Yeah, something like that."

"Fredrick was one of the military officers that were evacuating Cleveland. We took refuge in a large office building for almost three days, fighting off zombies. Eventually we ran out of ammo and Fredrick's whole team was killed."

"Fredrick and his team rounded up many survivors, including me, Braydon and Mark. A few of the people in this hospital are from that office building as well. When we were overwhelmed by zombies Fredrick found an alternative way out. We managed to get out with about twenty to thirty other people. The rest were presumably killed."

"Fredrick led us to a gun shop and asked for help in protecting everyone. Mark, Braydon and I all stepped forward. He gave us all guns and told us where he figured it would be safe. He said he and his team had a helicopter there; it is where they landed coming into Cleveland. Fredrick led us to the hospital and we decided to bunker down here."

Troy quickly changes the subject, "Alright, we're about halfway. Rest up."

April and I continue down the stairs to reach Troy. He was moving faster down the stairs, almost always a set of stairs ahead of us. When we reach Troy April and I both take a seat on the stairs, huffing and puffing while trying to catch our breath. While looking over at Troy I notice he is seemingly unaffected by the stairs, even with talking the whole time.

"So... What is the plan now?" I ask Troy.

"What do you mean?"

"Like, you guys plan to stay at this hospital your whole life?"

"Mark has made contact with other survivor colonies they say that they are developing a cure."

"There is no cure."

"The other survivor colonies said they have made great headway."

"Listen to me. Those people are dead. They used to be alive. Then they were killed and brought back to life with this shit. What do you think will happen to these people if you bring them back to life, again, from the undead state they are in? We're fucked if they inject someone and then turn them into something... else."

Troy places his hand on his chin and slightly nods, agreeing with the points I brought up. Troy peeks over the side of the rail, looking to see how many floors we have left. Right after he looks he starts back down the stairs, yelling back to April and I, "Let's go, break time is over."

April and I both roll our eyes. We pull ourselves back onto our feet and continue down the stairs, not even bothering to try and follow Troy closely. Occasionally I reach down and grab my right leg, able to feel the burn in it from all the stairs. While we're navigating down the stairs I turn to April and ask her,

"Think I pissed him off? It looks like I pissed him off."

"Yeah you pissed him off."

Both of us continue down the stairs until we reach the bottom where Troy is waiting for us. Once Troy sees us he opens the door at the bottom of the stairs and leads us down a short dark hallway. Right in the center of the hallway is a large ceiling light that is flickering. Making it almost perfect for a scary horror film, I thought to myself. April and I both hug Troy closely while making our way down the hall. Not wanting anything more than a three foot distance come between us. Both of us scared that something else may be in the hall besides us.

At the end of the hallway Troy opens a large door for us which leads into a very well lit room with computer equipment everywhere. In the center of the room is a large twenty foot monitor with weird symbols and pictures all over it. Below the computer monitor is a giant panel with hundreds of buttons on it.

In front of that panel stands a very tall man, he is about six foot five with short black hair. The man seems to weigh no more than two hundred pounds, giving him a very tall and lanky like figure. When we enter the room Troy walks over to the man and whispers something into his ear. After Troy whispers into his ear he turns around to look at us excitedly. He takes off his headset and puts on a pair of glasses as me and April walk over to him. I extend my hand and the man grabs it, shaking it.

"I'm Ryan."

"Mark", he replies before taking April's hand.

"April", She says with a smile.

"Mark."

Mark turns around and looks back at his computer monitor. Right after Mark turns around Troy looks to the ground shakes his head. He looks up and over to Mark before saying,

"You know it is very rude to ignore your guests."

"Yes, yes, I know. I have something I want them to see."

Mark starts hitting all kinds of different buttons on the computer until he finally brings up something that shows a large red blob on the Computer Monitor. The second the large red blob pops up he turns to April and I while pointing at the screen repeatedly.

"A few hours ago this was you. That is how we found you!"

I take a good long look at the computer monitor before saying, "I'm confused"

"The heat! The heat! Look at the screen, when you exploded the gas station the heat sensors went off the charts. Look, look." Mark says while seemingly jacked up on caffeine, pointing to the large red blob in the middle of the computer monitor.

"That's the gas station explosion"

Mark than leans over to the panel and starts to hit a lot of different buttons. This causes the screen to zoom out over top the large red blob. He turns to us, pointing around the area around it.

"See all these individual heat sensors? These are the zombies. They give off less heat than a human, since they're dead and all. But with how many you had around you, it is easy to see from a very far distance."

Mark turns back to the computer and starts to plug around with more buttons. While hitting buttons he reaches to his side and takes a sip from what seems like a cup of coffee. From the speed of which this man is talking he definitely doesn't need more caffeine.

"If we didn't set off the explosion, would you of still found us?" April asks Mark.

"Yes, no, well, maybe. I'm not sure. We didn't take any notice to that area until the large explosion. Once we had seen that we decided to investigate. As you can see, when we investigated we found you two."

"What is the range on this thing?" I ask Mark.

"Well we can see about halfway through Iowa and all the way over to New Jersey. It seems to be about eight hundred miles. Anything past that ends up being dramatically inaccurate."

"Can you show me all major cities around us?" I ask Mark

"Hah, I knew you were going to ask that!"

Mark hits a few buttons on the panel and uses an oval globe in front of him to zoom around on the computer monitor. He moves the screen up from Cleveland and down right onto another city. Still excited and shaking he turns around to the two of us. "Alright, this is Detroit. See this small little blob here, congested into the building?" Mark asks, "Yeah?" I reply curious as to what he is getting at.

"That is where the Detroit Survivor Colony says they are."

"Was the colony there before or after the disaster?"

April and Troy both break into laughter, understanding the joke that I just told. Mark turns to look at the two of them laughing before adjusting his glasses, "I'm sorry? I don't quite understand..."

"Nothing, nothing, what were you saying?"

"Uhm, alright so this is the Survivor Colony. As you can see this whole building is very red, but not much is outside the building. Now, let me try and find a pack of zombies so you can see the difference."

Mark starts to hit buttons on the large panel and uses an oval-like globe to scroll around the city. He occasionally takes his hand off of the globe to adjust his glasses.

I look over at Mark and ask, "Do they always travel in packs? Or do they split up?"

"Uhm, well since I can't really pin point them alone, it is much easier to find them in packs. But usually when they pick up a new scent they all pileup and walk over to it, forming a pack. Then once they find another scent, they all travel to it as a pack. Once they reach that scent, any other zombies there will join the pack and follow it to the next scent."

"This continues on until you get a large pack of zombies, much like the pack of zombies that surrounded you on top of the building."

After Mark finishes talking he focuses on the screen once again, looking for a group of zombies. Troy walks up to the screen and points around the center of it, "What is right there?" He asks.

Mark zooms into the area that Troy pointed to. He focuses on it for a second before zooming out and spinning around the area. Mark motions for April and I to come over while keeping his eyes fixated onto the screen.

"Look, look here. See how there is little green and orange dots all over the place?"

"Mmmhmm", April and I both mumble.

"Those are zombies. Their core is orange, since it is hotter than the rest of their body. The green is their outer layers, so to speak. Their heat output is much different than a Human, since, well, they're not human."

"Interesting.", I reply.

"So, everyone tells me you're really smart. So, what is your theory on how the zombie event happened?" I ask Mark.

"Theory, theory? No, no theory. Explanation yes."

I arch an eyebrow and tilt my head slightly to Mark, having my interests immediately perked. Everyone in the room takes a few steps closer to Mark, very interested to hear his explanation. Before Mark starts to speak he turns around and takes his glasses off, placing them on the panel behind him.

"There was a power plant in Delaware where scientists were experimenting with a very powerful neurotoxin called tetrodotoxin."

"Yes, yes! I heard about that! It comes from a, uhm, Puffer Fish, correct?" I exclaim.

"Yes, a few different species of Puffer Fish around Haiti as well as a frog species on Haiti. They were trying to find a way to bring the dead back to life..."

"Well it looks like they succeeded." Troy adds.

Mark continues, "Please don't interrupt. But yes. They did succeed. They figured the power plant would be perfect cover up. If anything went wrong they could blame the radiation. However, when the radiation leaked into the solvent, the outcome was, well, as expected."

"The first few people who came into contact with this new mixture would have mutated into something unimaginable within eight hours after being exposed. Anything they touch after being exposed will be infected. That's how it spread so fast. They had no idea they were infected at first. Then when they did know, well, it was too late."

"They already went home, seen their families, friends, strangers on the road. The ones who were taken to the hospital for radiation burns or anything else quickly infected every patient and visitor inside. Even now the original people who were exposed to the toxin are highly contagious and presumably much more powerful than the zombies we have already come into contact with."

"The remaining survivors have discussed using a nuclear warhead to possibly clean up the mess. However, the exposure of more radiation to the people who were originally affected... This would only make the problem worse. If you exposed them to more radiation they'd becomes stronger and even more demented. Pretend that radiation is like steroids to them. It is said these select few people maintained a part of their human selves."

"This means they can speak, feel and control themselves. It is uncertain if they can control the others that weren't directly affected by the toxin."

Mark pauses for a second before turning around and putting on his glasses again. Once his glasses are back on he sticks his hand up in the air and says out loud, "Alright, I'm done for now. I've got work to do. Troy can you please escort both of them back to their sleeping quarters?"

Troy nods and starts to escort us out. All of us somewhat puzzled by Marks abrupt end to the conversation and lack of people skills. April and I both follow behind Troy, through the scary hallway and back to the stairwell. None of us speak a word until we reach the stairwell. Once inside the stairwell Troy asks, "So, do you guys buy it?"

"Buy what?" I ask.

"Mark's explanation, I mean, it sounds believable right?"

"Yeah, I buy it."

"Well at least I know I'm not just gullible. What do you think April?" Troy asks.

"Yeah, it sounds accurate. Also makes me a little bit worried about the people who were originally infected."

"Yeah, I hear ya." Troy adds.

Everything is quiet until between us until we arrive on the floor that our sleeping quarters are on. When we arrive Troy opens the door and holds it for April and I as we walk out into the hallway. Once we're out in the hallway April turns to Troy and asks, "Is there any place me and Ryan can clean up?"

"Yeah, I'll show you to the showers. Follow me."

Troy leads us down a long hallway and past more survivors. Unlike the first time we walked by a group of survivors, this time we didn't get any mean looks. If any of the survivors do make eye contact with us it's to nod their head in greeting. At the end of the hall Troy rounds the corner and stops at the first door to the right. He grabs the handle and opens it for us, standing to the side to let us in.

"Alright, here are the showers. We got one problem though; we're low on water so there is only enough for one of you. We haven't figured out how to fix the problem, all the spickets turn on when you turn the water on, on one of them on. You two can always take a shower together, but that is none of my business."

Troy smiles and leaves down the opposite hallway that we came from. Before getting to far away he stops and turns around, smiling and scratching his head.

"Oh yeah forgot to add. Be sure to turn the water off, of course and your sleeping quarters are down the hall and to the left."

April and I both smile and nod to Troy, letting him know that we heard him. Before Troy gets too far away I yell out to him, "Hey Troy."

Troy stops and turns around again before responding, "Yeah?"

"Thanks for everything. We really appreciate it."

"No problem."

Troy smiles and does a slight bow before continuing down the hallway. April and I enter the shower area. We close the door behind us and lock it, wanting at least some form of privacy. I take a look around the shower area before turning to April and giving her a blank awkward stare.

A slight smile forms on my face before I ask, "So, how are we going to go about this without it being amazingly awkward?"

"I feel like I am in third grade playing the "you show me yours, I'll show you mine game." April says.

"I'll play that game!" I exclaim

April jokingly slaps me in the shoulder, lightening the mood a bit. After a minute or two we both go to separate corners of the room and undress. While we're getting undressed very few words are exchanged between us aside from "Hey!" and "No peeking!"

Once the two of us are undressed we walk into the shower and pick two different sides. Even though we told each other no peeking, both of us ignored each other's wishes. At first the two of us were shy of the idea but as time went on we got more and more used to it.

Both of us had a bottle of Shampoo and some Soap right by our spickets. After the water warmed up I grabbed the soap and lathered myself up. As I rinsed myself off the dirt and grime that I've accumulated the past few days can be seen spiraling down the drain below me. After I finish washing myself off with the soap I turn to face April and squeeze it, shooting it over at her. April turns her head to look at me, confused as to what hit her.

Before she can say anything I call out, "I dropped the Soap!"

"Don't bend over!" She says jokingly.

I reach over to the Shampoo bottle nearby and squirt a large amount in my hand before rubbing it into my hair. My hair was almost impossible to wash at first, the dirt and grime in it acting like an adhesive. Once I was able to wash out the first layer of gunk in my hair it was easy to continue washing it out. After I finished washing out my hair I stood in the shower forever, just spinning around and enjoying the feel of the water.

The feeling of the hot water caressing my cold body was just too good to give up. I couldn't help but smile as the water ran down my back; it was the best I've felt in days. The longer I stood under the warm water, the more I never wanted to leave it. I could tell April was enjoying the hot water from the shower to. She was constantly tilting her head from side to side; making sure it ran down both sides of her back equally.

The heat from the water successfully shook the cold from my body, allowing me to be completely warm for the first time in days. As time went on, what seemed like an eternity under the water only ended up to be about ten minutes. The water to the shower randomly shut off, ruining the fun for April and I. April and I both covered up the places that we didn't want each other to see before turning to each other.

Both of us started to shake, now cold with the absence of warm water. With both of us now uncontrollably shaking I turn to ask April, "What happened?"

"Don't know, did you touch your nozzle?"

"Whoa! That is a personal question!"

April sighs, "No, I meant..."

I quickly interrupt April, "I know what you meant. No, did you turn the water off?

"Why would I of asked you if I turned mine off?"

"Good point, let's get out of the shower to dry off then, I'm fuckin' freezing."

We rush out of the shower and over to the towel rack nearby, grabbing up towels for ourselves. Both of us dry ourselves off and get back into the clothes we were wearing before the shower. While looking around the room I spot a sink nearby with a razor and some shaving cream. My eyes light up like it is Christmas morning as I make my way across the room and over to the sink.

I check to see if the water works for the sink before wiping off the mirror. I take a look in the mirror, a bit taken back with how much my beard has grown in the past week. I lather my face up with shaving cream and start to shave away my beard. Since the blade is a bit dull it makes the process much more agonizing than it should be.

Before I finish shaving I accidentally cut myself in a few different places. When I am done I look over to April and hold up the razor, asking if she wants to shave. She shakes her head side to side, letting me know she doesn't need to. Once we're both clothed and dry we exit the shower and return to our sleeping quarters.

We arrive back at our bedroom and notice two spare pairs of clothes neatly folded and lying on the bed. April and I both jump in excitement when we see the clothes, happy to get out of the clothes we are in. April grabs her pair of clothes left for her and runs into the corner of the room before whispering to me, "No peeking!"

April giggles a bit as I turn around and look and look at the clothes they gave me. I turn the shirt around a few times and hold it up in the air, stretching it out and making a face. A little bit large, but it will work, I thought to myself. Moments later April turns around and says, "Alright I'm done, your turn."

I stand up and smile slightly while looking at April. They gave me clothes a size too big and April a size too small. She throws her old clothes into a corner, not caring what happens to them. April plants her hand on her hip and tilts her head at me, making it obvious that she is annoyed by me staring at her. Once I break my trance I walk over to the corner that April changed in and start to take off my clothes. I slip into the ones that were left for me on the bed and turn back around.

April and I clear the weapons, ammo and any other junk off the bed before crawling in. We both lay back and stare up at the ceiling. We can't help but think to ourselves that only a few hours ago we were on top of a building, firing down at thousands of zombies. The only thing on our mind at the times was how long until we run out of ammo and die. Now we're safely tucked away in a bed, warm and comfortable. It's funny how things work out. I thought to myself before falling asleep.

———————————————————

Around midnight April and I are awoken by the sound of knocking on our door. Just as I roll out of bed to walk over and answer the door Fredrick opens it and lets himself in. Once inside the room Fredrick turns on the light, almost blinding April and I.

"Ryan, survivors have been found fourteen blocks from here. They're surrounded by a large pack of zombies. We could use your help getting them out of there."

I nod to Fredrick before saying, "Alright April, lets suit up."

"Just you Ryan, we can only fit so many in the SUV and we need to keep room for the survivors. Meet me down stairs when you're ready. Be there in under five."

I scurry out of bed and throw on the tactical suit that Braydon gave me earlier. While I get dressed I continually reassure April that everything is going to be ok and that I will be fine. I take the knives that Braydon gave me and strap one around my right heel as well as one right around my waist. On the opposite side of the knife on my waist I strap on my Glock sidearm.

I toss the M4 around my shoulder and shove all the ammo April and I have in the room into my pockets. I toss April a smile before opening the door leading out into the hallway. I take a few steps out into the hallway before looking back at April, "I'll be back in time for dinner." I say sarcastically.

Those were the last words exchanged between April and I for awhile. Once out in the hallway I started to run in my full stride. About halfway down the hallway Troy bursts out of a room right in front of me. He slightly smiles to me as the two of us run side by side until we reach the staircase. We both enter the stairwell and quickly jog down the flights of stairs towards ground level.

Unlike last time in the stairwell this time I am keeping up with Troy. I even pass him while traveling down the stairs. About halfway down the stairs my heart is pounding from practically running down them. As I get closer and closer to the hospital's lobby I become more anxious, wanting nothing more to get out into the city and start shooting shit. At the bottom of the stairwell I burst through the door and into the hospital's lobby. The lights are shining so bright in the hospital's lobby that they almost blind me when I enter.

Fredrick and Braydon were waiting for Troy and I in the lobby. They greet the two of us as we enter from the stairwell and express the urgency of the situation. While Fredrick explains what is going on Troy and I continually nod our heads in understanding. After Fredrick is done talking we follow him out to the SUV outside.

Troy and I hop into the back of the SUV while Braydon gets into the driver's seat and Fredrick in the passenger's. Once everyone is inside the vehicle Braydon slams the car into drive and peels wheels. Fredrick leans into the back seat and hands everyone a set of night vision goggles as well as two clips of ammo for their rifles. Before he looks back out the front of the car he turns to me and says, "Alright rookie. Shoot to kill, aim for the head. Don't miss."

I nod to Fredrick, letting him know I understand and wanting to say I already know to aim for the head but still too winded from the stairwell. As we're driving down the road I glance out the window only to see buildings flying by. Braydon must be doing at least eighty.

"ETA one minute, suit up.", Fredrick calls out to everyone in the SUV.

Fredrick and Troy both pull the night vision goggles over their heads and slip a fresh clip of ammo their guns. I play around with my pair of night vision goggles, trying to figure out how they work. Just as I figure it out and turn them on Braydon comes to a screeching halt.

"Uhm, Fredrick, we got a problem." Braydon says.

"Yeah and what is that?" Fredrick asks.

"The zombies are packing the streets within a five block radius of our survivors. We're going to need to kill our way through."

"We don't have enough ammo for that." Troy adds.

"I'm not driving this car any closer; it will get completely destroyed by just trying to get there."

"We can't just leave them there!" Troy says out loud.

"Park the car, everyone out. We're going on foot." Fredrick says.

Braydon shifts the car into park and all four of us get out. Once out of the car Braydon quickly puts on his pair of night vision goggles before meeting everyone else around the passenger's side of the vehicle. Once we're all on the right hand side Fredrick informs us of his plan.

"Follow me close, don't make any noise and don't shoot unless we can't knife them. We don't want any unwanted attention."

We rush into a building nearby and quietly work our way through it. Fredrick leads us up onto a roof where we need to make a five foot jump to another nearby roof. We all jump across and wait for one another on the other side until we are all safely on the other roof. We continue this process until we are two blocks away from the building we need to be at and are unable to jump across any more rooftops. Fredrick walks around the building and looks for another approach while everyone else is panting and trying to catch their breath.

Unable to find any other approach Fredrick says, "We're going to have to go to ground level and take an alleyway to it."

Fredrick walks over to a metal door on top our roof that leads down into the building. He twists the handle and throws his shoulder into the door, trying to get it open. Unable to get it to budge he uses the back end of his rifle to knock the handle off the door, allowing us all entry. We rush into the building with Fredrick taking the lead followed by Braydon, Troy and then myself. Once we're inside the building I take a good look around. The building looks like it was used as an office building before the Apocalypse. There are filing cabinets everywhere with paper scattered across the floor. There is a long hallway on the second floor with office rooms on each side of it. Every one of the office doors is closed and it doesn't look like there was any sort of disturbance inside the building.

Fredrick and Braydon do a quick sweep of the visible areas on the second floor before quickly moving down to the first. Troy and I follow right behind them until we reach the front door of the building. We throw ourselves up against the wall and look out any windows we can into the street. When we look out of the window we can see ten to twenty zombies walking towards the building where the Survivors are said to be.

"It is too dangerous." Fredrick adds. "Let's check the back."

Fredrick runs across the building and over to the back door. The door at the back of the building is a large metal door, much like the one on the roof. Once we're at the back door we all plant ourselves against the wall. There are no windows nearby to get any type of visual in the alleyway.

Fredrick turns to us and says, "I'm going to open this door and see what is in the alley. Stay here until I clear it."

We all nod to Fredrick as he opens the backdoor leading out into the alleyway behind the building. The second Fredrick pulls the door out of its frame the alarm inside the building is set off. Everyone turns and looks around, caught off guard by the sound.

Fredrick shouts out, "Fuck! We got to go!"

Without any hesitation all of us rush out of the building and into the alleyway with Fredrick taking the lead. All of our guns are pointing in every which direction, ready to eliminate any zombie threat. "Clear, let's go." Fredrick says out loud after clearing the alley.

We all follow Fredrick down the alleyway running at almost full speed. All of us are extra careful to check every nook and cranny as we go. Doing this eliminates the chance of being caught off guard by any zombies. At the end of our alleyway we turn the corner into another alleyway which has a Zombie right in the middle of it. Without any hesitation Fredrick runs up to the zombie in the center of the alley and shoves his knife right through its temple.

The zombie's body goes limp as Fredrick slowly and quietly lowers it to the ground. Once the body is on the ground we continue following Fredrick around another corner and into another alleyway. This alleyway is clear, but it leads out to a street that we need to get across. All of us run up to the end of the alleyway where it dumps out into the street before throwing our backs into the wall. We make extra sure to keep our whole bodies concealed in the shadows. We look around the corner and into the street which is flooded by zombies.

We lean back into the shadows, our hearts racing faster than ever before now that we know what we're up against. All of us are out of breath and scared shitless of what is to come. Fredrick shakes his head before whispering the only plan he has. "Alright, there is about fifty of them out there. We're only going to have one shot at this. Run out, guns blazing. We need to get into the building across the street. From that building we can jump into the office building where the survivors are."

Fredrick doesn't even wait for our answers before propelling himself out onto the street with his gun blazing. The rest of us hesitate at first but quickly gather ourselves and follow him out. Once out onto the road our goggles light up, showing us zombies all over the place. I grip my gun tightly before simultaneously shooting at the nearby zombies with Braydon and Troy.

All four of us quickly make our way through the streets, killing any zombies in our way to clear a path. With the sounds of our rifles echoing off the buildings around us it makes it impossible to hear anything else. It doesn't take long for us to make our way across the street to the building adjacent to the one with the survivors.

Once we reach the building Fredrick opens the door and gets us all inside before shutting it and flipping a nearby bookcase in front of it. This will hopefully prevent any zombies from getting inside. We all take a much needed break, allowing us to gather ourselves and reload our guns. After we've all had a quick break Fredrick runs up the stairs of our building towards the rooftop, expecting us to follow.

Braydon, Troy and I all quickly finish our break and follow Fredrick closely. Fredrick finds the door that leads up to the roof but is unable to proceed since it is locked. The back of Fredrick's gun was a quick fix to this problem. After knocking the door knob off all of us bust out onto the rooftop and point our guns everywhere, ready to shoot anything that was there before us.

Now that we're all on the roof I run over to the front of the building and look down at the door. The hoard of zombies from the street have already conjugated to the front of our building. All of them are moaning and pounding on the door. Craving the flesh that they saw enter.

Fredrick calls everyone over before saying out loud, "Alright I found a way in. It is a long jump, probably seven feet. That is why only I am doing it. I'll find something inside to throw across to help you guys in."

We all nod to Fredrick and back up out of his way to give him even a slim chance of making the jump. Fredrick aims his gun at the window across the alleyway and fires, causing the glass on the window to shatter. He backs all the way up to the front of our roof, giving him a good forty feet to run before jumping the alleyway. Fredrick takes a few seconds to breath before running to the end of the rooftop and making one giant leap.

Fredrick makes it look easy as he clears the jump, landing a few feet inside the building. Seconds after seeing him enter the building he disappears, out of sight. We hear a burst of gun shots ring out from inside but they end abruptly. After the initial set of gun shots we don't hear anything for close to five minutes. All of us now starting to worry that Fredrick may have gotten into something over his head.

Seconds later we see Fredrick appear at the window holding a large, thick piece of wood. He slides it across the large gap to bridge our rooftop with his window. We all slowly make our way across the gap, one by one.

Once we're all across and into his building he says, "Part of the building is under construction. Be careful."

We all stay close to Fredrick, making extra sure to follow in his footsteps so we don't accidentally get hurt in the construction areas of the building.

"We're flying blind here. We have no idea what floor they are on. They could be anywhere!" Troy says out loud.

"We're going to split up.", Fredrick remarks.

"Whoa! That's a bad idea." I say.

"I'm with Ryan on this one Fredrick." Braydon adds.

"Listen to me! We're finding these people and we're going to do it fast. We're splitting up. We'll go in pairs since everyone here is a pussy. Troy, Ryan take the top floors. Braydon you're with me."

Fredrick makes his way over to the stairwell with Braydon close behind. They their search on the floor right below the one we came in on while Troy and I search the floor above. The first room Troy and I enter is under construction. The first thing either of us notice when we enter the room is a dead zombie on the floor in front of us. There is a large knife wound going right through the temple of the corpse. Troy and I look at each other and smirk, knowing this must be where Fredrick got the board from.

"Let's do a quick sweep of this floor. Fredrick was already here and I doubt he missed anything." I say to Troy.

The two of us take different directions in the room, double checking to see if Fredrick left anything alive. There isn't much room to clear on this floor, everything is covered in plastic. There are piles of wood stacked up all around the room, all of them neatly stacked aside from one. Chances are that is the same one Fredrick got the board from. Troy and I check each side of the room before meeting back in the middle.

"All clear." Troy says to me.

I nod to him before adding, "My side too."

We both enter the stairwell again and make our way up to the next floor. About half way up the staircase we're alerted by the sound of a door closing below. The two of us stop and look down to see Fredrick and Braydon running up the stairs towards us. As Fredrick passes us by he yells out, "We got the floor above you, get this one."

Fredrick and Braydon continue up to the floor right above us while Troy and I open the door next to us and enter a large room. The first room we enter looks disastrous. Blood is covering the walls, the floors and the windows. After taking a few steps around the room I notice that the blood is still wet. Meaning whatever happened hear happened very recently. Sitting in some puddles of blood around the roof are small pieces of flesh. It's very difficult to stomach everything in the room. Troy and I both swallow hard before starting into the room.

The two of us look around the room, moving slowly and very cautiously. Not too far into the room I accidentally kick something with my foot. When I look down I notice there is an arm lying on the ground, chewed off right at the elbow. I gag and cover my mouth, thinking I am going to puke.

"Troy... Hey Troy come over here and look at this." I call Troy over to look at the arm below me.

Troy walks over to me, a bit confused at first until he looks at the ground where I am pointing. When he sees the arm he is immediately revolted. He throws his hand over his mouth and turns to the side, trying his hardest not to vomit.

"Dude... an arm.... a fucking arm..." I say to Troy. "Let's stick together and clear this floor. We need to get the fuck out of here." I add.

Troy nods, sticking behind me while I move forward. This floor looks to be the floor where they did office work. Cubicles cover the whole middle of the room with offices and storage room doors all along the side. We slowly make our way through the room following a blood smear on the ground.

I shake my head before saying, "It seems like a body was dragged through here. Those zombies can't possibly be strong enough to drag a human body like this..."

Before Troy can respond we are caught off guard by the sound of gun shots up stairs. The shots come in bursts of three and only repeat four times. After the shots are fired everything goes silent. Troy and I both stare up at the ceiling in the direction we heard the shots, waiting to hear something else. After a few seconds of not hearing anything we both turn to each other. Just as we are about to speak we hear a loud bang at the other side of the room.

We both turn and look over at the office room that the noise came from. It sounded almost exactly like someone banging a metal door on his desk. The window to the office we heard the noise from is shattered and the blinds are torn apart and hanging down. While we both are still looking into the room a man stands up and looks directly at us.

The man has blood dripping from his mouth and his eyes are blood shot. His shirt and pants are both tattered with dried blood mixed with fresh blood all over them. One side of his cheek has large scratch marks down it while the other side has a hole right through it, fully exposing his tongue and teeth. The man tilts his head to both sides to crack his neck before throwing his arms back and letting out a painfully loud shriek. Right after the shriek he jumps out of the office and starts to run directly at us.

"Come on! We're here to get you out!" Troy yells to him.

"Troy, No! It's a Runner!" I say before pulling Troy back.

I throw Troy behind me and propel myself in front of the Runner. Once Troy is behind me I bring my gun up to my face to look down the scope. I set the crosshairs directly between the Runner's eyes before pulling the trigger and sending a bullet right through his head. The Runner collapses to the ground just feet in front of me.

I turn to Troy and ask in a very angry voice, "The snarling, blood covering his face and his mouth wide open didn't give you a fucking clue that it wasn't human?"

"It was running! They can't run!" Troy replies.

"Oh yeah? Tell that to the FUCKING corpse on the floor!" I yell.

Troy doesn't continue to argue with me, he can tell I am obviously frustrated since he didn't shoot. My anger doesn't last long, however, shortly after we finish arguing both Troy and I hear a noise coming from another office nearby. We both turn and look at each other, curious if both of us heard it or if it was just our imaginations. As we're both standing there staring at each other we hear the noise again, confirming that it isn't our imaginations.

The two of us walk across the room, following our ears. As we are walking across the room we continue to hear the noise once every few seconds. It sounds almost as if someone or something is shuffling on top of paper. About half way across the room Troy and I stop.

"Hello? Is someone alive in there?" I say out loud.

No answer.

Right when I finish talking the sound of the shuffling stops. I take a few more steps forward before saying, "If you are alive, please say something so we can find you and help you." Still no answer.

I roll my eyes, now highly becoming frustrated, "Why can people never fucking say anything, they always got to make it fucking difficult."

Troy doesn't comment when I talk so I turn to look at him. When I look at him I notice that he is looking at me all while pointing to his ear. I stop moving and listen closely, trying to hear exactly what he hears. Unable to hear anything I turn to him and ask. "What, what do you hear?"

"Nothing.", Troy responds.

"Then what was the point in telling me?" I ask.

"That is the point! You spoke and the noise stopped. Whatever it is, it heard us."

Before being able to respond I hear a loud shriek coming from behind us. Troy and I both turn around and see another Runner in an office across the room. It jumps through the window, sending glass flying everywhere. Troy opens fire on it, hitting it in the head, amongst other places. The Runner's lifeless body collapses to the ground. Seconds later we hear two more crashes coming from the office right next to us. Two more Runners come at us with their teeth barred.

Both of us point our guns at opposite Runners and fire at them, not letting them anywhere close. After we drop the two Runners we hear glass shatter from behind us. We spin around and aim at the room we heard glass shatter in, ready to kill whatever comes our way.

Two Runners jump out from the office and get their legs tangled in the blinds around the window. They fall to the ground and struggle before breaking loose and getting up. Once they're back up they run full speed towards us. Troy and I open fire on the two Runners, dropping them to the ground. Before the second one even hits the ground more glass shatters behind us. Troy turns and notices three more Runners out of the corner of his eye.

"Keep my back, keep my back." Troy calls out to me, wanting me to cover his back while he watches mine.

Runners are pouring out of offices all around us now. Smashing through the glass and running full speed at us. With Troy and I back to back it is almost impossible for any of them to get close. There are no signs of the Runners stopping any time soon. Every time we kill one it seems that two more come out of a nearby office in their place.

"We got to get out of here!" I yell to Troy

"There are too many!" Troy responds.

"Can you make it to the door?" I ask.

"No, they keep coming out of the offices by it."

"Let's slowly move over there, baby steps, take baby steps."

Both of us start making baby steps over towards the stairwell door. I have Troy's back covered while he watches mine. Troy and I don't let any Runners make it anywhere close to either of us. When we are within ten feet of the door we encounter a problem.

Troy calls out in between gun fire, "I can't get any closer! If I get any closer, when they come out of the door I'll be an arm's reach away."

"Fuck!" I reply.

Troy and I continue shooting at all the Runners that are coming out of the Offices around us. The situation was very easily controlled until we both had to reload at the same time. It only took a few seconds for both of us to reload but it allowed some Runners to get too close for comfort. Troy and I both got hesitant as the amount of Runners in the room increases and they start coming out of offices very close to us.

Just as we think it is all over Fredrick and Braydon burst in through the stairwell door. When they enter the room they pause for a second to look around the room and see the Runners. Fredrick and Braydon freeze for a second as they enter the room, unable to process what is going on. It doesn't take long for them to snap back to attention and help Troy and I kill any Runners in the room. With the help of Braydon and Fredrick Troy and I have just enough cover fire to make our way over to them and into the stairwell.

Troy and I quickly enter the stairwell to reload our guns. While Fredrick and Braydon hang back in the room and continue shooting at all the Runners until they need to reload. At which point they back up into the staircase and slam the door closed behind them. Back in the stairwell Fredrick and Braydon reload their guns before turning to Troy and I.

"Where those... Runners?" Fredrick asks.

"Yeah, I told you they existed." I reply.

Before we're able to say anything else we hear a loud slam against the door next to us. We all jump back and stare at the door, noticing dents starting to form in the hollow metal door. The slamming on the door starts to speed up and the dents become more rapid. We look at the hinges on the door and can start to see them bend and weaken as unbelievable amounts of pressure are being applied to the door.

"What the fuck... How are they..." Fredrick asks, unable to understand what is happening.

Fredrick doesn't even finish his sentence before he backs up and starts firing at the door. After the first burst of rounds blood starts to seep through the door and the banging stops. We can hear bodies slide down the door to the ground on the other side. It doesn't take long before the banging starts again, this time even more violent than the first.

I grab Fredrick by the shoulder and say, "We got to get the fuck out of here."

Right after I speak all of us snap to attention and start running down the staircase. While we are running down the stairs the banging on the door continues. Almost simultaneously upon reaching the second floor the door above us smashes in. The sound of metal skirting across the concrete stairs can be heard echoing throughout the stairwell. The growling and moaning the Runners make as they pour into the stairwell sends chills down my spine. The Runners can be heard traveling both up and down in the stairwell, covering all directions trying to find us.

I open the door leading to the second floor, the same floor that we entered on. I throw my back up against the door and fire at all the Runners that are visible in the stairwell. If they get close enough to shoot them in the head than I deliver a shot directly between their eyes. If I can only see them running down the stairs towards us and their head is just out of reach I aim for the knees. Once they're hit in the knees they come sliding down the stairs only to crash into the wall. This leaves a large streak of blood in their path and their head completely vulnerable.

I continue to fire at any Runners coming towards the door until I am well out of ammo. When I hear my gun click, letting me know I am out of ammo I take a step back. Before I can even get my first foot back onto the ground I feel a hand on the back of my neck. Fredrick grabs the back of my tactical suit and yanks me into the room.

The door slams shut in front of my face just as a Runner lunges at me. I stumble backwards into the room and continue to watch the door leading into the stairwell. The sound of Runners slamming into it is followed by large dents forming in the door. Now that we are all back in the room we rush over to the window we entered the room from. We all line up and walk over the board connected to the other roof single file. Everyone is careful not to break the board, taking their time over it and balancing themselves so they don't fall. Once we're all across Fredrick kicks the board off the roof and down into the alleyway below. Making sure it is impossible for anything to follow us.

Everyone stops and stares into the building we just came from, listening to the sounds from inside. The banging inside becomes more and more frantic until out of nowhere it stops. We all pause for a second and turn to each other, confused. Before any of us are able to say anything we hear a loud bang from inside the building. This is followed by the sound of the door sliding across the floor.

Runners can be heard pouring into the room of the building across from us, their moans and growls echoing out of the building and across to ours. Moments later the Runners come running out of the office building and plummeting down into the alleyway below. Very few of the Runners are smart enough to jump across the gap and make it onto our building. Any that do make it across are greeted with a bullet from one of our guns.

The Runners are relentless, they continue to run up to the gap while pushing and shoving each other out of the way. They seem to be growing smarter, instead of just running out the window every one of them is now jumping. Even with all of them now trying to jump the gap the outcome is still the same. Only a few are making it across and when they do, they are immediately killed by one of us.

About five minutes go by with the Runners continually coming at us in full force. And then out of nowhere they just stop coming. After the last Runner jumps out of the building and plummets to the ground below all of us go silent and stare at each other. We all stop and listen, waiting to hear something from the other building. With none of us able to hear anything we all let out a sigh of relief, thankful that the attack is finally over. However the danger isn't over yet, the Runners are still on the streets below us and the only way out of here is to go down there.

Before we are able to relish the fact that we survived the onslaught we hear a crash coming from the window in the office building we just came out of. All of us look up and are shocked to see Runners jumping out from the floor above us. With the extra height from the floor above us the Runners are easily able to make up for the distance between buildings.

"What the, how the fuck is that possible?" Fredrick yells.

We open fire at any Runners that land on our roof but within seconds we're out numbered. Braydon backs up to the door leading off the roof and into the building to open it up. Once he has it open he jams his foot into the door to brace it open for all of us.

"Let's go, inside, inside!" Braydon yells to all of us.

We all take baby steps backwards while continuing to shoot anything that lands on our roof. Once we're all inside Braydon leans forward to grab the handle on the door before slamming it shut in front of us.

Once the door is shut we all back up and run down the staircase in the building, returning to the first floor. The sounds of Runners vigorously pounding the door connected to the roof can be heard throughout the building. When we're all back down on the first floor we take cover anywhere we can and aim our guns at the stairs.

"Well. We're stuck in here." I remark.

"How much ammo does everyone have?" Fredrick asks.

Troy says, "I got another clip in my pockets and about half a clip in my gun."

Braydon says, "I still got two clips left."

I say, "Half a clip."

Fredrick says, "Aim for the head. Don't miss. If you miss, we die."

We all nod, gripping our guns tight while listening to the pounding on the roof. The pounding grows louder and louder, as does the tension in the room. As time goes on the amount of feet you can hear scurrying around on the roof grows. Time seems to pass slower than ever before as we wait for the impending doom to crash through the door. After a few minutes the door to the roof finally gives way and smashes open. The Runners from the roof start flooding into the building. We all aim carefully and take our time, making sure each shot is a headshot.

With the sound of every gunshot from inside the building a Runner slides down the staircase. We try to take turns shooting to prevent two people from shooting the same Runner but the bullets crossing paths is inevitable. Their bodies start to pile up on the staircase below, making it harder for them to reach us. This is probably the only thing still keeping us alive. As time goes on the hoard of Runners that were once violently flowing in from the roof starts to slow down and eventually stop.

When it is all over we breathe a sigh of relief. I look around the room while playing with my ears, which are still ringing from all the shooting. When I look at the bottom of the stairs I notice a good forty to fifty dead Runners piled up at the bottom of the stairs. With all of the dead bodies at the bottom of the stairs it is impossible to get back onto the roof. The only way out of the building now is right through the front door. Once Fredrick realizes this he starts to pace back and forth.

Fredrick says, "We need to stay put and wait for support. If we're not back by six a.m. they will come looking for us."

"Six a.m.? What time is it now?" I ask.

"It is about two-thirty."

"You want us to stay here for three and a half hours?"

"We have no other choice."

"The hell we don't!" I yell.

"They will find us by then. They will find us and kill us. We don't have the ammo for a defense." I add.

"And we don't have it for an offense either." Fredrick adds.

"Listen.", I say before going quiet.

"What?" Troy asks.

"Shh, listen. I don't hear anything outside. The Runners outside, that missed the jump, know we are in here. Why are they not at the door?"

Everyone nods their head and agrees with what I say. I lean my head up against the door before saying, "For that matter, I don't hear anything at all outside."

Fredrick goes quiet and listens for a few seconds before saying, "Alright then. Let's take a look outside."

Fredrick opens the door just enough to peek out with his one eye. After he gets a good look around he opens the door further and sticks his head outside. After a few seconds he pulls his head back into the room and closes the front door. Once his head is back in the room, Fredrick turns to us with a very confused look on his face.

"They're all dead... Every zombie and Runner is dead." Fredrick says, having trouble believing his own words.

I look to Fredrick and arch an eyebrow, puzzled by what he just said. Having to see for myself, I open the door and take a look outside. Bodies litter the street around us with puddles of blood surrounding each of them. Blood covers almost every inch of the sidewalk, road and building in the area. There is no sign of any type of movement outside. Everything is very still and quite, giving me an ominous feeling.

I lean back away from the door and let Troy and Braydon have a look outside while I converse with Fredrick. They peak their heads out for a few seconds before quickly pulling them back in. Both of their faces are now pale as they close the door that leads outside.

"What do you think could have killed all of them?" Troy asks.

"Don't know, but this is our chance to get the fuck out of here and we better take It.", I add.

Everyone nods, letting me know that they agree. Fredrick opens the door leading out into the street and holds it allowing us all to exit the building. Once we're all out in the streets we assume a square formation for protection, making sure we have all sides covered. While we are navigating the street I walk up to a zombie's body that is nearby. I stop next to the body and lean down to look at it, noticing it has a large bite mark on its neck. The bite mark is still oozing blood, meaning it must have been fresh.

I motion everyone over to me and say out loud, "Look. It has a fresh bite mark on its neck; I think the Runners are killing the zombies."

Everyone walks over to examine the bite mark and the zombie. Fredrick kneels down near the zombie and places his hand on the zombie's neck, checking for a pulse.

"Well, he has no pulse." Fredrick says after checking the zombie.

"We don't know if they have a pulse when they're even "alive", if you catch my drift." I add.

"Yeah, Ryan is right." Braydon adds.

"Either way, let's get the fuck out of here and back to the hospital." Fredrick adds.

Fredrick starts to jog in the direction leading to the hospital. We get about two blocks away from the building we were stranded in before hearing ear piercing screech. We all reach for our ears, covering them to dampen the sound of the screech. All of us spin around and look down our scopes to try and figure out what made the noise.

I point my scope at the street right outside the building we were just stranded in. I focus in on the middle of the street and notice that one of the zombies is starting to stand up. I stare at the zombie for a few seconds before turning away from the scope and looking at the zombie with my own eyes.

"You guys see that?" I ask.

"Yeah..." Everyone mumbles.

We all break away from our scopes and turn to look at each other, very confused as to exactly what is going on. When I look back down the scope I notice that now every zombie we thought was dead, has stood up.

"What the fuck is going on." Troy whispers.

"Don't know, but we should get the fuck out of here." I add.

Fredrick says, "Alright slowly and quietly let's continue towards the hospital. We're about fifteen blocks away."

We all start slowly jogging towards the hospital again. Every few steps someone turns around to check up on the zombies at the other end of the road. As we continue to get further away from the zombies another loud screech can be heard.

We all keep our heads turned to keep an eye on the zombies back at the building while still moving towards the hospital. As we are jogging Troy accidentally kicks an old soda can that is lying on the side of the road. The soda can rolls down the road and into a nearby sewer drain, creating a ruckus.

I turn and look at Troy while shaking my head in disappointment. After the ruckus we can hear a series of loud screeches coming from the zombie's outside the building we were just in. Everyone turns to look behind us at all the zombies. Almost simultaneously all the zombies turn to us and emit another ear piercing screech. The zombies jump forward and land on their hands and feet. They throw their arms out in front of them to pull themselves forward while using their legs to propel themselves along the ground. Everyone is frozen in fear as the zombies run towards us like some sort of Greyhound.

"What the..." Troy just barely mumbles.

"We've been spotted!" I yell.

"RUN!" Fredrick adds.

Everyone turns around and starts to run full speed towards the hospital. I occasionally turn my head to remind myself how much distance they are gaining on us and how fast. Giving me the extra motivation I need to push myself forward.

"We're going to have to hide. We can't out run them!" I yell out loud while we are still running.

"Oh and you don't think they will be able to break down a door? We don't have the ammo to defend ourselves." Fredrick adds.

All of us now out of breath and panting heavily from all the running. The creatures are on our tail and quickly closing the gap between us. We can hear a very low hum in the distance, coming from the direction of the hospital.

"Yes! A helicopter! Mark must be out looking for us!" Fredrick yells anxiously.

Fredrick grabs a flare from his waist and scratches it on an abandoned car that we run past. The flare immediately ignites and glows brightly, forcing us all to reach for out night vision goggles and throw them to the ground. Unable to see anything through them with the flare now lit. Fredrick waves the flare around in the air, hoping that Mark inside the helicopter spots it.

We can all hear the sound of the helicopter growing closer but none of us are able to see it in the darkness of the night. When I turn around to look for the creatures without my night vision goggles I am unable to see anything. But I can hear the pitter patter of their feet, like they are right behind us.

The hum from the helicopter can be heard all around us, meaning Mark must be close. A second later I see a large flash on the ground below us. The light on the helicopter lights up the whole ground around us. Everyone looks up at the helicopter above us, admiring the heavenly light from above.

Before we can relish the light, one of the creatures leaps into the light and tackles Fredrick to the ground. We all immediately stop running to help Fredrick, causing the light to leave us briefly but quickly come back over us. When the light comes back over top of us we can clearly see the creature on top of Fredrick. Fredrick is holding his face back using his elbow and gripping both its claws with his hands. When I actually focus my eyes on the creature I can see that the light from the helicopter is causing its skin to blister and burn.

As the light comes back over top the creature it unleashes an extremely loud screech. The screech is so loud that it forces everyone nearby to cover their ears to prevent permanent damage. Right after I cover my ears I notice Fredrick on the ground, his eyes clamped shut with his teeth barred. Blood is starting to gush out of Fredrick's eyes from the intensity of the screech. I uncover my ears and fire my gun at the creature's head. This causes the screech to stop abruptly and the creature to collapse on top of Fredrick. Fredrick throws the lifeless body off of him and into the center of the circle of light. Once the creature is off Fredrick and done its horrific screech everyone helps him up off the ground.

As the creature lies in the light his skin continues to blister and burn before eventually melting onto the ground. All of us continue to watch the creatures body melt away, dumbfounded by what we see and unable to explain it. Everyone looks around the area outside of the light. All the creatures that were chasing us are now hissing at us, staring at us from outside the light.

The creatures look like deformed humans but all the hair on their bodies is gone. From their transformation earlier, it seems like they have lost almost all of their clothing. Their bodies are much skinnier and shorter than a normal human body and you can see the bones through their extremely pale skin. The creature's face has become fully deformed and now looks nothing like a human. Its eyes are oval and have grown almost two sizes bigger than a normal eye. The area where a nose normally is now only has a very slight dent, the nose is almost nonexistent. The creature's tongue has grown much bigger than your normal tongue. It hangs almost three feet down and is swinging around in the darkness.

There are no ears on the side of their head; the only part of a human face that remained intact is the tongue and eyes. The creature's fingers are also completely deformed. They seem to have formed into some sort of sharp bone claws, each one looks to be about three inches in length. As we stand back in the light the creatures are all arched up on their hind legs, balancing themselves with their claws against the ground. They are waving their tongue around in the air and making a low hissing sound. As they stand there their bodies sway side to side, almost as if they were in a drunken stupor. But as minutes go by never do they once lose balance and fall.

I turn the light on that is duct taped to the side of my gun and step forward to point it at them out in the darkness. As I point it at them their skin starts to blister and burn. The second the light touches their skin they quickly scurry away, out of reach. I walk up to the very edge of the light from the helicopter and point my flashlight out at them. They are all standing a good ten feet back now, hissing a lot louder than before.

"I'd say that it is pretty obvious that light hurts them now." I say out loud.

Everyone turns on the flashlights attached to their guns and shines it around in the darkness. The creatures start to go wild, freaking out and running all over the place.

Fredrick says out loud, "Alright, enough fucking around. Let's get back to the hospital."

We all nod to Fredrick and agree that, that is our best bet. We all start to walk slowly back towards the hospital, making sure Mark is following us with the helicopters light. Once we can tell he is following us we pick up the pace to a jog. While we're jogging back towards the hospital we can hear the creatures following us. They're jumping along the sides of the buildings and throwing themselves all around.

It takes about fifteen minutes for us to reach the hospital. Once we're at the hospital Mark hovers over for a minute or two until he is positive we are all inside. Once we're all inside the helicopter flies up to the roof and lands.

Now that the helicopter is gone and we're all inside we stare out to the creatures surrounding the hospital. They are hiding behind cars and in alleyways across the street, being extra careful not to come into the light shining out from the lobby. Almost everyone takes a seat down in the lobby to catch their breath but Fredrick continues to stare out the windows at the creatures.

Fredrick turns to us and says, "What have we done? We led them back here. They know where we live now."

CHAPTER 6 - THE ESCAPE

Fredrick grabs his radio from his waist and holds it up to his mouth.

"Mark, come in, over."

No response.

"Mark, are you there? Over."

Still, there is no response.

Fredrick turns to Braydon and says, "Head up stairs to the Armory and grab all the ammo you can hold. I'm going to kill all these mother fuckers if it's the last thing I do."

Braydon nods and runs over to the stairwell, running up to the upper floors. I stand up and walk over to Fredrick, looking out the window with him at everything outside. I notice that Fredrick has his right hand made into a fist and is grinding his teeth. He is mumbling obscenities while watching the creatures jump around outside. In an effort to calm his nerves I decide to spark up a conversation with him.

"They're Night Stalkers.", I say.

"Huh?" Fredrick turns to me, confused.

"Night Stalkers that is what we're going to call them. Light hurts them, which means they can only come out at night. They're Night Stalkers."

The name sticks immediately.

Troy stands up and asks, "The Night Stalkers will go away in the morning, right? Can we hunt them then, so they can't devise an attack on the building?"

"Who knows?" I add

Braydon opens the door from the stairwell, almost tripping out into the room. He is carrying about twenty clips for our M4's, a couple of which spill onto the floor as he steps out into the lobby. Any that fall to the floor Braydon kicks across the ground over to where Fredrick and I are standing.

"This is all I could hold, hopefully it is enough." Braydon says to Fredrick and I.

Fredrick yanks a few of the clips out of Braydon's hand, causing even more to fall onto the ground. Fredrick jams a fresh clip into his gun and the rest into his pockets. Fredrick throws open the hospital's front door and steps back out into the cool winter air. He aims his gun at any of the Night Stalkers that are visible and starts firing at them. The only thing we are able to hear inside the lobby is the sound of gunfire and Fredrick screaming profanity after every kill.

When Fredrick goes to reload his gun I step outside and assist him in shooting the Night Stalkers. Upon first glance outside it looks to me that Fredrick has already killed four of them. The Night Stalkers that are still alive start to flee, proving that they may actually be smarter than there zombie counter parts.

The remaining Night Stalkers scurry off inside nearby buildings to hide. Out of our line of sight and out of the approaching day light. While the remaining Night Stalkers are fleeing for nearby buildings Fredrick and I managed to shoot six more of them. Fredrick is obviously frustrated that some of them got away. To prove this he fires the rest of his clip into a nearby car before stomping back inside the hospital.

I follow closely behind Fredrick and give Troy and Braydon a specific "Don't talk to him" look. Fredrick stomps over to the stairwell and starts to go down towards Mark's room. As Fredrick travels down the stairs he makes sure to slam his foot on each and every step. This causes the sound of each foot step to echo throughout the stairwell. When he reaches the hallway leading down into Mark's room he slams the doors behind him, causing the whole stairwell to shake.

Braydon, Troy and I all follow Fredrick down the stairs, through the hallway and into Mark's room. We make sure to keep a large distance between Fredrick, making sure not to let him know we are following him. Before we open the door leading to Mark's room we listen to the commotion inside. Fredrick can be heard throwing seats around and cursing at the fact that Mark isn't there.

We all sneak into the room and off to the side, being careful not to disturb Fredrick. Troy forgets to dampen the sound of the door behind us as we enter the room and lets it slam shut. When Fredrick hears the door he immediately spins around towards us, ready to rip someone's head off. Once he sees that it isn't Mark he grabs for his radio.

"Mark, are you there? Can you read me, over."

No response, just like before.

"Mark, come in."

Still, there is no answer.

"Mark, I swear to god if you don't answer this radio... I'm going to blow your fucking computer shit up."

"I'm on my way down the stairs Jesus Christ give me a minute."

Mark answers this time, apparently Fredrick's threat worked.

An awkward silence comes over the room as everyone waits for Mark. After a few minutes go by Mark finally enters the room, the second he does Fredrick stomps over to him.

"What the fuck were they?" Fredrick yells, getting up in Marks face.

"What were what?" Mark replies.

Fredrick grabs Mark by his shirt's collar and slams him against the wall. As Mark is slammed against the wall he drops his radio on the ground and raises both hands on each side of his head.

"What the fuck were they?" Fredrick asks him again.

"Uhm, I call them Light Walkers."

"Light Walkers?" I interrupt. "Why the fuck would you call them Light Walkers if they are hurt by the light? They're called Night Stalkers."

"I don't give a fuck what they are called! My question is how the fuck are they out there now and they weren't before?" Fredrick yells at Mark, pressing him harder against the wall.

"Well, I'd need a body to test. I'm not sure how they were created." Mark replies.

"Cross Pollination." I add.

"What?" Mark says before adding, "They're not plants."

"I never said that they were. The same logic applies though." I continue.

"What logic?"

"Look, we were surrounded by Runners and zombies. When the Runners fell to the ground, they attacked the zombies instead of us. When they attacked the zombies, their saliva infected them and mutated them. That is the only logical explanation." I say

Everyone looks at me as I talk, nodding their head in agreement. Mark puts his hand on his chin before saying, "You're actually right! It makes perfect sense. However I am unsure of why or how it mutated the zombies to look like that, instead of the Runners."

"Who cares about that? The better question is what happens when a Night Stalker attacks a zombie or a Runner." I add.

Fredrick asks, "What about their intelligence? They seem to be more intelligent then zombies."

"Well, I assume a part of their brain must remain intact when they are a runner or Night Stalker. As a zombie they have no human left in them. As a Runner or Night Stalker they must hold some part of their former selves, at least basic motor skills." I say.

Mark adds, "He is right. The Night Stalkers and Runners must be more human than we think. I don't think they have any compassion though, or remorse."

"We have bigger problems than this shit though. We need to start preparing for tonight." Fredrick says.

"What are you talking about?" I ask.

"Well they're intelligent right? They still retain part of their human brain? That means their memory is intact. This means they know where we live. They wanted us dead last night. They will want us dead again tonight." Fredrick says.

I nod to Fredrick, "You're right."

Fredrick says, "I'll start the preparations..."

Fredrick grabs the radio off his waist and starts to run down the hallway, back towards the stairwell.

"Can you put me over the intercom?" I ask Mark.

"Yes, why what do you want to say?" Mark responds.

"I want to warn everyone." I say to Mark before looking over at Braydon, "Braydon head to your armory, you're going to be getting visitors."

Braydon nods before running towards the stairwell leading up to his armory. Mark leans over to his computer and hits a button before motioning to me. This lets me know that our room is now broadcasting over to the whole hospital.

"Hello everyone, my name is Ryan. We have a bit of a problem and I need everyone's attention immediately. So please, stop what you are doing and listen to my extremely hot and amazing voice."

"We have discovered two new types of zombies; they are called Night Stalkers and Runners. The Night Stalkers, as their name suggests come out at night. They can crawl and jump in many different places. They are fast and deadly. Their main weakness is light. Picture them to be a vampire, you shine light on them, they get badly hurt."

"The second zombie is a Runner. These are zombies with the ability to run. They also can smash down doors. Light does NOT affect the Runners only the Night Stalkers."

"We believe that the Runners and Night Stalkers still retain part of their human brain, more specifically their memory. Our scouts found packs of them around the hospital last night scouting it out. We believe they may be planning an attack tonight."

"If you know how to shoot a gun and feel mentally capable please go to the Armory and speak with Braydon. He is on the fifth floor. Arm yourselves and barricade up your windows. If we remain calm we will be able to defeat them if they come tonight."

"We predict there are about two hundred and fifty of them coming. Count them as you kill them. If each one of us kill two, then we will be fine. If you have any questions please speak with Fredrick, Troy, Ryan or Braydon. Thank you for listening, Ryan out."

"Two hundred and fifty, scouts? What are you talking about?" Mark asks.

"Scouts, so they don't think we lead them here, can you imagine what people would do if they figured out we lead them here? They'd freak out, blame us for everything and revolt. Do you understand how much trouble that would cause? Two hundred and fifty, this way they have a number of how many they need to kill. If you just said they were coming they'd believe the whole city."

The door leading out into the hallway flies open and crashes against the wall. When I turn to look over I see April run into the room and look around, looking for me. When she sees me she runs over and excitedly throws her arms around me, glad that I am still alive.

"What happen last night?" April whispers in my ear.

I pull away from April and look to everyone else in the room.

"There were no survivors. The Runners put off a heat source very similar to humans. We were ambushed and attacked; we just barely made it out alive. Also we found out that the Runners attack normal zombies. When they do attack them a cross of some kind occurs. The zombies transform into Night Stalkers."

"Night Stalkers are these really ugly looking things that are hurt if they are exposed to light. They followed us back here last night and we fear they may attack again tonight."

As I talk April continually nods to me, letting me know that she understands. Right as I finish talking Mark walks over to his computer and starts to play around with a few of the buttons. He moves the picture around on the screen right over top our hospital.

"Look, look!" he calls out. "This is the heat source of our hospital. Notice how it is really red? Look around it..."

Mark points to the area all around our hospital. In the center of the screen there is a red blob, which is us, inside the hospital. Around the large red blob is a light orange and red ring, belonging to the Night Stalkers surrounding us?

"How many do you think?" I ask Mark.

"There looks to be about two to three thousand." Mark replies.

I walk over to the floor where Fredrick shoved Mark up against the wall and pick up his radio. I hold the radio up to my mouth and hold down the talk button.

"Fredrick, are you there? Come in."

"Yeah, who is this?"

"It's Ryan."

"We need to have a talk about your speech earlier. You pissed a few of the council members off.", Fredrick replies.

"Fuck the council members. We have a bigger problem. Get down here as soon as possible." I say.

Fredrick goes silent and doesn't broadcast anything else over the radio. About five minutes later he bursts into our room and looks around for me. I wave Fredrick over to the large computer monitor and point to the screen.

"Look." I say to Fredrick.

Fredrick slowly walks towards the computer monitor with his eyes as wide as saucers and his jaw dropped. "How many are there?" Fredrick asks in a fidgety voice.

"It looks to be two to Three thousand." Mark replies.

"Fredrick, I think it is time we think about evacuation, instead of trying to hold the hospital down." I say to Fredrick, hoping he will listen.

"We won't have enough time or even room for everyone." He replies.

"We can't fight them all off. There are too many." I say

Everyone in the room goes silent and ponders what to do to prepare for tonight. I turn to Fredrick and ask, "Can we have a day time team take out a good portion of them, and then fight off the rest at night? At least during the day the Night Stalkers will be vulnerable."

Fredrick shakes his head in disapproval, "Still too risky to send people out with that many. We don't know if they are all Night Stalkers or Runners. We can't risk it.", Fredrick continues by saying, "Best we can do is board up the hospital, hopefully hold them off until day light. Let's get to work because we don't have much time."

I throw Mark's radio back to him and exit the room, slamming the door closed behind me. April runs out of the room and catches up to me in the hallway before I enter the stairwell. She slows down next to me and asks, "Is everything ok?"

"No. Without evacuation we're going to die." I reply.

April stops dead in her tracks as all the information finally sinks in. I continue forward up the stairs, still angered from before. After a few seconds April snaps back to reality and yells out to me, before running up the stairs to follow me.

"Hey, Ryan, wait!" April yells. "Whatever you're doing, I want to help." She adds.

I nod to her while continuing up to the first floor. Back on the first floor I check up on everyone, making sure they are barricading up their rooms and any entrances into the hospital. Any room that doesn't have someone staying in it April and I barricade, making sure nothing can get in.

_____

As the day continues on we try and keep the same system going. Barricading up any entrances and windows leading into the hospital and making sure everyone is armed. Anyone that can wield a gun and fight is given a gun. We make sure every window and doorway that isn't used is barricaded with anything we can find. By the time we finish barricading each window and doorway it is already late afternoon.

The sun is starting to set in the sky as almost everyone gathers on the second floor. Each and every exit and entrance on or off the second floor is barricaded up. Making sure anything getting on or off the floor will have a very difficult time. We left a small part of one window towards the back of the building uncovered, allowing us to watch the sun set. As the sun comes down over the tallest building in the city a series of loud screeches can be heard outside. This sends an all too familiar chill down our spines.

As the sun continues to set the screeches continue, becoming more and more frequent. Silence comes over the room as everyone listens to the impending death that is waiting outside. Before the sun completely sets we board up the hole that we were using to look outside.

Once we're finished boarding up the last window all of us meet in the lobby and watch the stairwell door. Murmurs can be heard from the people in the crowd. People are saying prayers, begging god to help them in a time of need. Holding their loved ones close, promising them that everything is going to be ok. A few minutes later Fredrick and Braydon run into the lobby from the back hallway.

"Everything is secure." Fredrick says.

"Where is Troy?" I ask.

"He is coming."

I turn to look back at the stairwell again, just waiting to see something burst through that door. April and Mark are standing next to me, all three of us are fully armed, ready for whatever comes our way. Troy runs back into the room from the same hallway Fredrick and Braydon did earlier. He stops next to Fredrick and whispers something into his ears causing his eyes to light up like the sun.

Troy goes from person to person, whispering in everyone's ear. When he stops at me he whispers, "They're right outside." After Troy tells me I just confidently nod. Not wanting to cause a scene amongst the other survivors. Fredrick turns around and puts his hands up, getting the attention of every other survivor in the room.

"Alright, I need everyone's attention. I need eight people in each hallway, in case they come in through the windows. Everyone else will need to watch this stairwell and assist in the hallway if need be. Listen, don't be stupid and be brave. We will make it through this."

Fredrick takes people down into each hallway and gives them a quick debrief on what to do when the Night Stalkers come. I look up at the ceiling and take in a deep breath, hopefully not one of my last. A loud shriek can be heard right out front of the hospital, followed by the pounding on doors.

A few seconds after the banging starts Night Stalkers can already be heard climbing the side of the building. Their claws penetrating the cement and metal on the outside like it is nothing. Seconds after hearing them start climbing on the side of the Hospital we can hear glass shattering on the floor above us. It doesn't seem that the Night Stalkers know what floor we are on yet. Right after the glass shatters upstairs a shriek of agony echoes throughout the hospital. The shriek is the same exact shriek we heard when the Night Stalkers entered the light the last time.

The shriek from upstairs only lasts a few seconds before it immediately stops. More windows shattering can be heard across the hospital followed by the same deathly shriek. After the shrieks stop everything goes silent. Everyone uncovers their ears and looks around at the walls, waiting to hear the Night Stalkers climbing up the side of the building again.

Moments later the lights inside the hospital flicker before going out completely. We are all now standing in complete darkness. With the power now out the shrieks outside start again. The shrieks are followed by the sounds of Night Stalkers climbing the side of the building. The sounds of moans and crying fill the room as people tilt their heads up and pray that their death is swift and painless. Just as we've given up all hope the emergency reserves kick on in the hospital. The emergency reserves give us just enough light to see and boost our moral.

The emergency reserves aren't enough to keep the lights constantly lit so they are all now flickering and sparking. The lights have just barely having enough power to stay on. More windows start to shatter in the hospital, but this time they aren't followed by a deathly shriek. They are followed by the sound of clawing and ripping at the doors leading out into the hospital's hallways. The pounding on the front door of the hospital momentarily ceases before one loud bang. Runners smash the door open and shoot the desks we used to barricade it across the room.

Runners can be heard flooding into the lobby of the hospital and over to the stairwell door. They throw themselves up against the stairwell door, smashing into it, knowing exactly where they need to go to get to us. The stairwell door can be heard creaking and bending as the Runners are already starting to make progress. Everyone in the room grabs their loved ones and squeezes them as tightly as possible. Not wanting to ever let go of them because they may never be able to hold them again.

The Night Stalkers that got inside up stairs can be heard shattering and breaking everything they come across, looking for someone to tear apart. After a few minutes go by of the Night Stalkers trashing the floor above us a loud scream can be heard. The scream is followed by a loud shriek and the sound of tearing flesh. After hearing the scream gasps and awes fill the lobby that we are all standing in. Knowing that the Night Stalkers have found and killed one of our own the fear grows.

The sadness and despair is almost contagious in the lobby. When I look over at April I can see a tear rolling down her cheek. It is obvious that she is having a hard time grasping everything that is going on. The door leading into the stairwell on the first floor smashes in as the Runners start flooding the stairwell. They cover each direction in the staircase, looking for the floor we are on. Windows shatter across our floor as I grip my gun tighter, ready to shoot at anything that comes my way.

The Night Stalkers on our floor can be heard smashing and clawing at our barricades. Implying that they finally figured out what floor we were on. The sound of feet in the stairwell is accompanied by the growls and moans from the Runners. Shortly after hearing the first floor's stairwell door collapse the door in front of me starts to shake. Dents start to rapidly form in the door as the Runners start smashing it in. The hinges start to bend and break as they are violently being torn out of the frame.

More windows can be heard shattering on our floor as the first Night Stalker claws and bashes his way out into the hallway. The door is shot off its hinges from the force of the Night Stalker and collides with a survivor's legs. The sound of both of his legs shattering from the force of the door can be heard throughout the lobby followed by his yelp of pain. Right as the Night Stalker exposes himself gunshots ring out in the hallway. Kill the creature before it is able to do anymore damage.

The door leading out into the stairwell starts to bend and break as the hinges are finally starting to give way. I bring my gun up to eye level and open fire on the door, being careful only to shoot in small bursts. My bursts take out the groups of Runners as they approach the door and try to smash it down. Blood oozes through the door in sequence as the sound of bodies slide down it. Eventually my bullet holes accompanied with the Runners smashing the door weaken it enough, causing it to cave in.

The door falls to the ground as do bodies of Runners. April and Mark join me and open fire at the Runners as they pour into the room. When it comes time for me to reload my gun I rip the clip out of it and throw it across the room before slamming another into my gun. Mark and April are next to reload as I lay down suppressing fire for them, just like they did for me. A few more survivors run over to the three of us and join in with firing at any Runners that come into the room.

Every time we fire a shot our barrels provide us with just enough light to see the blood starved faces of the Runners. The Runners are unable to get anymore than a foot into the room as they trip and stumble across bodies of their own kind. The sound of gunfire and bullets penetrating flesh are the only sounds that can be heard throughout the hospital. The sounds echo and vibrate the ear drums of everyone inside.

Night Stalkers start to pour into the hallways of the hospital from every which way. They can be seen tearing through the ceiling, the floor and the walls. Once they are on the floor they are ruthless, tearing anyone apart that gets in their way. Since the Night Stalkers are so swift and agile it makes Friendly Fire a real concern. The flashlights that are attached to our guns stun the Night Stalkers just long enough for our bullets to rip them apart.

With all the bodies piling up at the staircase door the Runners are now having a lot of difficulty trying to get onto our floor. They are forced to climb over top six feet of bodies, making them easy targets for anyone looking. The real threat now is the Night Stalkers that are finding their way to us from everywhere. The floor beneath us starts to shake as a Night Stalker can be felt crawling on the ceiling below us. One of the survivors behind me that's been crying since the front doors were busted down, has a claw shoot up out of the floor next to him.

The claw reaches over and grabs the survivor's leg. The Night Stalker squeezes tight, cutting the leg off and causing blood to spray everywhere. After seeing the claw burst through the ground a panic breaks out amongst the unwounded survivors. They start to scream and dance around the room, trying to avoid any Night Stalkers that may be after them. A few other survivors think it is a smart idea to run down the hallway. Eventually crossing paths with a bullet and getting them killed. Complete mayhem sets in as the Night Stalkers start to tear through the floor below us.

As the Night Stalkers tear through the floor beneath me I kill each of them. Not letting them get anything more than their head through the floor. As my bullets penetrate their pale flesh their lifeless bodies slide out of the hole they created and back down to the floor below. Claws start bursting out of the walls and tearing apart any survivors that are within an arm's reach. Everyone starts to spin around frantically, firing anywhere and everywhere.

Just as everything starts to get out of hand Fredrick runs over to April, Mark and I and grabs us by the back of our shirts. He pushes us away from the stairwell door and towards the center of the lobby. Troy and Braydon follow right behind us, covering our backs. Fredrick pulls us away from the mayhem and over to an alternate, emergency, stairwell that is located in the center part of the building and leads up to the roof. None of us knew about the stairwell since the only entrance to it is on the second floor. Fredrick smashes a fire safety box nearby and grabs the Axe out of it. Once he has the axe he uses it to smash the door knob off the door and lead us all up onto the roof. Once we're all in the stairwell Fredrick uses the axe to block off the door as we all start to run up the stairs.

With all the adrenaline flowing through my body running up the stairs doesn't even cause me to break a sweat. As we get further and further up the stairs the amount of gunshots we can hear below decrease. Until eventually, right as we are on the second to last floor the sound of gunshots stop. Once everything is silent Fredrick stops on the staircase and pulls three grenades off of his waist belt. He pulls the pins out of all three out and chucks them down below.

The door leading into our staircase is busted open and the sound of Night Stalkers flooding in can be heard echoing throughout the stairwell. The sound of the Night Stalkers clawing their way up the floors is damped by the sound of all three grenades going off below. The explosion shakes the whole building, forcing us to grab onto the railing to risk not falling down. Shortly after the initial shock caused by the explosion we regain ourselves and continue up onto the roof. Once we're on the roof Mark runs over to the helicopter and quickly gets in.

We all follow Mark while Fredrick lays down suppressing fire at any Night Stalkers that find their way up onto the roof behind us. Once we're all onboard the helicopter and Mark has it running Fredrick jumps on right as Mark starts to pull away from the ground. We get about twenty feet up in the air before a Night Stalker jumps up and grabs a hold of the bar underneath the helicopter. Mark loses control of the helicopter as it begins to pull right and start to descend out of the sky.

I grab a hold of Fredrick, to give him support, as he leans over and fires down at the Night Stalker that has a hold of the helicopter. Fredrick's bullets make contact with the Night Stalker and cause it to loosen its grip and fall out of the sky. Once the Night Stalker is off the helicopter Mark regains control and continues to fly us away from the hospital.

As we get further away from the hospital we all look out the side of the helicopter and down at it. There are hundreds of Night Stalkers climbing up the sides of the building and thousands of Runners outside. The Runners have the hospital circled, filling the streets around us. Courtesy of the grenades from earlier the building is now on fire, the glow of the flames lighting up the whole area.

We all lean back in the helicopter and let out a sigh of relief, happy that we were lucky enough to make it out alive. A lot of sorrow is also noticeable in the helicopter, a lot of us sad that so many had to give their lives tonight. Almost a mile away from the hospital the shrieks of the Night Stalkers can still be heard, over the sound of the helicopter.

There are no words spoken between any of us for quite awhile. Everyone has their heads down, denying eye contact with anyone. None of us have any idea where we are going, not even Mark. The only plan was to get away from the hospital as quickly as possible. The only direction in mind was west.

We continue flying until the sun comes up behind us and early morning sets in. The heat from the sun is much warmer on our skin considering the fact that we are much closer than we normally are on ground level. Mark looks back into the helicopter and taps Fredrick on the shoulder before pointing to the fuel gauge. Fredrick looks at the fuel gauge and nods to Mark before pointing down to a field below.

Mark flies over to the field that Fredrick pointed to and starts to set the helicopter. After the helicopter makes contact with the ground everyone wait's a few seconds for Mark to shut it down before getting out. When we get out we do a quick sweep of the area, making sure everything is safe before getting comfortable.

After we check over the area we lower our weapons and turn to look at each other. It's the first time we've made eye contact since the roof on the hospital. A smile comes across all of our faces; finally all of us are able to enjoy the fact that we're all still alive. About a minute later the helicopter finally quiets down and allows us all to speak.

"Any idea what state we are in?" I ask.

"Indiana.", Troy replies.

"What is the game plan?" Braydon asks.

"We need to get the fuck out of here. That is the game plan." Fredrick adds.

"On a more serious note... We need to find a local city, grab a Greyhound Bus. Stock it with supplies and go west. That is our best bet.", I say out loud.

"Good idea." Troy replies.

"We should get moving we don't want to be stuck in the woods at night." April adds.

After we finish our conversation Mark finally climbs out of the helicopter and joins the group. Before setting out we grab any supplies out of the helicopter that may be useful to us. Like the first aid kit, blankets, ammo and the radio. Finally we look up into the sky and over to the sun, double checking our direction before going anywhere.

Once the sun helps us confirm the right direction we continue west, with our backs to the sun. About a quarter mile across the field in front of us is a tree line, which leads into a stretch of woods. The floor of the woods is covered with pine needles and leaves, whatever is left from the fall. Our pace through the woods is slow since we are forced to dodge fallen trees and broken branches.

After about an hour of walking through the woods we stumble across a vibrant flowing stream. We all stop next to the stream to get a drink and take a quick break. Everyone sets their gun down and takes a seat on any one of the nearby fallen logs. After about five minutes go by Fredrick interrupts our break and forces us all back up. We gather all our supplies and continue the trek through the woods until around noon. Right around noon, when the sun is highest in the sky we finally make our way out of the woods.

Right when we come out of the woods we see a desolate two lane road leading into a small town up ahead. As we continue up the road and closer to the small town I notice a large green sign on the right hand side of the road that says;

Welcome to Stone Village

Population 1257

The sign has a bit of graffiti on it; the most noticeable bit is the population number is crossed out. In a time like this, who would waste their time to cross out a population number? I thought to myself.

I point to the sign and say, "Well hopefully we have at least one thousand two hundred and fifty seven bullets."

I look at everyone around me, noticing no one laughed or even smirked at my joke. I tilt my head down and join the miserable crowd as we continue into town. Upon entering town the first thing we notice is that the destruction isn't that bad. Everything seems a lot tidier than the city we just came from. There is an occasional blood smear and abandoned car but nothing similar to what we saw in Cleveland. A lot of the cars in driveways look undisturbed, almost like nothing ever happened. One of the houses on the right hand side of the road even has their sprinkler system running in their front yard.

A lot of the homes on the street seem to have been fortified. Sand bags are on their porches and even some people have machine guns hanging out of their windows. Despite all the fortification everything still seems to be deserted. Apparently they thought evacuation was a better option after all.

We continue down the road, walking further into town. All of us keep an eye out for anything out of the ordinary that could use a bullet to the head. As we walk by cars on the side of the road Fredrick peaks into each of them, looking for a key.

"Can't we hotwire one of these?" I ask.

"Not if it's a newer car.", Fredrick replies.

"What does that matter? They do in movies." Braydon adds.

"This isn't a movie." Fredrick says.

"You make a good Point." I reply.

As we get further down the road I spot a diner on the side of the road. The lights inside the diner are on and the parking lot is filled with cars. I stop and get everyone's attention before pointing to the diner.

"Survivors?" April asks.

"Not sure. Good chance though." I reply.

All of us quickly and quietly make our way over to the diner, being careful not to make any noise as we approach. Once we reach the diner I run up to the window on the side and stand on my tippy toes to look in. There is no sign of life at all inside the diner. Everything looks neatly organized, no plates are on any tables and there isn't a drop of blood anywhere. After taking a good look around inside I set myself back down and turn to everyone. I shake my head and wave everyone over, letting them know it is safe.

Everyone nods and moves closer to the building. Fredrick runs up the stairs and over to the front door of the building. Once he is at the front door he begins a countdown with his hand. Fredrick starts at five and when he reaches zero he kicks down the door and rushes inside. Troy and Braydon follow closely behind him.

April and I sit outside with Mark, watching the three of them clear the building. About a minute goes by before we hear Fredrick shout, "Clear", at which point April, Mark and I all run inside. Once inside the diner I take a better look around the place. Everything inside is in pristine condition like it was recently cleaned polished and waxed. Nothing in the whole diner is out of place, not even a single salt and pepper shaker.

"The diner shouldn't even look this good when it is used..." I say out loud.

"Yeah, it gives me an eerie feeling too." Braydon adds.

"Nobody is here?" April asks.

"Nope, clear." Fredrick replies.

"Well that is odd." Mark adds.

"Nobody is here. No blood. No signs of a struggle. No forced entry. They even left their supplies... This is... I just don't understand..." I say out loud.

"Maybe the Army came and got them." Troy adds.

"No. The Army isn't still together and organized. The world is under shock right now. There is no such thing as diplomacy." I say out loud, trying to think.

April walks around the diner and double checks everything, not believing that no one is here. After April walks around the diner she comes back over to the group and leans up against a counter. Everyone sits silent in the diner for the next few minutes. All of us trying to understand what happened here and take another breather before we continue on.

After a few more minutes pass I stand up and say out loud, "We're not doing any good sitting here. Let's get bus, some supplies and get out of this place before nightfall. I got a bad feeling about this shit."

Everyone nods to me before exiting the building and continuing further into the town. As we continue down the street Fredrick still occasionally looks over into any cars that we pass. Hoping that someone left their key inside. About a mile down the street I notice a large sign that shows a silver dog jumping over top a bus.

"Guys check it out!" I yell out loud.

"That is Greyhound right?" I ask.

"Yeah.", Braydon responds.

After we rejoice we pick up the pace, now that we have the Bus Station in our sights. When we reach the Bus Station everyone splits up. We make sure to check underneath every bus and in between every bus for any zombies or Runners. After everything is secure we all meet up outside the Bus Station's building.

Once we're all here, Fredrick smashes the glass door and sticks his hand inside, allowing him to unlock the front door. Once it is unlocked he opens it and holds it long enough for everyone to get inside. After we're all inside we look for the rack that holds the keys for each of the buses. When we find it we take the key that says number eight before going back outside.

Back outside we look around for bus number eight. Once we find the bus we double check the area around it and underneath it for any zombies. After we make sure the outside is safe Fredrick opens the bus's doors and walks on board. He quickly searches the whole bus, checking each seat and underneath. After Fredrick clears the bus we all step on and find our seats.

"Alright, Troy, Braydon, Move the two buses that are behind us so we can get out." Fredrick calls out.

Troy and Braydon both nod to Fredrick before getting off the bus and running back inside the Greyhound building. Fredrick tosses Mark the key and has him start the bus to see if it works properly. Mark sticks the key in the ignition and turns it. The bus starts up flawlessly and the engine sounds nice and clean. After starting the bus Mark turns around and gives Fredrick a thumbs up, letting him know everything is good.

Shortly after Mark starts up the bus Troy and Braydon come running out of the Greyhound building. They both pick separate buses behind us and hop on board. Troy is the first to pull out of the station. After he shifts his bus into reverse he floors it, smashing into two other buses nearby and then into the fence across the street.

Braydon pulls out behind Troy, being equally as careless with his driving. Once the two buses are across the street and out of the way Troy and Braydon run back to our bus and come aboard. With everyone back inside Mark puts the bus in reverse and pulls out of the bus station and back onto the main road.

Everyone takes a seat on the bus while Fredrick stands up at the front of the bus with Mark. Making sure that Mark knows where he is going. As we are driving out of the town Fredrick points to a nearby shopping center coming up on the left hand side with a supermarket in it. Mark glances over to see the supermarket and nods before turning the bus into the shopping center.

We pull up to the supermarket and have everyone exit the bus aside from Mark who stays seated in the driver's seat. Once everyone is outside Fredrick says, "Ryan, April and Mark stay here and guard the bus. Troy and Braydon you're with me inside for supplies."

Braydon and Troy follow behind Fredrick into the supermarket, each of them grabbing a shopping cart before entering. April and I patrol around the bus, keeping an eye out, while Mark sits inside the bus pretending to do something productive. As April and I patrol around the bus I grow bored and spark up a conversation with her.

"So you missed me back at the hospital?" I ask April.

"Huh?" April asks.

"Oh come on, don't lie. When you saw me you were all excited." I say sarcastically.

"Yeah. When I heard the helicopter take off I knew you were in trouble." April says.

"Yeah... It was rough out there. We got pinned into a building. I thought we were going to die."

"At least you made it back though..." April replies.

"That we did. Too bad we led them all back to the hospital. So many people lost their lives..." I say in a condescending tone.

"Yeah... I'm just glad we made it out alive." April says.

"Same... At least now we got a bus too and can continue west." I add.

"Think they are going to buy into it and drive to Vegas?"

"Hopefully, if there is a survivor colony there, that is our best bet."

As April and I are talking Fredrick, Troy and Braydon come out of the supermarket with three cart full of supplies. They roll all three carts over to the front of the bus while Fredrick pounds on the doors to get Mark's attention.

"Mark you need to get the fuck out of the bus and do something." Fredrick yells.

Mark opens the buses doors and walks outside to help Fredrick, Braydon and Troy to unload the supplies. April and I walk around the bus to help unload the supplies but Fredrick quickly stops us and pushes us away.

"Whoa! Don't help us. Keep your eye out. That is more important." Fredrick yells out to us.

April and I both back away and leave Fredrick and his team to offload the supplies. We return to the other side of the bus and stare off at the empty parking lot, watching for any zombies. After all the supplies are unloaded into the bus Fredrick, Troy and Braydon head inside for another trip.

After everyone goes back inside the supermarket I walk around the bus and up onto it. Once I'm on the bus I start toying with the radio, checking each of the radio stations for any type of sound.

Mark turns to me and asks, "What are you doing?"

"I'm fucking with the radio." I reply.

"Yeah, I see that, but why?" Mark asks.

"Maybe Will Smith is broadcasting on the AM radio stations saying he is at the pier at noon, when the sun is highest in the sky." I say to Mark, sarcastically while trying not to laugh.

"What are you talking about?" Mark asks.

"*I Am Legend*? It is a movie, with Will Smith?" I say to Mark, while rolling my eyes.

"Who is Will Smith?" Mark asks in the most serious voice possible.

I stop what I am doing before turning to Mark and staring at him. I arch an eyebrow and ask in the most confused voice ever, "What? Are you serious?"

"I'm sorry my head isn't filled with useless knowledge like yours and that I actually know stuff that matters." Mark responds.

"This isn't useless knowledge. It is common sense. We're talking about Will Smith here, how can you possibly not know him?" I say while trying to comprehend Mark's idiocy.

"Wait, don't even answer that. I don't care. Better yet, tell me your address. The rock you've been living under for the last twenty years of your life that is where we're going." I say to Mark.

Mark rolls his eyes and gives me the finger. I laugh a bit before continuing to flip through each of the AM stations on the radio. Every one of the stations is broadcasting either static or silence. After I search all the AM stations I switch to FM and start to flip through them. I check each station quickly, being sure not to spend any more than a few seconds on each. While checking each of the stations I start to zone out and eventually wind up passing one that is broadcasting a voice. After hearing the voice I quickly go back to it and listen in. When I find the station again I turn it up as loud as it can go.

"Hello, my name is John. If anyone is out there that can hear this please come. A group of survivors and I are stranded at a church at the corner of Crescent and Church. We have food and water that we can supply. There are seven of us inside and about twenty to thirty zombies outside. They can't get in but are blocking our only exit. Please, if you can hear this we need your help."

Just as the transmission finishes Fredrick, Troy and Braydon come walking out of the supermarket with more supplies. Once I see them come outside the supermarket I rush over to them and tell them that Mark doesn't know who Will Smith is. After we finish laughing I tell them about the transmission that was broadcast over the radio. Right before I explain the situation the transmission repeats itself on the radio, saving me the trouble. I wave everyone over to the bus to listen in. When the transmission ends everyone stops and looks at each other.

"What do you think? Is it a trap?" April asks.

"Why would it be a trap?" I reply.

"They could pretend to want rescue, but they're a group of scavengers and they hold us at gun point and steal all our shit." Braydon interrupts.

"I don't know about you, but the sincerity in his voice sounded pretty real to Me.", I remark.

"I'm thinking a trap." Troy adds.

"Look. The least we can do is drive by and see if there are even any zombies outside. If there are we help them, if there aren't then it is obviously a trap." I say.

"I'm with Ryan on this one." April adds.

"Same.", Mark says.

"Alright, we're going to do one more run inside for supplies inside and then we will take a look at that church." Fredrick says.

Fredrick runs back towards the supermarket and motions for Troy and Braydon to follow him. After Fredrick goes back inside April and I walk around the side of the bus and stare off at the barren parking lot. After a few minutes go by, out of boredom of waiting I start to kick a rock around on the ground. April watches me while leaning her back against the side of the bus, thinking nothing of it. While I am side tracked, kicking the rock back and forth April and I heard gunshots ring out from inside the supermarket.

April and I rush around to the opposite side of the bus and stare off inside the supermarket. We only heard three shots fired but that could still signal trouble. After a few more minutes go by there is still no sign of Fredrick and his team yet. Nothing can be seen or heard from inside the supermarket, causing April and I to start worrying. April and I both raise our guns and point them at the supermarket, now expecting something else to come out.

As time goes by my eyes stay fixated on the supermarkets entrance until I see Fredrick and his team emerge from the darkness. After I see Fredrick, Troy and Braydon come out of the supermarket I let out a sigh of relief and lower my weapon, happy that the three of them are ok.

"What was the trouble inside?" I ask Fredrick

"Just a Night Stalker.", Fredrick replies.

"That gives me all the more reason to be long gone before nightfall." I add.

This time April and I help Fredrick unload the supplies. After we quickly unload the supplies Fredrick pushes the carts back towards the front of the supermarket and hops on the bus. When we're all safely back on the bus I tap Mark on the shoulder and say, "To the church!"

Mark nods to be before starting up the bus and plugging in the location of the church into the buses built in GPS. Fredrick walks to the back of the bus and sits down for a well deserved break.

"What is the ETA?" Fredrick shouts up to Mark from the back of the bus.

"Five minutes." Mark replies.

Mark turns the key in the bus to start it up and pulls out onto the main road before heading in the direction of the church. Everyone zones out and stares out the windows while driving towards the church. After a few minutes go by Mark yells out to the whole bus, "The church will be coming up on our right in about thirty seconds."

Everyone shifts to the right side of the bus to get a good look at the church. As we are driving past the church Fredrick yells out to Mark, "Slow down so we can see everything."

Mark slows the bus down to twenty five, giving us plenty of time to see the church's courtyard. As we drive by the church we all begin to nod. It was just like the survivors said over the radio there are twenty to thirty zombies are outside. All of them are pounding on the doors of the church, trying get in. Now that we know it is not a trap Fredrick yells out to Mark, "Stop the bus. Let's help these people."

Mark brings the bus to a complete stop about a hundred feet away from the church. Fredrick steps off the bus and starts to shoot the zombies one by one. I follow behind Fredrick while everyone else stays on the bus and shoots from inside.

With all of us shooting at the zombies they drop quickly and effortlessly. Once almost every zombie is dead outside and there is a safe path up to the church Fredrick runs up and bangs on the door. "Grab your supplies and load them onto our bus. We've cleared a path so you can do it safely and quickly. Hurry up before more come." Fredrick yells out to anyone inside.

Fredrick backs away from the door and lays down cover fire at any of the zombies still surrounding the church. A few seconds go by before the door to the church swings open. Five guys run out with their arms full with supplies while a girl holds the door for them.

After all seven people are out of the church with all the supplies she lets the door swing closed before following them onto the bus. When they are all back on the bus Fredrick and I start to slowly back up towards the bus. The two of us are still shooting any zombies that walk around the sides of the church. Once we're both back on the bus Mark closes the doors and pulls away from the church. After we're all back on the bus Fredrick turns to the new survivors and asks, "Everyone ok?"

All the new survivors on the bus nod, still a bit shaken up from making the trip from the church to the bus. After everyone shakes their head and let Fredrick know they are ok he continues by asking, "Is anyone injured and has anyone been bitten?"

All of the survivors shake their head side to side, some of them even mutter no, to Fredrick as well. After Fredrick gets an answer from everyone he smiles and replies, "Alright, good. My name is Fredrick."

Fredrick takes everyone's hand one by one and shakes it, further introducing himself. The process continues on around the bus as the survivors introduce themselves to everyone. After introducing themselves to everyone in the front of the bus they eventually work their way back to me, in the back. The first hand I shake is a short man; about five foot eleven in height.

"Hello, my name is Justin." The man says to me.

"Ryan.", I reply.

Justin has short brown hair and looks to be in his mid-twenties. He has on a pair of glasses very similar to Mark's and has a scar right between his eyes - which seems to have been caused by getting punched in the face with his glasses on. Justin has large gauges in his ear, about three quarters of an inch big. Aside from the self mutilation that the gauges imply, Justin seems to upkeep himself rather well. There is no facial hair at all on his face. It seems that after all that has happened he still shaves every day.

Justin has on a band T-shirt as well as a pair of jeans that are obviously too tight for him. Putting aside the obvious signs of starvation on him, it seems like he was thin even before the zombie infestation. After Justin is done shaking my hand the next survivor approaches me. He extends his hand out to me before speaking.

"Hello, my name is Luu."

"Ryan."

Luu is about the same height as Justin, maybe just a hair taller. Judging by how much hair on Luu's head is gray, he looks to be in his early thirties. Unlike Justin he is more on the heavy side, maybe just north of two hundred pounds. Luu has short brownish orange hair that gets a little bit longer in the front as it gets closer to his forehead. He has a small piercing through his left ear, nothing fancy just a little green gemstone.

Luu is wearing a baggy plaid, button up, shirt as well as a pair of baggy cargo pants. Luu seems to keep rather well groomed and is almost completely shaved aside from the goatee on his chin. After Luu is done shaking my hand the next survivor approaches me.

"Hello, my name is Zooey."

"Ryan."

Zooey is the only female in the pack of survivors that we just saved. She is about five foot six and looks to be about twenty-six years old. For her height Zooey is about normal size, looking to weigh about one twenty. She has long black hair, down to her shoulders and robust green eyes. Zooey has both of her ears pierced with little diamond gemstones.

She has a large diamond ring on her ring finger, but she doesn't seem to be attached to anyone here. Probably meaning she lost her husband sometime before she met us. Zooey is currently wearing a black sweat shirt and a pair of tight jeans. Seeming to be all the fad now a day. While Zooey shakes my hand she lets her eyes wander before shooting me a smile, checking me out.

Out of the corner of my eye I see April light up with jealousy. I finish shaking Zooey's hand as the next survivor approaches me. When Zooey turns around I shake my head side to side to April, trying to let her know that feeling isn't mutual. April ignores my gesture and turns around to sit down. I let out a sigh as the next survivor approaches me. The man extends his hand out to me before speaking.

"Hello, my name is John."

"Ryan."

John stands out amongst the new survivors because of his unique fashion sense. He is wearing a pair of black sunglasses as well as a gray hoodie sweat shirt. He also has on a pair of tight jeans that are almost in pristine condition. You can tell all of his clothes are top of the line designer clothes. Now whether he had the money to buy them before the zombie apocalypse or if he stole them from a store afterwards is the mystery.

Aside from his unique fashion sense John looks to be right around six feet tall and weighs about two hundred pounds. John has very short brown hair which almost perfectly matches his slightly tanned skin. Based on first impressions with John he doesn't seem like the preppy type that would buy top of the line clothing. After I finish shaking John's hand the next survivor approaches me.

"Hello, my name is Mike."

"Ryan."

Mike is the tallest of the new survivors standing up at about six foot two and about twenty years old. He has very short jet black hair, which perfectly matches his eyes. Mike looks to weigh about one eighty, which makes him appear to be skin and bone because of his height. You can start to see Mike's cheek bone a bit, letting you know he has been without food for quite awhile. Mike is wearing a baseball cap and a tight T-shirt, not really flowing right with his baggy jeans.

Mike has a clean shave, not a scrap of facial hair can be seen on his face. Mike has a small piercing in his left ear, much like Luu. I finish shaking Mike's hand as the second to last survivor approaches me.

The man extends his hand and says, "Hello, I'm Paul."

"Ryan."

Paul stands tall at about six foot one and looks to be in his mid thirties too late thirties. He has long blond hair that comes down to the top of his eyebrows. His hair is as straight as an arrow and seems to be very poorly cut, almost like Paul attempted it himself. Paul has dark green eyes which match the two emerald earrings he has in both ears.

Paul looks to weigh about two ten and has a full bushy beard, obviously not having shaved since the disaster happened. Paul's is very toned but not built. You can tell that he works out but he isn't going for the macho man look like Fredrick or Troy. I finish shaking Paul's hand, just as the final survivor approaches me from the church. The man stops in front of me and extends his hand.

"Hello, my name is Jeremy."

"Ryan."

Jeremy is about five foot eleven and looks to be about two hundred pounds. He has really short dark brown hair. It is short that at first glance he almost appears to be bald. Jeremy is clean shaven aside from his goatee and sideburns. Jeremy also has a pair of humongous ears, hanging a good few inches off of his head.

Jeremy has on a wife beater as well as a pair of baggy cargo pants. The cold weather apparently doesn't affect his bad fashion sense. Just by looking at Jeremy's face, you can tell he has been starving the past week. However, with all of his sniffing I think a much greater problem than zombies is at play. After I finish shaking Jeremy's hand all the survivors continue to the back of the bus and take a seat. I walk up to the front of the bus and stop next to April.

"Don't worry cutie pie, you're the only one for Me.", I say to April sarcastically.

April laughs and rolls her eyes at me. Before jokingly punching me in the arm a few times. After we're both done joking around I continue up to the seat behind Mark and sit down. Mark pulls away from the church and continues in our westward direction. When the bus starts moving again Fredrick stands up in the aisle and starts a quick speech,

"Alright everyone listen up. We're heading to Las Vegas. That is supposedly where the biggest survivor colony is located. We figure the trip will take a day or two and we only plan to stop for food water and gas. Any questions concerns or comments shout them out now."

No one answers Fredrick; everyone just goes about nodding their heads and talking to one other. After about ten seconds with no response Fredrick sits down across from me in the front of the bus.

After Fredrick sits down I look over to him and say, "We should probably make a stop at a gun shop before we get out of the small town. We could use more fire power."

"Good Point." Fredrick adds.

"Mark, take us to the closest gun shop." Fredrick says.

Mark plays around with the GPS for a minute or two before looking back to Fredrick and saying, "It's not finding any gun shops around."

Fredrick rolls his eyes before standing up and taking a look at the GPS. After Fredrick plays around with it for a minute or two until he realizes he isn't going to get it to work either. Before giving up hope he turns around and looks back to everyone on the bus.

"Alright, anyone here know where a gun shop is? We need some weapons for the trip." Fredrick asks everyone.

Justin stands up and says, "I'm a local here. There is a gun shop on the eastern side of town. It's maybe a five minute drive."

"Alright, get up here and show Mark the way." Fredrick says.

Justin walks up to the front of the bus and stands next to Mark to point him in the right direction. As we are driving to the gun shop I look back and notice that April is staring out the window of the bus. She has a sad look on her face, giving me the impression something is bothering her. I stand up and walk over to April's seat before sitting down right next to her. April continues looking out the window, not even caring that I came over to her.

"What is the matter?" I ask her.

"What do you mean?" she responds without looking at me.

"April, I can tell you're depressed. No reason to bullshit me!" I say in a sarcastic voice.

April turns to me and smirks before saying, "What if we get to Las Vegas and it is like everywhere else?"

"Then we will start our own survivor colony there. We will rebuild the city." I say to April.

April smiles to me a bit before putting her head back down. April fiddles her thumbs a bit before looking back out the window. I stay seated next to her and throw my arm around her, pulling her closer to give her some comfort.

A few minutes later the bus begins to slow down as we arrive at the gun shop on the east side of town. Mark opens the doors of the bus and lets Fredrick, Troy and Braydon head out into the shop. I decide to stay inside the bus with April, making sure she is ok.

A few seconds after they all enter the store I hear a single gunshot. Apparently there was a not so friendly zombie inside. After the initial gunshot no other noises can be heard until Fredrick and his team comes out of the gun shop with their hands full. Fredrick walks onto the bus and hands everyone who is unarmed a Glock pistol.

Fredrick warns everyone on the bus by saying, "If you point this gun at anyone that isn't a zombie. I will point mine at you and fire."

Braydon and Troy come up onto the bus right behind him carrying boxes full of ammo for each of the guns we have. They place the boxes on some empty seats in the back of the bus and go inside for another load.

When passing me on the bus Troy throws a M4 clip and two Glock clips into my lap. One of the clips is for April and the other one is for me. I reload my M4 and Glock as well as April's Glock. Just as I finish reloading April's gun and mine Troy and Braydon come out with another load of ammo. Fredrick follows behind them carrying a large sniper rifle in one hand and two boxes of ammo for his newly acquired gun in the other.

The sniper rifle looks to be a Barrett 50 cal. It has a long slick black body and is about four feet in length. Troy and Braydon are first to get on the bus. Much like before they walk to the back of the bus and place the crates of ammo down first before finding a seat. Fredrick comes on the bus and sits down right behind Mark before tinkering with his new toy.

Once everyone is back on the bus Mark closes the doors and beings heading west again, looking for the nearest gas station to fill up at. It is now late afternoon as the sun is starting to slowly drift down to the horizon behind us.

Towards the outskirts of town we finally find a gas station that has pump for diesel fuel. Mark pulls into the gas station and turns the bus off before getting out. I watch Mark from out of the window. After he swipes his card for the pump he gets frustrated and kicks it. After venting his anger Mark stomps back onto the bus.

"Anyone here have a debit or credit card for the pump? I need it to activate it but it is telling me mine has insufficient funds."

I nod to Mark before wiggling my way out from behind April, who is now asleep, and following Mark off the bus. Outside I swipe my Debit and punch in the pin, activating the pump for Mark. Mark and I shoot the shit outside for a few minutes until the buses tanks are fully filled. After we finish pumping the gas we walk back onto the bus and return to our seats.

After Mark is seated he sticks the key into the ignition and turns it, but nothing happens. Mark pulls the key out and sticks it in again before turning it again, still with no luck. Mark keeps turning the key, hoping that the outcome will change before finally giving up. After about a minute goes by of Mark continually trying to get the bus to start he snaps. He starts screaming profanities and vigorously punching the steering wheel.

Fredrick stands up and walks over to Mark before discussing the problem with him. Shortly after Fredrick walks up to the front of the bus Jeremy stands up in the back of the bus. He clears his throat before saying, "Uhm, I may be of assistance. I used to be an auto mechanic."

"Used to be? What happen?" Fredrick asks.

"Well, look outside, the same thing that happened to everyone's job." Jeremy replies.

"My job was to kill shit and judging by everything that has happened, we're short on staff." Fredrick replies.

"Uhmm well let me fix the bus so you can get back to work."

Fredrick rolls his eyes and motions for Jeremy to come up to the front of the bus. At the front of the bus Jeremy has Mark move out of the driver's seat so he can try to start the bus. Jeremy takes a seat and turns the key but has the same outcome that Mark had before. Mark dances around Jeremy continually telling him that he told him so. All while Jeremy looks around for a quick fix.

Unable to find anything Jeremy opens the doors to the bus and walks outside. He circles around the bus to the back and pops open the compartment that has the engine. With my curiosity now aroused, I get out of the bus and walk around to see what is going on. At the back of the bus I see the bottom half of Jeremy's body sticking out. The upper half is tinkering around with the engine inside. As I approach him he leans out of the bus and scratches his head.

"Hey Ryan, can you go into the luggage compartment on the side and grab me the bag of tools? Usually they keep one in there just in case."

I walk around the side of the bus and find the luggage storage compartment. I lean in and grab the handle to try and open it but it won't budge. "Locked, damn it." I exclaim. As I pull the handle and find out that it is locked Mark steps off the bus and starts to walk my way.

"Hey Mark, do you have a key for the luggage compartment?"

Mark holds up the key ring and shakes it, showing me that there is only one key on the key ring. Without any other options I take a few steps back and start to whack the lock with the bottom of my M4. After a few minutes I notice that I am actually starting to make progress. A few more minutes of beating it finally causes the lock to snap off.

With the lock now off I open the compartment and look around inside. There is about five empty gas cans and a bag of tools, just like Jeremy said. I reach in to grab the bag of tools and toss it to mark, allowing him to easily hand it over to Jeremy.

I pull the gas cans out from the luggage compartment and toss them over to the gas pump, getting ready to fill them up just in case. After all the gas cans are over by the pump I walk over and swipe my debit card to activate the pump. Once the pump is activated I stick the nozzle into the first gas can and stare off into the sky. After I finish filling the first gas can I close it up and slide it away from me before starting on another.

While I am filling up each of the gas cans almost everyone starts to walk off the bus and around to watch Jeremy work. When Troy and Braydon walk off the bus they come over and join me, instead of Jeremy.

When I look up I see Troy and Braydon standing around me I start to talk with them, "Man I really hope this zombie disaster never ends. Cause if it does at four seventeen a gallon my checking account is getting raped."

Troy laughs and nods to me while Braydon ignores my joke and walks over to see what Jeremy is up to. It takes me a few minutes to finish filling the gas cans. After I finish I place them all back into the luggage compartment and secure them with a bungee cord. With that done, I circle around to the back of the bus and stand with the crowd that has formed around Jeremy.

"So what is the damage?" I ask Jeremy.

"There seems to be a problem with the starter." Jeremy replies.

"What is the ETA?" Fredrick asks.

"Depends on if I need parts or not. Twenty minutes if I was at my shop, maybe four hours out here."

"Four hours?!? Not to be Buzz kill McGee here but we need to be moving by sundown. It's too risky with Night Stalkers out there to be in the open *and* stationary." I say.

"Ryan is right." Fredrick adds. "We don't have four hours."

Fredrick looks up in the sky and puts his hand out in front of his face. He starts counting hand lengths down to the horizon, checking to see how much longer until the sun comes down. After Fredrick realizes how much time we have until sundown he turns back towards Jeremy and says, "We got two and a half until sundown."

"I need more time..." Jeremy starts to say.

Fredrick interrupts Jeremy and says, "Anymore time and you're going to be ripped into two pieces by Night Stalkers. Tell me what my team and I need to get you to speed this up."

"You can't do anything right now." Jeremy says before continuing, "Just be calm and I may be able to finish it in time."

Fredrick lets out a long drawn out sigh before grabbing me on the shoulder. He escorts me over towards the front of the bus and whispers to me, "Have everyone come outside. We need to be ready for an attack and the extra fire power will be helpful."

I nod to Fredrick before quickly jogging back into the bus and looking down the aisle at all the inquiring faces. Once inside I stop for a second to catch my breath before clearing my throat. I look around at everyone and cause a dim look to come over my face. I take one final deep breath before saying out loud, "We're all going to die."

Everyone's jaw drops, as fear lights up in their eyes from the information I just gave them. I give them a few seconds to dwell on the thought of them dying before saying, "Just kidding! Oh my god! You should have seen all of your faces. That was priceless!" I say while letting out a hearty laugh.

I realize that everyone is quite pissed off so I continue by telling them the truth, "Jeremy is out there fixing the problem right now. He said he should be done in about an hour or two before nightfall. In the meantime Fredrick wants everyone to come outside in case any zombies do come.

Extra firepower never hurt anyone. Well, extra firepower did hurt someone at some point but not right now so let's go! Get outside!"

After I finish talking I back up into April's seat and let everyone off the bus before me. As everyone stands up and starts to walk off the bus they all give me mean looks as they pass me, apparently not liking my joke from earlier. After everyone is off the bus I turn around and look at April.

"Alright, it looks bad… We might not be able to get it fixed by nightfall. If we can't get it fixed by night fall we're going to have Night Stalkers up our ass, which is almost certain death." I say to April.

April turns to me and says sarcastically, "I'm really glad we have you around. What would we do without your negativity?"

April pushes by me and walks off the bus. A bit saddened by what she said I take a seat on the bus and stare out the window, into the sky. I scratch my head and wonder if I really put her down and she was just being nice about it. After a few minutes pass I am able to shrug it off and grab a few extra clips of ammo inside the bus for everyone. After my hands are full with ammo I walk off the bus and around to the group of people watching Jeremy work.

Back outside the bus I hand out the extra clips of ammo that I grabbed from inside. I make sure that everyone has at least a full clip in their guns as well as two in their pockets. Which will hopefully be enough if anything bad does happen tonight? Time seems to drag on as the sun is starting to set in the distance. As time goes on Jeremy is making little to no noticeable progress. Causing almost everyone to become upset and want to take a look at the problem for themselves.

The area around us is just barely lit with the oranges and reds from the setting sun. As time goes by Jeremy lets us know that he needs at least another forty five minutes to complete the repairs on the bus. Fredrick looks up into the sky and back at Jeremy, urging him to hurry up and reminding him that he only has thirty till sunset. Another ten minutes fly by as some of the new survivors start to become unruly.

Paul becomes angry and pushes Fredrick out of the way. He reaches up and grabs the back of Jeremy's shirt causing him to fall out of the bus and onto the ground. Right after Jeremy falls to the ground Fredrick throws a punch at Paul, hitting him square in the face and breaking his nose. Everyone cringes as they hear the snapping sound of Fredrick's fist colliding with Paul's face. Paul stumbles backwards and grabs his nose with both of his hands. The blood is now gushing out from between each of his fingers.

After watching Paul have his nose broken everyone calms down, now knowing Fredrick means business. Fredrick helps Jeremy up and motions for him to continue working on the bus, knowing there is no time to sit around. Jeremy looks over at Paul in disgust before listening to Fredrick and resuming work on the bus.

As Jeremy continues work on the bus I keep a close eye on the sun, noticing that it is now almost fully down. Very few rays of light are still piercing through the clouds onto the ground around us. As I wait for the impending darkness I click on the flashlight that is attached to my gun.

"Fifteen more minutes." Jeremy says out loud to everyone. "I just need to put it back together."

Everyone breathes a sigh of relief, thankful that we finally have a definitive time that we are going to get out of here. The relief is short lived, however, as a loud shriek can be heard from the woods just to our north.

"Oh fuck... The blood..." I say out loud.

"They can smell Paul's Blood." I add.

The look of gloom immediately crosses Paul's face. As he realizes his dumb ass just got himself killed. The sun now fully sets in the distance, not a ray of light can be seen around us. Troy, Braydon and Fredrick all turn on the flashlights attached to their guns so we can at least have some light. Everyone else stares off into the forest nearby, waiting to see whatever made the shriek come out. An eerie silence comes over us; the only sounds able to be heard are frantic breaths and the sound of Jeremy working on the bus.

"Ten more minutes." Jeremy whispers to anyone listening.

We all stand guard and make sure that someone is looking in every direction at all times, making sure nothing can get near us without us knowing. The sound of feet walking on dried leaves can be heard coming from the forest, in the same direction we heard the shriek from. After hearing the cracking of branches and crumbling of dry leaves I grip my gun tightly and expect the worst. I stare off into the woods but am unable to see anything. I take a few steps back towards the bus and into the crowd, feeling more secure and comfortable around everyone else.

The sound of branches cracking and leaves crumbling can be heard again. This time the sounds come from all over the forest. We all shine our lights into the forest, hoping to see them before they come out. Another minute goes by as we start to hear branches cracking and breaking from up within the trees. I swallow hard before turning to Fredrick and whispering, "It's them."

Fredrick nods to me, letting me know that he knows. As the sounds grow louder, everyone's breathing starts to become irregular. A loud crash echoes out from behind the gas station causing everyone to jump out of their skin. Every one of us is on edge and starting to stress about the seemingly inevitable attack. Luu can be heard grinding his teeth while Justin starts profusely sweating.

I get an ominous feeling from the woods as an eerie silence comes over us. Seconds later a loud bang can be heard from on top the roof of the gas station followed by the sound of a Night Stalker crawling on it. We are unable to get a visual on the Night Stalker that landed on the roof of the gas station but are still able to hear him move around. Everything goes silent on the roof for a few seconds causing our attention to drift back towards the woods. Before we are even fully focused back on the woods a loud screech can be heard resonating from the top of the gas station.

Before we even know what is going on Paul is tackled to the ground by the Night Stalker that was on top the gas station's roof. The Night Stalker sinks his teeth into Paul's neck and starts to rip apart his torso with its claws. Everyone opens fire on the Night Stalker, our bullets ripping through its body and into Paul's as well. The Night Stalker's lifeless body collapses on top of Paul's as he struggles to take his last breaths.

Paul is now lying in a puddle of blood on the ground. The puddle slowly grows bigger as the Night Stalker and Paul both fully bleed out. As the smell of blood fills the air loud shrieks can be heard coming from all over the woods. The Runners and Night Stalkers that were in the woods start pouring out as we all open fire.

Flickers of light can be seen all around me as the air is filled up with the sound of gunfire. Our bullets fly across the short field that is between us and the forest. Ripping apart any Night Stalkers or Runners that they make contact with. As the Night Stalkers come leaping out of the forest they are sometimes able to land on the back of a Runner and propel there selves closer to us. Nothing has yet to make it within thirty feet of us, giving us a false sense of hope and a slight moral boost.

As Jeremy is frantically trying to finish up we subdue everything that comes out of the woods nearby. His hands move quickly through his tool bag, throwing any tools he can't use out of it and onto the ground around us. While working on putting the engine back together he shouts as loud as he can to us, his voice barely able to be heard over the gunfire.

"ETA five minutes! Hold them off guys!"

We all nod to Jeremy's ETA while continuing to shoot any Runners and Night Stalkers that come out of the woods. After a few minutes of nonstop killing the amount of Runners and Night Stalkers starts to decrease until they finally just trickle in. When there are no more Runners or Night Stalkers coming out of the forest, zombies start to limp and stumble their way out. The zombies don't pose much of a threat since they move too slowly. It is impossible for them to close the distance between us fast enough to the point of where we can't kill them.

Our hearts are still racing from the gun fight as the adrenaline that is coursing through us finally starts to fade. Everyone lowers their weapons and lets out a sigh of relief, happy that we're safe for now. We all turn back to Jeremy but before we are able to say anything Justin is tackled by a Runner from behind. The Runner collapses on top of Justin and sinks its teeth into his neck, biting and tearing at his flesh. Fredrick shoots the Runner in the head, blasting its brains out all over the ground next to Justin. The lifeless body collapses on top of Justin before he frantically pushes it off and jumps to his feet. He throws his hand over the wound on his neck to try and slow the bleeding.

Fredrick aims his gun at Justin, knowing that it is only a matter of time before he becomes one of them. Though, before Fredrick is able to pull the trigger more Runners ambush us from behind. They tackle Justin to the ground again and tear into him. His screams of agony can be heard for miles as the Runners relentlessly tear limbs from his body.

Troy yells at the top of his lungs before dumping a whole clip from his M4 into the hoard of Runners tearing apart Justin's body. After Troy kills all the Runners around Justin's body he takes out his sidearm and fires a shot into Justin's head, making sure he stays dead. Those of us still alive form a little circle around the back of the bus. Three of us watch the forest and the rest of us watch the road in the front of the bus, to prevent and more surprise attacks.

April reaches into my back left pocket and grabs two clips of ammo for her Glock, knowing that I have plenty. After she takes my ammo she quickly reloads her gun before joining back in the fight. As time goes on a shortage of ammo seems to start becoming a very real problem. Zooey throws her gun away, finding it of no use without any. After she reaches down next to Justin's body and hesitantly grabs his pistol as well as the two clips of ammo that are in his pockets. With a new gun and ammo Zooey quickly rejoins the fight.

"Alright! Done!" Jeremy exclaims while throwing the bag of tools on the ground and shutting the back panel.

After the back panel to the bus is shut Jeremy jumps off the back of the bus and joins us in the fight as we work our way towards the doors to the bus. We form a half circle while moving up the side of the bus, making sure all directions are covered. We continue firing shot after shot as we slowly move towards the doors. When we reach the doors of the bus Fredrick hops on and does a quick sweep of it, making sure that everything is clear before inviting anyone else on. After he searches the whole bus he waves Mark on first to see if the bus will even start.

Mark runs up the stairs and jumps into the driver's seat. He kisses the key before sticking it in the ignition, hoping to give the key some luck. After Mark sticks the key in the ignition he turns it only to have the bus stutter and stall. Everyone's heart drops down into their chest as we all fear the worst. Mark says a quick prayer before turning the key again. This time the bus starts up and sounds nice and healthy.

"Alright, let's get the fuck out of here!" Fredrick yells to everyone, waving them onto the bus.

April and Zooey are the first two on the bus followed by Troy, Braydon and then finally me. Jeremy followed right behind me but right as he put his first foot on the step leading into the bus two claws descending from the roof and pierced through his body. The claws penetrate through his shoulder blades and come out the other end of his body, causing blood to squirt all over. As the claws are piercing through him and lifting him up Jeremy coughs and has blood shoot out of his mouth. Before any of us are able to do anything Jeremy is pulled on top of the bus.

Blood showers down around the bus as the Night Stalker tears apart Jeremy. Limbs are seen thrown from the top of the bus down to the hungry Runners below. "Come on, come on! Let's go!" I yell out to Mike, Luu and John. All of which are still outside shooting at the Runners. They all seem to ignore me as they are too focused on killing everything around. Mike starts to back up, away from the bus, and shoot at the Night Stalker on the roof that took Jeremy.

Just as Mike kills the Night Stalker on the roof that took Jeremy he is tackled by a Runner. As Mike falls to the ground; his gun slides off into the darkness. Before Luu is able to shoot the Runner off the top of Mike it has already torn into his neck and started to tear Mike apart. After Luu shoots the Runner on top of Mike he runs over to help him. As Luu leans over and starts to help Mike up. Mike lunges at Luu and sinks his teeth into Luu's neck before pulling him down to the ground. Runners run over and encircle Luu, relentlessly tearing apart his body. Everyone outside is dead now aside from John.

John freezes up outside, he is scared shitless after seeing so many people die. I reach out the front doors of the bus to grab John by the back of the shirt, trying to pull him onto the bus. But John weighs too much for me to be able to move him. While tugging on the back of John's shirt out of the corner of my eye I see Paul starting to get up off the ground. I swallow hard and yell to John while trying to pull him onto the bus but nothing seems to be working. I frantically look over at Paul again and see blood dripping down from his mouth as he tilts his head side to side to crack his neck. Paul lets out a loud screech before throwing his arms back and charging John.

Paul runs full speed towards John and slams into him, tackling him to the ground right in front of me. I jump backwards and pull the doors closed in front of me, trying to get away from everything outside. Within seconds of John hitting the ground Runners circle him and start tearing him to pieces. When there isn't enough room for them to get around John they start to pile up at the front doors to the bus, pounding and throwing themselves into it.

I turn to Mark and yell, "What are you waiting for! Go, go, go!"

Mark breaks out of his trance and slams his foot down onto the gas pedal. The bus peels wheels because of all the blood on the ground around it. I am caught off guard by the sudden acceleration and fall down on the stairs, almost tumbling out of the bus. Luckily, Fredrick's hand comes down and grabs me by the back of my suit before pulling me up to safety.

Once we're back on the main road Mark swerves in and out of both lanes. As Mark swerves what is left of Jeremy's body slides off the top of the roof and hits the pavement below. The Night Stalker follows right behind the body. It flails its arms in the air before it makes contact with the pavement below. All of us on the bus breathe a sigh of relief, glad that we made it out alive. I find the strength in me to pull myself to my feet and walk over to April. When I come over to April I notice that here is still some smeared blood on my face. It must have been from when Jeremy got mauled right in front of me. When April sees me she smiles at me before taking her sleeve and wiping the blood off my face.

After my face is clear I open my eyes again and see a tear rolling down April's face. She smiles at me and slightly tilts her head before throwing her arms around me. I pull April close and stare out the window at all the trees going by. After April sits back down I look around the bus and notice that everyone is staring at the ground, unsure how to handle what they just witnessed. After I take a seat I watch Fredrick walk up to the front of the bus and over to Mark before saying, "Don't stop until we're out of gas. Who knows how long they can follow us."

Fredrick takes a seat behind Mark and covers his face using both of his hands. I sit down next to April and lean my head against the seat before letting out a long drawn out sigh and staring up at the ceiling. My mind starts to drift off and think of something positive, trying to forget everything that just happened. Everyone on the bus is silent and stays silent for a long while.

Chapter 7 - Dawn of A New Era

As we continue driving for the next few hours, no one dares speak of the last gas station. Everyone is still on edge from what happened and trying to put the bad memory behind them. The first one to break the silence is Mark, letting Fredrick know that we are getting low on gas. Over the next few minutes all of us keep an eye out for a gas station and pray that it isn't like the last. A few more minutes go by before Troy spots a gas station coming up on the right hand side. Troy calls it out to Mark and he nods before starting to slow down and pull into the gas station. Once we're fully stopped Fredrick motions for Troy, Braydon and I to follow him off the bus and help secure the area.

Once we're all off the bus we quickly secure the area before Fredrick tries to start pumping the gas. Fredrick toys around with the gas pump, unable to get it to work. After a few minutes and a dozen second opinions he gives up and runs over to the luggage compartment to grab the gas cans. He empties the gas cans one by one into the gas tank before putting them back into the luggage compartment. When we are finished we all run back onto the bus where Fredrick peeks over Mark and takes a look at the gas meter.

After getting a good look at the gas meter he turns around and announces to the bus, "About three quarters of a tank. We'll make it easily till sunrise."

After Fredrick's words the moral is instantly lifted inside the bus. When Fredrick returns to his seat Mark shifts the bus back into drive and turns back onto the road before continuing west. Back in my seat April snuggles against me, putting her head on my shoulder and closing her eyes.

Shortly after April gets comfortable, Fredrick looks back at me and asks, "Anyone know what state we're in?"

"I figure about half way through Illinois." I say to Fredrick.

Fredrick nods and lays his head back on his bus seat before closing his eyes, trying to get some much needed sleep for the first time in days. I follow his example and lean my head on April's shoulder before closing my eyes. I listen to the sound of the buses engine as it soothes me enough to let me slowly drift off to sleep.

Hours later I am awoken by the sounds of the bus decelerating, stopping and eventually turning off. When I tilt my head up to look out the window I notice that we are at another gas station. I let out a loud yawn and wipe off my eyes as Fredrick, Troy and Braydon step off the bus to start pumping the gas and secure the area. I stretch my arms and crack my back before standing up and following them off the bus.

When I walk off the bus I am immediately blasted with the cool chilly air from the wintry morning. Once off the bus I look around and notice that more snow fell this morning. A few more inches are already on the ground and it still seems to be flurrying a bit outside. I form my hands into a large fist and blow into them, trying to warm them up before using them to rub my arms. I turn to look at the bus quickly and notice a large scratch that wasn't there before. It perks my interest so I walk over to the bus and look inside to Mark.

I tip my head to Mark before asking, "How hard is the snow making driving this beast?"

"Not that bad. It's a bit of a pain in the ass but nothing I can't handle." Mark replies.

"Yeah, I figured as much. Nice five foot scratches on the side of the bus, by the way." I say to Mark, sarcastically.

I tap the bus lightly before turning around and walking over to Fredrick and his team. Troy and Braydon are dancing around Fredrick. Both of them showing obvious signs of being cold while Fredrick stands there, seemingly unaffected by the weather. I walk up to Fredrick and tip my head before asking, "We still in Illinois?"

"Yeah we're right outside of some Davendart town." Fredrick replies.

"Davenport?" I ask.

"Yeah, that's it.", Fredrick says.

"Ahh, it's on the Iowa Illinois border." I add.

I turn around and look down the long and straight highway leading into Iowa. A large smile comes across my face as I mumble to myself, "Already half way there..." After getting a good look at the road ahead I turn back to Fredrick and everyone else.

"So, what happens if we get to Vegas and no one is there?" I ask Fredrick.

"You mean no Survivor Colony?" He responds.

"Yeah.", I answer.

"Guess we'll just have to start one then." Fredrick says as if he was stating something obvious.

"Thank you." I say before a large smile comes over my face.

"Huh?" Fredrick asks.

"You know, for everything." I reply.

"I'm not sure I quite understand what you mean." Fredrick says.

"Nothing, you just made everything so much easier for me and April. Without you I don't think I'd be alive." I say to Fredrick in a very serious way.

"Don't worry about it.", Fredrick replies.

After Fredrick finishes filling the buses gas tank he switches to the spare gas cans that are lying on the ground. As Fredrick fills each of the spare gas cans Troy and Braydon both take turns loading them into the luggage compartment. I continue by pacing around the area waiting for everyone to finish up before we can get back onto the bus. When Fredrick is finished he places the nozzle back into the gas pump and walks over to me. He places his hand on my shoulder and looks at me before saying, "You've helped me a lot too you know."

Fredrick pats me on the shoulder a few times before continuing up and into the bus. As Troy and Braydon pass me they shoot me a grin before getting back onto the bus. A large smile comes across my face before following Troy and Braydon back onto the bus. Once Mark sees that everyone is back on board he closes the doors and shifts the bus into drive. We pull back out onto the highway and continue driving west. The snow is now starting to come down a bit harder than it was earlier. "Hopefully we're driving out of a storm and not into one", I mumble to myself.

As the day continues on, so does the snow. The conditions outside are starting to get much worse, forcing Mark to drive slower and slower as the day goes on. However, the snow is not bad enough to the point of were travel is impossible. Mark is forced to drive at about forty to prevent losing control of the vehicle and careening off the road. We hold the speed of forty for a few hours until we come across the next gas station on our journey. Mark pulls into the gas station and Fredrick and I get out. Once we're both out of the bus we start pumping the gas.

It takes the two of us about ten minutes to finish pumping the gas, the snow on the ground making it hard to even walk around. As Fredrick and I are pumping the gas outside Mark finally decides to take a break from driving for a quick nap. After Fredrick and I finish up outside we walk back onto the bus and tap Braydon on the shoulder, letting him know that we're good to go. Braydon shifts the bus back into drive and slowly and carefully pulls out the gas station. There is about one foot of snow already down on the ground, forcing Braydon to do about fifteen miles an hour. Without anyone or anything plowing the roads it makes them almost impossible to navigate at a time like this.

With the storm being as relentless as it is everyone worries that we are going to get caught in the storm and be forced to spend a night stationary. If we are forced to stay in one place for too long then it increases the chances of us getting trapped and killed. We simply just don't have the man power to fight off a hoard as big as the one last night.

As the day continues on only our only fear starts to become more and more real. The snow storm is becoming worse, much faster than we originally expected. The conditions are so bad outside that it is almost impossible to see out the windshield. As we are driving down the highway we hear a loud shriek, the sound only a Night Stalker can make. Troy jolts out of his seat and looks around the bus with a look a fear in his eyes.

"Is that what I think it was?" Troy asks.

"Yup.", I reply.

"But it is the middle of the day..." Troy adds.

"The snow is blocking out the sun. That is the only thing normally stopping them from hunting in the day." I reply.

Zooey asks, "Well what about the snow? They can't possibly move faster than us!"

"Night Stalkers hop, the snow isn't an inconvenience to them." I say.

We all go silent as another loud shriek can be heard, this one sounding much closer than the last. Everyone peeks out their windows and looks around, trying to see where the Night Stalker is that made the noise. With nobody able to see anything we all breathe a sigh of relief and sink back down into our seats. The relief is short lived, however as a loud crash can be heard from on top the roof.

The sound of the Night Stalker landing on the roof echoes throughout the bus. Everyone ducks down for cover, the sound scaring everyone. I point to the roof as everyone on the bus nods, confirming that they heard it too. Using the same finger I place it over top of my lips, telling everyone to be quiet.

Every time the creature moves around on the roof the sound of its step echoes down into the bus. The Night Stalker continues to walk around on the roof for the next few minutes until out of nowhere he just stops, almost trying to convince us he left the roof. A few seconds later the same Night Stalker lets out an ear piercing screech. All of us are forced cover our ears, the noise almost unbearable.

Moments after the Night Stalker lets out its ear piercing screech another loud bang can be heard on the roof of the bus. "It sounds like one of its friends came to join the party", I mumble to April. There are now two Night Stalkers on the roof, each of them making weird low pitch clucking noises. It is almost like they are communicating with each other.

All of us on the bus stare at each other, confused by what is going on. I continue to listen to the clucks and chirps, realizing that no two sounds they make are the same. They continue to make their weird noises on top of the bus until they shriek one last time before jumping off. Everyone starts to look around and start to stand up but I motion for everyone to stay down, stay away from the windows and be quiet. If they're smart enough to communicate with each other, god knows what they're planning.

The five longest minutes of my life go by without hearing a single sound from outside. After a few more minutes go by I lean up and get on my knees to try and see out the windows nearby. I look around outside but am unable to see anymore than a few feet because of the white out conditions. After getting a look around outside I nod to everyone, letting them know it is ok to get back up. Everyone stands up before returning to their seats and looking out the window, wondering if they'll have better luck spotting the Night Stalkers.

As the snow continues to come down we're now unable to go any faster than five miles an hour. We're moving at a crawling pace, hardly getting anywhere any time soon. If the snow doesn't stop soon then we are going to be stuck here. Then the only option will be to stand around and wait for it to melt. Mean while, while it is snowing the Night Stalkers are free to hunt in the middle of the day. On top of starvation, freezing to death and dehydration, getting stuck is a very bad thing.

"Where are we going to end up at nightfall?" I ask Braydon.

"Somewhere around Des Moines, we're probably going to have to crash there." Braydon remarks..

"I have family that lives in a suburb right out of Des Moines.", I reply.

"You can't possibly think..." Braydon starts to say but I quickly interrupt him.

"No. I know. But it is a place to stay." I reply.

I stand up and walk over to bus's built in GPS and type in their address. It takes a few minutes to calculate the route. When it does, it estimates the time until we arrive at our destination to be five hours. I let out a sigh before returning to my seat and sitting back down next to April. As I sit down April puts her head onto my shoulder and gets comfortable before closing her eyes. With April taking a nap on my shoulder, I figure that we have five hours left to go and I mine as well get some shut eye too. So I lean my head against April's and close my eyes.

Later I am awoken by the sound of Troy's voice, "Ryan... Ryan... Hey Ryan wake up..." I slowly open my eyes and turn to look at Troy. The cold snow on top of his head is melting and dripping off from the inside of the warm bus.

"We're here." Troy says out loud.

"Why are you wet? Did you go inside?" I ask.

Troy pauses for a second and wipes some of the melting snow off the top of his head. He continues by saying, "Uhm... Uhhh.... Yeah. We went inside... Sorry."

I look up at Troy and swallow hard before asking, "Was anyone? ...."

"No... It was completely empty." Troy says, cutting me off before I can finish.

I nod to Troy and try to smile before pulling myself up out of my seat. I let out a long sigh before walking off the bus, a bit disappointed that my family isn't there. As I step off the bus I am a bit caught off guard by the cool chilly Iowa air. Once I'm off the bus I quickly make my way over to the house, trying to get out of the cold as quickly as possible.

Inside the house I stomp off the compacted snow on the bottom of my shoes before looking up and noticing that everyone is gathered around the kitchen table. They are still shivering from the wintry air outside, rubbing their arms and blowing into their hands. Fredrick is standing at the head of the table, not showing any signs of being cold.

I step up to the table and look around at everyone before saying, "It's getting late. Let's barricade up the windows and doors. Everyone will sleep in the living room on the floor. It may not be the most comfortable place but if we stay together we have the best chance to stay alive."

Fredrick nods before adding, "Ryan is right. We're going to stick together. We won't be here very long anyway."

Everyone splits up in the house and starts to barricade each of the windows with anything they can find. While everyone is barricading the downstairs I start up the stairs to go over to my cousin's room. While walking up the stairs I notice that some pictures are tilted and crooked on the wall. Below the pictures is a large black streak following the stairs down the wall to the bottom. Someone must have been carrying something big down the stairs in a rush.

At the top of the stairs I walk over to my cousin's room and slowly slip inside of her room before quietly closing the door behind me. When I take a look around I notice everything is a mess, she must have left in a hurry. A lot of her clothes are thrown across the floor as well as the drawers that held them.

Her bed is also a complete mess. It looks like she ripped a few layers of covers off her bed and left the others lay sloppily over top of it. After looking around her room I walk over to her bed and search for an old photo album from the last time that I seen her. I look under her bed and pull out a few assorted items before I notice the photo album in the back corner. I stick my arm under the bed and reach all the way across the floor over to the photo album. Once I have it in my hand I pull it out and lay it on top the bed. Afterwards I stand up and take a seat right next to it on the bed.

I pick the photo album up and set it on my lap before flipping a few pages until I find a picture that was taken of us together. The picture was an older one, taken a few years back, from when we first met in New Jersey. As I look at the picture of us together tears start to form in the corner of my eyes. The last time we spoke we got into a huge argument, one that I now wish I could take back. It was over something so stupid and the two of us couldn't think of anything to do but blame each other for it.

I was constantly being childish and over protective while she was lying and being immature all while swearing on her life that she wasn't. In truth, it was both of our faults, equally. She was too young and immature to see my point while I was too childish and hardheaded to see hers. As we grow older we seem to forget that when we were young, we thought we knew everything too. Then as we grew older we started to realize how much we don't know. I figured maybe a few years would go by and she would grow up and maybe we could still remain friends.

While looking at the picture now, I wish I could go back to that night and just have bit the bullet. Instead I got angry and threw my ego out there and told her the truth. Why is it that we can never find it in us to apologize before it is too late? I pause for a few minutes and think about everything from my past before flipping a few more pages from the album. Tears continue to fall from my face as I am reminded by all the fun that we had together. Before I am even able to reach the end of the photo album the door to my cousin's room opens and April steps in. I try to quickly organize myself by sliding the book back under the bed and wiping the tears from my eyes but April catches on.

April lets out a sigh before walking over to me and throwing her arm around my shoulders. I don't make eye contact with April and keep my eyes focused on my hands which are clamped together in my lap April turns her head and whispers into my ear, "Don't worry Ryan... You'll see her again."

"That's the thing though..." I say out loud to April before continuing, "Some people just aren't meant to be together. She is too much like me, a friendship is impossible to salvage out of It.", I hear April snivel a few times so I turn to look over to her. When I turn my head my eyes lock perfectly with hers, I can almost see the sorrow in her face, almost like she is sharing my feelings. As tears start to form her eyes glisten like diamonds.

In this moment in time it felt like we had a connection, something that made us more than just friends. Unable to resist the urge I lean in and place my lips against hers. April's lips were so savory and plump, I never wanted to let go. April takes the kiss at first, slowly moving her hand up to the back of my head. Then she stops and breaks it. She backs her head away from me while shaking it side to side.

"Something... Something just isn't right... I'm sorry." April says to me before standing up.

April runs over to the door and opens it; she takes one last look at me before stepping out of the room and closing the door behind her. I let out a long sigh before placing my forehead in my palm, wondering if I made the right choice. My heart feels like a glass that was dropped off the empire state building, only to shatter a mile below.

It takes me a few minutes before I pull myself together but when I finally do I stand up and flip my cousin's bed against the window, barricading it from any intruders. I turn and start to walk towards the door before looking back at her room. A slight smile comes across my face before I open the door and exit her bedroom. Once outside the room I slide the nearby bookcase over the door, stopping anything from getting into or out of that room. After her room is secure I had back downstairs and look around. After looking around the room I notice that April is missing.

I turn to Fredrick and ask, "Hey, where did April go?"

"She went outside; she said she needed some fresh air." he replies.

I immediately fill with anger towards Fredrick. "And you thought that would be a good idea?" I say while raising my voice to him.

"Calm down. She said she needed air and some room. So she went outside."

I start to get more frustrated at Fredrick, raising my fist in the air, wanting nothing more than to place my clenching fingers upside his head. Fredrick senses my frustration and starts to loosen his grip on his gun, ready to fight me. Troy and Braydon are moments away from stopping the fight but a loud shriek from outside interrupts us.

We all immediately stop whatever we were doing and listen. Another shriek can be heard from outside followed by April's scream. A chill runs down my spine as the scream almost mirrors the same one I heard the first night we met. I am now being driven by anger as I rush out the front doors of the house and jump off the patio into the snow.

I run out to the middle of the yard before stopping to scream April's name at the top of my lungs. After yelling I hear a loud scream coming from my right side, the snow is falling so hard I can't see more than a few feet in front of me. I yell April's name again at the top of my lungs. This time I get a response.

"Ryan! Please help me!" April screams back to me.

"I'm coming April! I'm coming!" I yell back to her while frantically making my way through the snow as quickly as possible.

As I get further away from the house I spot a long drag mark through the snow. The snow was pressed down in that area but there was no blood which is a really good sign. I follow the drag marks as well as April's scream, praying that it will lead me right to her.

I can hear Fredrick, Troy and Braydon following behind me. The sound of their guns hitting the metal on their uniforms as they try and travel through the snow is distinctly clear. About thirty feet away from the house I am able to start to see April in the white out conditions. My eyes light up with hope, happy to have her in my sights but the worst is still not over.

There is a Night Stalker right on top of April, biting at her face and clawing at her body. The tactical suit that Braydon gave her seems to be protecting her quite well from the Night Stalker's claws. The Night Stalker is just inches away from April's face, the only thing holding it back is her gun pressed against its neck. The second I get in sight of the Night Stalker and have a clear shot I aim my gun at its head and fire. My bullet penetrates the creature's skull and immediately changes the color of the snow on the other side of it.

I help April up right as Fredrick, Troy and Braydon arrive to help. We all breathe a sigh of relief, happy to see that everyone is ok. I help April up and escort her back towards the house; all of us walk at a much slower and more relaxed pace on the way back to the house. Once we're all back inside I close the door behind us and slide the dryer over the front door.

The sun outside is starting to set. Causing the little rays of light that did make it through the snow storm to start disappearing. All of us inside round up blankets before meeting back in the living room. We're all well aware that it is going to get awfully cold tonight and we're going to need them. We all lie down on the floor and make ourselves comfortable, almost forming a sea of blankets.

As we all try to fall asleep minimal amounts of conversation can be heard amongst us. The drive has made everyone exhausted as well as the stress from everything over the past week. We all just want to fall asleep on some much needed solid ground.

In the middle of the night I am awoken by the sound of the wind blowing against the house. Without thinking anything of it I roll over and snuggle back against my arm, trying to fall back to sleep. While trying to fall back asleep I hear a cough come from the kitchen. After hearing the cough, I tilt my head up and open my eyes to look around. Through the darkness I am just barely able to make out April sitting down in the corner of the kitchen. She has her back to the wall and is staring at the ground, seeming to be depressed about something.

I wiggle my way out from underneath the blanket and quietly walk across the living room, trying not to disturb anyone. April doesn't even know that she woke me up until I am standing right next to her. When she looks up at me I notice that she has tears rolling down her cheeks. Without any idea what to say to me April sits there and just looks up at me. A smile comes across my face before I sit down next to April and toss my arm over her shoulder. After I pull April into me, the fresh tears rolling down her cheeks are now landing on my shirt below.

"What's the matter?" I ask April.

After asking April what is wrong she chokes up a bit before starting to cry even more. I gently pat her on the back of the head and constantly reassure her that everything will be ok. I also move April's hair away from her face to prevent her from crying on it.

"It's ok April, you can tell Me.", I ask again.

After asking April a second time she starts to choke up even more. Giving me the impression that prodding for information right now might not be the best idea.

"I'm sorry for earlier, I shouldn't of ki..." I start to say but April interrupts me.

"It's not that... It's not your fault... It's me..."

April pulls her hand up to her face and wipes away some of the tears before saying, "By going outside... I put everyone in danger... I don't think I can do this anymore..."

"What?!" I remark before continuing with, "Listen April... Don't worry about that we're all safe and more importantly you're safe now. We'll be in Vegas at the Survivor Colony in just a few days, maybe even a week. Then everything will go back to normal."

April sniffles a few times before turning her head and looking up at me. Her cheeks are rosy red from the cool air in the room and she has small tears rolling down her face. When April turned to look at me it was almost like I was infused with sorrow. It felt like all of our emotions are being shared with one another. We both go silent and stare at each other; it feels like hours go by before either of us is able to speak a word.

"Is it wrong...? Is it wrong that I don't want it to go back to normal?" April asks me.

"No, it's not wrong at all. I don't want it to go back to normal either. That is why I plan to form a team and drive around to find survivors all over the country." I say to April, trying to reassure her.

I pause for a second and see April starting to smile now. Neither of us brings up the moment from earlier, as we are both questioning what we even felt and if both of us felt it.

I continue by saying, "Before all this, I was your average day zombie. Get up, eat, work, shit, eat again and sleep. My life didn't consist of anything fun. I felt meaningless, useless. But, after the zombie disaster, after I met you... I felt like I had purpose. Someone actually needed my help for once and couldn't get it from anywhere else."

"This all might sound stupid and sick. But this is the best thing that has ever happened to me. It may be scary and it may threaten my life every day. But god damn am I enjoying myself like never before." I say to April with a large smile across my face.

April smiles to me, indicating that she feels similar about the zombie disaster. She puts her head back down and snuggles into my chest before closing her eyes. I place my hand on the back of her head before leaning mine against the cabinets in the kitchen. I stare at the ceiling for a few minutes, unable to stop thinking about the connection I felt with April just a few minutes ago. As it starts to get later I eventually close my eyes and try to get some sleep before the morning comes.

Early in the morning I am awoken by the sound of people trying to quietly rummage around the house. When I am awake and look around the house it looks like everyone is awake aside from both me and April. After I wake up a bit more I shake April a few times to wake her up and get her ready for another long day.

Fredrick catches me stretching and starting to move around out of the corner of his eye. He smiles to me and tips his head, almost like saying good morning. I wipe my eyes and yawn again before shaking April some more, trying to get her to wake up. I look over to Fredrick and ask, in a very low voice, "What time is it?"

"It is eleven in the morning." Fredrick replies.

"What about the snow?" I ask Fredrick.

"Stopped and turned to rain. It's a bit icy outside but we can get on the move." Fredrick replies.

April sits up and yawns before stretching her arms. After April is up off of my lap, I am able to stand up and walk over to the window in the kitchen. When I look out the window I see that the rain is coming down pretty hard, clearing quite a bit of the snow on the ground. All of the snow on the ground from the day before has turned to slush and isn't much to worry about for our bus.

While still looking out the window I say to Fredrick, "We should get moving now, at night it is going to freeze up and make traveling very difficult."

"That's the plan." Fredrick adds, "We hope to get ahead of the storm and dodge the freezing roads by nightfall."

After Fredrick finishes talking he slides the Dryer that was blocking the front door into a room nearby. Troy and Braydon grab any water and canned food from the house and place it into shopping bags that were left lying around. While Mark and Zooey collect the blankets we used from the night before and neatly fold them to carry them out to the bus.

Fredrick holds open the door for Mark, Troy, Braydon and Zooey since each of them have their hands full with supplies. Once they're all outside and on their way over to the bus Fredrick motions for both April and I to hurry up. Before leaving the house I stop and take a look around, knowing it will be my last.

"Come on Ryan, let's go!" Fredrick calls out to me, snapping me out of my trance.

I shake my head side to side before quickly remembering what is going on. As I walk by Fredrick on my way out of the house I slightly tip my head, thanking him for waiting. Once I'm back outside I quickly jog over to the bus where everyone else is waiting for me. Mark is the only person not on the bus beside Fredrick and I. He is preoccupied with emptying the gas cans into the bus. With a full tank of gas we won't have to worry about stopping for a few hours once back on the road.

Once back on the bus I return to my original seat right next to April. Just as I sit down Fredrick walks onto the bus with Mark following right behind him. Fredrick sits down right behind the driver's seat which is quickly filled by Mark. After Mark sits down Fredrick looks up and taps him on the shoulder before saying, "Alright Mark, follow the roads west!"

Mark nods and turns on the bus before shifting it into drive. We pull out of the development and onto the main road. As we're driving Mark keeps a close eye on the GPS while trying to navigate his way through the streets. Before we get back on the highway and continue west I stand up and walk over to Fredrick and Mark to discuss travel plans.

After sitting down next to Fredrick I say, "We should go south at this time of the year. Through Missouri, Kansas, Oklahoma, Texas, New Mexico, Arizona then up to Nevada. If we continue west then drop down we're going to be going through Denver, which is the mile high city, as they call it. This also means a lot of fucking snow. Our best bet is to go the extra two hundred miles and avoid the snow."

Fredrick arches an eyebrow and questions me, "How do you know all this?"

I respond to Fredrick with, "I drove to Iowa in December before in a huge snow storm. Twice. The second time I drove to Iowa I decided to continue by going to Vegas. It was spring time, maybe March or April. I took the southern route there. It was peaceful and not really that cold. On the way back from Vegas to Iowa I took the northern route. I hit a shit ton of snow right around Denver and had to reduce my speed dramatically to continue."

Fredrick nods his head while I am talking, understanding and agreeing with almost everything I am saying. When I am finished talking he leans up and taps Mark on the shoulder before saying, "Alright, you heard the man. Take the southern route."

"What should I plug into the GPS?" Mark asks.

"Oklahoma City.", I remark.

Mark leans over and starts to hit buttons on his GPS, figuring out the route he needs to take. In the mean time Mark slows down the bus, giving it time to calculate. It takes a few seconds before giving Mark a new route. Once the new route is calculated Mark is forced to turn around and continue south.

Fredrick looks to me and smiles before saying, "Good thinking."

I smile back at Fredrick and nod before standing up and returning to my seat, right next to April. Now that the rain cleared most of the snow off the roads Mark is actually able to do the speed limit. Everything outside has a light fog over it, accompanied with the freezing rain it makes for an overall miserable day. The rain is coming down pretty hard and the bus has a few leaks, letting the cold water seep inside through the roof. The wind isn't much better than the rain either, especially with how drafty the bus is.

With the cold drafts coming inside the bus and the freezing rain dripping on me my whole body starts to quiver from the cold. It seems like I am not the only one affected by the cold as well. Everyone on the bus is reaching for blankets from the house and any spare clothes lying around to cover themselves with. While Braydon and Troy are constantly blowing on their hands and rubbing them together, trying to warm up.

The day drags by; it is almost three in the afternoon by the time we make it to our first gas station of the day. After Mark pulls up to the gas station Fredrick, Troy and Braydon all run off the bus and secure the area before starting to pump the gas. April and I follow them off the bus to get some fresh air and stretch our legs. Everyone standing outside, aside from Fredrick is blowing on their hands and jogging in place to keep warm.

Fredrick is standing there, holding the nozzle with one hand and his M4 rifle with his other hand. He is perfectly relaxed and calm, not showing any signs of being cold. After Fredrick is done filling the bus with gas Troy hands him each of the gas cans for him to fill up. Unable to take the cold any more Braydon yells out, "I'm going back inside the bus. It's too fucking cold out here."

April and Troy watch as Braydon runs back onto the bus. The two of them pause and stare off at the bus for a minute before following right behind them, obviously unable to handle the cold either. Fredrick and I are now the only two still outside. He looks over to me and notices that I am shivering a bit but not totally effected by the cold. He pulls his nozzle out of the gas can and closes it up, sliding it over to me before placing the nozzle into another.

"Cold doesn't bother you either?" Fredrick asks me.

"Nah, not really, I usually wear shorts in shit like this. Unless it is windy I'm normally not affected." I respond.

"Good, I'm glad someone can still help me outside in this shit." Fredrick says before sliding another gas can over to me.

I pick up both cans that are in front of me and place them in the luggage compartment on the bus before walking back over to Fredrick.

"So you think this whole going south thing is going to help us dodge all the snow?" Fredrick asks, continuing his conversation with me.

"Positive, the further south we go the closer to the equator. It's going to be warmer just by default. Not to mention Texas, New Mexico and Arizona are all desert states."

"Good point. I'm just worried it will put us behind in time."

"Eh, it's about two hundred and forty miles extra, meaning if we travel at least sixty-five miles per hour we will arrive at least four hours later."

When Fredrick finishes filling up the final gas can and carries it over to the luggage compartment and slides them all in before closing it up. After loading all the gas cans back into the luggage compartment Fredrick places the nozzle back into the gas pump. Before stepping back onto the bus Fredrick looks around outside to see if he is forgetting anything. Without anything catching his eye he steps back onto the bus and taps Mark on the shoulder. Letting him know we're all finished up and ready to go.

Mark closes the doors to the outside and shifts the bus back into drive before pulling away from the gas station and continuing south through

Missouri. The further we get away from Iowa the amount of snow and slush on the roads starts to decrease. But the amount of puddles starts to increase. It seems the storm that gave Iowa a ton of snow just gave Missouri a ton of rain.

The further south we go through Missouri, the closer we get to Kansas City. The scenery throughout Missouri is quite boring. The only scenery for us to look at in Missouri is a bunch of farms followed by an occasional farm house. Of course in the large fields there are cows and other wildlife, which is a very good sign. If the zombies started to tear into the cows, than we would have a very serious problem. Let's just say, as of now, there still is no cow level. Before we get too close to Kansas City I stand up and walk to the front of the bus.

I sit down next to Fredrick before asking, "How are we on gas?"

"About a half tank, why?" Mark responds.

"We're getting close to Kansas City and I think it would be smart to stop outside the city for gas instead of going in and stopping in there."

"That's a good Point." Mark adds.

Mark and Fredrick keep their eyes out for a gas station while we drive closer to Kansas City. While looking out the passenger's side of the bus I spot a large green sign that says, "Final stop before Kansas City!" I bring it to Mark's attention as he switches lanes to get onto the deceleration ramp. When we pull into the gas station we notice that there is a truck sitting at the gas pump.

It is a Toyota Tundra, black in color with an extended cab and an extended bed. In the bed of the truck they have a large tarp over what seems to be many boxes. There is no one sitting inside the truck but you can tell the owner is around because the truck is still running. Mark pulls up to the gas station and goes very slow past the Toyota Tundra, letting Fredrick get a good look. Mark pulls up alongside the gas station and lets Fredrick, Troy and Braydon out to scout the area to see who the truck belongs to.

After Mark drops all of them off he circles around again to drop me off. After I'm out of the bus I run over to join Fredrick and everyone else. Mark continues around the building again but this time to park on the side. Once we're all ready Fredrick nods to us and we all run over to the truck. I run up to the back seat of the truck and look inside. Lying on the back seat is a green duffle bag that looks to be packed tight with guns. Next to that duffle bag in the backseat sits at least three cases of shotgun shells.

After looking into the back seat of the truck I turn around and point to my gun before nodding to Fredrick. This lets Fredrick know that the survivors inside are armed. After letting Fredrick know they are armed he motions for Troy and Braydon to follow him inside the rest station. While Fredrick and his team go inside I stay outside and watch the truck to make sure no one leaves in it. While I am waiting at the truck April comes running out of the bus and over to me with her pistol drawn, in case she sees anything.

"What is going on?" April says when she gets close to me.

"We think there might be survivors inside. Fredrick, Braydon and Troy are going to go check it out."

"If they're survivors why are we going in armed and taking so many precautions?" April asks.

"Remember the group of Scavengers we met? Who knows who these people are? We're taking every precaution necessary."

April nods to me, letting me know that she remembers the scavengers as a very un-fond memory. Almost two minutes have passed since Fredrick and his team entered the building. Since Fredrick entered the building I haven't heard a single noise from inside. This could mean something really good or something really bad. Another five minutes go by without any sign of Fredrick from inside the building.

"I'm giving him another two minutes... If he doesn't come out by then, I'm going in after him..." I say out loud.

Right as I finish my sentence I see Fredrick walk out of the gas station with two men I've never seen before. The man to the left of Fredrick is an older man at least in his late forties. He has a sturdy build, seems as if he worked out quite a bit. He also has boyishly blue eyes and brown hair. Almost his whole natural hair color is gone and has been taken over by gray.

The man is wearing baggy clothes and has another green duffle bag thrown over his shoulder. Judging by how long everyone took inside the duffle bag is probably filled up with supplies that they were collecting from inside. The other man to Fredrick's right is a younger man. He shares a striking resemblance to the older one, maybe even father and son.

The younger man is about the same height as the older one, right around six foot two. He looks to be in his late twenties, maybe even early thirties. He has light blond hair, short and spiked back. Around his forehead is a dark brown bandana which is helping to hold the hair off his forehead. He also has an unlit cigarette hanging from his mouth, something I'm usually disgusted by, but it fit his character nicely.

Fredrick and the two new survivors approach April and I before introducing themselves. The older man shakes my hand before saying, "Vincent". "Ryan", I reply back to him. Vincent now introduces himself to April while I move over to the younger man and shake his hand. "Cid", the younger man says to me. "Bob", I add jokingly.

"Didn't you just tell him your name was Ryan?" Cid asks.

"Yup, I was just seeing if you were paying attention!" I add with a laugh.

Cid gives me an odd look so I ask, "You guys coming with us?"

"Yeah, where are you heading?" Cid asks.

"Las Vegas." I say out loud.

"Vegas? It's nothing but a ghost town... We heard the east coast is uninfected though." Cid replies.

"We just came from the east coast. There is nothing but Runners and Night Stalkers." I add.

"Runners and Night Stalkers?" Vincent asks.

"Yeah, the ones that run and the ones that come out at night." I reply.

"Oh, didn't think they had names." Cid says.

"Yeah, I named them!" I exclaim.

"But really, you've been to Vegas?" I continue by asking Cid.

"Nah, but I heard from a friend that it's a ghost town."

I turn to Fredrick and say, "We still need to go there ourselves. We need to at least see. If not we can start a colony!"

Cid Interrupts, "I'm down for going where ever, as long as we don't go back to Kansas City."

"What is in Kansas City?" I ask.

"Death.", Cid replies with an ominous tone.

Cid continues by saying, "We were all at the hospital in town and then we got attacked. Vincent and I are the only survivors. Well, as far as we know."

"Would it be safe to even just drive through?" I ask.

"Maybe, but this highway will take you right past the hospital and if they stick around in a specific area for awhile... Trust me you don't want to go there." Cid says.

"We're full up on gas, we can drive right by without stopping and it isn't even night time. So the worst threat won't even be out."

"Alright, we better get a move on then before night." Cid adds.

Cid turns to Fredrick behind him and says, "Fredrick is your name right?"

"Yeah.", Fredrick responds.

"Can you and your guys help us with the guns and ammo in the backseat? Shits' heavy."

We all walk over to the truck and begin to unload everything out of it. Fredrick opens the back door of the truck and grabs the boxes of shotgun shells out of the backseat. After Fredrick is out of the way Troy reaches into the backseat and grabs the duffle bag full of guns that were sitting there. Everyone else that isn't holding something grabs as many of the boxes out of the back of the truck they can hold.

In the mean time Vincent turns the key in the truck's ignition to turn it off. After the truck is off he places the keys down onto the front seat of the truck and closes the door. He leaves the keys in the truck in case any more survivors come along and need it. Once we have all the supplies from the truck we all work our way back to the bus where Mark and Zooey are both waiting.

As we all return to the bus Cid and Vincent introduce themselves to Mark and Zooey. Back on the bus I let Mark know about Kansas City. I also tell Mark that night fall is coming soon, so now would be a good time to get back onto the road. After we're all back on the bus and we've offloaded all the supplies Mark stands up and says, "One last thing here. First, I'm thirsty. Second, we still need gas."

Mark sits back down as I reach for the bottle of water that is sitting next to me. Before Mark even puts the bus into drive I chuck the bottle of water in my hand up at him. It slams into the windshield in front of him and causes Mark to jump. He lets go of the steering wheel and flails his arms in front of him. Everyone on the bus breaks into laughter, except for Mark. Mark looks back to us and says, "ha, ha, ha, ha..." in a very sarcastic tone.

As we're all still laughing Mark circles around the rest station again before parking in front of a diesel pump. Once we're at the diesel pump Fredrick and Troy get out of the bus to fill the tank up. Since we've been at the gas station awhile there is no reason for anyone else to get out since we won't need the extra protection.

While Fredrick and Troy are outside I turn to ask Cid, "So you really heard Vegas was a ghost town?"

"Yeah, everything there is dead or undead." Cid replies.

"Where are you from?"

"Dallas Texas."

"What you doing up here?"

"We were on our way to the east coast, we heard it wasn't infected."

"You know this originated in Delaware, right?"

"Delaware?" Cid asks in a shocked voice.

"Yup, I'm surprised it moved to the west coast so fast." I reply.

"Yeah, I am too."

Once Fredrick and Troy are done filling the buses gas tank they walk back on board. As Fredrick passed by Mark he taps him on the shoulder, letting him know we're good to go. Mark shifts the bus back into drive before pulling back out onto the highway and continuing southwest towards Kansas City.

The Mile Markers keep us up to date on how close we are getting to the city. As we get closer to the city I can't help but worry that Cid is right and we should go around it. When we pass Mile Marker five the tension rises. Mark increases in speed up to about sixty five, making sure almost nothing can stop us or catch us.

As we start to enter Kansas City, Cid looks out the windows on the right hand side of the bus, waiting to see what still surrounds the hospital. Everyone follows Cid's example and gathers on the right hand side of the bus, ready to see what he was talking about. As we continue another few miles up the road Mark speeds up even more, now pushing seventy.

"Alright, it's coming up in about a mile." Cid calls out to everyone on the bus.

As we continue driving up the highway Mark starts to come up on a large bend ahead. As we approach the large bend Cid looks back to everyone and says, "Alright, its right around this bend on the right hand side."

I hover around the right side of the bus and watch out the window as Mark rounds the corner. As we round the corner everyone stares out the window at the hospital on the side of the road. Almost every window in the five story building is shattered; there are claw marks and streaks of blood that can be seen along the sides of the building and on the pavement below.

There are bodies hanging out the windows of the hospital, harmlessly flailing in the wind. Outside the front doors of the hospital it is impossible to see the pavement because of the blood and bodies that litter the ground.

The bodies on the ground look to be from both zombies and survivors, anyone who was at the hospital during the time of the attack. Outside the hospital I notice that there are some zombies roaming around. It is almost like they are oblivious to anything around them.

As we drive by the hospital the Runners throw their heads up and look at the bus. Without any hesitation they stop what they are doing and chase after the bus. They have their arms back and at their sides as they run full speed towards the bus. Their mouths are wide open with drool gushing out of them as they snarl and bite at the air. They must know that there is food for them on the bus.

Luckily our bus is moving at close to seventy miles an hour and they are topping out at around ten. This makes it almost impossible for the Runners to catch up to us. As we gain distance on the Runners everyone looks back and laughs at them. Some of us even taunt them by waving goodbye to them. As the hospital is now barely visible out of the back window of the bus we can all breathe a sigh of relief.

Well after the hospital and the Runners are out of our sight we all start to return to our seats, glad that the little scare is all over. After I return to my seat I look out the window and up into the sky. The sun is starting to set and it is more beautiful than ever. The dark oranges in the sky and the light reds make this a perfect sunset.

Without a drop of pollution in the sky above us, it is just simply beautiful. There have been no factories pumping out their noxious fumes into the sky for almost a week now. Along with very few cars running the skies are almost untouched by any form of pollution. Giving us the cleanest air we've breathed in a long time as well as the best sunsets and sun rises ever imaginable.

Over the next twenty minutes everyone on the bus admires the sunset, basking in its beauty until it is gone. Now that the darkness is upon us everyone gets comfortable in their seats before tilting their head back and falling asleep. It takes me a lot longer than usual to fall asleep tonight. I continually toss and turn for almost an hour, every time I get close to sleep all I can think about is everyone I've ever known being dead. Eventually I am able to clear my mind long enough to fall asleep.

"Holy shit.", "What the fuck was that?!"

Was the first thing I asked myself after being woken up by the loudest gunshot I have ever heard. The gunshot came from outside of the bus and was so loud and powerful I could hear all the windows of the bus shake. My eyes are as wide as saucers as I look around the bus and notice that no one is on board.

A few seconds after hearing the gunshot outside I hear a round of applause followed by many cheers and praise. Confused at first, I look out the window and see everyone standing around Fredrick. Fredrick is holding the large fifty caliber sniper rifle that he took from the gun shop the other day. I stand up and pound the window of the bus to try and get everyone's attention outside but they all cover their ears as Fredrick prepares to fire another shot.

Fredrick fires another shot, this one startles me so much that it knocks me off my feet. I tumble to the ground and land with a loud crash. Unlike the last shot, instead of praise and applause I can hear everyone asking each other, "Did you hear that?"

"What was that?"

"Let's go look!"

Everyone reaches for their guns and runs over to the bus. With my head still hurting from the fall, I wait for someone to come onto the bus before yelling doesn't shoot! Troy is the first one to walk on the bus. The second Troy walks on the bus he points his gun at me, not realizing who it is at first. Once Troy realizes who it is he lowers his weapon as I raise my hand to give him the middle finger. Troy laughs before motioning to everyone else behind him that it is safe. Troy walks over to me and gives me a helping hand up from the ground.

"What is going on?" I ask as he is helping me up.

Braydon interjects by saying, "The gas station up the road has zombies all over it. So instead of risking anything we figured we would kill them from afar."

"Interesting..." I reply.

After I stand up and brush myself off I follow everyone back outside where Fredrick gets into position again and lines up another zombie. As Fredrick prepares for another shot we all cover our ears and look towards the gas station. After Fredrick fires we all uncover our ears and stare off into the distance. A very small figure almost a mile away can be seen exploding with blood flying everywhere.

"Oh shit!" I exclaim, having never experienced anything like that before.

"I know! It is awesome isn't it?" Braydon asks.

"Ears.", Fredrick says.

Everyone quickly covers their ears again as Fredrick takes another shot. After the shot is fired everyone stares at the zombie in the open and watches the bullet as it rips the zombie's torso in two. After the bullet hits the zombie we all jump around like children on Christmas morning. Who knew that something so serious would be so much fun!

"Ears.", Fredrick says again, interrupting our cheers.

When Fredrick speaks we all stop jumping around and cover our ears again, waiting for the next shot. After we hear the loud gunshot we all stare off at the gas station, much like before. Only this time we don't see any body parts flying in the air or a tidal wave of red coming from one of the zombies.

"Did you miss?" I ask Fredrick.

"Yeah. There are only six more of them. Keep your ears covered I'm going to speed this up.", Fredrick says.

After he finishes talking, Fredrick slides a fresh clip of ammo into his sniper rifle before looking down the scope again. Everyone takes Fredrick's advice and covers their ears. Over the next minute the loud sound of his fifty caliber erupts again and again and again. Each time Fredrick fires he hits a zombie in the distance, giving us a gruesome spectacle of body parts and blood flying through the air.

After killing the sixth and final zombie Fredrick breaks away from his scope and starts to stand up. He takes the clip out of the gun and empties the chamber before putting the rifle around his shoulder and walking back over towards the bus. Once Fredrick is done shooting the zombies we follow him onto the bus. Mark takes his usual seat behind the steering wheel before starting up the bus. With everyone back on board we pull away from our lookout area and drive over to the gas station. On the drive over to the gas station I take a look around outside and realize that it is early morning. Which means I finally got my first full night's sleep in days.

"What state are we in?" I ask April.

"We are in the southern part of Kansas, almost in Oklahoma." She responds.

"What? Already? Holy shit I slept awhile."

"Yeah you were out all night. Braydon wanted to draw faces on you but we couldn't find a permanent marker at the gas station.", April says while giggling.

"Praise the lord." I remark sarcastically.

When we arrive at the gas station, Fredrick, Troy, Braydon and I all get off the bus to help fill it up. Fredrick puts Troy and I on look out duty while him and Braydon pump the gas. We didn't stay very long at this gas station because of the blood bath we caused just moments ago. After we finish pumping the gas we toss the nozzle onto the ground and run back onto the bus. Once we're all back inside the bus we pull away from the gas station and back onto the Highway. Mark gets bored while driving and starts to play with the dials on the radio as we are driving.

"Hey look!" I shout out while pointing at a large sign in the distance.

As we all look out the windows we can see that the large sign that reads: "Welcome to Oklahoma!" After reading the sign a large smile comes across everyone's face, now we are only states away from our destination. The chatter starts to pick up on the bus as we start driving through Oklahoma, over the next few minutes you can hear the "We're not in Kansas anymore..." joke muttered dozens of times, most of which by me. Before I'm done joking around Mark interrupts my fun by yelling into the back of the bus.

"Shut up! Everyone shut up! Listen!" He screams out loud in an overly excited voice.

Mark turns the radio up to full volume and we all go silent and listen. Under the static we can hear a song playing. None of us are able to make out the song that is playing but we can definitely hear something there. As time goes on I continue to listen to the sound but it is almost impossible to distinguish what it is.

"Mark what FM frequency is this?" I shout up to the front of the bus.

"100.5", Mark responds.

"That is a radio station in Oklahoma City..."

"How do you know that?" April asks.

"Lots of useless knowledge up in my head... Lots..."

I stand up and walk over to Mark before saying, "Oklahoma City is in the center of Oklahoma. Someone must be at the radio station. Take us there."

Mark turns to Fredrick and awaits his approval. Before nodding to Mark Fredrick looks over to me and asks, "If there someone is at the radio station and alive, wanting to be saved, why would they playing music and not asking for help?"

"Good question, I thought of that too. They may have a broken microphone?" I reply.

"Hmm..." Fredrick says while rubbing his chin.

"We got plenty of time to think about it. We're still a few hours away from Oklahoma City. Sit on the idea and decide in an hour or two." I say to Fredrick, hoping he will make the right choice.

As we continue driving south, closer and closer to Oklahoma City we are able to start making out the song that is being played on the radio. Almost another thirty minutes go by with all of us trying to decipher the static we're hearing until finally one part of the song comes in clear

"Please stay, until I'm gone.
I'm here hold on."

After that little bit of the song is played it goes back to static without any other parts of it able to be recognized... I stare at the bus seat in front of me running hundreds of songs through my head until it finally hits me.

"They need our help!" I stand up and yell out loud.

Fredrick turns to me and says, "What are you talking about?"

"The song! The song is a message!" I say in an excited voice.

Everyone on the bus stares at me as if I have lost my mind. I start to wave my hands in the air, as my excitement level goes through the roof. I continue by saying, "*Blink 182*? Anyone? The band?"

Everyone on the bus shakes their head side to side, letting me know they have no idea what I'm talking about. I spin around and look to everyone on the bus, shocked that they never heard of the band I am talking about.

"Oh come on! It's like the best band ever!" I yell out loud.

"Oh yeah, now I remember! They did *All the Small Things* right?" April asks.

"YES!" I shout out, no longer able to control my excitement

"Can you just cut to the chase?" Fredrick asks, getting frustrated with my childish games

I clear my throat and place my left hand on my chest while raising my right into the air, preparing to sing. I start to sing to everyone using a falsetto.

"Come here; please hold my hand for now,
Help me, I'm scared please show me how,
To fight this, God has a master plan,
And I guess, I am in his demand."

Before starting to sing the verse I increase the pitch in my voice and point to Fredrick and smirk for the next part of the song,

"Please save me, This time I cannot run,
And I'll see, you when this is done."

When I stop singing I look to Fredrick and wait for his response. He looks back at me clueless, having no idea what I am trying to get at. Everyone else on the bus gives me a blank stare as well. While looking around the bus I start to get frustrated that no one else understands what I am trying to get at. So I raise my hands in the air and yell out loud the part of the song that I think will get their attention.

"Come here; please hold my hand for now,
Help me...
Please save me, This time I cannot run?"

Without anyone showing me signs of understanding I start to get frustrated before asking, "Seriously, no one gets this?"

"It's just a song dude..." Braydon responds.

"It's just a song that says, please save me and help Me.", I remark.

"We will check it out, but I don't think your song has anything to do with It.", Fredrick adds.

Without anyone else seeing what I do in the song I sit back down next to April and stare out the window, frustrated that no one believes me. As we get closer to Oklahoma City the song starts coming in clear and it can be heard playing on repeat. April looks over at me and can tell that I am still highly frustrated so she leans over and whispers into my ear, "I think you're right with the song"

She is obviously lying but at least she is trying to cheer me up. While we're still driving towards Oklahoma City the radio cuts out and goes silent. It stays silent for a few seconds before running a commercial advertising the radio station,

"Weekday mornings here at *100.5 KATT radio...*"
The radio station cuts out again before going back to a part of the song,
"Please save me"
A little bit of static can be heard followed by,
"Email us or write us at P.O box,
388 Commercial Street
73102, West Oklahoma City"
It cuts out again before continuing with the song,
"Come here, please hold my hand for now, Help me..."

Everyone turns and looks at me, already knowing what is about to come. Within seconds after hearing the radio I jump out of my seat and around the bus. I point to everyone as I am jumping around and laughing at them all while saying, "I fucking told you so!" Before I am done jumping around the song comes back onto the radio and plays in its entirety.

Fredrick looks to me and says, "Alright, I hate to admit it but... I'll give you this one. You were right."

Fredrick looks up at Mark and says, "Mark, take us to 388 Commercial Street."

Mark nods to Fredrick before typing in the new destination on the GPS. It calculates us at about twenty six miles away from the radio station. We spend the whole twenty six miles suiting up and discussing evacuation plans for getting any survivors out of the radio station that may be in there.

It doesn't take too long for Mark to get us within eye site of the large building. We stop on an overpass near the building to get a bird's eye view of the area. Right outside the radio station there is a pack of zombies pounding on the front doors. Up in the window of the fourth floor a large foam board is visible that has, "Please save me" written on it.

"This is too risky." Fredrick says.

"What are you talking about?" I ask.

"He says, please save me, implying it is only him. God knows how many zombies and Runners are down there." Fredrick replies.

"We can't just leave him..." April starts to say before Braydon interrupts us.

"Look! Look!" Braydon yells out.

When we look to Braydon we see that he is pointing up to the window with the large foam poster board in it. When we all look up to the room we notice at least five survivors that are all waving down to us on the highway, trying to get our attention.

I look over to Fredrick and ask, "Does that make it worth it?"

"Yes, yes it does." he replies before saying, "Round up boys, we're going in."

Every one of us has a rifle or shotgun and at least two side arms. Thanks to Cid and Vincent's duffle bag that we brought along with us, there are plenty of guns to go around. Once everyone is armed we start the short trek over towards the radio station. All of us besides Mark and Zooey head over to the radio station. Those two decided to stay back to watch the bus in our absence.

We continue towards the radio station until we are about two blocks away. We are now the perfect distance away from the zombies to take them out easily and safely. Once we're close enough to the radio station I can see that there are at least thirty to forty zombies pounding on the front doors. None of them have even noticed that we're behind them yet. Fredrick has us all aim at them and start shooting, making sure to kill all of them before we get close.

As we open fire the zombies start dropping like flies. Almost half of them are dead before they even realize what is going on. Once they do finally spot all of us they start to limp towards us, with only about ten of them left alive. The sound of gunfire echoes between buildings as we are all lined up behind a car shooting at the zombies. By the time all the zombies are dead we've all used at least a half clip of ammo. Now with all the zombies dead we have a clear approach up to the radio station.

All of us start to run up towards the radio station, checking every side street and alleyway, not taking any chances. As we reach the front doors of the radio station Fredrick looks around inside before trying to open the front doors. After pulling on the handle to each door he turns around and says, "Locked."

After letting us all know the door was locked Fredrick backs up and points his gun at the door. Before Fredrick fires at the door everyone turns their head away to protect themselves from the shrapnel. Finally Fredrick fires his gun, shattering the handle on the door and the lock that was keeping us outside. With the door now unlocked Fredrick kicks it open and runs inside, all of us following closely behind. Once inside the building I notice that their power is still on, meaning we don't have to depend on our flashlights for light.

As we walk through the lobby of the radio station we are taken off guard by how normal everything looks. There is nothing out of place, nothing is damaged and there is not a drop of blood anywhere. The survivors have apparently done a good job keeping the Zombies on the outside. On the other side of the lobby Fredrick hits the call button on the elevator but nothing lights up. He lets out a sigh before motioning for us to follow him over to the stairwell. Fredrick opens the stairwell door and looks around inside before stepping in. After getting a good look around inside he walks into the stairwell and starts heading up.

We hastily make our way up the stairs until we reach the fourth floor where Fredrick is waiting for us. When we all reach the fourth floor Fredrick lets us catch our breath before giving us a countdown with his hands. When Fredrick reaches one he pulls open the door and exposes the hallway leading to the survivor's room. Instead of entering the room Fredrick freezes up, unable to believe his eyes.

Compared to downstairs, this hallway was fucked up. There are claw marks along the walls and the floor. The claw marks on the walls are easily distinguishable to be a Night Stalkers. The claw marks along the floor are much different and look to be human. It appears that someone was dragged along the floor for the whole length of the hallway before being torn to pieces at the end of it.

There are body parts littering the hallway, emitting a horrible stench and are equally as horrifying just to look at. There are forearms with bite marks so deep that you can see the bone traveling through. Feet are left lying around with the bone sticking out of them, without any leg attached. Entrails are scattered throughout the hall, decorating the walls and floors like a loose spindle of yarn.

Unable to handle the gruesome sight in the hallway, April turns away from the room and throws up over the railing of the stairwell. I pat her on the back to comfort her and let her know there is nothing to be embarrassed about.

"Everyone reload. We're going to need It.", Fredrick says.

Even though my clip is only half empty I pull it out and stick it in my back pocket before slipping a new one in. After we all finish reloading we look to Fredrick and nod, letting him know that we're ready to enter the hallway.

"We're going to enter on my mark." Fredrick says out loud.

"Three..." Fredrick says as the tension in the room immediately rising.

"Two..." He continues as I squeeze my gun much harder.

"One!"

Fredrick yells out before rushing into the room. Without any hesitation Troy and Braydon follow right behind him with Cid and Vincent bringing up the rear. I decide to stay in the stairwell with April and wait for her to feel a bit better. "It's ok, don't feel embarrassed." I say to April while continually patting her on the back.

April does a half ass nod to me, knowing she shouldn't feel embarrassed but she still does. While I am standing in the stairwell with April I hear a gunshot coming from the opposite end of the hallway. I quickly spin around and look down the hallway but am unable to see anyone at the other end. While I am still looking down the hallway the gunshot is followed by a few more, causing me to worry.

I tap April on the back and say, "Wait here, I'm going in". Without waiting for a response I rush into the hallway. I keep my head plastered against the scope on my gun, ready to fire at anything I see that isn't human. I step out further into the hallway and point my gun down all three junction hallways, frantically looking for Fredrick and everyone else.

"Fredrick!" I yell out, hoping for a response.

My call out for help to Fredrick was like signing my death warrant. Runners start to pour out the hallways on either side of me. By the time they round the corners of their hallways they are within five feet of me, just within lunging distance. I open fire on the Runners, holding the trigger down in the gun and frantically pointing it where ever I see a Runner. While squeezing the trigger I am caught in a long drawn out scream with Fredrick's name.

Time seems to slow down as the sound of my voice is being muffled by the sound of my gun. The only two things I can see are the faces of Runners. All bloodied and drooling with their eyes blood shot and the empty bullet casings. They're flying out of my gun and lightly bouncing off the walls before rolling along the ground. I continue to pray that Fredrick can hear my screams and come to help me as more and more Runners start to flood into the hallway from around the corners. I start to sweat profusely and squeeze my gun so hard that my fingers begin to hurt.

Just as I think it is all over April grabs the back of my suit before pulling me back into the stairwell. Once I am back in the stairwell April slams the door shut in front of me. Right as the door closes Runners start pounding on it, wanting to get inside and tear me apart. Emotions fill up inside of me, knowing that Fredrick, Troy, Braydon, Cid and Vincent are all still out there. April places her hand on my shoulder and tries to comfort me but I refuse and shrug it off. I reload my gun and point it eye level at the door and fire in small bursts. Every time I finish a burst the pounding stops briefly until another Runner can take its place

This process continues until I use all the bullets in my magazine. When I run out ammo I reach into my back pocket and grab another clip. I slide the clip into my gun but instead of firing I slam my gun against the door and collapse against it.

"God dammit! They're dead!" I scream at the top of my lungs.

Out of frustration I start banging the door with my gun, each swing forming a massive dent in the door. Right before I give up hope I hear the radio kick on in the stairwell. I look up at the megaphone in the corner of the stairwell as a very familiar song fills my ears. I light up with excitement as April continues to ask me, "What? What is it?"

"It's Dammit!" I exclaim jumping around with joy.

I turn to April and ask, "You know what this means right?!"

"They're Alive!!" I scream at her before placing both my hands on her shoulders and dancing around with her.

"How do you know that from just one song?" April asks me, confused.

"Context clues... context clues miss M.I.T. Not only did I say *Blink 182* was my favorite band on the bus, but the song goes with it!" I say to her.

April looks at me, giving me the same confused face that she did on the bus. I start to sing along with the song as both of us now are completely ignoring the Runners that are pounding on the door next to us.

"And it's happened once again,
I'll turn to a friend,
Someone that understands, sees through the master plan,
When everyone is gone, I've been here for too long,
To face this one my own, Well I guess this is growing up."

April rolls her eyes at me, finding my theory to be silly and childish, just like everyone did on the bus. I back away from the door and bring my gun up to eye level before shooting any Runners on the other side. The song playing in the background gives me the motivation and adrenaline rush that I need to push forward. When I no longer hear any more Runners in the hallway I turn the handle on the door and try to open it.

But too many bodies are blocking the door from opening and even with a few good shoves I am unable to open it. After shoving the door I attempt to kick it, hoping to maybe move some of the bodies, but still no luck. Without any other options I back away from the door and shove April behind me. I take a deep breath before aiming my gun at the top hinge of the door and firing.

The Bullet I fired blasts the hinge off on the door but also ricochets off into the stairwell. April and I both dance around in the area, keeping constant motion to try and dodge the bullet. Once the bullet is done bouncing around in the stairwell I have April stand directly behind me, so if anything happens I'll be the one taking the bullet. With April safely behind me I am at the second hinge and fire, causing the hinge to fly off

2012: The Zombie Apocalypse

the door. The second the hinge is off the door two Runners smash through and into the stairwell.

As they make their way into the stairwell they trip and fall over the bodies of the other Runners. The two Runners collapse to the ground and flap around like fish on land, trying to get back up on their feet. With both of them immobilized on the ground I carefully aim at each of their heads and fire, killing them instantly. After they're both dead I run up the stairs and back into the hallway. Once I am back in the hallway I turn to the right and spot a Runner coming straight towards me. The second his blood ridden face gets in the center of my scope I pull the trigger causing a red mist to come out of the back of his head.

After killing the Runner I spin around to check the left hallway only to see two more Runners coming straight at me. I fire off two more shots at them, dropping them to the ground. Right after they both fall to the ground April comes out of the stairwell and fires a single shot straight down the hall, killing a Runner that had me in his sights. April starts down the hallway where she killed the Runner just seconds ago but I get ahead of her and push her behind me. Feeling that the emergency lighting in the hallway isn't good enough I decide to turn the flashlight on that is taped to the side of my rifle.

As we continue down the hall we're forced to step over the bodies of all the dead Runners. I continue through the hall very slowly, double checking each corpse to see if it is indeed dead. My face stays plastered against the top of my gun the whole time, my right eye staring down the scope, ready to shoot anything that gets inside my crosshairs. When I reach the end of the hallway I stop at the three way intersection and look both ways.

"Clear.", I say out loud to April before motioning for her to follow me.

I look into both hallways before picking the one that goes right. The decision was an easy one, I have this theory that right is always the right way. The hallway to the right is covered in blood, still fresh and dripping off the walls. A very good sign that Fredrick and everyone else have been here recently. At the end of the hallway I round the corner and continue left, down the new hallway. The new hallway is a long straight and narrow hallway with no doors on either side of it and much like the hallway before it; this one is covered in blood as well.

At the end of the hallway I can see a door that has light shining all around it, meaning there must be a large window on the other end. Based on our current progression through the building this must me the room that the survivors are trapped in. About halfway down the hallway April and I hear a faint snarl from behind us. After hearing the snarl I spin around and shine my light in the direction we came from. There is a Runner back at the end of the hallway with his arms down at his sides and his fingers curled to form the shape of a claw.

The Runner is standing in the dead center of the hallway and is panting heavily. The Runner and I both stare at each other for a few seconds without either of us making a single move. After a few more seconds the Runner throws his hands back and snarls at April and I before charging towards us. April raises her gun and aims it at the Runners head before firing; her shot was a direct hit. Blood sprays out from behind the Runners as his body slides across the ground towards us.

After April fires the shot the sound of growls and moans erupt from the hallway that we came from. Before we even have a chance to gather ourselves Runners start to pour around the corner and into our hallway. As the Runners come pouring around the corner they come straight towards us, not stopping for anything. April and I start to back up towards the room with the light as we open fire on the Runners that are coming around the corner.

April stops shooting and backing up for a second as she needs to reload her pistol. While April is reloading I try and hold the Runners off but too many of them are coming around the corner and into the hallway. I reach out and grab the back of April's suit with my free hand while using my other hand to grip my gun and fire at any Runners coming up the hallway. With April now in hand I continue to back up through the hallway.

After April finishes reloading she shrugs off my hand and starts to back up with me while shooting any Runners that come up the hall after us. When we reach the door at the back end of the hall I turn the knob and realize that it is locked. My heart drops into my chest as I kick the door a few times, praying that it busts open. On my third kick the door swings open, causing me to stumble backwards. Fredrick leans out of the room and grabs April and I by the back of our suits before pulling us into the room.

He fires a few shots into the hall as April and I fall onto the floor in the room. Troy slams the door in front of April and I while Braydon, Cid and Vincent slide the Radio Equipment that was barricading the door back over it. After the door is secure Fredrick turns around to April and I who are still lying on the floor and says,

"So glad you could join us!"

CHAPTER 8 - THE FINAL STRETCH

"I thought you were dead!" I yell out to Fredrick. "And then you played Blink and I knew you were alive!" I quickly add.

"Yeah, I figured I'd play Blink because you're the only idiot that would think it means we need help." Fredrick says while laughing at me.

Everyone in the room laughs with Fredrick while I pull myself up onto my feet and help April up behind me. Once I'm up I am able to take a look around the room. It is a small room with some radio equipment and only one door in and out, the same door that we entered from. The room is on the corner of the building, two of the walls are large glass windows and the other two are walls. One of the windows gives us a perfectly visual of our bus and the other gives us a look at the highway we came to the radio station from.

The windows cover the whole wall and look to be made out of some sort of thick tempered glass. After I am done examining the room I turn back to Fredrick, who still has everyone laughing and giggling about my theory with the songs. As I go to say something to Fredrick I realize that there are six new faces in the room. "Oh! How rude of me!" I exclaim. I walk over to the first survivor and extend my hand to him.

"Hello, I'm Ryan." I say out loud.

"Ben" the man responds.

The man has short black hair which is gelled and spiked. He is about five foot nine and one hundred and eighty pounds. A little on the pudgy side for his height but give the man some credit, he works on his ass in a radio station all day. Ben has a few piercings going down his ear, all just plain silver hoops. He also has bright green eyes, which stick out like a sore thumb on his face since they don't match it at all.

Ben is wearing a black *Lamb of God* T-shirt with a pair of baggy tan Cargo pants. Based on Ben's general appearance and his posture I'd say he is a little bit of a poser. Since he doesn't look like the hardcore Death Metal type. After I've finished my introductions with Ben I turn to shake another man's hand.

"Hello, my name is Ryan."

"I'm Brad."

Brad stands tall at about six foot two and has long dirty blond hair, down past his shoulders. Brad has a full beard, with side burns to go with it, and small gold gauges in his ear. He looks to weigh about two forty, if I had to guess almost all of his weight is muscle.

When Brad introduced himself to me I noticed that he has an extremely deep voice, one that would put Michael Clark Duncan's to shame. Brad is wearing a baggy black shirt as well as a pair of baggy ripped up jeans. You can tell by the way he dresses himself he doesn't care what people think about him. While still shaking Brad's hand I chuckle a bit, unable to resist asking him a question.

"How many people call you the white Michael Clark Duncan?"

Brad laughs out loud, now topping my list for weirdest laughs I've ever heard. After he is done laughing he answers me with, "You're the first... But that's funny!" I give Brad a half assed smile while still chuckling at my own joke. After saying goodbye to Brad, I walk over to the next survivor and shake her hand.

"Hello, my name is Ryan." I say to her while trying to hold in any remaining laughter from my joke with Brad.

"Stephanie.", she responds, smiling and chuckling from my joke earlier.

Stephanie is rather short, right around five foot six. She looks to weigh about one hundred and twenty pounds and has the same type of figure as April. Stephanie looks to be in her late twenties and has darker hair, coming down a little bit past her shoulders. Stephanie gives me the impression that she is more of a normal girl. She isn't dressed to impress or displaying any overly arrogant attitude. Stephanie also has dark blue eyes, almost the same exact color of the ocean.

She wears very little jewelry, only a few earrings and a ring. The ring is located on her Ring Finger and is a beautiful large emerald. Based on first impressions Stephanie seems to be a bit close to Brad in the room. She always hangs around him and often turns to him for comfort. After I finish my introductions with Stephanie I turn to the other female survivor in the room before extending my hand.

"Ryan."

"Emily."

Emily has long bleached blond hair, coming down to her shoulders. She looks to be the youngest of the survivors, probably just turned eighteen not too long ago. Emily has Freckles that cover her cheeks as well as a little bit of acne on her forehead. Her eye color stands out the most on her face though. Her eyes are dark green, almost the same color of a pine tree needle.

Emily is the shortest survivor here as well, looking to be about five foot two and weighing right around one hundred pounds. Emily is rather flat chested and seems to be very embarrassed by it. This perfectly explains why she is wearing a sweat shirt in such a well heated room. She is also wearing a pair of short-shorts, the teenager's way of saying "Hey! Look at my ass!" After my introduction with Emily I turn to the first African American survivor I've seen in over two thousand miles. I extend my hand out to him and say,

"Ryan"

"George."

George is a very tall and thin man. He looks to be in his late thirties, is about six foot four and roughly a hundred and eighty pounds. He is a very well groomed man, there isn't a scrap of facial hair on his face and is also completely bald. George isn't naturally bald, but bald by choice, based on the small hairs growing out of his head. George has dark brown eyes, almost perfectly matching his skin color.

George is wearing a white buttoned up T-shirt accompanied with a tie and a pair of black dress pants. In his right hand he has a tuxedo shirt wrapped up which looks to be about his size. Giving me the impression that George was probably here for an interview when the zombie disaster happened. After shaking George's hand I turn to the final survivor. He is an older man, looking to be in his late forties maybe even early fifties. The older man is sitting on the ground with his back to a desk. He has a bandage wrapped around his arm, giving me the impression he was injured recently.

I extend my hand slowly and carefully to him and say, "Hello, I'm Ryan."

He grabs a hold of my hand and says, "Lewis."

Lewis has a full head of hair but almost all of it has gone gray, thanks to his age. His skin seems to be a little pale, possibly becoming sick from an infected wound or from the loss of blood. Aside from the wound Lewis seems to be a healthy older man. He looks to be about two hundred pounds and six feet tall.

Lewis has the same outfit as George. However he portrays himself more as a CEO and not someone new that is looking for employment. After I finish shaking Lewis's hand I tilt my head up and ask him, "How did you hurt yourself?"

Lewis looks at me, his hands shaking a bit from the blood loss, "One of those damned things bit me!"

My face goes pale when Lewis tells me what caused his injury. I briefly look away from Lewis and try to wipe the fear off of my face before turning back to him. I ask Lewis again, hoping I misheard him the first time, "Did you say.... b-bitten?"

"Yeah! One of those sons of bitches snuck up on me and bit me right in my arm!" He says again.

I back away from Lewis and pull out my gun before pointing it at him. I gently put my finger over the trigger as Fredrick, Braydon, April and Troy all turn away. Lewis' eyes light up with fear as he yells out, "What the fuck do you think you're doing?"

"You've been bitten. You're becoming one of them." I say.

"You can't just kill me in cold blood!" Lewis exclaims.

Emily interrupts us, "He is right! You can't just kill him! We don't even know if there is a cure!"

"There is a cure. It's sitting in the chamber of my gun." I add.

Emily starts to walk over to Lewis as I spin my gun and point it at her, causing her to stop dead in her tracks, "I'll fucking shoot you too." I remark.

"I thought you were coming here to help us! Not kill us!" Stephanie says before putting her arm around Brad.

"We did. What do you think I'm doing now? He is going to turn and kill someone!" I yell out.

"We don't know that!" Emily says.

"Fredrick?" I ask wanting his approval.

Fredrick sighs before responding, "Bind his legs and hands. It's only a matter of time before he turns and I'm not going to let him hurt anyone. Troy, Braydon, Use the straps from your guns to tie him up."

Troy and Braydon nod to Fredrick before escorting Lewis over to a corner of the room. They bind Lewis' arms and legs so if he turns, when he turns, he won't be able to hurt anyone. While Troy and Braydon are binding Lewis, Brad yells to us, "This isn't right! I want you guys to leave, now!"

"Yeah!" Ben adds.

"We're stuck here together whether you like it or not!" Fredrick says.

"Fuck this, I'm leaving! I'd be safer out there with those *things* then in here." George remarks.

George starts to walk over to the door leading out back into the hallway but Fredrick intercepts him and slams him against the wall. Fredrick's pins George against the wall by pressing his elbow up against George's neck.

"You even get near that door and I will put a fucking bullet right into your head." Fredrick says to George through his teeth.

Fredrick uses his free hand to roughly poke George's temple, showing him where the bullet will go. Right after Fredrick slams George to the wall; Ben walks over to the door and starts to move the Radio Equipment that is barricading it out of the way. Before Ben is even able to move the Radio Equipment out of the way I grab him and throw him into the corner.

Fredrick looks over at the fight between Ben and me, taking his eyes off George for no longer then a few seconds. While he is distracted George head butts him, knocking Fredrick back and disorienting him. While Fredrick is stunned George grabs Fredrick's side arm and points it directly at me. Troy just finished tying up Lewis when he looks up and sees that George has a gun pointed at me. Without hesitation Troy raises his gun and shoots George, hitting him in the chest, causing him to collapse to the ground.

As I hear the gunshot in the room I turn to look at George, not even aware he had a gun pointed at me in the first place. Ben is still lying on the ground right below me, with my hand tightly gripping his neck. When I look at George he is already on the ground with both of his hands grasping his chest. Blood is now soaking his shirt and he is starting to cough up blood. You can tell that George is in excruciating pain as he grips his chest, savoring his last few seconds of life.

When I turn back to Ben who is still right below me the first thing I see is his fist flying towards my face. I don't have any time to react before it connects with my left cheek, stunning me and knocking me back. After stumbling backwards I shake my head side to side, realizing what just happened. Without thinking twice I grab for my rifle and aim it at Ben's chest before firing two shots. The first shot hits in his lower chest, only wounding him but the second lands directly in his heart which kills him on impact.

I quickly spin around and point my gun at everyone else in the room as I wait for another person to rebel. Fredrick spins around to Lewis who is still lying on the ground. Fredrick aims his gun at Lewis' head, ready to pull the trigger, but Emily in front of him. She kneels down next to Lewis and throws her arms around him.

"Get the fuck out of the way." Fredrick says, obviously pissed off with everything that just happened.

Emily shakes her head before yelling, "No! You're not killing him!"

Fredrick's face goes pale as he starts to back away from Lewis. Everyone else in the room covers their mouth and closes their eyes, not wanting to witness what is about to happen. Emily starts to notice something is out of place so she looks around the room and asks, "What?"

After a few seconds go by she realizes it's not her, its Lewis. When she turns her head to look at Lewis her eyes light up with fear. Lewis' eyes are blood shot and staring right into Emily's, his mouth also foaming as he just finished his transformation into a zombie. Emily panics and locks up in place, unable to escape the impending death. Lewis cracks his neck to loosen himself up before snarling at Emily and lunging for her neck.

Emily lets out a scream of anguish right before Lewis sinks his teeth into her neck. After Lewis bites Emily I walk in front of Fredrick and point my gun at Lewis' head before pulling the trigger. As my bullet rips through Lewis' skull Emily jumps back away from his lifeless body and holds onto her neck which is now gushing blood all over the floor. A look of disappointment comes across my face as I aim my gun at Emily next.

"You should have just listened..." I say out loud.

"I'm sorry... Oh and by the way, since that is a really dim note to end on I figured I'd let you know you're really hot. If it wasn't for all this I'd so totally be into you." I say sarcastically, trying to lighten the mood.

"Ryan!!" April yells at me as she starts to get frustrated.

"Ok, ok, ok." I say out loud.

Emily holds her hand up in front of her face, wanting to say stop but unable too since blood is gushing down her throat, almost choking her. I tilt my head to the side and close my eyes before pulling the trigger on the gun. When the bullet makes contact with Emily's head all the new survivors gasp and look away, not wanting to believe what just happened.

When I turn around I say out loud, in an oddly uplifting voice, "If I was going to die, last thing I'd want to hear besides I'm sorry is hey you're totally hot!"

Everyone looks at me and is filled with anger due to my immaturity. I shrug to myself, never understanding why everyone is always mad at me. I walk over to the corner and lean against the wall while I wait for everything to cool down. No one inside the room speaks for almost two minutes, at which point the tension finally starts to subside. As time goes on and everyone seems to have calm down Fredrick decides to be the first to break the silence.

"Alright, well putting all this bullshit aside, we still need to find a fucking way out of here." Fredrick says to us all.

"We could do something like a jail break." I add.

"What are you talking about?!" Fredrick yells at me, angered, unable to tolerate my childish games anymore.

"W-we could take all our gun's straps, belts and some clothes and make a rope ladder down to the ground." I say to Fredrick, trying to show him that I was serious.

"Well that's just fucking brilliant!" April yells out in a sarcastic voice, "Let's have bras and panties hold two-hundred pound men climbing down a building." she adds.

I point at her before saying, "I never said Bras and panties! Everyone needs to calm the fuck down!"

"How the fuck can you possibly expect us to calm down?!" Stephanie says, still crying, "Look at everyone who is dead!" she adds.

After Stephanie yells at me I throw my hands up into the air, almost like motioning surrender. As I am trying to calm down I walk circles around the room. Still distraught about the current situation we're all in. It takes me a few minutes to calm down but after I do I come up with a plan. I take the strap off of my gun and my belt off my waist before tying them together. After they're both tied together I give them a few pulls to test their durability. After I'm certain it will hold us I toss one half to Fredrick and say, "Come on big boy, give it a pull!"

Fredrick smirks at me, happy that he gets to possibly injure me and it was my idea. Fredrick catches his half of the belt and pulls it as hard as he can. I stumble toward him, caught off guard by his strength. Now that I know Fredrick means business I grip the belt tightly and pull back with all of my strength. Both of us grunt and groan at each other as we enter a testosterone driven childish tug of war match.

We pull back and forth on it for almost twenty seconds before Fredrick gets bored with my game and yanks me to the ground. Thanks to Fredrick's yank, I fall face first onto the ground, practically face planting the floor. As I am lying down on the floor Fredrick tosses the belt onto my back and chuckles, gloating over his victory. After pushing myself back up onto my feet I wipe myself off before looking over to Fredrick.

"Between you and me... We probably put well over five hundred pounds of force onto the strap and belt. No one here weighs five hundred pounds, meaning it can carry us down the side of the building with ease." I say to Fredrick, trying to make a point.

Fredrick nods to me, after seeing the demonstration he now fully agrees with me. He pulls off his belt and takes the strap off his gun before motioning for everyone to do the same. As people take off their belts they hand them to me, allowing me to weave them into the makeshift rope. After collecting everyone's belt and strap I spread out the makeshift rope across the floor to see how long it is. After seeing the belt fully spread out I let out a sigh, realizing that it is still much too short.

"We only got about twenty feet here." I say a bit depressed about the length.

"What are we going to do now?" Stephanie asks.

"Clothes.", I reply. "Strip the dead and any clothes you can spare, well... spare."

I take off my tactical suit and throw my civilian clothes onto the ground, starting a pile for the rope. After I take my shirt and shorts off I am left with only my pair of underwear left on. To save further embarrassment I slide my tactical suit back up my now almost naked body. Cid and Vincent help Fredrick strip down George, Emily, Lewis and Ben. Any of their clothes that aren't covered in blood are thrown into the pile. Once all of the bodies are stripped of all their clothing Fredrick turns them over, showing the dead some dignity.

After counting everything in the pile Fredrick says, "Alright, so we have four more belts, two from Lewis, one from George and another from Ben. We also have a gun strap from Lewis, from when we tied him up and four shirts. In addition we also have three pairs of pants as well as some underwear."

Fredrick holds the underwear up while holding his nose, showing me that he actually has a fun side. I laugh a bit and say to Fredrick, "Hey look, you actually have a fun side! All holding your nose and shit while holding the underwear. I had you figured wrong Fredrick."

Fredrick shakes his head side to side before responding, "No really. We got skid marks."

"Huh?" I ask a bit confused at first.

Fredrick spins the pair of underwear around to reveal a long streaked shit stain on the back. A look of disgust crosses my face as I quickly turn away from the underwear Fredrick is holding and yell, "Oh no! What the fuck!" Jaws drop across the room followed by the sounds of dozens of people awing at the sight. Anyone who isn't gagging from having seen the underwear is busy mumbling to themselves, "Oh my god... That is disgusting." Fredrick tosses the dirty underwear into one of the corners of the room, far away from everyone.

I look over to Fredrick and ask, "Who's... Who's were they?"

"Ben's..." Fredrick responds.

"Oh no! He punched me with that?!" I yell before wiping the side of my face.

"I bet he scratched his ass right before hitting you", Troy says, laughing to himself.

"Uhh! That's nasty!" I remark.

Troy lightens the mood in the room, quickly changing it from disgust to laughter at my expense. After everyone throws the clothes they're willing to give up into a pile I combine them into my pre existing makeshift rope. It takes a few minutes for me to finish combining all of them but when I do I spread the rope out across the room, just like before.

"Well it looks to be about fifty five to sixty feet down." I say before looking over at Fredrick for a conformation.

Fredrick nods to me, "Yup. That's about right. It should get us down."

Fredrick walks over to the window and looks down to double check the length the rope will need to be. After Fredrick is done checking the distance to the ground below he backs away from the window before shooting it three times. Each one of Fredrick's bullet holes forms a corner of a perfect triangle. After Fredrick feels the window is weakened enough he lowers his weapon and kicks the center of the triangle that he formed in the window.

It takes Fredrick a good five to ten kicks in order to finally knock the piece of glass out of the window and down to the pavement below. Now, with the large opening in the window, Fredrick tosses the rope out the hole and to the ground below. Fredrick watches the rope as it falls down the side of the building, slowly unraveling. When the rope hits the ground it coils up a few times, letting Fredrick know we have a few extra feet of slack at the end.

After seeing how much slack we have Fredrick ties the rope to a desk in the room before wedging it into a corner with more desks. With the pile up of metal and wood in the corner of the room it makes it almost impossible for the desk we have the rope tied to, to slide out the hole. After all the desks are piled up in the corner of the room Fredrick yanks on the rope as hard as he can to see if he is able to make anything budge.

After a few good yanks and nothing budging Fredrick hands the rope to me before saying, "I think you should do the honors, it being your rope and all."

I nod to Fredrick, "Seen that coming. Well pull it back up and lower me down. I don't think I can climb down that far myself."

Fredrick chuckles a bit before starting to pull the rope back up into our room. While Fredrick is pulling the rope back up I turn around and stretch a bit. Making sure I am limber for the long descent down. While I am stretching Brad motions me over to the corner him and Stephanie are standing in. I shrug to him, asking why.

"I got something to tell you..." Brad says to me with a hesitant tone.

I get an ominous feeling as I walk towards the corner Brad and Stephanie are standing in. When I am just a foot away from them Brad leans in towards me and whispers, "This is for Lewis, Ben, Emily and George." I pull my head back away from Brad and arch an eyebrow before responding to him by saying, "Huh?"

Right as I back away from Brad I feel a sharp pain in my chest. I reach down and grab a hold of the knife that is now sticking out of my body. I stumble backwards before pulling the knife out of my chest and dropping it at my side. I fall to my knees with both of my hands covering my fresh wound. I take a few more breaths before closing my eyes and collapsing onto my side. Once I am down on my side it doesn't take long for everyone to realize what has happened.

After Fredrick sees me on the ground in front of Brad he points his gun up at Brad and fires twice. The first bullet enters his heart, killing him instantly and the second goes through his head. The bullet that tears through Brad's head causes blood to spray all over the walls around him and onto Stephanie. Stephanie jumps in shock as the blood sprays all over her, but then stays motionless, as she stares at Brad's corpse. Without any hesitation Fredrick switches targets to Stephanie and shoots her directly in the chest. No one questions Fredrick's brutality in the matter, knowing Stephanie was a co-conspirator.

April runs up behind me and falls to her knees. She scoops me up into her arms where I lay, looking up at her and gasping for air. April puts her hands over my wound and puts pressure on it in the hopes to slow the bleeding. But even with April's extra pressure my wound is still gushing blood which has already soaked my tactical suit and the floor all around me.

Everyone in the room gathers around me, a few people even starting to cry while watching me lay in April's arms. As I lay there, coughing up my own blood, April continues to brush my hair off to the side and tell me everything is going to be ok. I take my hand and place it over top of April's before making eye contact with her for the first time since I've been stabbed.

"My life... didn't flash... before my eyes... like they said... it would..." I say to April while having to pause periodically throughout my sentence for air.

"It didn't because you're not going to die!" April says to me, trying to believe her words.

"You're a bad liar..." I say before coughing up more blood.

I manage to make April smile as a tear is just finishing rolling down her cheek. After I see April smile I tilt my head back and close my eyes, finding it very hard to stay lucid. Once April sees my head tilt back she breaks into tears, thinking that I am dying on her. After a few more seconds go by I cough up some more blood, finding it hard to stay with reality. There is a drop of blood running down my cheek as I smile at April.

"Just kidding, I'm not dead yet." I say to her.

April tries to laugh but can't find it in her to battle past the tears. I take my right hand and hold it up to April's face. I lightly place it on the side of her cheek and am just barely able to squeeze out another smile before asking, "Am I... Am I... Hot?"

"Huh?" April responds to me, not fully realizing why I am asking that.

April then turns to the side and notices Emily's body. April smiles as she remembers the last thing I told Emily before she died. When April turns back to look at me she nods, causing the tears to rush down her face making it impossible for her to talk. Moments later my body goes limp and I lose consciousness. As I drift in and out of a lucid state for the next few minutes I am able to understand the conversation in the room but can't make out who is talking.

———————————————

"I can't believe he is dead..."

"He got us all this way... This just isn't right..."

"I knew we shouldn't have helped these people..."

"Yeah."

"There is nothing we can do now..."

"It's too late. He is gone..."

"Wait guys, look!"

I feel two cold fingers press against my neck as they check for a pulse.

"He has a pulse!"

"He's alive!"

"Hang in there Ryan, just hang in there!"

"Troy, Braydon. Go down first and secure the area. We'll lower Ryan down behind you."

"Alright."

"We're going to get you to a hospital! I promise!"

After that all the talking in the room stops for awhile. The only thing able to be heard is people scurrying around the room and the sound of the desk creaking as people lower themselves down the rope. The very next thing I feel is my body being dragged a short distance across the floor before being set down. After I am set down I feel a cool draft coming from my right hand side. It immediately cools the blood that has soaked my tactical suit and sends a chill through my body.

I can feel a rope being tied around my waist as the draft from the hole in the window grows colder. I black out for a few minutes, the very next thing I feel is my body being lowered down the building. It is bending and contorting while it travels down parallel to the building. As they are lowering me down, my body smacks the side of the building periodically. This sends waves of immense pain to vibrate throughout my body. With the rope tied around my waist and no support anywhere else on me, my body is arched, almost like a crescent moon. That accompanied with my knife wound is the most uncomfortable thing I've ever experienced in my life.

As my body gets close to the ground I feel two sets of hands reach up and help balance me, gently lowering me to the ground. My body is set back down on solid ground as I feel the rope being untied from around my waist. Everything goes silent as I black out again. I drift in and out of reality, only being able to hear grunts and groans while feeling four sets of hands carrying my body.

"Oh shit... What happened to him?"

"Someone stabbed him; help me get him onto the bus."

"Zooey come down here and help too."

After arriving at the bus I feel two more sets of hands touch my body. They carefully guide me up, onto the bus and over onto a seat nearby. After setting me down in the seat I hear everyone leave the bus but no commotion outside. I start to worry that they left me here to die until I hear the footsteps of people coming back onto the bus.

"Is he still alive?"

"Don't know."

"Check his pulse."

I feel two cold fingers press up against my neck.

"He's still got one, but it is light."

"Good."

"Mark get us to a fucking hospital. We need to seal him up."

"On it, closest is five miles away."

I drift in and out of reality for the next few minutes. The next thing I remember seeing is patches of bright light on the ceiling as I am being wheeled through a hospital on a stretcher. I blackout again and wake up on a table with a light being shined right in my face. I am unable to see anything but I can feel sharp pokes and prods right around my wound.

While they are stitching me up I black out again and don't wake up until the following day, in a bed. After I wake up I tilt my head to the side and see that April is sitting down in a chair right next to the bed taking a nap. A smile comes across my face, knowing that April cared enough to stay with me through the night. I reach down and feel my wound which is still tender from the day before. I gently rub over it to feel the stitches that were put into it.

"Mmmphf", I mumble as I feel my stitches.

Now that I am awake I lift my arms up into the air and stretch them, trying to get rid of some of the cramps from being lowered down the building. When I lift my left arm I see a large bandage over where I bit myself on top the gas station. I let out a long sigh before throwing my head back into the pillow, wondering how I am going to explain this one. Not wanting to stay in this hospital for any longer I lean over to April and shake her to wake her up.

"Hey April!" I say to her.

"Mmm? Huh?" She responds, still a bit disoriented from just waking up.

"Oh, you're up?" April says out loud before jumping out of her seat. "Everyone! Ryan's awake!" April calls out.

Everyone runs into my room, anxious to see me. They all crowd around my bed and ask dozens of questions like, "How are you doing?", "Do you feel ok?" and "Does it hurt?" As each person walks into the room I become more and more surprised no one is pointing any guns and asking about my bite. Fredrick and Mark are the last two to enter the room. As Fredrick enters the room an awkward feeling comes across me. Before getting close to the bed Fredrick tilts his head up to me and asks, "Why aren't you one of them?"

"It was self inflicted." I say out loud to Fredrick.

"I'm not buying it.", Fredrick replies.

"When I was on the roof with April, she was inside the store and the zombie's were pounding on the glass to get in. I bit myself and stuck my arm over the side. The blood distracted them long enough, giving April enough time to get back onto the roof." I say out loud.

"Mark?" Fredrick asks.

"Based on tone of voice and willingness to give the information... I'd say it's the truth."

"You're in the clear than! Welcome back, Ryan." Fredrick says before sticking his hand out and shaking mine.

"Where are we?" I ask, still a bit disoriented from the loss of blood.

"We're at the Oklahoma City hospital." Mark replies.

"Now it is time for the million dollar question. How am I still alive?" I ask.

"Luckily, the knife missed all your organs on the inside, causing very little damage." April responds.

"How long do you think until we can get on the road again?" I ask.

"I'd recommend taking a few days break." April replies.

"I'm not asking for a recommendation." I remark.

"You're good to go now, if you wanted." Mark says.

"No he isn't!" April yells out at Mark.

"Start the bus.", I say to Mark

"I'm not letting you leave like this!" April yells at me.

"It isn't your decision. I'm not going to waste eight people's time. We're leaving today."

Even though April is against me leaving she assists me in getting out of the bed and hands me my clothes which were in a pile on the ground. After I am up out of the bed I struggle to put back on all of my clothes, my body still sore from being lowered down from the window. While I am putting on my clothes Braydon hands me my tactical suit and says, "Here you go, I fixed it up for you." I nod to Braydon and thank him.

Braydon hands me the suit and points to the area on it that he had to stitch up. I take a good look at the area and notice that Braydon made it look like I was never even stabbed. While I am putting my tactical suit back on over top all my clothes my wound starts to bleed again. A small red spot has formed on my shirt from the bleeding wound.

After feeling the wound and getting some blood on my fingers I look around the room and say out loud, "Can someone in here get me some fucking Percocet or Vicodin? This shit hurts."

April nods before running out of the room to find some pain pills in the hospital. After April leaves the room, I limp out into the hallway and towards the exit. Almost everyone that came to visit me in my room is walking behind me, ready to catch me if I stumble or fall. As I am still hobbling down the hallway April runs up to me and hands me a bottle of pain pills that she found. I dump three of the pills out into my hand and toss them into my mouth, not caring what the proper dose is.

I swallow the pills without hesitation and continue to walk down the hallway towards the lobby. Upon entering the lobby I see that Fredrick is waiting for me by the front doors. As I approach Fredrick he asks, "You sure you want to leave like this?"

I ignore Fredrick's question and ask, "Is the bus started?"

After asking Fredrick my question I look out front of the hospital and see our bus parked right outside and Mark running towards the doors. Once Mark is inside he nods to Fredrick before saying out loud, "Bus is started!"

"Alright, let's get the fuck out of here." I say out loud.

I hobble over to the front doors and push them open using my right hand while keeping my left hand firmly placed over my wound, which is still hurting. Once I am outside I continue to limp over to the bus, the cold chilly weather not making my trek any easier. When I reach the bus and walk up the stairs each step I take sends a shiver of pain into my abdomen.

Making each step on the bus excruciatingly painful. Back on the bus I walk over to the seat right behind the driver's seat and sit down. I slowly and carefully swing my body to the side before lying down across the seat and gently placing my head against the window.

I close my eyes and let my legs hang off the seat into the center isle of the bus. As others start walking on the bus the only conversations that are able to be heard are about me. I struggle trying to figure out who is saying what but some voices stick out like a sore thumb.

"He is so pale."

"Are you sure we should let him leave like this?"

"It's not our decision."

"But he can barely walk!"

That's the one voice I recognize... No other voice out of everyone with us is as distinguishable as April's. Accompanied by the amount of concern in her voice, it's easy to tell who is talking.

"I do not agree with this *at all*. He needs rest, if the wound tears open again it can get infected and we don't have the right antibiotics for that." April says out loud.

"I'll be fine. Stop talking about me like I am not here and I can't hear you. Get everyone on the bus and get it the fuck moving." I mumble to everyone on the bus.

Shortly after hearing the doors to the bus close I can hear Mark shift the bus into drive and start to pull away from the hospital. The sound of the bus accelerating roars through my head. Causing some pain thanks to the pounding headache I have from the shortage of blood. Even with my pounding headache it doesn't take long for me to fall asleep as I am still restless from the night before.

I wake up a few hours later while the bus is still in motion. It feels like I've slept for days, maybe even weeks. Once I'm awake I struggle to sit upright. When I am sitting up I turn to Mark and ask him what state we are in.

"We just entered Texas, before you woke up.", Mark replies.

"Oh boy we're in Texas? It has been awhile since I've been here." I say out loud.

"Any luck with any more radio transmissions?" I ask Mark.

Fredrick interrupts us and says, "Yeah. One was playing *Blink 182*. We're going there right now."

"What?! Really?!" I ask while almost jumping out of my seat.

"Oh yeah, they're in Dallas." Fredrick tries saying with a straight face.

"You're bull shitting me aren't you?" I ask.

"Of course I am who the fuck would play that shit besides the people we just tried to save." Fredrick says out loud.

I manage to let out a soft smile, trying to take what Fredrick said with a grain of salt. Since nothing important is going on I lie back down in my seat and lay my head back against the window. As I Listen to the sound of the engine and the road beneath us it almost soothes me for the time being. I begin to close my eyes and try to drift off into sleep but the sound of Mark's voice catches me off guard and keeps me awake for the time being.

"Quarter tank, we should probably get some gas. That sign back there said it was the last gas station for close to thirty miles."

"Good eyes Mark. Take us there." Fredrick says out loud.

Fredrick stands up and walks over to the front doors of the bus, anxious and ready to go. When Mark turns down the deceleration ramp it throws Fredrick's balance off a bit but he quickly regains it. As we pull into the gas station I extend my hand out to Troy so he can help pull me up out of my seat. After I am up on both feet I walk over to the opposite side of the bus and look out the window. The gas station we are at is in complete shambles. Almost every pump at the gas station is completely destroyed and shattered glass litters the ground.

All across the front of the gas station's store you can see dried up blood streaks, from where someone was brutally killed. The front door of the gas station is completely barricaded off by a large SUV that was driven right into it. After getting a good look at the whole gas station I walk a little bit closer to the side of the bus to look down at our diesel pump. It is the only diesel pump at the whole gas station and from where I am standing the line looks severed.

I turn to Mark and say, "We aren't going to be able to get gas here... The line is severed."

"Let's get out and check anyway. Troy, Braydon, on me.", Fredrick says out loud.

Fredrick says before rushing out of the bus with Troy and Braydon following behind him. As I watch them all scurry around outside the bus I let out a long drawn out sigh. As if there was something they could even do outside to salvage the gas pump. A few minutes go by with the three of them outside, trying to find a way to fix the gas pump. As they walk back on the bus without having pumped any gas the moral is immediately lowered. Everyone knows we need gas and need it now. Fredrick gets everyone's attention when he gets back on the bus and breaks the bad news to us.

"We can't get gas here. There is none available to us."

"What about a nearby town? Or even another gas station?" I ask.

"Going into a city is too risky, especially with the very little gas we have. If we were to become attacked, we would barely be able to defend ourselves."

Fredrick continues, "What we're going to do is continue driving in this direction until we run out of gas. When we do we're going to walk to the nearest gas station and fill up our cans. With them full we will return to the bus and dump them in. This will give us enough gas to drive the bus to that gas station."

"Mark, start up the bus and let's go." Fredrick finishes his talk before sitting down.

As we continue to drive further west the time seems to fly by. Every mile we drive we get closer and closer to running out of gas. Less than ten minutes after leaving the gas station Mark yells out to the whole bus, "Low gas light is on."

"Keep pushin' her till she stops!" Fredrick says while pondering to himself how much further the gas we have will get us.

Mark nods to Fredrick while continuing down the long straight road, hoping that the fumes in our gas tank will carry us to another gas station. The fumes in our gas tank carry us for another four miles until the bus finally stalls. After the bus stalls Mark lets it roll downhill for almost another mile until we come to a complete stop at the bottom of the hill. Once we're at a complete stop Fredrick stands up and motions to everyone on the bus to get up.

"On your feet let's go, everyone, If we travel together, we stay alive together." Fredrick calls out.

I stand up and look to everyone on the bus before saying, "Grab all the supplies you can hold, guns, ammo, water, food, anything. We have to plan for the worst and hope for the best."

April runs over and grabs me by the arm before saying, "Are you sure you're up to this?"

I nod to her, "Hey, you're supposed to be the damsel in distress here. Don't worry about me! I'm a big boy now."

April smiles at me, wanting to believe that I'll be safe. Before following Fredrick and getting off the bus I grab my rifle and stick at least three clips of extra ammo into my back pockets. After I collect the extra ammo I grab a bottle of water from the bus and drink three quarters of it before throwing what is left of it into the back of the bus. Now that I have all the ammo I'll need and am very well hydrated I exit the bus.

I am the last one off the bus, after I walk off Mark forcefully closes the doors, making sure nothing can get on while we are gone. After the doors are closed and secure we start our long trek down the road hopefully towards a nearby gas station. As we walk down the road anyone who isn't having a conversation keeps themselves entertained by kicking anything they find lying on the road. Stones, cans and bottles are the most common choices.

About a mile down the road Troy finds a rotting head along the side of the road. Just like it was a rock he starts to kick it along while walking down the road. As Troy is kicking the head down the road he is giggling and having a good time. Sometimes he even pretends that he is playing soccer. Everyone stares at Troy as we walk down the road. Watching him kick the head and questioning his sanity. There are Veins and arteries hanging out of the bottom of the head as well as other stringy shit that I don't even know what the fuck it is. A few more minutes go by with Troy kicking the head along the road. After about five minutes in all he gets bored and punts the head off into a field to our right, acting like he just kicked a field goal. As the head flies off into the distance it ends one of the most disgusting chapters of my life.

Further up the road we come over top of a large hill and get a good look at a little bit of a valley below. At first glance I don't see anything but after looking again I notice a small gas station right off the side of the road.

"Look!" I yell out loud while pointing to the gas station up the road, "A gas station!"

The moral of the group is immediately lifted when I point out the gas station in the distance. The gas station is surrounded by a forest, which I thought was quite odd for Texas. The gas station doesn't offer the best safety value since it is surrounded by a forest. It would be almost impossible to see anything coming until it was practically right on top of us. Before saying anything, Fredrick takes a look into the sky and back at the gas station.

"It's about a two hour walk. With the amount of day light left, it looks like we're going to be spending the night there." Fredrick says out loud to everyone.

After Fredrick breaks the bad news to us, sighs can be heard amongst the crowd. No one likes the idea of spending a night inside an abandoned gas station. As we continue down the road the rugged terrain and long walk is starting to get the better of all of us. Complaints about the heat, people's feet hurting and the distance we have to walk can commonly be heard muttered amongst us all.

It doesn't take the full two hours that Fredrick thought it would to reach the gas station up the road. Once we're at the gas station we all walk over to the only diesel pump and stand around it. After verifying that it is in good condition we stick the nozzle in the gas can to start pumping the gas. Fredrick squeezes the trigger on the nozzle but nothing comes out. After a few minutes of playing with it we come to the conclusion that the power is out.

"Cid, Vincent, Head inside and see what is up with the power situation." Fredrick says while motioning for the two of them to go inside.

Both Cid and Vincent nod before entering the building. While Cid and Vincent are inside figuring out what is wrong with the power everyone else tries to find someplace to sit outside. The long walk to the gas station has obviously taken its toll on everyone. A few minutes go by until Cid and Vincent finally come out of the building. As they walk out of the building and back towards us they are both shaking their heads side to side.

"No power." Cid says.

"Dead as a fucking door nail." Vincent adds.

Fredrick looks up into the sky at the setting sun and uses his hand to see how much time we have until sunset. After checking how much time we have left he turns back to all of us and says, "Alright, let's head inside and barricade up the store. If we're going to spend a night in there we want to make sure nothing can get in."

After Fredrick is done speaking we all follow him into the building. The only form of light we have inside the building is our flashlights and about twenty more minutes of sunlight. While everyone is barricading up the building I walk over to the counter and sit down behind it. After sitting down I pull my tactical suit up to look at my wound. Right after I pull my tactical suit up to see my wound April comes over and sits down next to me.

"You're bleeding again..." April says to me, in a very concerned voice, while looking at my wound.

"I told you not to worry about Me.", I mumble to her.

April places he hand on the bottom of my chin and tilts my head up to look into my eyes. I am just barely able to keep them open long enough for her to get a good look at my pupils.

"Your pupils are dilated... You've lost too much blood... You could really cause some damage like this..." April says to me.

"I'll just take a nap. Everything will be fine tomorrow..." I say to April.

April nods, taking my word for it as I close my eyes and fall asleep behind the counter. As I am asleep everyone else boards up the gas station and makes sure all exits are secure. I drift in and out of my sleep as they are boarding up the gas station from all the noise they are making. After everything is boarded up it all goes silent, allowing me to drift off into a deep sleep. The next time I come to my senses is right around midnight.

A loud scraping sound can be heard coming from the roof, waking me up from a dead sleep. As I pull myself up and look around the room everyone is holding their finger up to their lips while looking at me, telling me to stay quiet. I nod to them before standing up and slowly and quietly making my way to the center of the room with everyone else. Once I am in the center of the room I sit down next to April and whisper into her ear, "What is it?"

"It sounds like a Night Stalker." April replies.

I nod to April before leaning back against an aisle in the center of the store. After leaning against the aisle I join the other survivors in staring up at the ceiling. All of us follow the all too familiar noise around on the roof. As the Night Stalker drags its claws across the metal roof a faint screeching sound vibrates throughout the building. The Night Stalker on top the roof periodically stops to emit a very faint clucking sound. It's the same clucking sound that we heard on top the bus a few days ago.

Shortly after hearing the clucking sounds on top the roof everything goes quiet. Everyone in the room shares the same very curious look, wondering what is going on outside. A few more seconds go by before a loud bang echoes throughout the building, as another Night Stalker lands on the roof. The bang scares me and many other survivors, causing us all to jolt forward. After hearing the second Night Stalker land on the roof an eerie silence comes over the whole area. Not a single sound can be heard from outside, even the bugs that were chirping outside are now deathly silent.

Everything stays silent for the next twenty seconds until an obnoxiously loud screech can be heard from on top the roof. The screech is so loud that it sends a chill down my spine and forces me to cover my ears to prevent permanent damage. Immediately after the first Night Stalker lets out his chilling shriek the second follows his example. Over top the shrieks of the Night Stalkers on our roof you can just barely hear dozens more in the distance. When the horrifying shrieks end the Night Stalkers begin to dig and claw at the top of our roof.

"They must know we're inside!" April yells out.

Everyone nods to April, fearing that she may be right. The Night Stalkers begin to rip and bend the metal on top the roof as they try to find their way inside the building. Fredrick aims his gun at the ceiling where he hears the noise originating from and then fires. The sound of Fredrick's rifle echoes throughout the building as his bullet rips through the ceiling. After the bullet pierces through the ceiling we hear a loud thump followed by the Night Stalker's blood seeping through the bullet hole. After seeing the method being quite effective, Braydon follows Fredrick's example and points his gun at the clawing sound on the ceiling.

When Braydon pulls the trigger the sound of his rifle is followed by the thump of a Night Stalker, just like before. As blood seeps through the bullet hole in the ceiling everything goes quiet again... but not for long. Night Stalkers can be heard landing on the roof from all sides. The sound of them landing is quickly followed by them clawing and digging the second they land. I've notice that once the Night Stalkers land on the roof and start tearing at the metal ceiling they don't stop. Even after being shot they don't move and continue to tear at the ceiling.

Once the Night Stalkers start digging at the roof they become easy targets for us inside. All we have to do is aim where ever we hear noise and fire. It's very rare that the first shot doesn't kill the Night Stalker, if it doesn't; it is very easy to tell. If the first shot isn't a kill shot the Night Stalker screams in anguish until it is killed. Every one of us that has a gun walks around the store with it aimed at the ceiling, waiting for a noise. Over the next few minutes more and more Night Stalkers continue to land on the roof.

With the bodies of Night Stalkers piling up on the roof they start to get in the way of the Night Stalkers trying to tear into the roof. In order to get an open area on the roof to dig at the Night Stalkers are forced to toss the dead over the side of the building. After about twenty to thirty minutes after the attack started it is impossible to hear them walking around on the roof anymore. The bodies of the dead Night Stalker's dampen the sound and equally disperse the weight across the roof. Each time they take a step on the roof we can get a general idea of where they are but not an exact location that is needed to kill them.

Time seems to fly by as we sit in the store and shoot at the Night Stalkers on the roof. Oddly enough, being attacked by the Night Stalkers on the roof was much more fun than it was scary. Everyone takes turns killing the Night Stalkers that land on the roof, even arguing with each other with who goes next. Almost an hour after the attack on the store started it ends. Before anyone is allowed to go back to sleep Fredrick sets up guard rotations to make sure someone is always awake incase the Night Stalkers come back. The only reason Fredrick decides to exclude me from having to stay guard is because of my injury. A good night's sleep is needed in order to restore a lot of lost blood back into my system.

Braydon is the first one required to stay up and keep an eye out for any returning Night Stalkers. After the attack is over I sit back down in the middle of the aisle and lean back against the shelf. As the adrenaline starts to leave my system and I start to calm down it becomes really easy to fall back asleep.

When I wake up the first thing I notice is that the front door isn't barricaded anymore and sunlight is finding its way back into the building. After letting out a small yawn I pull myself up and onto my feet, feeling much better than the day before. Once I am up and mobile I walk outside where everyone is waiting around the gas pump.

"No go?" I ask.

Everyone shakes their head side to side while looking down at the gas cans lying on the ground. With everyone now awake and outside Fredrick says out loud, "There is no reason for us to go back to the bus if we don't have any gas. We need to continue west and the most direct path is through these woods. We'll eventually find a small town with another vehicle that we can use. Is everyone ok with that?"

"Guess we don't have any other choice." I reply.

Everyone is a bit upset with having to walk again as we all are still worn out from yesterdays trek to the gas station. Even though no one wants to walk through the woods, everyone follows Fredrick without much of an argument. Trying to navigate our way through the woods is rough at first. Since we are required to step over fallen trees and branches we are only moving at about half our normal pace. While walking through the woods I become a bit bored. So I decide to spark up a conversation.

"You know... we are probably going to get killed by a fucking water buffalo or some shit out here."

"What do you mean a water buffalo?" Zooey asks in a very confused voice

"Yeah, that big ox thing with fucking horns." I reply.

Cid joins in, "Oh yeah? You're talking about the species that is indigenous to Africa? Just happens to be here in Texas?"

"Coulda' swam across the ocean," I reply in a very sarcastic voice.

"They can't swim across an ocean...," Cid replies, not detecting my sarcasm.

"Oh, yeah? Then why do they call them water buffalos?" I say again, in a very sarcastic voice.

"I don't know, but they sure as hell can't swim across an ocean," Cid adds, starting to get frustrated.

"What about a sea water buffalo?" I ask.

Cid lets out a long drawn out sigh and shakes his head side to side, finding my question too stupid to even warrant a response.

"What do you think about a zombie water buffalo?" Troy asks.

"Now that shit would be fucked up." Troy adds.

"Hell yeah man!" I yell out before stepping over a large log blocking my path. Once over the log I turn around and help April over it behind me followed by Zooey and Braydon.

With everyone over the log I start talking again, "With those huge horns and shit, they'd fuck someone's shit up."

"What about a lion or even a zombie lion?" I say out loud.

"What makes you think a lion would ever be in Texas?" April asks.

"Escaped from the zoo? Come on, get with the program here." I say out loud.

"What about a pack of rabid zombie dogs? Is that more Texas for you April?" I ask sarcastically.

April looks over at me and gives me a half ass smirk, nicely blowing me off.

"What about zombie rattlesnakes?" Braydon asks.

"A zombie rattlesnake, are you serious?" I ask.

"Yeah, why?" He replies, a bit confused.

"Who cares about a zombie rattlesnake? I mean seriously the snake is going to kill you anyway..."

"Wait! I got it! Zombie grizzly bear! Oh man can you imagine that?" I say out loud.

"Can we cut the childish shit?" Fredrick says out loud, obviously getting a little annoyed.

"Alright, alright..." I say out loud.

Over the next few minutes I stay quiet and obey Fredrick's wish. But as we continue to walk through the woods I grow more and more bored as time goes on. Eventually I am unable to resist opening my mouth again.

"What state are we in again?" I ask.

"Texas...", at least two people respond.

"Alright, alright. What about a zombie Chuck Norris? He did *Walker Texas Ranger* and we're in Texas. I mean come on! A zombie with ninja fighting moves. We'd all be screwed." I say.

"Nah, no zombie on this planet could get close enough to Chuck Norris to turn him." Braydon says out loud.

"Tru dat.", I reply in a very sarcastic voice.

"What do you think about a zombie George Bush?" Troy asks.

"Oh yeah, I forgot George lived in Texas." I say out loud.

"I call dibs on zombie George Bush." Fredrick yells out.

"Aww man, that's so not cool!" I remark.

"I call Sarah Palin.", Braydon says.

"We're not in Alaska, we're in Texas you dip shit." I add.

"Oh, what, Palin's are indigenous to Alaska?" Braydon asks.

"Lol, you said Palin was a species." I reply.

Braydon laughs, "Why did you just say lol?"

"It's a sarcastic, non-rude way to say your joke wasn't funny." I reply.

"This is by far, the dumbest conversation I have *ever* taken part in.", April says.

"It's only dumb because you're part of It.", I say to April.

"Can sharks be zombies?" Troy asks, changing the subject.

"More like can animals be zombies..." I say.

"I saw a zombie dog a few days back. It was a pit bull, foaming at the mouth and its body was all torn up.", Cid says.

"Sounds like rabies, not a zombie."

"No, no, no, no. This was a zombie, trust Me.", Cid adds.

"Well then that answers that question." I say.

"What question?" Mark asks.

"The question if animals can be zombies." I reply.

Our childish conversation carries on for quite awhile as we continue through the woods. The only time we stop for a break is when someone has to go to the bathroom or the five minute rest period Fredrick gives us every hour. With the dumb jokes and amount of conversation amongst us all the time we spend walking through the woods seems to fly. It's already now later in the evening and with the sun setting Fredrick starts to look for a place to make camp. We would continue on through the night but the sun is our only source of direction when walking through the woods. Without it greatly increases our chances to get lost.

There is about another hour until sunset when Fredrick finds a nice opening in the forest. The opening has no trees or bushes growing in the middle of it and is mostly padded by moss that is growing on the forest floor. Fredrick walks out into the middle of the opening and spins around to look at the woods around him before setting down his baggage. After he sets down his supplies he turns back to everyone and starts to speak.

"We make camp here. I need at least five people to collect firewood, lots of it. Everyone else should clear the area right in this ten by ten clearing. I want all Sticks, Branches, and Leaves, everything off the ground. Make sure nothing is around that we can sit on that will injure us as well as nothing the fire can spread to. We have about an hour till sundown. Let's get crackin'."

April, Vincent and I all form a little group to look in the woods around our camp for some firewood. April collects small Logs and Sticks while Vincent and I both drag the bigger and heftier logs back into camp. Braydon, Troy and Fredrick collect firewood from the opposite side of the camp. Which leaves Cid, Zooey and Mark to clear out the area where we will build the fire and sleep.

After Cid, Zooey and Mark finish clearing out the camp area they assist the rest of us in collecting firewood for tonight. Once we have a couple dozen logs and plenty of tinder to get started Fredrick stops collecting wood and returns to the camp area. He starts to construct a large bonfire, wanting to make something that will not only keep us warm but also keep us safe. After we finish collecting wood we return to the camp where Fredrick has a roaring fire waiting for us all.

We all gather around the fire and take our seats on logs that Fredrick laid out for us. The discomfort of our seating isn't what most of us are worried about. Most of us are worried about being exposed on all sides, able to be attacked from anywhere at any time. The fire offers some solace but not enough to make us feel at ease with spending the night here.

With all of us grouped around the fire we share stories of our lives before the whole zombie apocalypse. Fredrick mentions his two kids that lived in Chicago with his wife. He said his kids names were Milo and Sarah. He joked about how Milo looked just like him, without the full beard. Fredrick told us that Sarah reminded him of his wife, Christine. They both had the same eye color and the same vibrant smile. When Fredrick was done describing his family he pulled his wallet out of his back pocket and took out the picture of his family. He passed it around to all of us, allowing us all to see his family.

After Fredrick showed us all a picture of his family it was Braydon's turn to tell his story. He mentioned his wife, Alicia, back in Georgia. She was pregnant with his first kid on the way. Neither of them had any idea if it was going to be a boy or a girl yet but they wanted it to be a surprise. Braydon was joking how he had the pre-daddy jitters even though Alicia was only three months pregnant. Braydon said he hoped that he would be able to love, take care of and support his child more than his father did to him.

Braydon shed a few tears during his story but before we knew it, it was Troy's turn to talk. Troy mentioned he lived in Minnesota his whole life, right outside of Minneapolis. He said that he was married once but it didn't last very long. They got married right out of High school; he said it was amazing until college which just tore them apart. Troy didn't have any kids and both of his parents died when he was at a very young age, forcing him into a foster home. Troy was just like me, a loner, he didn't like being around other people and could never really become attached to anyone. And when he did it never worked out.

Right after Troy it was my turn. I explained my website to everyone, how it worked, what it has accomplished and how much I really started to hate working on it. I explained that I lived in New York, had some family in New Jersey but really no friends anywhere else. I mentioned that I dreamed to be a Musician, which is what drove me to New York. I wanted to be somebody one day, not just a random person on the face of the earth. I wanted hundreds and thousands of people to chant my name as I walked on stage. I didn't care about the money or the fame, I wanted to have fun. Wake up every day and have it be drastically different then the last, new city, new faces and nonstop fun.

I continued to explain how much the zombie apocalypse changed my life for the better. It may have even saved my life, made me into a new person. I was grateful for everything that happened, regardless of how fucked up it sounded. I also mentioned how I was happy to of met everyone sitting around this camp fire and how I will dedicate my life to getting us to safety. Before getting too preachy I passed the spotlight onto April.

April quickly took the lead by explaining that she was a med student at M.I.T before the disaster. She talked about her family in New York City and some other family that she had in Russia. April mentioned a cute little white poodle she had before the apocalypse, ironically named Killer. She was in New York City for vacation; her college was closed because of some sort of shootout.

After April was finished talking we discussed the possibilities of the zombie threat not being in other countries. Since April mentioned Russia we all became side tracked with a whole different conversation. We discussed the possibility of only America having zombies and the other countries not being contaminated. After a few minutes of discussing the topic we drop it. Figuring it would be nearly impossible for the zombies to be isolated to one country.

Next up was Cid and Vincent, who both spoke together. They mentioned that they were indeed father and son. Vincent explained that he lost his first wife at a very young age because of a drunk driver. A few months before she was hit by the drunk driver she gave birth to Cid. Since Cid was only a few months old at the time he doesn't remember his mother at all. Vincent said that he remarried later in life but it didn't work out and he got divorced. Cid mentioned that he had a kid of his own that he was battling to get custody of. He didn't talk much more about the girl that had his kid or the kid himself. He seemed very troubled about the subject.

Mark was the next person up. He mentioned that he was originally from Connecticut. He was in Cleveland on a business trip for his company when the zombie apocalypse occurred. He did not elaborate on what type of work he was doing or much on his field. He just explained that he was a Biomedical Engineer and graduated from the University of Connecticut. Mark's whole back story was about his recent life, how he got into Cleveland and about his old college. He didn't ever mention his family or friends.

The last person to speak was Zooey. She mentioned that she was single and has been for quite awhile, never able to find Mr. Right. She's always wanted to have a few kids, maybe three or four since she was the only child growing up. She lived in Seattle Washington but was visiting family when we found her. She thanked us all again for helping her and protecting her from everything out there. She added that without us, she would probably be dead right now and for that she owes us her life.

After all of us told background stories of our selves we joked around the fire and commenced in small talk, just passing time before it was late enough to go to bed. As the night went on we all started to become more and more scared of the woods around us. Over the past hour an eerie silence started to settle in. Everyone noticed the silence around us but no one brought it up. Even the bugs around our camp were silent. Every time we stopped talking the only thing able to be heard was the roaring fire.

We tried to always keep a conversation going for this exact reason. However when it was finally time for bed we were forced to listen to the eerie silence around us. It was very hard trying to fall asleep without any ambient noise and having to keep one eye open at all times. But I did. Just knowing I was in the company of others for protection and that Fredrick was going to be up all night on look out duty. This was enough to help soothe me and allow me to drift off into sleep.

We're all awoken hours later by the sound of an extremely loud screech. However it was nothing nearly as loud as the Night Stalkers screech.

Troy jolts up from the ground and yells out, "What the *fuck* was that?"

Without any warning I break into laughter. Everyone looks at me with a very confused look.

I look to Troy and try to say between laughs, "You... you ever see *My Cousin Vinny*?"

"What are you talking about?" Troy asks.

"You know the movie... with Joe Pesci?" I add.

"Uhm, yeah. I saw it.... why?" Troy asks.

"Remember the part with the Screecher Owl?" I ask.

"Yeah? ..." Troy responds.

"That was you right now. With your "What the *fuck* was that?" "Pow, pow, pow." I say while still laughing my ass off.

Troy rolls his eyes at me and sits back down onto the ground. Even Fredrick starts to chuckle a bit before saying, "You know you're not usually funny but that one was pretty good."

"It still doesn't explain what that was though..." Braydon adds.

"Ryan is right, probably a Screecher Owl." Fredrick says.

"Don't worry, I'll keep watch. Get some sleep." Fredrick adds.

Everyone nods to Fredrick before laying their heads back down. It is easy for everyone to fall back asleep after the scare. It takes me a bit longer though, still chuckling about the Screecher Owl. When I finally do fall back asleep I don't wake up until the following morning.

The warm feeling of the sun shining through all the Tree Branches onto my face awakens me. The Campfire that was once roaring the night before is now reduced to ashes and the only light emitting from it is the hot embers from the previous night. I stretch my arms and look around the Campfire, everyone aside from Fredrick is still asleep. I sit up and look over to Fredrick before asking, "How much longer we going to let everyone sleep?"

"I am going to wake them up right now." Fredrick says.

Fredrick stands up and loudly claps his hands together, waking everyone up around the fire. Once everyone is awake and alerted by the clapping Fredrick says, "Five minutes till we leave, grab your shit and get ready."

With Fredrick's deadline, everyone scurries around and grabs anything they brought with them. Once we're all ready we meet up around the campfire before following Fredrick west. No one talks the whole morning as everyone is still trying to wake up during the journey. The morning goes by quickly as we slowly make our way through the forest.

Walking through the woods today was much easier than the previous day. The woods were more open and cleared on this side. With everything being so clear there were very few obstacles for us to dodge. We walk through the woods until noon, when we finally find a large clearing where the woods stop and dump us out into a large field. The field has grass that comes up to our waists and is majestically blowing in the wind. It's impossible to see to the other side since the grass is so high and there are dozens of hills going through the field.

We all walk cautiously through the field, having to hold our guns up in the air to prevent them from getting caught and tangled up in the large blades of grass. While I am walking through the grass I continually check the area around me, worrying that something may be hiding in the tall grass. While walking through the grass our feet and shoes are constantly getting caught, forcing us to travel at about half our normal pace. While walking through the field I grow a bit bored and decide to spark up a conversation with everyone.

"So, anyone care to explain why there is a fucking field in Texas?"

"Cattle farm is my guess." Fredrick replies.

"Alright, well that doesn't explain why there was no fence around the area and why the cattle fail at eating the grass."

"What do you mean, fail at eating the grass?"

"Look at it! It's up to our waist! If the cattle were doing their jobs it'd be little stubs on the ground." I say out loud, like I am stating the obvious.

"I feel like I'm in fucking *The Happening*... Next thing I know I am going to be reaching for my gun to shoot myself." I say, changing the subject.

"Or even *Jurassic Park*. You remember the one where the raptors kept picking them off through the field? Good thing there are no raptors."

"Uh oh, guys..." I say out loud before stopping in my tracks.

"What?" Fredrick asks in a worried voice.

"What about a zombie raptor?" I say.

"Oh Jesus fucking Christ not this again..." April says out loud.

"Wait! Guys! Think about it! ...." I yell out.

The conversation continues on for another thirty minutes until we come over top of a large hill and see a small town below. There are about two dozen buildings in the small town, giving me the impression that the town wasn't very well known. All of us stand at the top of the hill and look down at the small town, worrying about the danger that could be ahead. Before any of us leave the top of the hill I say out loud, "With a town that small, no way did they evacuate or even know to evacuate for the zombie shit. They're all still there."

Fredrick nods his head while I am talking, letting me know he has come to the same conclusion. Not wanting to delay the inevitable any longer Fredrick starts down the hill towards the town with everyone following right behind him. Instead of holding our guns up in the air to prevent them from being tangled in the tall grass we keep them eye level and watch for any zombies. It takes us close to thirty minutes to travel the short distance across the field to the small town. When we finally reach the small town we take refuge behind the first building we come to. Interestingly enough it happens to be a giant red barn. Judging by the location of the barn, the person who owned it probably owned the field we just came across to the town.

Before moving out into the streets Fredrick glances around the side of the barn to make sure it is clear. After checking the streets and making sure everything is clear Fredrick bolts out from behind the barn and into the open. The rest of us follow closely behind Fredrick, being extra careful to stay quiet and close to Fredrick. Once we're all out from behind the barn and into the streets of the town we look at the houses around us. Most of the houses on the street are in horrible condition. Their windows are shattered with screens hanging off of them and blowing in the wind. Blood spatter covers most of the houses like a very poor paint job.

There are large spots of dried blood all along the street of this small town and on the sidewalks. You can tell they were caused by someone dying and bleeding out but there were no bodies in the center of the dried up spots. Meaning whatever did die there, is now up and walking around somewhere around us. Almost every house has a car parked in the driveway, implying that not many people got away from whatever happened here. As we continue further down the road Troy notices a School Bus that is parked down a side street. After spotting the bus Troy motions Fredrick and I over and points the bus out to us.

Fredrick and I nod to Troy before turning down the side street. As I follow Fredrick I look inside every window of every house that we pass to make sure nothing is inside. When we reach the bus Fredrick tells Mark and Braydon to head on first and make sure it is safe. Braydon gets on first and sweeps the whole bus, making sure no zombies are on. After Braydon clears the bus and notifies us that it is safe Mark gets on and checks for a key. After checking the ignition Mark turns around to Fredrick and says, "Key must be inside the house."

Fredrick has Braydon and Troy head inside the house and search for the key while everyone else outside starts to board the bus. After everyone is on the bus Fredrick and I stand guard outside while we wait for Braydon and Troy to get done inside. Almost a minute after Troy and Braydon entered the house we can hear gunshots from inside. Only three shots were fired but it was enough to catch everyone's attention on the outside. After hearing the shots Fredrick and I both turn to look at the house that Troy and Braydon are inside of. We both stare at the house and wait for some sort of conformation that they're still alive inside. Before we see any sort of conformation from inside Zooey screams out from the bus.

"Look! Over there!"

Fredrick and I both spin around and look at Zooey. She is pointing across the street at a mustard colored house with a white picket fence. As Fredrick and I turn to look at the house Runners are pouring onto the front lawn from the right hand side of the house. With the new threat racing towards us Fredrick and I open fire on them. We make sure each shot is a headshot, only using three bullets to kill all three of the Runners. Thanks to the commotion Fredrick and I have caused Runners start to come at us from all directions.

Fredrick and I keep the front of the bus well protected while Cid, Vincent, April and Mark pull down the windows on the bus and cover every other side. With all the gun fire outside it puts the fire in Troy and Braydon's step. They scurry around the house, opening all the drawers they come across, looking for the key to the bus. With the Runners coming from all directions it is very difficult to defend the bus. A little bit into the fight one Runner comes from around the corner of the house that Braydon and Troy are in, catching us off guard. By the time Fredrick and I even see him it is too late. I am able to fire off one shot at it, hitting it in the chest before it lunges at me and tackles me to the ground.

When I land against the hard pavement below my gun is knocked out of my hands and across the front lawn. The Runner lunges at my neck but I am able to stop him from sinking his teeth into it long enough for Fredrick to kick him off of me. After Fredrick kicks the Runner off of me he places a bullet right between its eyes. When the Runner is dead Fredrick extends his arm down to me and quickly helps me back up to my feet. Right as I get back onto my feet Troy and Braydon emerge from the house with the key to the bus held high.

Troy and Braydon run right past Fredrick and I onto the bus. Troy hands the key to Mark and Mark sticks it into the ignition in almost perfect sequence. When Mark turns the key the bus starts up without any problems. After Fredrick and I hear the engine we start to slowly back up to get onto the bus. Fredrick lets me get on the bus first as he hangs back and kills any Runners that come at us. After I'm safely on the bus Fredrick slowly backs up and gets on next. Once Fredrick is back on the bus Mark slams the doors closed before shifting the bus into reverse and backing out the driveway. While backing out the driveway Mark runs over two Runners that were coming towards the bus. This causes blood to spray all up the back windows of the bus.

Once we're back on the road Mark shifts the bus into drive and pulls away from the house. He makes sure to hit any Runners that dare step out into the road in front of the bus. There is only one road leading out of the small town and it is a very long dirt road. As we turn onto the dirt road and start to leave the small Texan town all the Runners stop chasing us. Now that we're safely out of the town Mark uses the windshield wipers to clear the blood and guts off the front of the bus.

With the town behind us we can all breathe a sigh of relief before sinking down into our seats. The dirt road we're on has many bumps and ditches, each time the bus goes over one we're thrashed around in our seats. With all the bumps and ditches Mark is forced to go slow to prevent losing control of the vehicle. The dirt road is only a few miles long but with how slow we're going it takes us almost ten minutes to drive those few miles. After we're off the dirt road Mark looks up into the rear view mirror of the bus so he can see everyone. Once he is looking at all of us he says, "Sorry to be the bearer of bad news, but we need gas."

Chapter 9 - The Fabulous City of Las Vegas Nevada

Almost five minutes after Mark notified us that we needed gas, we came across the first gas station. When we turn into the gas station Mark pulls up to the diesel pump and lets Fredrick, Troy and Braydon out. Once all three of them are off the bus I walk towards the front to get off as well and help them secure the area. As I pass by Mark he leans over and lightly grabs my arm.

"Hey, while you're out there, grab a map book. There is no GPS in the bus so we're going to need It.", Mark says to me.

I nod to Mark before stepping off the bus and sliding a fresh clip into my gun, just in case. After I am off the bus I walk over to the little store at the gas station and take a look around inside before opening the door. Everything in the store is highly disorganized, aisles are knocked over and everything that used to be on them is now scattered all over the ground. The stench of rotten eggs is seeping out from the store. With no power and the heat of Texas I can only imagine how fast they spoiled.

Aside from the obvious signs of a struggle inside the store there doesn't seem to be anything harmful to me inside. After fully checking over everything I open the front door to the store and walk inside. Once inside the store the first place I go is right near the cash register. At the cash register I take a look around at the floor and look for a map book.

"Come on! The map book has got to be right around here!" I yell out loud.

I continue to mumble profanity while searching around the counter that the cash register sits on. After a few minutes go by I notice there is a fallen rack right next to the counter but an aisle from the store has fallen onto it. I pull the shelves up before pushing them out of the way and revealing the floor below. There are half a dozen food products, smashed, smooshed, opened and smeared on top of the selection of map books. I let out a sigh before leaning down and brushing the mess off of all the books. Finally towards the bottom of the stack I find a map book almost unscathed by the food spillage.

When I find the cleanest map book I grab it with both hands and hold it up in the air like it is gold. After my quick, self celebration moment I run back out to the bus with the book in hand. When I arrive at the bus Fredrick, Troy and Braydon are just finishing up filling the bus with gas, as I pass them I shoot them a smile before getting back on board the bus. Once we're all back onto the bus Mark closes the doors and pulls away from the gas station. I take a seat behind him and to his right before opening up the map book to give him directions on where to go.

"What road should I be looking for?" Mark asks.

"Uhm, Looks like... Route forty." I reply.

"Yeah, we follow route forty until we come to ninety three north, which then will take us into Vegas."

"Alright, where does it say ninety three is?"

"Uhm, it says Kingman Arizona has a branch going north out of it."

"How many miles does it say until Kingman?"

"Uhm, what?" I ask confused.

"Use the little Inch measurement thing and your finger at the bottom of the page."

"I suck at those things." I remark.

"Oh my god just give it to me!" Mark says as he is starting to get frustrated.

"Wait! It's like two hundred miles until Vegas so like one fifty until Kingman. Just read the damn signs!" I yell out to Mark.

Mark rolls his eyes at me as we board the route forty acceleration ramp. Once we're on route forty I lean back into my seat and stare out the window. I can't help but be amazed by looking at the landscape around us. From someone who has lived on the East Coast his whole life the West Coast's landscape is amazing. It is filled with large rocks piled up onto more large rocks and actual crevices, valleys, plains and ravines. There are actually long stretches of land with no houses to be seen. The huge ravines and crevices are so deep that if you made a wrong step, you'd fall to your death. Everything is different out here, the trees, the shrubbery and even the wildlife.

For one of the first times in my life I am able to see a cactus in its natural environment. I mean sure, I seen them while driving to Vegas for the first time but not like this. Then I was focused on the road and worried about getting to my destination, not some cactus on the side of the road. And we're talking a real cactus here, one that is not stuck in a store in some pot or planted in a Museum exhibit. This is an actual Cactus, out in the real world, in an actual desert. The experience was similar to that of someone who lived in Florida their whole life then came north to New York or Manhattan and experienced snow for the first time in their life.

You feel so childish and juvenile for finding something so simplistic, so interesting, but you can't help but to be amazed. Even though you see it in pictures, on TV, in movies and in stores nothing compares to seeing it in person. Now that I am not the one driving, seeing a desert for one of the first times in my life was quite exhilarating. I stared out the window of the bus for hours, just taking in the whole environment around me.

One of the biggest differences of the East Coast and the West Coast are the highways. Out here they have signs like beware of falling boulders, back east the only signs you're going to find are deer crossings. It was so much more serene on the West Coast. We could travel for miles and miles without seeing any signs of people even being there, no houses, no cars and no trash. Back east there wasn't any uncharted land, every five feet was a house, trash, road, car or a person. There wasn't a single stretch of road you could travel down without seeing some sort of sign that people have been there.

As we are driving down the highway I notice that almost everyone has their eyes glued to the windows. With a lot of us have never having left the East Coast in our lives; experiencing the West Coast is just a mind blowing experience. As we continue west down the highway towards Las Vegas everyone acts like a tour guide. We all point out rock formations near the road that look cool or even slightly inappropriate.

An hour seems to fly by and before we know it we're already in New Mexico. Just at first glance I can tell that the sights in New Mexico are even better than they were in Texas. Out here there are tons more rock formations for us to look at and many more cacti to admire. After we are about a quarter ways through New Mexico Mark notifies us that we need gas. Everyone keeps an eye out on both sides of the road for a nearby gas station.

A few miles further down the road we come across a small gas station on the right hand side of the road. Mark pulls up to the diesel pump before letting Fredrick, Braydon, Troy and I off the bus to check the area and see if it is safe. Once we're off the bus we quickly scan the area around us before letting Mark know everything is safe. When we're done checking the area Fredrick sticks the nozzle into the bus and start the pump.

Everyone decides to get off the bus to stretch their arms and legs at this gas station. With the weather being so much nicer and everyone cramped up from the long bus ride a good stretch is well needed. While we're all off the bus and stretching our legs a few of us decide to walk over to a cactus alongside the gas station. I poke and prod the Cactus a bit with my gun, feeling so childish that I am amazed by such a simplistic piece of nature. After a few minutes go by of playing with the cactus a few others gather around me, amazed by it as well.

"We should break it in half, see what is inside."

"I heard water is inside of them."

"Nah, its all slime."

"Slime?"

"Yeah it is similar to Semen."

"That's nasty."

"Hey, you asked..."

Everyone continues rambling on about the Cactus, sharing what they know about it. Some people even grow daring and stick their hand near it, just barely touching one of its spikes. Regardless of who touches it, the outcome is always the same. The second they feel the spike enter their skin they quickly pull back and yelp. Placing their finger inside their mouth and sucking on it, nodding to everyone, letting them know that it is sharp.

It doesn't take long for me to get bored from just looking at the cactus and grow curious of what is inside. Unable to resist my curiosity anymore I stand up and kick the cactus, causing it to break in half. With the cactus now broken in half I plunge my hand inside and get some of the slimy juices onto my fingers. I bring my fingers up to my nose and smell them a bit, curious of its scent. As I smell my fingers everyone is staring at me, waiting to hear my verdict. After smelling it a few times I shake my head to the crowd around me before saying, "I can't smell anything."

After I speak almost everyone bends over and sticks their hands inside the cactus to get some juices on their fingers, wanting to smell for themselves. Once they have some of the slime on their fingers they bring it up to their nose and smell it. After smelling it they nod their head, confirming what I told them. Some of us, after smelling it, stick our tongues out and very lightly touch them against our fingers, curious what the slime tastes like. Anyone who was daring enough to stick it in their mouth gags before spitting out whatever got on their tongue.

Once we're done playing with the Cactus we all walk back over to the bus and get onboard where Fredrick is patiently waiting for us. As we're all walking back onboard the bus, Fredrick asks, "You children done playing with your Cactus?" All of us laugh and smile at him while walking by him and back to our seats. Once we're all sitting down Mark closes the doors before pulling away from the gas station and back onto route forty. As we're pulling out of the gas station I lean forward and tell Mark, "We'll need to make another stop for gas right after Albuquerque. After that we're good until Arizona."

Mark nods to me, letting me know that he heard me. Afterward I lean back into my seat and stare out the window at the setting sun. I stare off into the horizon at the reds and oranges that fill the sky. The colors of the sunset fit perfectly with the New Mexico landscape, matching beautifully with the rocks and dirt all around us. Over the next few minutes my eyes stay glued to the sunset. Amazed that after all that has happened to the world these past few weeks something can still be so beautiful. After the sun is fully set in the distance I lay my head back into my seat and stare up at the ceiling before letting my mind drift off. Once I finally get tired I lay my head against the window and close my eyes before falling asleep.

Smack! The sound of my head hitting the window of the bus can be heard by everybody onboard, followed by me screaming profanity at the top of my lungs. I grip the side of my head before standing up and pacing back and forth on the bus, trying to shake off the pain. While walking back and forth on the bus I continue to grunt and groan before stopping next to Mark.

Once I am standing next to Mark I say to him, "Hey, you know those big round things in the road? They're all deep and shit? Well they're called Pot Holes and you're not supposed to hit them, so next time let's try to fucking go around them, ok?"

Mark sticks his hand up behind him before giving me the finger. As Mark gives me the finger I grumble to myself, half tempted to break it off of his hand. I pace back and forth down the aisle a few more times before stopping next to Mark again.

"Where are we at?" I ask Mark.

"We are going through the Rocky Mountains now, coming up on Albuquerque."

"What's the ETA?"

Before Mark is able to respond we come up over top a large hill that looks directly down at Albuquerque, New Mexico. As we come over the hill and see Albuquerque my jaw drops down, the sight almost indescribable... There are thousands of lights still on in Albuquerque, almost convincing us that there are still people living there. Before we get too close to the city and ruin the spectacular view I call everyone up to the front of the bus. The sight was simply breath taking. To see the city from up high was breath taking. It seemed so quiet and serene, almost like it was untouched by destruction. The lights in the city were so bright that you could see the clouds in the darkest parts of the sky.

As we continue to descend down the hill and towards the city the signs of destruction become more and more obvious. The visible destruction starts off large scale, such as, large buildings with all their windows smashed out and large amounts of structural damage. Some of the things that we thought were beautiful lights while driving down into the city turn out to be dangerously large, roaring fires. The fires are relentlessly burning everything in their path. As we get even closer still to the city, the small scale destruction starts to become noticeable.

There are hundreds of cars that are left abandoned. Most of them have their windows shattered, leaving the glass to cover the ground like confetti. As with every other city, bodies litter the road. They are torn apart or still being torn apart by the zombie's feasting on them. While driving through the city Mark steps on the gas pedal and increases in speed. Making extra sure nothing we don't want on the bus can get on. Also as we're driving Mark aims for any zombies or Runners that get in his way, making sure to splatter their guts all over the front of the bus. The mess they make across the front of the bus is a quick fix for our windshield wipers.

It doesn't take long for us to drive through all of Albuquerque and before we know it we're looking out the back of the bus at it. Now that we're out of the city I return to my seat and stare up at the ceiling. The whole time I am staring at the ceiling I am nothing but perplexed of how the city looked so beautiful on the outside but so hideous on the inside. Every mile closer that we get to Vegas I can't help but think about my friend John. I constantly ask myself, is it wrong for me to actually believe that I am going to find him when I come to Vegas? Or is the false hope I am giving myself perfectly justifiable? Either way, I'm still going to keep my fingers crossed.

Once we're about thirty miles out of Albuquerque Mark pulls onto a deceleration ramp leading down to the first gas station we come across on the outskirts of town. As we approach the gas station we go slow, worrying that there could be some zombie wanderers. Or even some over spill from the infestation in Albuquerque. After we scope the area around the gas station Mark parks next to the diesel pump and lets Fredrick, Braydon and Troy out of the bus. Once they're off the bus they double check the area before starting to pump the gas.

While I wait for them to finish pumping the gas I walk over to the opposite side of the bus and look out the window. As I look out the window my eyes light up with fear. There are twenty or so zombies hobbling towards the bus from the highway. After seeing the zombies I reach for my gun before pulling down the window and sliding it outside. I start by killing the zombies that are closest to the bus first and then working my way out. Right after Fredrick hears the first gunshot he sends Troy and Braydon around the side of the bus to investigate.

Troy and Braydon run around to the front of the bus and immediately stop when they see all the zombies. The two of them hesitate before bringing their guns up to eye level and shooting at the zombies they see. As Fredrick is just finishing up pumping the gas more zombies come towards the gas station from over the highway. When Fredrick is done pumping the gas he throws the nozzle of the pump on the ground and bangs the side of the bus. Letting Troy and Braydon know it is time to go.

After Fredrick bangs on the side of the bus Troy and Braydon quickly turn around to get back onboard. When everyone is back onboard Mark slams the doors to the bus shut and punches the gas, accelerating back out onto the highway at a dangerous speed. Once we're back onto the highway and a few miles down the road Mark is able to safely return to his normal speed. Now that we're in the clear I return to my seat before tilting my head back and staring off at the ceiling.

"Almost there Ryan, almost there..." I say as I try and reassure myself for the short journey ahead.

After sitting down I bring my hands up to my face and rub my forehead, trying to calm myself down so I can fall back asleep. Before placing my head back against the side of the window I look up at Mark and hope he heeded my warning about the pot holes. I close my eyes with my head placed against the window and toss and turn for close to ten minutes before finally falling asleep.

————————————————————————————

"Get up!" I hear a familiar voice say while their hand is on my shoulder, shaking me.

"Ryan! Get up!" I hear the same voice call out again, this time sounding a bit more agitated. "We're at a gas station right outside of Kingman and we need directions."

Once I'm awake I rub my eyes before looking out the window. The first thing I notice is there is a large gas station right in front of us. Every one of the gas station's windows is shattered with tumble weeds accumulating where the glass used to be. That gas station is so destroyed that there is even an American flag colored RV parked over a pump.

Shockingly enough the only operational pump at the gas station just so happens to be the diesel pump we are at. I guess we happened to luck out for the first time in over two thousand miles. While Troy and Braydon are still outside pumping the gas I grab the map book at my side and flip to the page that has Arizona on it. Once I am on the page with Arizona I look over the whole page until I find the city of Kingman.

I look up at Mark before starting to talk, "Alright... So... Towards the ass end of Kingman you'll want to take route ninety three, which branches off of route forty to the west. It says it is called W Beale Street. So keep an eye out for that. That will take us all the way up to Vegas."

As I am talking Mark writes everything I am saying down so he can keep it in front of him at all times. Right after I finish giving Mark directions, Troy and Braydon finish up pumping the gas and walk back onto the bus. As Troy is walking by me on the bus I stand up and ask him, "Are we sure we're approaching Kingman and not Flagstaff?"

"Yup, you slept through Flagstaff." Troy replies.

"Good thing! What a shit hole that place was..." Braydon remarks.

Troy chuckles a bit at Braydon's remark before the two of them continue to the back of the bus. As Mark pulls away from the gas station and back onto the highway I sit back down in my seat and breathe a sigh of relief. We have officially just made our last stop before Las Vegas. A few minutes after pulling back onto the highway Kingman is visible in the distance. As we start to approach Kingman I am a bit taken off guard by the condition of the town. Before the zombie apocalypse the town looks like it was ruled by poverty. It is hard to tell if a lot of the destruction happened before or after the apocalypse.

But, just like all the other towns we've driven through, almost all of the windows are shattered and buildings have tons of structural damage, mostly from explosions. The only recent sign of the apocalypse is blood spatter and the bodies that litter the roads throughout the city. About half way through the city everyone stands up and starts to question the bodies that are lying on the ground, wonder why they aren't up and walking around. Out of all of us, April is the first to bring the subject up.

"If zombies did this, why isn't everyone turned?" April asks.

"Good question. It must have just happened recently." I reply.

"Do we even know how long it takes for someone to turn?" Zooey adds.

"No idea." I reply.

"Lewis turned pretty darn quick if you ask Me.", I add.

Mark calls out on the bus, "The amount of time it takes to transform depends on the person. Just like different doses of medicine are prescribed depending on the person."

"Wait, look at their bodies..." Troy adds.

Troy points out one of the bodies we're driving by that is impaled on a broken pipe sticking out of a building. On the body there are deep, noticeable claw marks across the man's throat and torso, penetrating at least an inch down. The man's ribcage is visible through the torn flesh on his torso. Flies have found their way over to his body and started to hatch maggots in it, making the site uglier than it should be. As we drive by the body the wiggling and squirming of the maggots is just barely noticeable. After seeing the maggots I turn away from the window and gag.

"Night Stalkers..." I mumble out loud.

"Those bodies have maggots, if they were going to turn... They would of already..." I add.

Everyone nods, letting me know that they agree with my statement before turning to look out the windows again. While driving through Kingman we are forced to pull all the windows of the bus up. The stench of the decomposing bodies and the burning flesh is too much for any of us to stomach. We keep the windows up until we're out of Kingman at which point we put them back down to let the stench escape out. While we wait for the stench to leave the bus everyone has their shirts pulled over their noses, making us all look like bandits.

219

After driving about twenty miles outside of the city the stench finally starts to leave the bus. While we're all busy coughing and trying to endure the smell none of us are paying attention to where we are going. In between coughs when I tilt my head up I see a sign for ninety three west pass us right by. After seeing the sign I turn to the front of the bus and yell out to Mark.

"Mark! You passed it!", after I yell Mark snaps to attention and looks around.

"What? Missed what?" Mark asks.

"The turn Mark, the turn!" I yell out loud.

"Oh. Shit! Well, where should I turn to get to ninety three from here?" Mark asks.

"Around.", I say.

"Huh?" Mark replies.

"Around! Turn Around!" I yell at Mark as I start getting frustrated that we're now almost a mile past our turn.

"But that is illegal!" Mark remarks.

"Who is going to pull you over, the fucking zombie cop?" I yell out to Mark.

"Oh... Right..." Mark says, remembering that almost everyone is dead.

"You're such an idiot..." I say to him.

Mark slowly decelerates before moving as far over to the right on the highway as he can. Once we're almost at a full stop Mark swings the bus to the left to do a K-turn and turn back around. During the K-turn Mark almost drives us into a ditch on the side of the road before backing us up and fully turning back around. Once we're turned around and driving back in the direction we came from Mark passes the turn yet again.

"Hey, Mark. You passed it again..." I say out loud.

"Yeah, I know. How do you expect me to turn this gigantic vehicle onto that small ass lane without turning around?" Mark yells out at me.

"I'll let you slide on this one." I respond.

After Mark turns on to ninety three I lean back in my seat and look out the window. I look up into the sky and notice that it is mid day and that we are only about an hour outside of Vegas now. As we get closer to Vegas I stare out the window of the bus to try and conceal my excitement. After a few minutes go by I am unable to conceal my excitement any longer so I decide to stand up and start a conversation to help pass time.

"So, it's been bothering me..."

"What makes Night Stalkers so much different then zombies and Runners that their bite doesn't change you?" I add.

"Who knows? We don't know these things well enough to make any kind of guess." Troy replies.

"Mark?" I ask, wanting a more educated opinion on the subject.

"Well, maybe they don't carry the same toxin that the zombies or Runners do." Mark answers.

"Toxin?" I ask.

"In order for the zombies or Runners to change you they carry a sort of virus or toxin in their blood and saliva. When exposed to that you will be infected and it will eventually take over. Apparently the Night Stalkers don't have it." Mark says.

"What that means to me is if a Night Stalker bites you, I don't have to shoot you in the head." Fredrick says out loud.

"Good call Fredrick, good call." I say.

When the chit chat comes to a close I sit down and toss my head into the back of the seat while still chuckling at Fredrick's response. While staring out the window I start to day dream, losing myself in the ups and downs of the terrain. I don't pay attention to anything outside until we pass a sign that catches my attention, "Hoover Dam five Miles". After seeing the sign I snap back to reality and stand up and start talking to everyone on the bus

"Alright everyone we're approaching the Hoover Dam, I'm your tour guide for the day, my name is Ryan."

"Hoover Dam was created by some guy at some time and it blocks water. Tour's over, enjoy the sites!"

After I'm finished talking I sit back down, very few people giggling about my quick presentation. About a minute after sitting down we finally make our approach up to the Hoover Dam. As we get closer to the Hoover Dam everyone on the bus stands up to look out the side windows with Lake Mead now visible in the distance. We all take a minute to look at Lake Mead in the distance - the way the mountain reflects off the lake is unfathomable. It looks exactly like one of those pictures you see hanging up in someone's office. The large mountain with trees all around it and the snow capped peak reflecting off the lake is something you don't see that often in your life. But for right now, it's in front of you and you're witnessing it with your own eyes.

For a manmade lake, Lake Mead is one of the most beautiful things I've ever seen in my life. We continue our approach up to the Hoover Dam, climbing the hill leading up to the large concrete highway going over top of the dam. All of us are too busy and side tracked to pay attention to the Hoover Dam all of us are still staring at Lake Mead and the surrounding mountains. When we reach the top of the Hoover Dam and start to drive over Mark starts to slow down. With the intention of yelling at Mark I look up to see why he is slowing down, but then notice a barricade in front of the bus.

Mark stops in front of the barricade and turns the bus off, leaving it running and wasting gas would be pointless if we can't go anywhere. Since now we're unable to go anywhere we all step off the bus to do some sightseeing. The first thing I do is run over to the side of the dam facing Nevada and look over. The dam is still channeling water through it, meaning there is a chance it could be still supplying electricity to Las Vegas.

With that question answered I walk over to Fredrick and Mark who are both looking at the barricade. The two of them stand there, still and stare at the barricade. You can tell by the looks on both of their faces that they are not happy that the barricade is there. I stand right next to them and stare at the barricade as well, trying to think of a way to get through. The barricade consists of two police SUV's parked parallel on the road which is covering up both lanes of the highway. Both of the police SUV's have been torched in a fire, probably from an angry citizen throwing a Molotov. In front of the police SUV's sits two concrete barriers, which is a bigger problem than the SUV's in our way.

"Well, the police SUV's won't be a problem." I say out loud.

"It looks like someone burned them to a crisp, only the frame of the vehicle is left." I add.

Fredrick nods while still staring at the concrete barriers, wondering what we can do. After a few more minutes go by with Fredrick just staring at them he changes it up a bit. Fredrick walks over to the barricade and starts to kick it and whack it with his gun, testing its durability. After about a minute of beating on it he manages to break off a large chunk of one of the barriers. Fredrick picks it up off the ground and holds it in his hand to show Mark and I.

"The barriers aren't very strong." Fredrick says out loud.

Fredrick takes a few steps back and away from the barrier. While Fredrick is backing up he pushes Mark and I back as well, getting us all away from the barrier. Once we're all about twenty feet away from the barriers Fredrick starts shooting the one on the right. Every one of Fredrick's shots blasts a large chunk off the barrier. When Fredrick finishes shooting his clip into the barrier we all walk up to see the damage he did.

While we're all standing around the barrier I brush the dust off of it and the small chunks to see the damage Fredrick did.

"You blew about a quarter of it off.", I say out loud.

Mark and Fredrick walk over to the barrier and help me clean off all the dust and break off any large chunks that are loose. After the three of us clean up the barrier that Fredrick destroyed we back away to let him start shooting again. Knowing it is going to take awhile for Fredrick to bust through the barrier I walk to the other survivors and stare off into the distance at Lake Mead.

"We are very creatively working our way through the barrier." I say to everyone to answer their question as to why we're shooting at a concrete wall.

While looking into the distance at Lake Mead I feel soothed, almost like the lake is reassuring me that everything is going to be ok soon. Quite a bit of time goes by with all of us just standing on the sidewalk next to the highway. Our arms are hanging over the railing as we just stare off into the distance at the lake in front of us. All of us throw our heads up into the air and take in the smell of fresh air for the first time in a long awhile. The sound of the water flowing through the dam beneath us is just barely audible over the sound of Fredrick's gun. The only time it is possible to hear the dam and the sounds of the wildlife around us is when Fredrick stops to reload.

After Fredrick's fifth clip into the barricades he stops firing and lets his gun hang at his side. Fredrick walks over to the barricade and checks out all of the damage he has done to it before walking back towards the bus.

"Alright, that's about it. We should be able to smash through it now." Fredrick says while walking past us and onto the bus.

All of us take one last look off at Lake Mead before following Fredrick onto the bus. When we're all back on the bus Mark starts it up and slowly inches forward until we reach the barricade. Mark uses the front of the bus to lightly push the barricade out of the way, while being careful not to get us stuck. The pressure that the bus is putting against the concrete barrier is ever so slightly pushing it forward. Mark gives the bus a bit more gas which causes the right tire to lift up on onto the barricade and the bus to slant dramatically to the left. As the bus tilts to the left we all start to slide out of our seats and down to the left side of the bus. This causes the bus to tilt even more and even start to roll.

"Everyone move to the right! Move to the right!" Fredrick calls out before propelling himself to the right hand side of the bus.

As we are all trying to get back onto the right hand side of the bus the right wheel can be heard spinning in the air as it is unable to gain traction on the barrier in front of us. As more people make their way to the right hand side of the bus I can feel the front right tire catch back onto the ground and pull the bus forward. The bus quickly climbs over the concrete barrier in front of us and smashes into the police SUV's that are in front of it. Just as we expected the police SUV's were no match for the bus as we quickly shoved them out of the way.

When the front end of the bus lands on the other side of the barricade and pulls the bus forward the underbelly grinds along what's left of the concrete barriers. When the back end of the bus reaches the barrier it gets caught and stops the bus dead in its tracks. Mark hits the gas and causes the wheels on the front of the bus to screech against the ground. While the back wheels are left up in the air on the other side of the barrier.

Mark puts the bus in reverse and backs about halfway up as we all shift to the front of the bus to help the front tires keep traction. Once the bus is sitting on the barricade like a teeter totter Mark shifts it back into drive before stomping on the gas pedal. This time when the back end hits the barrier it smashes it into a dozen different pieces. Now without any trouble the bus is able to hop over the barricade and free us from its clasp. We now can continue down the Highway, getting even closer still to Las Vegas.

Shortly after passing the Hoover Dam we are already starting to see signs for Boulder City, the final city we will be driving through before Las Vegas. As we approach Boulder City everyone stares out the windows, amazed. The houses are all in perfect condition and there is no noticeable damage done to them, no destruction and no blood. Not only are all the houses in perfect condition they are all huge. Almost all of them are two stories tall with two car garages, pools, sheds and perfect front lawns, the grass is even still a dark green color without being up kept. None of the houses are something an average Joe could afford.

There are a few cars parked in the driveways of each house but for the most part it looks like almost everyone was evacuated. While driving through Boulder City we don't see a single person or even any signs of life. Driving through the city without seeing anything gives us all an eerie feeling that is hard to shake.

It only takes about ten minutes to drive through all of Boulder City before it dumps us out onto a very long, straight and perfectly flat highway. It is a four lane road, two going in and two coming out with sand in the center for a divider. While we're driving down the highway everyone leans back and relaxes, knowing that Vegas is just ahead. There are very few buildings located along the highway, most of them are convenience stores but there is also a junkyard or two.

At the very northern end of the highway sits two large mountains. Both the mountains are standing tall up into the sky, with both of their peaks bright white from the snow on them. The highways road that we are on right now travels in between both of the mountains and weaves through them. It seems like only seconds later that we're driving through the mountains and looking up at the rocks all alongside the mountain. Each one of the rocks has little holes dug out in between them or through them that little creatures call their homes. All along the mountains you can see hundreds of caves, most of them are up high but some are down low. The last time I was in Vegas everyone would tell us stories about homeless people living in these caves.

The stories always seemed a bit farfetched at the time but as we drive through the mountains they start to become more believable... There are clothes hanging up on the rocks that were left out to dry as well as shopping carts hanging out of some of the caves. With everything that has happened I highly doubt someone lives in the caves now but it is obvious that someone did. On the outside of one of the caves it has "HLEP ME" written in white paint. My guess is it meant to say help me but the person who wrote it had a lack of an education.

We continue through the mountains, weaving and zig zagging through all of them until finally we come out into a large open valley. In the valley we are able to get a quick glimpse of Las Vegas before being overwhelmed by highways that lead into the city. As we're overwhelmed by highways Mark slows down, unsure of where to go and scared to make a wrong turn.

"Hey, Mark! Find Sunset, Arville, Flamingo or... uhm... The Palms just get us near that and I can find my friend's house!" I yell out to Mark, trying to give him a sense of direction.

"What is the Palms?" Mark replies, confused of where I am asking him to go.

"It's a big ass Casino, you can't miss It.", I say to Mark.

While Mark drives around and looks at each of the Casinos, checking to see if it is the Palms, everyone else has their faces plastered against the windows. For a lot of us this is the first time any of us have seen Las Vegas. And it sure is the first time we have ever seen it deserted. We're all amazed by the design and upkeep of the city also the fact that it is still in perfect condition despite everything that has happened. While driving through the streets we pass an occasional zombie, usually dressed in torn and baggy clothing and walking with a serious limp. Probably just a homeless guy that was unable to evacuate in time.

Almost all of the buildings in Las Vegas have very little structural damage, which surprises almost all of us. The only signs of the recent zombie disaster are cars parked in the center of the road and left abandoned. All of the cars are pretty beat up, most of them have shattered windows with blood covering a lot of the car. Some of the cars even have blood trails leading away from them and into an alleyway off the side of the street. None of us question what happened in the alley, we figured it was obvious based on the blood trail. While we're driving through the city Mark hits any zombies that are caught walking down the center of the street. Even someone as boring as Mark needs to find a way to keep themselves entertained.

As Mark continues to drive around the city he is completely clueless to where he should be going. Almost thirty minutes go by of us driving around Vegas until we finally spot the Palms off in the distance. After spotting the casino I point it out to Mark and have him navigate his way over to it. Once Mark has the casino in his sights he tries to keep it there while navigating his way through the city. From the distance we're at, the Palms looks to be in rather good condition. A few windows of the casino are cracked and damaged but other than that there isn't much structural damage done to the building.

As Mark drives us closer and closer to the Palm casino certain buildings and street names start to catch my attention. When Mark reaches the Palm's casino he stops right out front and awaits further directions from me. I walk up to the front of the bus and point out my friend's house to him which is visible from right outside of the Palms. Mark nods to me before taking us over to the house I pointed at.

Mark stops the bus in the middle of the road, right out front of my friend's house. When I look up and see his house tons of memories rush back into my head. Mostly all of them are good ones of the short week of fun I had when I visited him in Las Vegas. After Mark puts the bus into park he turns it off before standing up and leaving the key in the ignition. We all exit the bus as everyone follows my lead up to my friend's house. I stop in front of his door and raise my hand like I am going to knock before catching myself.

"Who are we kidding...?" I chuckle to myself as I lower my hand and turn the knob.

The door to my friend's house opens after just slightly being touched. Whoever was here last must have been in a real hurry. When I walk into the house I notice that the whole house is completely trashed. The last person here completely trashed the house when they were looking for something. While I search the house I keep my gun ready at my side, in case someone didn't trash the house and *something* did. After clearing the whole house I set my gun down on the kitchen counter and take a seat on the nearby couch.

"I'm going to take a nap. All this driving has me worn out." Mark says out loud before entering one of the bedrooms and closing the door behind him.

"We need to devise a plan." I say while looking to everyone.

"First things first we all should get long range radios to communicate with each other. I'm sure there is a hobby shop around here somewhere with ear buds and radios." I add.

I continue by saying, "Second thing we need is a headquarters. This house simply won't do, it will work for the night but we need something bigger. Something people can come to and know where it is. My vote goes to McCarran airport. It's big, wide open and there are signs pointing to it all around Vegas."

"Third thing we need to do is tell people we have a survivor colony at the airport. We need to bring people in. The best way to do this is over the radio. We need to find a radio station around here and have a tape play on repeat that we have food, water and shelter." I add.

"Fourth on the list is, as I just said, food and water. We need to stock the shit out of that place and get it ready." I repeat.

"Fastest way to do all of this is split up into groups of two. April and I will go for food and water. Cid and Vincent I want you two to find us some radios. After you do, if you have any room left, grab food and water. Braydon and Troy, find a GPS so we can get around easier and then grab weapons. Zooey and Fredrick, grab weapons from another gun shop away from Braydon and Troy. Anybody have any rejections?" I say out loud.

Everyone shakes there head side to side, letting me know they agree with their tasks.

"We will meet back here before nightfall. Anybody have any questions?" I repeat.

"Where are we going to get our cars?" Zooey asks, curiously.

"Steal them." I say as I am walking out the front door.

April follows me out of the house and over to the street. Once I am on the sidewalk I look down both ends of the street at all the cars that are parked on the roads. Wondering what one I want to drive. A Mustang GT at the other end of the street perks my interest but I decide to settle on the SUV next to it since it is able to hold more. Once I have my vehicle picked out I jog down the street towards it before stopping next to it and looking inside.

"Keys aren't in it.", I say to April.

"Let's check inside." I add.

After checking out the car we both walk over to the front door of the house and look around inside. "It looks clear." I say out loud.

April nods, confirming that she doesn't see anything inside either. After looking around inside I try to open the front door but am unable to because it is locked. Without hesitation I take a step back and use my foot to kick the door out of its frame, allowing me access into the house. As April and I are entering the house I hear a car peeling away behind me. When I turn around to take a look back I see that Fredrick and Zooey have already found a van. I chuckle a bit to myself before walking through the doorway I just opened up. Once inside the house I check the drawers closest to the door but only find checks and bills, no keys.

After checking around the door I walk over to the kitchen and find the key rack right next to the refrigerator. There are two sets of keys on the key rack; one has a picture of a Mustang and the other a SUV. I grab the keys to the SUV and make a strong mental note that the Mustang keys are inside. After I have the keys in my hand I direct my attention to the refrigerator before opening it. The first thing I notice when opening the refrigerator is that the power is still on inside. The second thing that comes to mind is that the home owner had really bad taste for food. veggie burgers, soy milk and diet coke. I couldn't take looking around inside any more before I was forced to shut the door. I gag a bit to myself from their shockingly bad taste for food. Now that I feel I have seen enough in this house I return to the SUV outside.

Back outside I run over to the SUV and stick the key with the picture of the car into the lock before turning it and opening the door. I step inside the SUV before hitting the unlock button to unlock April's door and allow her entry. Once we're both inside I start the vehicle up before shifting it into reverse and pulling out of the driveway and back onto the road. Before I am fully in the road Cid and Vincent pull out in front of me in an Acura.

I race up and get directly behind Cid and Vincent and start blowing my horn while screaming, "Go! Go!" out the window.

On my way out of the development I stop and look both directions before putting on my blinker to indicate that I am going right. It takes a few seconds for me to realize that what I did was stupid and there is no point in stopping, or even putting on my blinker. After realizing this I pull out of the development and make my first left into a convenience store. Once at the convenience store I park the SUV out front before opening the back. I leave the engine running as I run into the store to grab some supplies. Before touching anything in the store I walk around with my gun drawn as I make sure everything is clear. After everything is clear I wave April inside. The first thing we grab is every single case of water and water bottle inside the store. All the water from inside the store fills the SUV about half way up.

The second trip we make inside is to grab any canned or bagged food to carry back to the car; it takes us a few more trips to grab everything we need from inside the store. When we're done raiding the store we end up with tons of different supplies. About a dozen cases of water, thirty different types of potato chips, some pretzels, a couple dozen power bars... We also found boxes full of different canned foods such as chicken noodle soup, chicken and stars, chef Boyardee and baked beans. After we're done with the store we load everything into the back of the SUV and return to the house to park it out front.

I turn the car off and leave the keys in it before getting out. Feeling that we could still use more supplies I scan the streets for another SUV that April and I can load up. After looking up and down the street a few times I finally spot one that I like. I run inside the house it is parked outside of and grab the keys for it before hoping inside. April and I take the vehicle to another convenience store nearby before loading it up, just like last time. After we've gotten everything useful from inside the store onto the SUV we drive it back to the house. Once we're back at the house I look up into the sky and notice the sun is just now starting to set.

"We've got time for one more." I say to April before scanning the street for another car.

The only car that is now left on the road that I'd like to drive is the jet black Mustang GT with a bright white racing stripe going over the car. Of course the car won't hold much for supplies but it will be damn fun to drive. I run over to the house and grab the keys for the car before returning to it and opening the door. Once it's open I hop inside and start it up before revving the engine a few times to hear it. After hearing the engine I step out of the car and look over to April.

"You may want to sit this one out." I say to April.

"Nah, I feel safe with you." April says with a smile.

I chuckle a bit from what April said before putting the car into reverse and looking behind me before peeling wheels out of the driveway. Once we're out in the street I spin the wheel to the right which swings the front end of the car into the dead center of the street. I place my left foot on the brake before shifting the car into drive and punching the gas. I use my right foot for the gas pedal which allows the car to smoke its tires for a few seconds. After I have had my moment of fun I release the break and continue to peel wheels until I am well out of the development. Once out of the development I continue to drive like an animal all around town, pulling my emergency break around almost every turn. On a turn just down the road from my friend's house I pull the emergency break but lose control and smash into another car on the opposite side of the road.

"Man if this was my car, I'd be *pissed*." I say while laughing the whole event off.

We drive for close to five minutes before finding another convenience store where April and I both load up on supplies. The two of us mostly grab food this time, since we have an over abundance of water. After we fill the car up with supplies we get back inside before returning to my friend's house. As we come screeching around the corner Fredrick and Zooey are standing next to the van that they have stocked with tons of weapons and ammo. Fredrick and Zooey both stare at me as I come tearing around the corner, the ass end of my car sliding all over the road. When I regain control of the vehicle I pull up next to Fredrick and Zooey with my bumper hanging off the back of the car and scratching against the ground.

"You're a good driver I see." Fredrick says to me, sarcastically, while pointing at the bumper.

I give Fredrick a half ass childish smile before turning the car off and getting out.

"All that time and you only filled a Mustang?" Fredrick asks.

"Don't forget that Black SUV right there and the Tan one right there." I say out loud.

"Oh yeah? Well take a look at my goodies." Fredrick says.

It is easy to tell that Fredrick is almost as excited as a kid on Christmas Morning. When Fredrick opens the back of his van to show me all the weapons and ammo he collected my jaw drops. My eyes grow wide as I am just barely able to open my mouth.

"Dude, that's like the whole fucking store!" I say to Fredrick, shocked by how many guns he has.

"Hah, yeah, I know. It is." Fredrick replies while laughing a bit.

As Fredrick opens the back doors of the van I reach in and go through a lot of the guns to see what Fredrick has collected. All while being amazed by how much Fredrick managed to grab in such a short period of time. While going through the guns I hear a loud obnoxious Pickup Truck come around the corner behind me. When I turn around to look at it I see black smoke pillowing out the back of it as it continuously backfires while coming around the turn. By looking through the windshield I can see that Vincent is driving the truck and Cid is in the passenger's seat. Vincent pulls up next to us before Cid and him step out of their pickup truck. The back of the truck is filled with cases of water that are being held down by bungee cords going over top of them.

After Cid gets out of the passenger's seat he hands each of us a small headset and a transmitter that straps onto our waist.

"We're going to use signal seven. They have an eleven mile radius and take double-A batteries. We grabbed a twenty five pack of batteries, for whenever we run out."

"What happen to the Acura?" I ask.

"We filled it up, it's parked somewhere over there." Cid says while pointing down the street.

Before putting the headset on all of us strap the transmitter to our waist. The headsets that Cid grabbed for us are clear. They have a microphone that runs down right next to our cheek and stops right next to our mouth. After we have everything hooked up we walk around and talk into the headsets to see if they actually work. In order to transmit anything through them you're required to press in a button on the piece that goes into your ear. Just after we finish talking to each other through the headsets Troy and Braydon come around the corner. They are driving a slick black SUV which is so over filled with supplies that the bumper is dragging along the ground. As they pull up next to us Troy hops out of the SUV holding a *TomTom* high in the air.

"The *TomTom* was in the SUV when we found It.", Troy says while walking towards us.

"Also, we just grabbed ammo, I figured Fredrick would go ape shit and grab almost the whole store of guns." Braydon says while getting out of the car.

All of us laugh, knowing that Fredrick did actually grab the whole store. Now that we're all back at the house we agree that it would be a good idea to head back inside before sunset. After we're back inside I set my gun down on the kitchen counter before opening the freezer. I look around inside the freezer before spotting a few frozen pizzas. After seeing the pizzas I reach into the freezer and pull them out before un-wrapping them and sticking them in the oven. Once they're in the oven I crank up the heat to three hundred and set the timer for twenty minutes.

"Pizza is in the oven!" I call out to everyone in the room.

"You found some pizza? That's awesome!" April yells out.

"This will be my first real meal in over a week!" Troy adds.

After the pizza is in the oven I walk over to the Bathroom and hit the light switch before walking over to the shower. I say a quick prayer before turning the knob in the shower and feeling warm water coming out of the spicket from above. Feeling the warm water caress my hand gave me a feeling of ecstasy. Almost everyone is able to hear the running water in the house and when they do they race over to the bathroom and pile up outside the door.

"Oh my god a shower too!?" April yells out.

"This is amazing!" Braydon yells out loud.

After seeing that the shower works everyone jumps around in celebration, like we've all just won a million dollars. Before stepping out of the bathroom I turn the water off and push back the crowd that has gathered around the door.

"Hey, hey, hey!" A few people say while I push them away from the door.

"We can all take showers but they can't be any longer than five minutes. We got to make sure there is enough water for all of us and we don't know how much water there is for the shower. So, when it is your turn, even though it feels amazing, clean yourself and get out." I say to everyone and wait for each of their nods to let me know they understood.

After everyone nods I lean my head back into the bathroom and look inside at the shelf in the shower. There is a bottle of shampoo on the shelf as well as a bar of soap and some conditioner. After looking inside the shower I say, "It looks like they left us shampoo and conditioner as well as some soap. Don't be a whore when using them; remember others have to shower too."

"As far as who goes first... You guys fight over that, I couldn't care less." I add.

Dozens of petty arguments break out as people debate who should be the first one to take a shower. After a few minutes go by they decide the order for the shower will be Zooey, Cid, Vincent, Troy, April, Fredrick, Braydon and then finally me. It was my decision to go last since I will be checking on the pizza every few minutes. Plus, if I go last it means I get to take as long of a shower as I want.

In between Vincent and Troy's showers the pizzas in the oven finish cooking. After I pull them out of the oven and set them on the table everyone digs in. Nobody has the patience to wait until it is cut or even cooled off before grabbing a few slices and shoving them into their mouths. I turn away from the table to grab the other pizza out of the oven. When I turn back to put the second pizza on the table I notice that the first whole pizza is already gone. The only thing that remains from it is a few crumbs and a strip of cheese covered in tomato sauce.

I place the second pizza down on the table and pull off three slices for myself before anyone is even able to get near it. After securing my slices of pizza I reach into the freezer to pull two more pies out and throw them into the oven, figuring we'll need more food by the end of the night. While waiting for the pizza in the oven to cook I walk around the kitchen and eat the three slices I took for myself. Right as I finish eating Troy gets out of the shower and April gets ready to go in. Once I finish eating I check on the two pieces in the oven to make sure that they're ok and aren't getting burned. After checking on the pizza I walk over to the back door and stare out. It is now fully dark outside as night has now fully set in.

"We should probably board this house up, just in case. Someone help me with this bookshelf." I say as I lean over and grab the bookshelf next to the back door.

As Troy and I slide the bookshelf over the back door I notice that it is a perfect fit, making it so there is no way that anything could see inside. After barricading the back door I walk around the rest of the house and make sure that something sturdy is in front of all the windows. We hope that if Night Stalker's can't see inside and we stay quiet, maybe they won't bother us. After the whole house is barricaded up I return to the oven and pull out the two freshly cooked pizzas. Once they're out of the oven I slide them onto the table before grabbing a slice for myself.

I almost inhale the slice of pizza as Braydon is just getting out of the shower, leaving only I left. When Braydon leaves the bathroom I rush in right behind him. Once inside I lock the door and strip my clothes off before throwing them into a corner of the room. After getting undressed I turn to the mirror and take a look at myself and am a bit surprised. Before all this started I was about two hundred and thirty pounds. Now my rib cage is completely visible and my cheeks are even thinner. I shrug after looking into the mirror and turn towards the shower. Unable to wait any longer I hop inside the shower and turn it on.

After turning it on I can immediately feel the warm water caressing my body. The water quickly flows through my hair, soaking it before trickling down my back. After the water runs down my back it chooses one of two legs to run down before ending up in the drain on the floor. A large smile forms on my face as I spin around in the shower, making sure water touches every single spot on my body.

After allowing my body to soak in the shower for a few minutes I reach over and grab the soap before lathering it onto my body. After the soap covers my body I step back under the water and allow it to rinse off before applying the shampoo. I mix the shampoo into my hair before washing it out underneath the shower head. I repeat the same process with the conditioner, taking my sweet ol' time since no one has to shower after me. After I finish rinsing out my hair I stay in the shower for another ten minutes, making sure to fully enjoy the warm water.

After I am done I exit the shower and dry off with the only towel remaining in the room. I slip into my old dirty clothes before leaving the bathroom. Back in the living room everyone is laying down on the floor. With a blanket or and pillow they managed to grab off a bed or from the couch. They are all still awake and chit chatting about the city amongst other things. Before walking out into the living room I peek into the only other bedroom in the house to see if it is occupied.

Without seeing anyone in the bedroom I say out loud, "I'm going to take the last bedroom, since it is my friend's house.", afterwards I look around to see if anyone disagrees.

Everyone nods, letting me know they don't mind if I take the only available bedroom for myself. After getting the approval of everyone to sleep in the bed, I walk into the bedroom and close the door behind me. Wasting almost no time I slip under the covers and close my eyes, drifting off into a sleep.

When I wake up and look outside I notice that it is about mid day the following day. I yawn and sit up to stretch my arms before realizing that April is lying in bed right next to me. She must have been really quiet, to not have waken me last night, I thought to myself. I quietly roll out of bed and look out the window. Rays of light from the sun are shining through the blinds, making it very difficult to see outside. Before leaving the room I walk around to the other side of the bed and shake April to wake her up. When I walk into the living room the first thing I notice is that everyone else is still sound asleep on the ground. Not wanting to waste any more of the day I pound on the wall in the living room to wake everyone up.

"Today is going to be a long day, everyone up, let's go!" I yell out loud as everyone rolls over and glares at me miserably.

I walk over to the refrigerator and reach in to grab both egg cartons before looking at the expiration date on them. "Eh.", I say out loud, noticing they only expired yesterday. "Should still be ok." I mumble to myself before throwing a pan onto the stove and some butter into the pan. Before turning the oven on I grab a bowl out of the cabinet and start cracking eggs into it. After I've cracked both full cartons of eggs I turn the stove on before mixing the eggs. By the time I finish mixing the eggs in the bowl the butter is fully melted and starting to sizzle. I dump half the eggs into the pan before searching the nearby drawers for a spatula. After finding the spatula I slave over the stove, mixing the eggs until they are done.

Once the eggs are done I pull three different plates out from the cabinet above the stove before evenly pouring the eggs onto them. After I've finished I turn around and slide all three plates onto the table behind me.

"Breakfast is served, possibly the last batch of good eggs you'll ever eat." I yell out loud before turning back to the stove.

I continue to cook eggs until everyone has a plate in front of them. Before sitting down to eat my eggs I open the door to Marks bedroom and yell in to him. "Get the fuck up! Your eggs are getting cold!" After yelling to Mark I return to the kitchen to begin eating my eggs. When I am about halfway done eating my eggs Mark finally stumbles out of his bedroom. As he walks towards the kitchen he is constantly rubbing his eyes, still trying to wake up. Mark puts his elbow on the table and leans his forehead into his palm before sticking his fork into the eggs. With everyone awake and together I decide now would be a good time to discuss today's plans.

"Alright, so now that everyone is out here, let's discuss today's agenda." I say out loud.

"We need to send out a radio frequency as far as possible to anyone that can hear us. The second thing we need to do is barricade all but one entrance to the airport. After the airport is fully sealed, of course we need to make sure we're the only things inside. It's already about mid day so we should split up into two teams. One team will go to the radio station and the second team will go to the airport. Fredrick will lead one team and I will lead the other." I add.

"Now, who wants to go to the radio station with me?" I ask as Troy, Mark, Cid and April all raise their hands.

"Alright, so that leaves Vincent, Zooey and Braydon with you Fredrick." I remark.

"Is everyone ok with this?" I ask. Everyone nods their heads, letting me know they're ok with the teams.

"Alright, let's head out. We'll meet you at the airport before nightfall. Keep the main entrance open." I say to Fredrick.

Now that we all know what we're doing I walk outside and over to the Mustang from the other day. April and I get inside the Mustang while Mark and Cid choose the tan SUV that April and I stocked up the other day. Troy runs over to the SUV that Braydon and he drove back the other day, the one with the GPS. As Troy is trying to figure out the GPS I pull up next to him and roll down April's window.

"You're going to have to lead us there, you got the GPS." I yell out to Troy.

"Yeah, I know." Troy says, as he is toying around with the GPS.

After Troy figured out how to work the GPS and it finds the nearby radio station he starts up his car and pulls in front of us. Troy goes slow at first and allows all of us to catch up to him and start following him. After Troy sees that we're all following him he accelerates to normal speed before leading us to the nearest radio station. April is able to admire the beauty of everything around us as we drive through the city. But I am forced to keep my eyes on Troy who is in front of me and the road around me. The radio station was only a five minute drive away from my friend's house.

When we arrive all three of us park out front of the radio station. Before exiting our vehicles we grab our weapons and look over at the radio station's lobby. There is no movement inside or any signs of recent destruction. Without seeing anything inside that could harm us I motion everyone to follow me inside. Once inside I make my way over to the elevator and look at a piece of paper hanging on the wall that gives a floor layout. On the piece of paper I look for the floor that shows the radio transmitter or DJ area. After finding the room and floor they host their morning show I hit the call button on the elevator and wait for it to come down.

"Fifth floor, let's go." I say motioning for everyone to follow me onto the Elevator as it arrives.

Once we're all on the elevator I hit the number five button before backing up and watching the lights. With every passing floor I grip my gun tighter, hoping that this radio station is nothing like the last. As the elevator dings and we reach the fifth floor I grip my gun tightly as the doors start to open. When the doors are open I propel myself out into the hallway, clearing all three directions before quickly moving down the hallway. As we pass each office I look inside to make sure it is clear before passing it and continuing down the hall.

At the end of the hallway I look both ways, making sure it is clear before doing anything else. When I look up I see a large sign on the wall right in front of me it that is pointing to the right. It says, "Be Quiet Live on the Air." When I look to the right I see a room at the end of the hallway that has metal double panel doors. I slowly make my way towards the room at the end of the hall while having flash backs of the other radio station. Each step sends chills down my spine and a sharp piercing pain throughout my chest. When I reach the room at the end of the hall and open the door I see that it is filled with tons of radio equipment. The equipment comes up about four feet off the ground and is covered with hundreds of different buttons. In front of each piece of equipment is a pair of chairs and a microphone that is hanging in front of it.

"Well, this is going to take awhile." I say before sitting down and starting to read the labels over each button.

Some of the labels above each button are torn and some are even faded. A lot of them have words I don't recognize or even understand. But sometimes I get lucky enough to find one I can actually read and understand. However after close to five minutes of searching I still can't find one that is as simple as an on or off switch or even an on air button.

"Oh come on, can it really be this hard? Mark where the fuck did you go?" I yell out loud, realizing that I will need some help finding this button.

Mark walks over and hovers over me to help examine the radio board. He slowly moves his hand over the board and hits a few different buttons. "Alright, try now." Mark says while backing away from the microphone. I pull the microphone over to my face and continue to speak in a different tone of voice, "Why hello there, you're listening to... Um... 133.7 Radio Uber. I'm your host, Ryan..." I pause and think for a second before turning to Mark.

"Wait, how do I know if people can hear me?" I ask.

"Hmm, good point." Mark adds.

"Oh, I know! Let me turn on the radio over in the corner." Mark says before running over to a little portable radio in the corner of the room.

After turning the radio on Mark tunes to our frequency before giving me a thumbs up. This lets me know that if I am transmitting, we will be able to hear it.

"Testing, one, two, three. Testing, one, two, three." I say while trying to keep it old school this time.

"I am still not hearing anything." I say out loud after not hearing myself repeat through the radio.

Mark walks back over to the radio board before hitting a few more buttons, scratching his head in between each to give himself time to think.

"Look, Mark, shouldn't this light thing be lit up at the top next to the on air label?" I ask.

"Hmm, good point." Mark replies.

Mark looks around the radio board before hitting even more random buttons. As time goes on and Mark is making little to no progress I become highly frustrated. Right before Mark can hit another button I swat his hand away from the panel. Mark and I start arguing about who is smarter while April plays around with the panel right next to ours.

"Look, Mark, go find an Instruction Manual or something! No reason to keep hovering over me like a fucking helicopter and hitting random buttons hoping that they work!", I say to Mark.

"I'm trying to figure this out, haven't you ever heard of trial and error?" Mark replies.

"Have you ever heard of being punched in the face? You can play trial and error with my fists and tell me which one hurts more." I reply to Mark.

"....one hurts more." Both Mark and I pause for a second after hearing my voice echo in the room.

"What the fuck was that?" I ask.

"...What the fuck was that?" My voice echoes back into the room.

"You're on air dumbass." Mark remarks.

"...You're on air dumbass." Mark's voice echoes back.

"Hey! Go fuck yourself! It's my voice on the air, not yours!" I say.

"...Hey! Go fuck yourself! It's my voice on the air, not yours!" Echoes back.

"Live on the air making yourself look like an idiot!" Mark replies.

"...Live on the air making yourself look like an idiot!" His voice echoes back.

"Hey!" April yells out before slamming her hand against the panel in front of her to make the echoing stop.

"Will you two grow the fuck up? Let's get this signal broadcast so we can get over to the fucking airport." April says to Mark and I.

"It was Mark's fault!" I say out loud.

"No it isn't." Mark answers.

April rolls her eyes at Mark and me before hitting a button and putting us back on the air. After putting us back on the air April also hits a button to record everything that I say.

"Is so..." I mumble to Mark before quickly starting the message that will be broadcast.

"Hello. My name is Ryan and I am a member of the Las Vegas Survivor Colony. If you're hearing this then turn your radio the fuck up and listen." I smirk as April rolls her eyes.

"We are stationed in Las Vegas, go figure, at the McCarren airport. Once you're in Las Vegas you can follow the signs to the airport. We will let you in through the front doors. We have food, water, and shelter, everything a growing boy needs. If you're alive and need help, come to McCarren airport in Las Vegas. We can and will help you. I advise that you come during the day, at night there are Night Stalkers out. It simply isn't safe enough to travel, If anyone is out there, please come to McCarren airport in Las Vegas. This message will be on repeat incase for any reason you need to hear it again. Thank you and I hope to see you soon." I finish my message on a more serious tone.

After finishing the broadcast I motion my hand across my neck in a slicing fashion. This lets April and Mark know that I am done talking and to stop the recording. April hits two buttons before nodding to me, letting me know that I am off the air.

"Alright, so how hard is it to get that on replay?" I ask April.

"It will take a minute or two but I can figure it out." April responds.

"Are you sure you don't want to re-record it? You sounded like an idiot..." Mark says.

"Hey, Mark, go fuck yourself. Figure it out." I say to him sarcastically, joking about the first sentence.

About a minute or two later my recording plays on the radio in the room. As it plays back we all listen to it and make sure it repeats before making any noise. Right as the recording starts again I burst out and say, "Yeah, I sounded stupid, can I re-record it?"

"No.", "No.", April and Mark both say at the exact same time.

"That sucks. Alright, saddle up, let's get to the airport." I say out loud.

I grab my gun from next to the chair before opening the door leading out to the hallway. When I bust out into the hallway I walk down it with my head held high. As my voice is now being broadcast to over five hundred miles. Some of that distance even covers one of the largest cities in the world. At the end of the hall I hit the button to call the elevator to our floor. Once the elevator arrives I get on board and hold the doors for everyone else. After everyone is on board I hit the button to take us down to the lobby before stepping away from the panel.

"So, did you know *My Chemical Romance* held a contest in this radio station for best song and the band *Escape the Fate* won? Then they got to open for *My Chemical Romance* on their very next tour?" I say out loud.

"You left out the part of why we should care." Mark replies.

"Hey, Mr. Marky Mark. I will shove that gun right up your ass!" I say jokingly.

"Is busting my balls like your new past time activity?" Mark asks.

"Right next to eating seeds." I say to Mark jokingly.

"Huh?" Mark asks.

"*Eating seeds as a past time activity...* You don't know that song?" I ask Mark, surprised.

"Uhm, would anyone but you?" Mark adds.

"*The toxicity of our city, of our city?*" I continue.

"Nope don't know it.", Mark says.

"*NOW!*" I scream while jumping in Mark's face before continuing.

"*What do you own the world, how do you own disorder?*" I sing the next verse.

"Still don't know it, sorry." Mark says.

"What rock did you grow up under?" I ask Mark in an extremely serious tone.

"What do you mean?" Mark replies.

The elevator dings and the doors open as we arrive back on the first floor. Mark, April and Troy follow me as I walk out into the lobby. When I reach the front doors of the radio station I push them open before walking across the street over to my car. While walking across the street I yell back to Mark, "*Toxicity*, by *System of a Down*."

"Ahhh.", I hear in the distance, acting as Mark's verbal reply.

"Troy you're guiding us." I say before hoping into the driver's seat of my car.

I start up the car and put it in drive while holding down the brake and waiting to see which direction Troy goes first. When Troy pulls away from the radio station I follow right behind him. We follow Troy all around the city, making it feel like we're traveling in one giant circle. About ten minutes after leaving the radio station we finally arrive at the airport. We pull up right out front of the airport so that it is to our left with a large parking garage to our right. The vehicles that Fredrick and his team drove here are all parked out front with their door's wide open. The vehicles still have supplies stock piled in them, meaning Fredrick hasn't done much since he got here.

I turn the car off and pop the trunk before getting out and walking around to grab some supplies out of the back. I grab two cases of water out the back of the Mustang and carry them inside the airport before setting them down. Inside I look around for any signs of Fredrick or anyone else. Without seeing anyone I press in the button on the side of my headset and start to talk into it.

"Fredrick, where are you guys at?" I say into the headset.

"We're boarding up the other side of the place. We're locking the doors and shoving a bunch of shit in the little room in between the outside and the lobby, why?" Fredrick asks.

"Roger, how long will it take you guys to finish up?" I ask.

"We've already blocked off two entrances, I think Braydon said we have three more to go. Maybe another thirty minutes?" Fredrick replies.

"Alright, I'm going to start unloading shit." I remark.

"Roger that. You got the radio broadcasting?" Fredrick asks.

"Sure did, anyone out there can hear us loud and clear." I reply.

After talking to Fredrick I lean down and grab one of the cases of water and carry it back outside. I open the front door as wide as it can go and set the case of water down in front of the door to keep it open. After word I help Mark, April and Troy carry in countless numbers of supplies into the airport. In the middle of carrying in all the supplies Cid and Vincent arrive in their beat up pickup truck with even more supplies. They join in helping us carrying supplies into the airport over the next thirty minutes. For the time being we just put the supplies anywhere, having no idea where we will have room in the future or where we will put them.

Right as we finish carrying all the supplies into the airport Fredrick and the others walk down an un-operational escalator and across the lobby. As Fredrick is walking towards us we all decide to take a seat and rest as carrying all the supplies has worn us out.

"So glad you could join us!" I say as Fredrick is walking over to us.

Fredrick gives me a half ass chuckle before looking over all the supplies in front of us. After looking over all the supplies he turns and looks out front of the airport. The sun is just barely visible through the parking garage as it is setting in the horizon.

"We should move these cars, in case anyone needs to quickly pull up.", I say out loud, wanting to be ready if anyone comes by.

Fredrick walks outside and gets into the car in the front of the line before pulling it around and into the parking garage. Others follow Fredrick outside and pull around to the parking garage as well, making sure that the front of the airport is clear in case anyone needs to pull up. Once all of the cars are out of the car pool lane that is in front of the airport we all head back inside and lock the front doors.

"So, where are we going to sleep?" I ask, a bit curious of what everyone had in mind.

"Well, there is a storage room up there. Before we barricaded all the entrances we found a store with a few sets of sleeping bags. We threw them into a storage room up there for our bunks." Fredrick points to a solid metal door up the escalator near where he came down.

"Let's carry all these supplies up there and into our room, then we can go to sleep for the night." I say to everyone as I grab a case of water off the ground.

Every one of us grabs something as we make our first trip up the escalator and over to the storage room. I place the case of water down in front of the door before opening it and looking around inside, to make sure it is safe. After I clear the room I nod to everyone and hold the door open as they all carry in their supplies. We all have to make about a dozen trips up and down the escalator in order to get everything up to the storage room. Now that we're all done it is safe to say that we're all exhausted. We each pick a sleeping bag from a nearby camping store before returning to the storage room and rolling them out on the floor. There is just enough room on the floor for all of us. After we've all rolled out our own sleeping bags we snuggle inside of them before falling asleep.

"Ryan! Ryan! We've got company! They heard your message!" I'm awoken by the sounds of April yelling out to me.

I roll over and stare at April while rubbing my eyes. Trying to shake off whatever has formed on them thanks to the dry air in Nevada. April is standing in the storage room doorway, looking in at me. April has a large smile on her face as she dances around in the doorway excited that a new group of survivors has come. When I look around the room I notice that I am the only person that is left in the room. Everyone else must have gotten up early to start organizing our supplies.

"What?" I ask April, still a bit confused with what is going on.

"Survivors! There are more survivors that came when they heard your message, come meet them!" Aprils yells out in a hurry.

April runs out of the room before I am able to respond. Once she is gone I pull myself up out of the sleeping bag and readjust my pants. They must have gotten twisted up from the night before. I grab my M4 from right next to the sleeping bag before opening the storage room door and walking outside into the lobby. Once outside of the storage room I look over the railing and down into the lobby of the airport. I can see Fredrick talking to four different people that I've never seen before.

One is a young boy, probably right around ten years old. He has light brown hair coming down over his forehead and is wearing baggy jeans with a plaid shirt. There is another child with the new group of survivors; this one is a small little girl. She looks to be right around seven years old and has the same hair color as her brother. Just her hair travels down past her shoulders and stops right near her upper back.

The other two survivors that are with the children look to be their parents. Both the mother and father seem to be in their late thirties maybe even early forties. The dad has short brown hair and a clean shave to go with it. He is wearing a pair of baggy jeans and a plain white T-shirt. The Mother has dirty blond hair coming down to her upper back, about the same length as her daughter. She has on a pair of tight jeans and what looks to be some sort of old classical band T-shirt. As Fredrick is talking with the new survivors April runs over and introduces herself before motioning for me to come down and over to her. I mumble to myself before walking down the escalator and over to the new survivors.

"Hello, my name is Ryan.", I say while putting my hand on my chest and announcing it to everyone before extending my hand out to each of them to further introduce myself.

"Jaina.", The Mother replies as she takes my hand.

"Tom.", The Father replies as he firmly grips my hand.

"Jen!" The little girl says excitedly.

"Hey, my name is Ryan too!" The little boy replies but is reluctant to take my hand.

"My dad said to never trust someone with a beard! You don't know what they're hiding!" The little kid exclaims.

A curious look comes over my face as I turn to Fredrick and think to myself, but I don't have a beard. Fredrick smirks and gives me a slight nod as I bring my hand up and feel my chin. My eyes light up when I feel nothing but hair with my fingers. I chuckle a bit before leaning down and looking into the kid's eyes.

"Well, your dad is a smart man.", I say while reaching around into my back pocket. I pull out a Kit-Kat bar that I grabbed from one of the convenience stores yesterday. I smile before handing it to the kid.

"It may be a bit mushy, but it's all yours now." I say to the kid.

"Thank you mister!" The kid exclaims before tearing into the Kit-Kat bar.

"So, do you guys have supplies you need carried in?" I ask the parents while standing back up.

"Yes, we have some but not many." They say while pointing outside to their SUV.

"Alright, we'll unload them for you." I say before walking out to their SUV.

"Thank you for everything!" I hear the man say as I'm walking outside.

I turn around and start walking backwards to reply, "Not a problem."

I walk out front of the airport and over to the survivor's SUV before grabbing anything out of the SUV that they have. After I have a hold of everything I kick the door shut before walking back towards the airport. On my way back inside I pause for a second and look into the sky."Hmm." I mumble as I look into the sky and realize it is mid afternoon already.

Shrugging it off I continue inside with the supplies in hand. As I pass by Fredrick I tell him to move the car into the parking garage in case anyone else arrives. He nods and runs outside before driving the car around and parking it into the parking garage. Back inside the lobby I slide the survivor's supplies up against the wall before pressing the button on the side of my headset.

"Mark, can you hear me?" I say into the headset.

"Yeah, what do you want?" Mark replies

"I figure you're in the security room with all the computers and shit, where is it?" I ask.

"Over head in the lobby look at the flight times." Mark replies.

I tilt my head up and look at the flight time board. There is a large red arrow pointing up the escalators and towards the storage room. I follow the arrow up the escalators and then look around clueless.

"Where do you want me to go from here Mark?" I ask.

"Turn around and look at the advertisement in the lobby." Mark says.

I spin around and look at a light board that is normally used to cycle through advertisements in the airport. It now has an arrow pointing down the hall, leading away from the storage room.

"Dude this is some Eagle Eye shit." I say to Mark while looking for another arrow.

At the end of the hallway the last arrow pointed down I find a door that says "Security" written on it. When I open the door and walk inside I see Mark is sitting in front of at least two dozen monitors with color pictures on them of almost every room inside the airport. As I look into each monitor I am amazed that you can spy on everyone. While looking through each of the monitors I notice that Braydon is in one of the monitors, scratching and picking his nose.

"Hey Braydon! Stop picking your nose!" I say while holding down the button on my headset.

Braydon doesn't respond but instead spins around in the room and looks around, confused as to how I see him. Eventually he spots the Security Camera in the corner of the room and smirks before giving it the middle finger. Mark and I both break into laughter as Braydon walks away.

"Got anything to eat in here Mark?" I ask as my stomach grumbles loudly.

"Yeah there is food and water in the back on the metal shelf." Mark replies while pointing back to the shelf.

I turn around and browse all the goodies Mark has. I look over almost every item on the shelf twice, starting to lick my lips wondering what I'd like to eat. About a minute goes by until I decide on a bottle of water and a bag of Doritos. With my food in hand I turn around and watch the monitors again with Mark. While I am looking over them all I notice a small amount of movement on the monitor in the lower right hand corner. I point to it to get Marks attention.

"Where is this monitor located? I saw something." I ask Mark.

"Uhm, the label is torn off but I think Victoria's Secret." Mark replies.

"There is an underwear store in an airport?" I ask.

"Yeah, so you look pretty for the mile high club." Mark replies with a chuckle.

"Wow! Mark knows some pop culture! My little boy is all grown up!" I say while patting him on the back.

Mark snaps to attention and looks into the monitor I pointed out earlier. After adjusting his glasses he hits a few buttons on the large panel in front of him to zoom in on that one monitor.

"Is that, what I think it is?" Mark asks.

"Yes... Yes it is..." I add.

"Fredrick. We've got a streaker zombie in *Victoria's Secret*", I say while holding down the button on my headset.

"A Streaker zombie?" Fredrick asks.

"No clothes. She is naked." I respond.

"Ahh, Alright I'll take care of It.", Fredrick says.

"Braydon, Troy, I want you guys to meet me there." Fredrick adds.

Mark and I watch Fredrick, Troy and Braydon as they run across almost every monitor in the room towards the one with the zombie. In less than a minute they all arrive at *Victoria's Secret* before slowly making their way inside.

"She is in the back, near the underwear." I say to everyone while munching loudly on my bag of chips.

"Look! There they go!" I yell out to Mark as we both sit there and watch the monitors impatiently.

Once they spot her Fredrick aims down his scope before shooting. With the positioning of the camera Mark and I are only able to see the flicker of light from Fredrick's gun and the blood from the zombie's head spray all over the wall.

"BOOM HEADSHOT!" I scream as the bullet hits the zombie in the head. As I yell I shake my bag of chips, causing them to fly out of the bag and all over the room. When I yell Mark jumps a little bit out of his seat, taken a bit off guard.

"That was awesome! Look for another zombie, look for another zombie!" I say out loud while looking at each of the monitors, hoping to find another zombie.

When I look back at Victoria Secret's monitor I notice that Fredrick, Troy and Braydon are wrapping up the zombie they just killed in a tarp. Allowing them to drag it outside and dispose of it easily and without anyone seeing. Over the next hour I review each of the cameras with Mark, looking for any anomalies. As time goes by, without noticing anything out of the ordinary I get bored and leave the security room. Once outside I look out the front doors of the airport and notice that it is already dark outside.

"Hmm, what time is it?" I say to myself as I am a bit curious.

I run down the escalator and over to the board where it shows the flight times. Right next to the board on the large wall there is almost a dozen different clocks showing different times all around the world. I scan over each of them until I find the one for the east coast.

"Eleven o'clock? What? Are you kidding me? Already?" I say a bit frustrated.

"Oh wait, that's right. We're West Coast now. So, it is eight." I say, remembering that I am not on the east coast any more.

After getting a look at the time I hold my hand over my mouth and yawn, the long day starting to take its toll on me. Figuring now is a good time to turn in for the day I walk back up the escalator and over to the storage room. When I open the door I notice that Cid and Vincent are both already inside sleeping. After seeing them I quietly close the door behind me and tip toe over to my sleeping bag. Before getting in and getting comfortable I take off my belt which has my sidearm and knife on it as well as my headset.

After I get into the sleeping bag I stare up at the ceiling for hours thinking about almost everything. My mind is mainly focused now on our first group of survivors. With us now officially being a Survivor's Colony, we have people to protect, people who can't protect themselves. More mouths to feed, children that we have to look out for. Within one short period of time we've been bestowed with undeniable responsibility. Responsibility that I'm not even sure I can handle.

Chapter 10 - The Grand Finale

Almost a week has passed since the first family of survivors has come to our colony. Since then we've been getting trucks, SUV's, cars and even bus loads of survivors coming in from all over the place. If they can hear our message being broadcast across the FM radio stations they come to our Survivor Colony. We've had people come from as far as Utah to our Survivor Colony. The word that we're a functional and friendly Survivor Colony is spreading fast.

We've got upwards of a hundred people here now. With all the new survivors always coming in it is hard to remember everyone's name but we all do our best. We've started to set up jobs for all of the new survivors that came to join us. Every day we have a few people drive around and collect water, food, weapons, beds, clothes and any other essentials that we may need. Of course with the influx of new people there have been some arguments and disagreements. But it was nothing we couldn't handle just by sitting them down and talking to them. We haven't quite picked a leader for the Survivor Colony yet but everyone answers to either me or Fredrick.

The storage room that originally served as sleeping quarters for all of us is now private sleeping quarters for April and I. We ditched the sleeping bags and stole two beds from nearby houses to bring back to the storage room to use. We also managed to find two dressers to keep any clothes we managed to take from local clothing stores or abandoned houses. Since April and I took this storage room for ourselves everyone else had to branch out across the rest of the airport. With the amount of storage rooms and shops there is almost an unlimited amount of space to sleep.

Almost all new comers are required to spend their first few nights in the lobby until we find a place where they can sleep. They either sleep on the benches in the lobby or with a sleeping bag that we provide them, which ever they prefer. As more people arrive we've discussed branching out further from the airport to nearby houses and buildings. However we don't have enough people to provide the protection required for branching out. Even with our best attempts to protect everyone inside we've had a few accidents. Sometimes someone tries to hide a bite and then changes during the night only to attack someone else. Or sometimes someone thinks it would be a good idea to go outside at two AM to have a cigarette. Only to be torn apart by a Night Stalker that got a whiff of them as they were outside.

After a few idiots got themselves killed by sneaking out for a smoke we've had to assign trust worthy survivors to watch the doors for us at night. Anyone of the original nine watches the front doors of the airport, or sometimes any new survivors that we trust. The original nine is what we call ourselves now, the nine of us that started the largest survivor colony in the U.S.A. As far as transportation goes, we've started to fill up the parking garage with all different types of vehicles. Anything that the survivor's arrive in goes into the parking garage after we've unloaded any supplies and are done with it. During the day Mark has also managed to steal a few helicopters' from the local hospital's and police stations. The only place to land in the helicopters was the air field right outside the airport. This is where Mark put all five of the helicopters he managed to steal.

One of the very small storage rooms inside the airport now serves as our Armory. We put all the guns anyone brings as well as ammo inside and seal it with lock and key. Mark keeps an eye on the room almost all day to make sure no one tries to break into it. As for right now Braydon is the only one with a key to the room. We take any guns away from the Survivors as they come and don't give any out unless they prove themselves to be trust worthy enough. This has obviously caused some problems amongst the survivors but it is the safest way to go about things.

With all the new survivors coming to the colony our specialties are quite spread out. We've gotten a few very friendly chefs that decided every morning to wake up extra early and cook everyone breakfast in the food court. Around seven every morning the chef's head down to the food court and start cooking a gigantic breakfast for everyone. No matter where you are in the airport the smell of the food being cooked will find you and fill your nostrils. Around eight Mark makes an announcement for everyone to head down to the food court to get some Breakfast. Less than five minutes later the table with the food is surrounded and everyone acts like a pack of savage hyenas as they fill their plates and stuff their faces. When everyone is done eating they all chip in and help clean the dishes and silverware. Everything has to be cleaned before five in the afternoon, which is when they start cooking dinner.

Throughout the course of the day, Troy, Braydon and I can most commonly be found walking around the airport. You can call us Enforcers, we like to make sure order is kept throughout the building and that no one is causing any trouble. As for Fredrick, he spends most of his day atop the MGM Grand Casino. He has a little shack he built up there with a couch, a few cases of water, some food, a pair of binoculars and his beloved Barret 50.cal Sniper Rifle. As much as he would like to, Fredrick doesn't sleep up there. At night it would just be too risky with all the Night Stalkers out.

As for today, it began just like any other day at the Survivor Colony. Until early on in the morning I got a scrambled radio transmission from Fredrick. "Ryan... Come over to the MGM and meet me on the.... roof.... There is something you.... need to see..."

It was right around eleven a.m. when I left the airport to go meet Fredrick atop the MGM Grand. When I arrived Fredrick was standing on the roof waiting for me. He motioned me over to his 50.cal that was hanging part way off the side of the building. I look down the scope of the gun which he has pointed at a highway to the far west of the city.

"See that?" Fredrick asks impatiently.

Around the area Fredrick had his gun pointed there are only about thirty zombies, limping and stumbling around on the highway. After seeing them I look around the area more, figuring I had to miss something. Without seeing anything else I break away from the scope and look at Fredrick.

"What are you talking about, the small amount of zombies out there?" I ask Fredrick.

"Yeah, there was two of them two days ago. Then yesterday there was fifteen and today thirty some." Fredrick says out loud.

"I'm sorry, but what are you getting at?" I ask.

"They're out there, standing around, waiting. They're planning something." Fredrick says.

"I think you're just paranoid, you should probably get off the roof out of the Sun.", I say to Fredrick.

"No! This is abnormal. We need to do something about It.", Fredrick yells out.

"Alright. If there are more there tomorrow then we can inform the colony. Otherwise it is not worth scaring everyone." I say to Fredrick.

"Alright.", Fredrick agrees with me before Troy contacts me through the headset.

"Hey Ryan, get back here. We have two more batches of survivors. It looks to be another thirty or so people." Troy says over the radio, calling me back to the airport.

"Well, they're calling my name. Be safe Fredrick." I say before walking back towards the stairs.

Fredrick nods as I leave the MGM Grand and return to the airport. Back at the airport I help unload the supplies the survivors brought and introduce myself to everyone. The group of survivors came in two large school buses, much like what we came to Vegas in. Both of them had at least fifteen people in them as well as tons of supplies, ranging from food, water and weapons. With all of the new survivors still on or around the bus it is very easy for me to publicly introduce myself to everyone. While they are still unloading I give them a quick speech about how we run the colony and exactly what they can expect by being here.

From this point on, the day continues on much like any other day. We get another load of survivors later that evening but it was much smaller than the last. Only three of them came and they were in a beat to hell pickup truck with no supplies.

Early in the morning the following day Fredrick calls me back up to the MGM roof to show me that there is nothing left to worry about. The pack of zombies he was worried about gathering on the highway leading west out of Las Vegas is now completely gone. Later that morning some of the new survivors that arrived yesterday took a school bus out to gather supplies. They insisted on showing us how thankful they were for us taking them in and helping them. The group of survivors was gone almost the whole day before coming back later that evening.

When they came back the whole bus was filled with enough food and water to last us a month. As we were unloading the supplies another bus pulled up with roughly twenty new survivors. They didn't have many supplies with them so they helped us unload the bus that was already here.

We continued to unload the bus until later that evening when the sun started to set in the distance. At which point we agreed to finish the rest tomorrow, knowing that it was too dangerous to continue.

In celebration of all the new survivors recently we cooked an extra big dinner; to show everyone how thankful we are to have them. Dan, one of the chefs that are nice enough to cook for us found a full wine rack of one hundred year old champagne in a house outside of the airport. He brought the bottles out of hiding and to the food court to celebrate this very special occasion. All of us stayed up far into early morning hours, getting drunk and celebrating that we were all still alive. I slept like a rock that night until around ten AM the following day. I was awoken by Braydon screaming into my room that Fredrick wanted to speak with me again on top the MGM. After I got out of bed and got dressed I drove over to the MGM and climbed up the stairs to the roof where Fredrick was waiting for me.

"We have a problem." Were the first words out of Fredrick's mouth.

Fredrick slams a pair of binoculars into my chest and points over to the same area he showed me the pack of zombies a few days ago. After looking down the binoculars I almost shit my pants. The day Fredrick was concerned about thirty zombies was nothing compared to this, now, there are thousands. After seeing all of the zombies I drop the binoculars to the ground before turning to Fredrick. My mouth is wide open as the terror in my eyes is noticeable.

"Yeah, I know. We need to warn everyone." Fredrick says out loud.

"Yeah..." I answer, unable to find a better word to answer with.

Knowing that everyone needs to be warned I run back down the stairs and get into my car. Ten minutes later I come to a screeching halt outside of the airport before running out of my car, not even bothering to turn it off. Once inside the lobby I get tunnel vision on Mark's security room. I ignore everyone and everything as I run straight towards the security room and burst through the door.

"Mark. I need to use your intercom right now." I say in an angry, frantic voice.

"For wh..." Mark starts to respond but I quickly interrupt him.

"No need, press the button NOW." I yell out at him.

A bit confused Mark presses the button on the Intercom, which broadcasts me live over the whole airport.

"Everyone needs to come to the main lobby of the airport *immediately*. This is an emergency and *not* a drill. I will explain more there." I say over the intercom before Mark releases the button.

"You come too Mark." I say to Mark before walking out of the security room and into the lobby.

Out in the lobby I stand up on one of the baggage terminals and wait for everyone to gather around. It takes a few minutes for everyone to make their way out to the lobby. But once they do I start a long speech, the fear in my voice very noticeable.

"We have a problem, a really big problem. There are thousands of zombies mobilizing to our west. The only logical explanation for this is they all came from LA or some other city in that direction. It will take about a day for them to get here, unless they are Runners, which then we're going to be attacked within a few hours. We will keep you updated via the Intercom. Troy and Braydon here will give you all a gun and some ammo. If you point the gun we provide you at anyone besides a zombie, Runner or Night Stalker you *will* be shot. No questions asked." I say to everyone.

"Ryan, they're starting to move towards the city. They aren't zombies, they're Runners. We got about five hours before they reach us." Fredrick says to me over the headset.

"Alright, Troy and Braydon, get everyone weapons. Be prepared for an attack tonight! Go, go!" I yell out before jumping down from the baggage terminal and running over to the armory.

There is now a huge crowd around the Armory as I am forced to push and shove my way over to the door. When I finally reach the door I ask Braydon for a M107 Sniper Rifle and two cases of ammo. After getting what I want I push and shove my way back through the crowd and out to the car pool lane outside the airport. I throw everything into the back of my car before getting in and peeling wheels away from the airport. I drive over to the western part of Las Vegas and into the first neighborhood that I find.

I drive through the neighborhood until I find a house that doesn't have a door leading up to the roof and is at least two stories high. The house I choose is overlooking the western highway in and out of Las Vegas, the same highway that the Runners are on. Once I am at the house I grab a nearby twenty foot ladder and prop it against the building, to give myself access to the roof. I climb up the ladder and toss my gun on the roof before making two additional trips for each case of ammo. After getting everything up onto the roof I pull myself up and kick the ladder away from the house, making sure nothing else can get up.

"I'm in position." I say into my headset.

When I look down the scope of my sniper rifle I can see that the Runners are now only a few miles out of town. They are making good progress and will be here right around nightfall. This makes perfect timing for the Night Stalkers to come out and help them. Maybe they are more intelligent than we originally thought?

Night settles in.

The Runners are now about a mile out and my bullets are just barely able to reach them. Every bullet I fire manages to kill at least two or three Runners. Each shot from my sniper rifle is so powerful that it penetrates through one Runner and keeps going. The bullets sometimes even tear through two or three of them before landing in the pavement below. Luckily with how the Runners are cramped together I don't even have to aim in order to hit them. With them covering so much of the road it is literally impossible to miss a target. As I am just finishing up the first case of ammo the pounding headache the sniper rifle gave me is noticeable. Each shot going off next to my unprotected ear sends a shockwave through my head, almost as if it was rattling my brain.

Within the next fifteen minutes Runners are almost finished closing the gap between them and the city. The highway is filled with Runners leading all the way back to the mountains and around the bend that goes through them. Without being able to see the end of the line we still don't have a definitive answer of how many of them there are. A few more minutes go by before the Runners reach the outer boundaries of the city. As the Runners start to pass me and enter the city I can hear the sounds of Fredrick's rifle in the distance. Each shot echoes through the night, the sound of death so distinguishable.

With how close all the Runners are to me my heart rate dramatically increases. Every time I look down the scope of the sniper rifle I can see over a dozen bloodshot eyes. All of them are staring forward down the highway with their teeth barred and only one thing on their mind, tearing us apart. As the Runners find their way down the highway they disperse throughout the city. One of the large groups from the highway works their way through my development before eventually finding my building. From the ground the Runners claw and jump at me but I am far too out of reach for them.

It only takes a few minutes for the Runners to find and smash down the front door of the house I am perched on. After they do I can hear them scurrying around inside the building, smashing and breaking anything inside that gets in their way. As the Runners find the windows inside the house they jump through them only to plummet to the ground below. They probably thought that the window would lead them out to me. While the Runners are trashing the house below me I continue to kill any of their friends that are still out on the highway. Close to ten minutes later I finally run out of ammo for my sniper rifle.

Unable to use the gun without any ammo I pick it up and toss it off the side of the building. As the gun falls to the crowd below the back end hits a Runner in the head and cracks his skull, killing him instantly. With the sniper rifle now gone I reach up and grab both sides of my head. The headache from all the shooting is still excruciatingly painful. After complaining about the headache I reach down and grab the M4 that is lying on the roof next to me. With the M4 in hand I look over the side of the building and start shooting at any of the Runners below. Making sure each and every bullet kills at least one of them. After finishing the first clip in my gun I reach down and grab the other two. I stick one of the clips into my back pocket and the other into my gun.

When one of the Runners is killed the others push and shove its body out of the way. A lot of the time the Runner is pushed to the ground only to be trampled by all the other Runners. But sometimes their bodies are surfed over top the hundreds of Runners around my building, just like a concert. When my M4 is out of ammo I am forced to switch to my Glock sidearm. Once the Glock is out it only takes me a few seconds to empty the clip inside the gun. With all my guns now out of ammo I reach up and press the button on my headset to contact Mark.

"Mark, I need an Airlift out of here immediately." I say into the headset.

"Next time, I really got to pack more ammo..." I mumble to myself.

Psssh! Is the first thing I hear after I finish talking to myself. When I look down at my feet to see what made the noise I see a bloody hand sticking through the roof. After seeing the hand I jump up in the air and yell, just barely missing its attempt to grab me. As I land I bring my foot down on top of the hand, causing it to break off at the wrist. The bone is now visible through the arm and blood is now spraying all over the roof. After smashing the first hand flat against the roof I start to dance around. I am careful not to keep a foot down on the roof for any longer than a few seconds as more hands are starting to break through to the roof. After the first hand busted through the roof it didn't take the Runners long at all to start making a giant hole for their whole body to fit through.

"I should have kept some fucking ammo..." I mumble to myself as the Runners are starting to break through the roof.

I reach up and press the button in on the side of my head set before talking, "Mark, I needed an airlift *yesterday*. Where the fuck are *you*?"

Without hearing an answer from Mark I leap to an adjacent rooftop. Once I'm safely on top the roof I turn around and look at the roof I was just on. There are a handful of Runners that are flooding onto the roof from the hole that they created in the attic. As they pour out onto the roof it only takes them a few seconds to realize that I am not there. Once they realize I am on an adjacent rooftop they begin to propel themselves towards me. Most of them plummet to the ground below but some of them are smart enough to jump at the edge of the roof. As the Runners start making their way across the roofs I have no other option but to continue jumping across them too.

The Runners continue to follow me; all of them are slowly but surely making their way across each rooftop after me. The Runners on the ground below follow me as well, switching houses as I switch roofs. I am able to continue evading the Runners until there are no more roofs for me to jump too. When I am out of roofs I pull my knife out and stand ready, ready to kill anything that comes my way. It takes a few minutes but the Runners eventually get the hang of jumping across the roofs. Some of them take short cuts by smashing through roofs closer to mine and even starting to work on mine. I press the button in on the side of my headset to try and get in contact with Mark one more time.

"Mark... I need you here now or I'm fucking dead." Still there was no response.

"Fuck!" I yell out loud.

I tightly squeeze my knife as the Runners are now starting to jump across and onto my roof. The second they land is when they're the most vulnerable. I take advantage of the short period of time that I have to slash their throat and kick them off the roof to the other Runners below. After killing almost twenty Runners one gets lucky enough to knock me over as he is jumping across. As the Runner knocks me off my feet my knife flies out of my hand and across the rooftop. Almost immediately after landing on my back a Runner throws himself on top of me. I grab the Runner's throat with my left hand and firmly press my thumb against his Adam's apple. While fully extending my right arm out and trying and grab my knife.

Once I finally manage to grab a hold of the knife I firmly press it against the Runner's neck. The Runner doesn't seem to be bothered by the pain as he pushes his face closer to mine. This causes the knife to cut even more into his throat. His face is just inches away from mine as I can feel his hot breath on my neck, accompanied with the smell of rotting flesh in his mouth. The Runner's face is covered with dried blood and his teeth are stained from all the flesh they've seen. As I stare into his blood shot eyes I swallow hard. Almost positive this was one of my last few seconds alive.

Just as I thought it was all over I hear a loud gunshot echo in the distance. I clench my eyes shut as the Runner's head explodes in my face, spraying blood all over me. Its lifeless body collapses against me before sliding off and into an alleyway below. With the body now off of me I am able to quickly wipe the blood off my face. I am extra careful not to open my eyes or mouth to risk getting blood into them and getting infected. While I am distracted with cleaning the blood off of my face I can hear more gunshots in the distance. Each shot comes from the top of Fredrick's building and is followed by the sound of tearing flesh nearby.

"Ryan! Get Up!" Fredrick screams to me over the radio.

I push myself up onto my knees before crawling to the other side of the roof. As I am crawling to the other side of the roof, I can hear the sounds of a helicopter in the distance. By the time I reach the other end of the roof the helicopter is right over top of me. Mark hits the spotlight and lights up the whole roof around me. Right after the spotlight is turned on me a loud shriek echoes across the neighborhood followed by the horrible smell of burning flesh. When I look up at the helicopter I can see a rope ladder spiraling down towards me.

"Grab a hold of it and let's go!" Mark yells over the intercom of the helicopter.

"Oh, now you decide to talk!" I yell at the top of my lungs up to Mark, knowing he can't hear me.

As I grab a hold of the rope ladder and climb up it, Mark starts to pull away from the rooftop. Before the rope ladder is able to fully leave the rooftop a Runner makes a giant leap and grabs a hold of it. With the sudden shift of weight Mark temporarily loses control of the helicopter. The Runner starts to throw himself up the ladder towards me, surprising me with his ability to climb. When the Runner gets close enough I proceed to kick him in the face until I knock him loose and watch him plummet to his death.

After the Runner falls to its death a large caliber gun starts firing from above me. I look up at the helicopter and see the large barrel of a machine gun sticking out of the side. For a second I am also able to get a glimpse of Troy inside on the other end of that machine gun. As the barrel spins around and unleashes hell on the crowd of Runners below it lights up the night. The hot shell casings from the gun cascade down around me, stinging my unprotected skin before bouncing off. I turn my head away from the burning hot shell casings and look back at the rooftops below.

Down below there is a light red mist over top all of the Runners as their body parts fly through the air. The smoking bullet's from the helicopter's machine gun relentlessly tears through the crowd of Runners below. As Mark pulls away from the building Troy continues to unleash hell upon all the Runners in the streets until we're out of reach. Mark flies me all the way across the city and over to a building right next to the MGM where Braydon is waiting for me.

"We're leading a group into the MGM to protect Fredrick." Braydon yells to me over top the sounds of the helicopter above.

Braydon runs over to a nearby ammo case and grabs six clips out of it before tossing them to me. I shove each of the clips into any available pockets that I have before looking around to the other survivors. I borrow a bottle of water from one of them so I can wash my face off before leaving the roof. Making sure the sweat off my forehead doesn't run any of the blood from the Runner into my eyes or mouth. After cleaning myself up I follow Braydon and his team down the staircase and out into the streets. Once we're out in the streets we all open fire on any Runners that we come across, making sure nothing gets even close to us. Mark is still hovering over us with Troy on the machine gun in case we need extra support. While those of us on the street pick off any Runners outside of the pack, Troy unleashes hell on any large groups that are coming our way.

By the time we get across the street the front doors to the MGM are shattered and Runners are already all over the lobby. With the Runners all over the place in the lobby danger is inevitable as they can come from any direction and ambush us. As we make our way through the lobby we see that the door leading up to the roof is already smashed in. Runners can be heard making their way up the stairwell as their growls and snarls echo across the room. Everyone but Braydon and I stay back and guard the stairwell and make sure nothing can ambush us from the back. Braydon and I give all five of the people that are staying back our extra ammo before running up the stairs to Fredrick.

The journey up the stairwell only takes a few minutes but by the time Braydon and I reach the top we are pretty much exhausted. At the top of the stairwell Braydon and I find four Runners pounding on the door leading out to the roof. We both take all four of them out, quickly and efficiently, only using four bullets. After they're all dead I use my headset to get into contact with Fredrick, letting him know that it is safe and to open the door for us. Fredrick thanks us for killing the Runners after opening the door for us.

With Fredrick now safe Mark and I call for an airlift off the MGM. It takes a few minutes for Mark to arrive but when he does we quickly board the rope ladder. On the flight over to a neighborhood on the west side Mark lets us know that April is in grave danger. She is trapped in a house that is surrounded by Runners. When we arrive Mark hovers over the house long enough for Braydon and me to climb down the ladder and onto the roof. After we safely make it onto the roof Troy tosses out an extra case of ammo for us before flying away. As Braydon reloads and restocks I run over to the front doors on the house and look down. The doors are completely barricaded off by the bodies of Runners. It would be impossible to try and open them with just the two of us.

"April, are you ok inside of there?" I yell into my headset.

"Yeah! But I can't hold them off much longer!" April replies.

As the helicopter gets further away from the house I can start to hear April's gunshots from inside the house. After reloading Braydon runs over to the side of the house and shoots any Runners that try to get in the side window. With Braydon holding off the Runners for now I quickly reload and restock on ammo before jumping to an adjacent rooftop. On the adjacent roof I am able to see into the second floor window where April is standing. She is frantically shooting any Runners that come up the stairs and try to attack her.

Unable to think of any other option I throw my gun through the window and into the hallway that April is standing in. The window shatters as glass covers the floor inside the hallway of the house. I swallow hard before backing up and running towards the house that April is in. At the end of my roof I leap off the building and through the window of April's building. When I land inside April quickly spins to face me before shooting her gun, not knowing who it was at first. After hearing the gun go off I quickly duck as I am just barely able to feel the bullet wiz by my head.

"Whoa!" I yell out loud.

"Sorry!" April replies with a smile before turning back to the staircase and killing any Runners that come up.

Before coming up with an escape plan I assist April in killing any Runners that Braydon misses and lets inside. After about a minute passes so many bodies of Runners pile up on the stairs that they temporarily block off access to the lower floor. I take this brief opportunity to grab April's hand and pull her over to the window I jumped in from. Luckily, right outside the window is a large rope ladder hanging down from the helicopter with the spot light shining over it. I help April out of the window and onto the rope ladder before following her myself. After we're both on the ladder Braydon jumps on and gives the queue to Mark that we're good to go.

As Mark is pulling the helicopter away from the building Runners begin to climb onto the rope ladder from the ground below. April looks back and starts shooting any Runners that are climbing up the rope ladder towards us. Each one of her bullets just barely misses me and hits one of the Runners below. With April shooting from right over top of me I grip the ladder in fear. Not trusting her abilities to aim that well yet. As April is shooting the Runners off the ladder Mark broadcasts over the intercom of the helicopter.

"It's too much weight for the helicopter! I can't hold you guys, I'm going to have to set you down on a building nearby! Hold on!" Mark yells out.

Mark flies us a few neighborhoods over before setting us down on a nearby roof. After we're all off the ladder I look around us and notice there are no Runners, But not for long. The Runners from the other neighborhood start to pour into this one. They presumably followed the sound of the helicopter over here. In no time at all they surrounded the building we are stranded on before pounding on the walls. It takes them less than a minute before they break down the front door and shatter all the windows to the house, trying to find a way up to us. As I jump across to the adjacent rooftops looking for a nearby car I motion for April and Braydon to follow me.

A few rooftops over I spot a truck parked in the driveway of a house at the end of the neighborhood. The house is right near the road leading out of the development and has absolutely no Runners around it. After spotting the truck I call Braydon and April over to show them my escape plan. They nod after seeing it, figuring that it is our only chance of getting out of here alive. As we jump across the rooftops throughout the neighborhood none of the Runners are following us. All of them are still unaware that we left the first building.

In between each building I yell to Braydon and April, "This reminds me of that movie, *Tremors*. You know where they had to pole vault across the rocks to get to that girls truck. Just now we're jumping across buildings."

When we reach the pickup truck at the end of the neighborhood I jump down from the roof and land in the bed of the truck. I bend over and look inside before yelling out to Braydon and April who are still up on the roof. "Keys are inside, let's go!" Both of them jump down into the bed of the truck with me, the suspension on the truck helping to break everyone's fall. After Braydon lands on the truck he jumps out and hops into the driver's seat before turning the truck on. April and I both sit down in the back and grab a hold of anything we can to keep us in. Both of us place our guns on the side of the truck and keep an eye out, ready to shoot whatever comes our way. Braydon puts the truck in drive before pulling out onto the road and hitting a zombie that was out walking the streets. To finish the job he backs up over top of the zombie and punches the gas pedal, causing the truck to peel wheels

Instead of leaving tire marks from peeling the wheels Braydon leaves a large spray of blood out the back end and a solid red line for about twenty feet in front. After the minor amount of fun killing the zombie Braydon takes us straight to the airport. Any zombies, Runners or Night Stalkers that are in our way on the route back to the airport are hit with the truck by Braydon. Anything that Braydon misses with the truck April and I take care of by shooting them from the back.

While driving back towards the airport I yell out to April, "You know what this reminds me of?"

"What? *Tremors*?" April replies.

"No! That was the rooftops earlier! This reminds me of the crazy motorcycle chase in *Final Fantasy 7*. You know where everyone is in the back of the truck and Cloud has to defend it while racing down the highway."

"Do you ever have anything productive to say?" April asks.

"Not really." I reply.

As we get closer to the airport we notice that the road leading up to it is almost impassable. Hundreds upon hundreds of Runners were killed in the area, making it very difficult for us to navigate up the road. In order for us to continue towards the airport Braydon is forced to shift the truck into four wheel drive. As we drive over all of the bodies it feels like we're trail riding up a mountain. Every foot we travel up the road sends the truck bouncing up in the air or side to side in all different directions. Sometimes the bodies act like soft sand. Causing us to get stuck and forcing us to find a quick way out before we're surrounded.

As we get closer to the airport we can see everyone grouped outside the front doors. They are surrounded by benches, trash cans and anything else they could find and use as a make shift bunker. Braydon pulls up right outside the front doors of the airport before putting the truck in park. With the truck now in park April and I hop out followed closely behind by Braydon. Once Braydon is out of the truck he turns around before wedging his gun between the seat and the gas pedal. After doing this the truck starts to rev like crazy, as it backfires repeatedly. With the gun wedged in between the seat and the pedal Braydon shifts it back into drive before jumping out of the way.

The truck rubber bands forward and plow through a large pack of Runners that were headed for the airport. After smashing through the Runners the truck continues down the road, scraping the concrete barrier all the way down. We lose sight of it after a few seconds but hear it crash into something big about a quarter mile away from the airport. With the truck out of the way Braydon, April and I all take shelter behind the barricade. We restock on ammo before helping repel the zombie onslaught from the airport. A few minutes after the three of us arrive at the airport, the sound of Mark's helicopter can be heard from above.

When I look up into the air I see the large spotlight from Mark's helicopter coming right towards the airport. The rope ladder is hanging down from the helicopter with what looks to be Fredrick holding onto it as it sways in the air. Fredrick has the rope ladder tightly gripped with his left hand while his other hand is holding his M4. The light flickering from Fredrick's gun is easily distinguishable as he kills everything he is able to see from the ladder.

When Mark stops the helicopter above us Fredrick hops off the rope ladder and joins us behind the barricade. Troy pulls the ladder back into the helicopter before having Mark circle around so he can get a better look of the area. After circling around the airport Mark stops and hovers in between the parking garage and lobby of the airport. This gives Troy a perfect line of sight with the machine gun of both the roads leading up to our barricade. We hold our positions over the next ten minutes, not letting any Runners get within ten feet of us.

The longer we're stuck behind the barricade killing all the Runners the more repetitious it all becomes. The sound of all the guns firing echoes throughout the area. Without anything but the sounds of gun fire ringing through my ears I constantly zone in and out. Barely able to focus on or pay attention to anything that is going on. Until, out of nowhere, I am caught off guard by the sound of tearing flesh from above. When I look up to the helicopter I see a light red mist drifting towards the ground. Chunks of pale flesh and body parts are scattered throughout the sky, burning up the second they enter the light around the airport.

Seconds after hearing the first Night Stalker get shredded by the blades of the helicopter another leaps from the roof and into the blades. Just like the first Night Stalker this one is torn to pieces as well. Less than a second after hearing the sound of grinding flesh from above an alarm sounds from inside the cockpit. "Mayday, mayday!" Mark yells over the intercom as the helicopter spins wildly out of control. Both Mark and Troy bail out of the helicopter and jump into the nearby parking garage. Once Mark and Troy are out of the helicopter it continues to spiral out of control before crashing into a building near the airport.

"Mark, come in, are you ok?" I say into my headset.

No response.

"Mark, are you there? Please respond." I reply.

Still there is no response.

A few seconds later Mark finally responds, "No... My legs broke... I can't walk...."

Without even checking to see if anyone is following me I bolt forward and make a run for the parking garage. April, Fredrick and Braydon all follow closely behind, knowing that I will need the help when I find them. As I make my way up to Mark I have to stop frequently to kill the Runners that are in my way. Apparently they are curious as to what made all the noise from above. When Mark is finally in my sites I see that he is sitting with his back to the concrete wall. He has both of his hands wrapped around the thigh on his right leg.

As for Troy, he is laying face first on the ground right in front of Mark. I run over to Troy first and drop to my knees before rolling him over. He has blood all down the right hand side of his face and large deep scratch marks from the rocky pavement on his cheek. All of them are guaranteed to leave scars. After rolling him over I place my fingers on his neck to check and see if he has a pulse.

"Guys! He has a pulse!" I yell out loud.

"Come on Troy, wake up!" I say to Troy while lightly tapping the side of his face.

"Troy! Come on! Wake up!" I yell to Troy, now shaking his body.

"What? What's going on?" Troy says right after opening his eyes.

"We got to get out of here, can you walk?" I ask Troy.

"Yeah, I just need a minute..." Troy replies.

Troy sits up and puts his hand on his face as he is regaining consciousness. After touching his face he looks at his now blood soaked hand before letting out a sigh. As the realization that he is pretty beat up sets in. While Troy is coming back to his senses Fredrick and I lift Mark up. We have him put one arm around Fredrick's shoulders and the other around mine to make it easier to carry him. Once we have a hold of Mark, Troy stands up and picks up his M4. With his gun in hand, he nods to us, letting us know that he is ready to get out of here. With Fredrick and I carrying Mark back to the terminal Braydon, Troy and April all keep an eye out. They make sure that no Runners or Night Stalkers are able to catch us off guard.

Back outside the terminal Fredrick and I set Mark down in a corner before giving him a pistol for protection. Throughout the night there are very few Night Stalkers that try and attack us at the airport, since it is so well lit. The main danger for us though, was the relentless wave after wave of Runners all night long. Throughout the night Cid and Vincent were forced to run back inside a couple dozen times for more ammo. In the early morning, just as the sun peaked on the horizon the attack ended. Finally the onslaught of Runners has stopped.

Even though we've been up all night, none of us are tired. With all the adrenaline still flowing through us it would be impossible to feel anything but wired. As the morning continues on everything starts to very slowly calm down. Finally around ten AM almost everything starts to return to normal. April takes a look at Mark's leg to determine how broken it was from his fall last night. As April is doing that I do a head count of everyone inside the lobby to determine how many people survived the attack. After doing the headcount I found that the results were rather depressing. I double checked, even triple checked the amount of people we have but the number was always the same. Only twenty of us survived the attack last night. Which means we lost way over half of our colony during the night.

The whole day following the attack was spent cleaning up bodies from around the airport. Anyone who survived last night and is not injured helps us clean up the bodies that litter the outside of the airport. All of the bodies that we collect are taken to an empty field near the airport. At the end of the day, after accumulating over a thousand bodies, we pour gasoline over all of them before lighting them on fire. This is to guarantee that they could never come back to life.

The black smoke from the pile billowed up into the sky, there is no doubt you could see it for miles. There was also a rancid smell from the pile after we burned it. The smell of burning and rotting flesh was impossible to avoid and even harder to get off of our clothes. There were no new survivors that arrived that day. Not even like they could, with all the bodies around the airport. Or that they'd even want to, with the smell of burning flesh all around. No one spoke almost all day and I rarely even joked around. The atmosphere just didn't feel right, everyone was too uptight and worn out from the long previous day. After the very long and depressing day everyone decides to call it a night right around eight.

CHAPTER II - A NEW BEGINNING

It's now the third of June; three months have passed since the attack that night where we lost so many of our own. Every day since then new survivors have been coming to our colony. So many new face and names, most of which I can't even remember. Eventually allowing us to rebuild and regrow what we had and even surpass it. We have people coming in that specialize in many different fields. Allowing us to start rebuilding a civilization and re colonizing the city.

Not many zombie attacks have happened since that night. If they do it's normally a Night Stalker grabbing someone at night. Or someone wondering too far away from the colony, unarmed and getting attacked by a Runner. With the assistance of a few new survivors we were able to reconstruct the houses and roads that were damaged the night of the attack. This allows transportation to continue in and out of the airport like normal. With the massive influx of people we ran out of space in the airport and were forced to start reconstruction on the MGM, where we've started to send new survivors to create a second Survivor Colony.

The one Survivor Colony at the airport is now lead by me. The MGM's Survivor Colony is lead by Fredrick, who has upgraded his shack on top the roof to a small cottage. He still looks out every day, down at the whole city below. We call Fredrick our watcher, from atop the MGM he watches out for all of us. All the bodies from three months ago were placed in a field just west of the airport. Most of the bodies were burned but some of the survivors wanted to bury their loved ones. This field has now become the Graveyard for all those lost over the last three months. It's a place for friends and family can go to mourn the loss of the dead.

Our Survivor Colony has become widely known now. We've been told that people all across the country know about it and we're the only functional Survivor Colony left. We've also been told that the zombie disaster across the country is growing worse. As the zombies infect different types of Animals, weird kinds of mutations are starting to happen.

Since we are the biggest and most well known Survivor Colony we decided to start a mural inside the terminal. The mural is someplace everyone can write their name down with a short passage. That way anyone passing through or newly arriving can check to see if they have any family or friends that have been here or are here. The mural started out to be a very small portion of one of the walls but quickly grew as it became more and more popular. Now the mural takes up almost every wall inside the terminal and has over two thousand different names written on it.

With the massive influx of people coming and going from the Survivor Colony we've had to promote some people to help us keep order. With all the people now at the survivor colony it is much harder to keep everyone happy. There are petty brawls that break out over almost anything. Someone taking more food than someone else thinks they should, someone looking at someone the wrong way and even someone sitting down in the wrong place. My solution to all the problems is either kick the person out or shoot them, Fredrick mostly agreed. But sadly, that didn't win the popular vote.

Surrounded by all the death outside it was only a matter of time before it hit close to home. A little over a month ago Vincent had a heart attack in the middle of the night and died in his sleep. Cid was a wreck the first two weeks, but now, almost a month later he seems to have gotten past his father's death.

Vincent's death was the main reason behind starting the graveyard outside the airport. The same field we burned bodies in three months ago is now fenced off with at least five constant guards outside of it at all times. The guards make sure no undead get in to reanimate the dead. We have a special rule for the graveyard, which has been argued many times amongst the survivors. Your body is only allowed to be buried there if you die of natural causes. If you were bitten or turned your body is burned, no questions asked.

They graveyard has served its purpose quite well though. Every day Cid goes down to it early in the morning to visit his father's grave. He usually spends ten to twenty minutes there before leaving and returning to his daily assignment. Every week, once a week Cid places a new bouquet of flowers at his father's grave. One of the newer survivors that came to our colony from as far as Florida is a Florist. She makes Cid a bundle of flowers every Wednesday to take to his father's grave.

But as they always say, with death comes new life. Zooey announced about a week ago that she was pregnant and that Mark was the father. Zooey and Mark became close after the attack three months ago. I always bust Mark's balls and say it was the broken leg that did the all the work. But Mark still thinks it was his charm. They've been together for almost two and a half months now. Even though it hasn't been that long all of us already bugging Mark when he is going to pop the big question to her. Three months usually isn't a long time but in the world we live in now, three months is equal to three years.

After Mark and Zooey got together many people were curious when April and I were going to do something about the obvious signs of affection between us. To be honest, the conversation hasn't even come up yet. Neither of us care to be bothered with the drama behind a relationship and even if we did, neither of us have time for it. Regardless of being in a relationship or not, April and I still do everything together. Most of our supply runs every day are two man jobs as are the rescue missions that we go on. At the end of the day we still share the same room and even the same bed now that April so kindly donated hers to another survivor. Maybe one day, I tell everyone. You never know what the future may hold.

As the day starts to come to a close I can hear the final bus of the day pulling up to the front of the airport. After the bus pulls up the sounds of all the survivors unloading their supplies and introducing themselves can be heard throughout the airport. "Hey Ryan, come down here. Someone wants to see you." April says to me through her headset.

I leave the storage room and walk down the escalator. Saying hi to anyone as I pass and also welcoming any new faces into the Colony. When I finally make my way past the crowd and get outside I look around for April. After I spot her I walk her way before I hear someone call out my name from behind me.

"Ryan!" I hear a very familiar voice call out from behind me.

"Is that... who I think it is?" I say to myself while slowing turning around.

When I turn around my jaw drops down as my eyes start to sparkle with tears when I see who called out my name.

"John? Is that you?!" I yell out loud.

John doesn't say anything, instead he just drops the bags he is holding and runs over to me. He throws his arms around me as he isn't even able to describe how happy he is to see me.

"No homo?" He says after leaning back to look at me.

I nod before saying,

"I told you I'd come for you."